Hitler was dead. Never again would his ranting hyp-
notize millions. This time, the Nazi leader would be
as American as apple pie. But the terror would be just
as real . . .

Of course, if you told anyone that, you'd be called
crazy. Especially if you were a woman lawyer too
smart, too sexy and too stubborn for your own
good . . .

"A SUSPENSE-CRAMMED THRILLER!

. . . *a feisty lady with the delicacy of a machine gun,
Sylvia ricochets from one peril to the next in this
headlong saga . . ."*

—COSMOPOLITAN

SUSPICIONS
The electrifying new thriller by
BARBARA BETCHERMAN

SUSPICIONS

BARBARA BETCHERMAN

BERKLEY BOOKS, NEW YORK

This Berkley book contains the complete
text of the original hardcover edition.
It has been completely reset in a type face
designed for easy reading, and was printed
from new film.

SUSPICIONS

A Berkley Book / published by arrangement with
the author

PRINTING HISTORY
Putnam edition published May 1980
Berkley edition / May 1981

ISBN: 0-425-04839-X

A BERKLEY BOOK ® TM 757,375

PRINTED IN THE UNITED STATES OF AMERICA

To Brian

PROLOGUE

The building sat inconspicuously in the middle of the big city. Its suites were rented by small companies, fly-by-night operators who didn't notice who moved in or out. They came when they had amassed the cash for two months' rent in advance and left when they had no money for the collectors who haunted the building daily.

The offices were dingy and dirty. No one had funds for unnecessary overhead like cleaning ladies. Or if some did, they preferred to live in filth or make their own arrangements rather than subject themselves to the gaze of a curious charwoman.

There was one office that stood out from the others, but only once its decrepit anteroom was passed. And no one passed who didn't have business in the inner sanctum.

A dozen men sat around the long table in the inner room. They hadn't minded the dirt outside and they weren't impressed by the paneling and the art inside. They had very little in common. Their ages ranged from the thirties to the seventies. They were tall, short, thin, fat. They had met each other only that afternoon, all except for the man at the head of the table. He knew every one of them well.

Each man had a piece of paper in front of him.

"Have you read the letter, gentlemen?" The leader spoke in slow, measured tones.

He was accorded instant nods and respectful murmurs.

"This meeting is now open for discussion of the operation."

One of the younger members spoke first. "What do we do if the papers don't print this?"

"They will. We have a great many friends in the newspaper business. And this makes news. They'll print anything that raises the circulation."

"But if some don't?"

The leader smiled coldly. "It will be published widely enough for our purposes."

The oldest man in the room nodded gently.

1

"Max. Did you want to say something?" The leader made a point of deferring to his older colleagues.

"It's a good letter. But what effect do you expect it to have?"

A bald man beside him answered. "An organized attack like this will bring people into the open. We'll be contacted by many who have secretly thought as we do but were afraid to say so. We'll be raising the issue again. For the first time in a big way since the war. If we don't do it now, it will be too late. Perhaps for forever."

"This is only a small part of our plan," the leader interjected. "We've been very successful all along the line. Most importantly, our people have achieved infiltration of all desired pivotal positions. Our most decisive takeover is due to happen in a few weeks. It has taken thirty years, but we're finally ready to act. It will soon be time to come into the open. We have friends everywhere, friends who will support us openly if we show them that our movement is strong enough to destroy its opposition. We are ready to give the people a powerful alternative to the miserable system that is corrupting the country."

He paused.

"Our day is dawning again, gentlemen. There can be no mistakes now. We are too close to permanent success. Soon we will control the most influential organization in the government. And after that . . ." He looked at the dapper man at his right hand.

The man raised his water glass. "After that, the White House, gentlemen."

They all stood and drank.

As they filed out, leaving by several doors and at irregular intervals, the dapper man stayed behind.

"Our friend is still being pursued. They're getting close to him."

"Then kill the hunters."

"And if we can't find them?"

"Remove our friend. He knows too much."

ONE

Traffic was already easing up, by New York standards at least, when Sylvia West dashed out of her Madison Avenue office building. On summer Fridays everyone came up with a reason to leave early, so rush hour started shortly after lunch. Sylvia stood at the corner, impatiently tapping her foot at the red light, a bulging briefcase in one hand, the other hand pushing her shoulder-length auburn hair out of her eyes.

A few men eyed her, surreptitiously, because of the unwritten rule that female executives be treated with some appearance of equality. Without the briefcase, she would have been the object of overt ogling. Even in Manhattan, a six-foot woman with slim hips and large, hooded eyes in a sculptured face was noteworthy.

The light changed and Sylvia strode across immediately. She was late for a dinner party and things weren't going well. Her briefcase was thick and it continually banged against her legs, slowing her down. The parking lot was several blocks away, and at each corner, the lights perversely stayed red for double their usual time. She was breathless when she arrived at the parking lot; the attendant was nowhere in sight.

"Hello?" Sylvia tried to curb her irritation. The attendant wasn't responsible for her tardiness. Furthermore, if she annoyed him, she'd be there for half an hour. "Hello? Anyone around?"

A voice answered her from across the concrete floor. "Just hold your horses, lady."

Sylvia had deliberately avoided looking at her watch but the clock in the office was so positioned that it forced itself upon her consciousness. It was almost seven, the party had been set for six-thirty, and she had at least forty minutes of driving ahead of her. Had it been hosted by one of her friends, she wouldn't have worried about the hour. For one thing, the starting time would have been much later, and anyway, it would have been understood that emergencies arise in the life of a

3

criminal lawyer. Tonight's host was one of her husband's law partners. For all she knew, Stuart wouldn't care either about her punctuality but John had been most insistent over breakfast that she be on time tonight. She disliked it when he overlooked the pressures of her job, but liked it even less when he was angry.

"Key's in the car." The attendant meandered over to her, flipping through a sheaf of parking tickets. "What's the license?"

Sylvia told him, holding out the exact change. "I have to pay the maximum anyway, so here's the money."

"Naw. I gotta find the card."

Sylvia took a deep breath. Then she took another. Hyperventilation was better than murder.

"Here it is. That comes to..."

"Yes. Here you go." She escaped, running awkwardly with the briefcase toward the back of the lot. "You'll move the other cars?" she shouted over her shoulder.

Eventually, the car jockey cleared her way and she pulled out to the street. Although rush hour had theoretically passed, the roads were still humming as the commuters returned to the city for their Friday night on the town.

Sylvia smoked incessantly as though the activity would speed her up. When she finally pulled up outside the trendy Greenwich Village brownstone, forty-five minutes had passed and she was measurably closer to lung cancer.

"I'm sorry I'm late," she apologized to Doris Paliano, her hostess. "Just before I left, I got an emergency call from the jail. A murder."

Doris, a skinny, expensively dressed woman with the leathery face of the overtanned and overdieted matron, nodded disinterestedly. Sylvia could just as easily have excused herself on the basis of her mother having died. Doris never listened to anyone, a habit Sylvia could understand given a lifetime with Stuart.

"John's here already. Would you like to go to the washroom first?"

Sylvia could feel the soot and dried perspiration under her tailored but regrettably creased linen pantsuit. "Uh, no thanks. You'll have to take me as I am." It would take more than five minutes to repair the damage.

"What will you have, Sylvia?" Stuart had his arm around

her shoulders, hand hanging down just a bit too far.

"Scotch, thanks." She moved out of range. "Sorry, I'm late but—"

"No trouble. We won't eat for another hour. I just wanted us all to get together for a really good chat," he boomed. Stuart was a barefaced liar. Chatting implied two people talking. And he never engaged in any reciprocal activity if he could help it.

Sylvia looked around the room. She'd been in it many times but getting to know it was not the same thing as getting to love it. Teams of decorators, armed with instructions no more specific than generous financial limits, had obviously swept into the house and like locusts had stripped everything in their path. They'd left their droppings behind, a color scheme in the living room of hot pink and white dotted with lime green, an enormous velvet sectional sofa hemmed in by too many glass and marble coffee tables, precious lamps that gave off very little light, art on the walls that was so modern it had scarcely had time to dry. The aridity of the furnishings went poorly with the gracious old house, the high ceilings, the moldings between wall and ceiling that must have been too difficult to remove or else, certainly, they would have been. It was not a room to feel comfortable in; it was designed to overwhelm even large parties.

"You know everyone?" Stuart clearly wanted to move on. "I'll let your hubby take you around. He's been waiting anxiously for you. Still honeymooners, after, it must be ten years?"

"Yes, ten," Sylvia answered absently. She wasn't keen to confront John. From where she was standing, his glare didn't much resemble the gaze of an ardent new husband.

Al Pennell, another guest, saved her. "Hi, Sylvia. I don't think you've met my wife, Susan?"

Sylvia smiled at a younger version of her hostess. Susan Pennell could be no older than thirty-five but already her skin was showing the effects of countless fad diets, too many trips to the sun, too much makeup. Her dress wasn't attractive enough on her scrawny body to justify the price tag. Sylvia knew how much it had cost because it was the kind of basic black sheath that John was forever urging her to buy.

"I've heard so much about you, Sylvia," Susan gushed. "A lawyer and a mother! I admire you so much! Wherever do you find the time?"

"She doesn't." John had joined the group.

Sylvia ignored the sour note. "Al tells me you're a tennis star."

"Imagine that! Boasting about little me." Susan laughed nervously.

Actually, Sylvia and Al had had a case together and they'd run out of small talk early on. Sylvia had asked about his wife in desperation.

"I've been playing for ten years," Susan confided. "And you know, my game's improved more over the past year than in the first nine! It's the new tennis pro at the club."

Sylvia could tell she wasn't the only bored guest. Both Al and John had glazed eyes too.

"Here's your little drinky," Stuart said coyly, thrusting a tumbler half full of Scotch into Sylvia's hand.

She took a gulp. With enough of the stuff, she could survive the evening.

"Did John introduce you to everyone?" Stuart had poured himself a few generous drinks as well, if his slightly slurred speech was any indication.

"I don't think I've met the couple talking to the Thompsons." Sylvia gestured toward a foursome leaning elegantly against the fake-marble fireplace.

"That's Herb Dutton. An old friend of Rupert's and mine. He's a big muckymuck at State. In Washington." Stuart couldn't hide his elation at landing a big fish. "Very involved with the real decisions, you know. He asks my advice from time to time."

Sylvia tried to hide her concern for the future of American foreign policy. Maybe she underestimated Stuart. Maybe he was a gifted tactician.

He led her over. Sylvia smiled hello at Rupert Thompson and his rather faded wife whose name entirely escaped her. She could hardly ask, having met the woman at least a dozen times. Rupert was a thin man with the cavernous face of a modern and somewhat sexy Abe Lincoln. Even assuming that he'd gotten better-looking as he'd aged, which was probably the case, it was hard to understand why he'd chosen to marry the dowdy, prissy woman at his side.

Stuart made the introductions, recalling just in time that courtesy required that he introduce Pat Dutton as well as her husband. Stuart had difficulty remembering people who had nothing to offer him. Dutton was a small, slender man with one of the perfectly round faces that defied remembrance. He looked about forty but since his matronly wife looked at least fifteen years older, Sylvia had to assume that he, like Thompson, had aged well.

"Pleased to meet you." Dutton smiled broadly. "I read about the Cavendish trial last year and I wanted to meet the great lawyer."

Cavendish had been charged with masterminding a loan-sharking operation. He'd protested his innocence to a generally unbelieving audience, but Sylvia had accepted his story and had defended him successfully on the basis of it. In fact, his tale of being framed, incredible though it sounded, had since proved true, and two of his brothers-in-law were enjoying the hospitality of the State because of it.

"Another drink, folks? Before we go in for the little lady's meal?" Stuart was flushed with his dinner party's success. He'd landed two big-time lawyers, three if you counted Sylvia which he was unlikely to do, a senior mandarin in the government, and as the *pièce de résistance*, Thompson, who was the director of the Wandling Institute, the most prestigious think tank on the Eastern Seaboard. Stuart had gloated for months after the Institute had become a client.

"I believe you know Margo Whitten?" Pat Dutton spoke softly as though she was used to being ignored.

"Yes," Sylvia smiled, resisting the impulse to bend down to speak to the small woman. "We went to school together."

"I knew her mother well. She died years ago but I've kept in touch with Margo. We both think the world of her. Herb usually asks for her when he needs advice from a lawyer in Justice."

"I wish I had the time to keep in touch. We were inseparable at law school but I hardly ever see her nowadays."

"Dinner is served." Doris was showing a little animation. She loved the idea of food although she seldom allowed herself to swallow any.

John was at Sylvia's elbow. "Don't drink any more. You've had enough," he muttered with a fixed smile as though exchanging sweet nothings.

"I have not." Sylvia spoke wearily. John had persisted for the last ten years in thinking she'd embarrass him in public. All because she had once, in reaction to their first serious fight shortly after their marriage, become plastered at a party. Since then, she'd been scrupulous about booze. Not to mention that she'd become somewhat more hardened to their disagreements,

"What a beautiful couple you make," Susan Pennell cooed.

It was true. Sylvia had hardly noticed that John was fifteen years older than she when she met him. Nor had the fact of his Swiss background and European outlook bothered her. She'd had eyes only for his broad shoulders, the thick lashes around his gray eyes, his height which gave him a good four inches on her. His sideburns were silver now and his face was lined but he was still downright handsome.

All in all, the men in the room were a good-looking bunch, disproving the theory that high-pressure jobs kill. The men here were far more attractive than the women, they were sexier, appeared to age more slowly, and she'd take odds on them living longer. Being the wife of a Great Man was a harder life by far.

Susan was eyeing John covetously. "You can't take your own wife in to dinner. It's just not done."

"Well, then I'll have the pleasure of taking you." John was a formal person, a little stiff when he attempted gallantry, but it never seemed to faze his female fans. Sylvia smiled and watched them head off to the dining room.

"May I escort you?"

"Thanks, Rupert." Sylvia took his arm, wondering not for the first time about his motives as they walked into the dining room. Rupert was about an inch shorter than she, but in good physical shape. More importantly, he had charm. Real charm. Not the kind John had shown in their courting days, which turned out to be an old-world gallantry based on the premise that women were fragile and none too bright. Sylvia had only herself to blame. Even her usually vague mother had pointed out that a man born and bred in Switzerland was unlikely to have American views about women. Rupert amused her, taking the trouble to make her laugh. If she ever did step out, it would definitely be with someone who made her laugh.

"Sylvia, you sit there." Stuart was fussing about self-importantly.

She took her seat at the long rosewood table between Dutton and Al Pennell. John had been placed on the opposite side between their wives. If she tried, she could avoid his eyes and enjoy the wine. She decided to do so. They'd have a hell of a fight later anyway, about her tardiness. Might as well be shot for a sheep as for a lamb.

For once, Stuart didn't dominate dinnertime conversation.

He was apparently somewhat awed by Thompson and Dutton who seemed to know everyone worth knowing, at least in Stuart's estimation, and their version of gossip was high-level enough to be published on the front page of the *Times*.

The only flaw was that Sylvia wasn't interested in high-level gossip. She enjoyed the meal, which was excellent as it should have been since it was catered by the most expensive outfit in town, and otherwise occupied herself by worrying about her cases.

"Do you know Lorne, Sylvia?" Rupert was smiling at her daydreaming. John was not.

"Uh . . ."

"Lorne Reyes," Rupert helped her out. "I was just saying that he's in line for a very cushy appointment."

"I don't believe I've met him. Is he a lawyer?"

"Yes, but he never practiced. He mentioned he'd been at Columbia with you when I said I'd be seeing you tonight. You and John," he added.

"Oh, I see. Well, I was one of very few girls at law school. I'm afraid that I didn't know all of the guys' names though they knew me." It was still a problem. Sylvia was forever running into lawyers who greeted her familiarly and whom she couldn't recall having laid eyes on before. She took to calling them "there," as in "hi, there." Sometimes, to avoid the possibility of snubbing a former classmate, she was friendly to total strangers in elevators.

"Lorne's done very well, even if I do say so myself," Rupert commented.

"I should say so. He's been with you at Wandling for six years now?" Dutton asked.

"Nearer seven. It couldn't happen to a nicer guy. Will you be dealing with him once he gets to the White House, Herb?"

"Probably. We use informal conduits to the President whenever we can get them. With Lorne at his right hand, I'm sure we'll be seeing a lot of each other."

A vague picture of a blond, rotund boy in a sweatshirt was forming in Sylvia's mind. Presumably, Lorne had dropped the sweatshirt for a jacket immediately upon being called to the Bar. He must have, to earn the respect necessary for an appointment to the White House.

"He'll be staying in his own field?" Sylvia asked, implying that she had some notion of what that field might be.

"That's right. Foreign Affairs. He's worked in that almost

exclusively for the last two years."

Stuart was feeling left out. "I understand he did a hell of a job on the terrorist conference."

Dutton and Thompson nodded.

"You had a conference with terrorists?" Susan Pennell creased her forehead.

"Not with them, dear." Al was very embarrassed. "About them. A conference about terrorists."

"Oh." She nodded unconvincingly. "I see."

Doris stood up. "If the women would like to retire with me, we can leave you men to your dull politics."

Sylvia was appalled. She hadn't been placed in this position for years. Every principle screamed no, but John was distinctly staring at her in an effort to will her out of the room.

"Uh, why don't we stay and share the enlightenment?" she suggested tentatively. With a weak smile at her host.

"Sure. Why not?" Herb Dutton came to her rescue and Stuart had no option but to reverse direction.

"Of course. That's old hat, nowadays. Sit down, Doris."

She shrugged and sat. Sylvia couldn't help but admire her absolute lack of concern over the conduct of the party.

It turned out that Doris had been right after all. The conversation was dull, duller even than it had been during dinner. Sylvia thought about dinner parties she used to attend. In her younger days she had been very unconventional, and if anyone had suggested that she'd find herself, one dreary day, in a group like this one she'd have laughed. Or cried. Her parents, somewhat nonconformist themselves, had encouraged her to travel, to work at unusual jobs, to experience a world somewhat broader than that dreamed of by middle-class America in the fifties. It had been partly her fear of parties like this that had kept her from marrying John for three years. She gave in when her fear of losing him overcame everything else. Sylvia tried not to get wistful.

Afterwards, she walked out with the men to get the car, leaving John who didn't drive standing at the door with the women. For one brief moment she imagined herself avoiding the impending battle by simply driving off.

She regretfully pushed the unuxorious thought out of her mind. She and John smiled and waved good-bye. As soon as she'd put her foot back on the accelerator, the atmosphere changed.

"Okay, John, out with it." Anything was better than cold silence.

"I don't think there's any point in saying anything. You apparently have no idea how one should behave and nothing I say will change you." John proceeded to outline her faults in detail, both in general and with specific reference to the evening.

"And," he finished up, "you not only appear late and badly dressed, but you make a scene when your hostess suggests a time-honored division of the party."

"Time-honored, my foot." Sylvia snorted in disgust. "I didn't go to law school so I could retire to talk about my children while brilliant men discuss affairs of the world." This was not the moment to mention that the men had been as uninspiring as the women would have been.

"It would be a good thing if you were interested enough in your children to want to talk about them." John's nostrils were flaring and his face was pale. Signs of real anger.

"Look, I'm sorry but Dutton agreed with me. If it's any consolation, I'd have disappeared like a good little girl if no one had spoken up. For your sake."

"Don't give me that! If you cared about my sake you'd have taken some trouble tonight. Even to dress right! These men are important to me. Dutton's the guy who asked me to sit on the Presidential Commission on Securities Regulation—"

"Which you turned down," Sylvia interrupted, "for some unknown reason."

"I've told you, corporate clients don't like their lawyers to be in the news too much. And Dutton can send me a lot that I do want! Moreover, Thompson's an important client, not to mention one of the most influential men in the country! I hear he's in line for something really big, the announcement's due any day now. So you could have acted like a help to me. Instead of . . . of . . ." Words failed him.

Sylvia lost her temper. "You listen to me for a minute! I've been working since seven-thirty this morning and I stopped only because of this goddamn party which I didn't want to go to and didn't enjoy. I went for only one reason, because you wanted me to!"

The rest of the drive passed in silence. Sylvia's stomach was killing her and the cigarettes she chain-smoked weren't helping.

She drove through the dark, winding streets of their Long Island village. The car lights caught the large trees and hedges, pinning them against the backdrop of bucolic frame houses and frothy gardens. Very pretty, but she'd never pictured herself as a commuting suburbanite. She'd loved their eight-room apartment on the upper East Side facing the park, and in particular she'd been happy with the short cab ride that took her to the steps of her office.

The car turned into the driveway. Their house was a white-trimmed gray stone affair, just beyond the village limits. The inside lights were off, but the floodlights that illuminated the entire lot somewhat lessened the rustic flavor. She'd assumed that at least there would be one advantage to the move to the suburbs, a move she'd fought tooth and nail, namely that life would be simple and safe. In fact, every break-and-enter artist worth his salt knew where Long Island was and almost every house had burglar alarms and floodlights.

John stalked into the house, clearly headed for his study where when angry with her he bedded down. Not that it made much difference. Even when nothing specific kept him from the conjugal bed, he showed little interest in anything but his bedside reading.

Sylvia should have been used to it by now but she wasn't. She watched his retreating back, feeling as though she'd been kicked in the stomach. It took her a long time to fall asleep.

The telephone woke her just after six in the morning. It was kept on John's side of the bed, and it took a few rings before she gathered her wits together sufficiently to realize that he wasn't there to answer it.

"Hello?" Sylvia wanted to be angry but she was too tired to express hostility. "Hello?"

The line went dead.

"Who was that?" John stood in the doorway of their bedroom. His face looked pale and strained.

"I don't know. Wrong number." Sylvia turned over to go back to sleep.

"What did he say?"

"Nothing." It was going to be difficult to relax again.

"Tell me exactly what he said!"

John seldom raised his voice. Sylvia sat up again in surprise. "What's the matter, John? It was a wrong number. When I answered, whoever it was hung up. No big deal."

John turned on his heel and left.

"Hold it," Sylvia called after him. "What was that all about?"

He didn't respond.

Sylvia was now awake. She went downstairs to make the first of her several pots of coffee, wondering what was bothering John. He certainly couldn't blame her for the call. Unless he thought it was her boyfriend. And the way things had been lately, even if it were, he probably wouldn't give a damn. It looked as if it was going to be a long weekend.

TWO

Sylvia closed the door behind her on Monday morning with a thankful sigh. Her feelings about the weekend had proved correct. John had maintained an icy silence and the boys, whose antics were usually a relaxing pleasure, had picked up on the atmosphere and had wrangled and whined continually. The high points of the weekend had been her normally detested mile-long jogs in the mornings.

She walked away from the sounds of her sons' roughhousing and got into the car, lighting a cigarette and enjoying the feel of the early sun through the windshield. She made a mental note to bring the children a treat tonight to make up for their parents' moodiness.

John strode out and crammed his long legs into the space beside her.

"Is it absolutely necessary to smoke at this hour? It smells disgusting."

"Sorry." Sylvia put it out. An auspicious beginning to the day. "How did you manage to get away from the children?"

"Not easily. Jay wanted me to punish Carl for scraping his bicycle yesterday."

"Did you solve the problem?" It was vaguely amusing to picture cool reserved John trying to separate two screaming little boys.

"I did my best."

Sylvia maneuvered the car into the already-heavy expressway traffic. "And we had two so they'd be friends for each other."

"They would be if they had better manners." The implied criticism of her methods of child-rearing didn't have to be spelled out. It had been, often enough.

Sylvia cast around for a safer topic. "What's your schedule today?"

"The usual. Half a dozen appointments and a tax seminar to write. What about you?"

14

"I'm . . . oh, damn!" Traffic had come to a complete stand-still. "John, I can't bear this commuting. The house is gorgeous but I'm becoming hysterical over the drive. I wish you'd reconsider the idea of living in the city again."

John was silent. She looked over at him. He was staring out the side window.

"Did you hear me?"

Eventually he turned. "The city is out of the question. The children get little enough from you. The least we can provide for them is a healthy neighborhood." He didn't speak loudly but his coldness was a good hint that he considered the subject closed.

Sylvia was about to argue the point but decided that the matter was best pursued after work. "I started to say that I'm beginning the Larson trial today."

It was depressing that John had so little interest in her life that he had forgotten a major jury trial. If they didn't start talking to each other soon, there wouldn't be anything left to talk about.

Sylvia turned to him conciliatingly but John was furious.

"I suppose that means that your children won't see you for days. I'll take a taxi home so they won't be all alone."

Sylvia tried to lighten the atmosphere. "One of these days, John, you're going to have to learn to drive. Your annual cab bill would pay for a Mercedes."

"I don't want a Mercedes."

Sylvia gave up. She lit a cigarette and continued the drive without speaking.

The car crawled along Broad Street and pulled up in front of a slightly grimy, elaborately decorated stone skyscraper. John muttered good-bye and opened his door.

"I remember holding up traffic in the old days. I guess the honeymoon's over." Sylvia smiled as she spoke but John got out as though he hadn't heard.

She watched impassively as he entered the building.

Sylvia's firm had large offices behind a security door on the twelfth floor of a stodgy Madison Avenue building. Clients announced themselves to a receptionist cunningly caged in a bullet-proof bubble who then, if the spirit moved her, would press the magic button that opened their way to sage and conservative counsel. Sylvia had joined the firm after practicing on her own for a year, mainly because John had convinced her that that was the only conceivable route to respectability and security, two items he regarded as akin to godliness. Her partners, commercial and corporate practitioners for the most part, had hoped that she would defend white-collar crime, specifically the peccadilloes of their triple-A clients. She did so, but in addition she maintained her rawer clientele to the disapproval and sometimes horror of her colleagues.

"Morning, Sylvia." Her secretary had followed her into the inner office. Bess was a colorfully dressed, plump, vivacious woman in her late forties with black eyes and hair and a quick, sharp tongue. She'd been with Sylvia for more than ten years, ever since Sylvia had started to practice law. Over that time, they'd become fast friends. When Sylvia thought about it, Bess was probably her only close friend because she hadn't had the time to keep up with any of the others.

"There are several messages about the Larson case, Sylvia. Davidson from the D.A.'s office wants an adjournment. Something's come up. And the duty counsel at the jail called. Larson wants to see you before court."

"Mmm." Sylvia had grabbed a cup of coffee on her way in and was sipping it as she chewed three Riopan. Her stomach was on fire.

"Had a bad morning?" Bess was scowling at the black coffee.

"What? Oh, yes, I guess I did. Never mind." She sat behind the desk. "Get me Davidson on the line. No, on second thought, just tell him I've gone straight to court. That bastard isn't getting another adjournment with my man in custody. I'll do some of the mail now and then I'll go see Larson."

She picked up her package of cigarettes and debated whether to light one. She put them down, feeling virtuous as hell. A minute later Bess walked back in.

"Davidson wasn't happy."

"I've got other problems right now," Sylvia said grimly. "Did you see the mail? Hereford skipped bail, the State's appealing the Butterworth acquittal, and Mrs. Fellowes wants me to know that a five-year-old could have won her son's trial and she intends to sue me."

"Why don't you have a nice cup of tea and relax for a while?" Bess spoke soothingly as she wandered around tidying up. The office was furnished with two pale-blue couches facing each other, framed by two wing chairs covered with a blue and yellow print. Except for the desk, a large walnut affair inlaid with tooled leather, it might have been a living room.

It was actually a lot nicer than Sylvia's living room. Which was a sore point with John who couldn't accept that her work was more important than the traditionally female task of fixing up the nest.

"The office is getting shabby, Sylvia." Bess grimaced at the grease marks left behind by a few of the less attractive specimens who had visited. "We should redo a few things."

"Whatever you think," Sylvia said absently. Bess had decorated the office in the first place and Sylvia was only too happy to allow her to carry on.

"How's your stomach now?"

"Better." If you preferred dull pain to sharp spasms.

"Sylvia, you can't go on like this." Bess looked unhappily at the strain lines around Sylvia's eyes and mouth. They were getting deeper by the day. "Why don't you take some time off?"

"It wouldn't help."

Bess nodded reluctantly. She'd been married too. Once upon a time. It had not been a notable success, a volatile Jewish woman married to an inhibited Presbyterian accountant. She'd become something of an expert in recognizing the signs of a losing matrimonial battle, and every one of them could be seen on Sylvia's face. Bess had watched with dismay as Sylvia's home life had disintegrated along with her stomach lining but she'd kept her mouth uncharacteristically shut.

She'd opposed the marriage in the first place, an attitude which at the time had resulted in serious tension between the two women. Those scars had healed but it still wasn't wise for her to criticize John.

Still less to point out that she'd been right. Bess had figured from the beginning that a man who arrived fully grown in the New World, who cut himself off from his mother, his only living relative, who never made any close friends, was a bad marital bet. Moreover, she'd sensed immediately that John chose to marry a woman fifteen years his junior so that he could mold her to his taste. Unfortunately, he'd miscalculated. He had never counted on Sylvia becoming such a big success.

"Go away by yourself for a while," Bess suggested. "I did, right after that bastard took off, and it was the smartest move I ever made. By the time I got back, I didn't give a tinker's damn about him."

"I can't. First of all, John's not a bastard and besides, I've got two kids. You were in a different position."

"Yeah. To have children, you have to get laid." Bess snorted. Murray had not been the passionate type.

"Let's get back to work." Sylvia didn't want to pursue the topic. It was too sore a point these days. "I've got to get to court soon."

Forty minutes later Sylvia stood and gathered up her paraphernalia. It wasn't even ten o'clock and she was exhausted. Matrimony and motherhood didn't exactly enhance a law practice.

Bess picked up a memo slip as Sylvia passed. "Oh, one more thing. An Inspector Friedman called while you were working. He wouldn't say what he wanted. He just asked if you were in town today and when I said yes, he asked if you'd be here tomorrow too."

"Well, I haven't got time now. I'll call after court."

"He didn't leave a number but I guess the police switchboard will connect you."

THREE

Sylvia nodded at the guard as she entered the dingy holding cell. As usual, the smell of ground-in urine and sweat caused her to long for the camouflage of a cigarette. Six men dressed in rumpled, unwashed T-shirts and jeans lounged on splintering benches, waiting to be taken upstairs to the courtrooms for their trials. Larson was one of them.

"Come on over to the bars," Sylvia said so that the two of them could have at least the illusion of privacy. "Now, what's the matter?"

Larson had a lengthy criminal record. If he went down on his present charge of robbery, he stood a very good chance of going away for life. Whatever macho bravado he mustered on the street didn't show in custody. He shuffled his feet with a sheepish expression as he informed Sylvia that he'd assaulted a guard in the prison yard with a stone he'd picked up.

Sylvia sighed. This case could have been very exciting because she actually had what might amount to a defense in law, something that occurred rarely in a criminal practice. She'd been working like a mad woman to prepare for the trial and she'd been looking forward to it. This latest development could force her to make a deal with the prosecutor.

"Have you been questioned yet about the assault?"

"Not exactly." Larson shrugged vaguely.

Sylvia took a closer look at him. Larson wasn't in the prime of life but he'd looked better the last time she'd seen him.

"Did they rough you up?"

"Some." Larson, like many experienced cons, was philosophical about the use of force. When on his own, he employed it himself. He didn't think it strange that the authorities on their turf did the same.

Sylvia warned him to keep his mouth shut about the incident, repeating her caution twice to be on the safe side. Larson had served time because of informers, but he still tended to forget that every second inmate of the holding cells was a stoolie.

She trudged upstairs to eat crow with the D.A.'s man. Sometimes she thought about a real estate practice with longing.

The assaulted guard had just died. Sylvia had long since hardened herself not to think about the victims. Otherwise, it would have been impossible to practice criminal law. She answered her conscience, on the rare occasions when it raised questions about the morality of her work, with truisms about everyone's right to a defense.

She sighed and agreed to an adjournment of today's trial.

Bess was happy to see her return early. Their paper work was way behind and now Sylvia had no excuse to avoid it.

Sylvia glumly sat down at her desk. She hated paper-pushing. She'd never had a sedentary job. She'd worked in bookstores, been a waitress, sold artsy crafts, and in one particularly memorable semester been a go-go dancer. Never behind a desk. In fact, John's strongest argument when he'd convinced her to leave her sole practice for the firm had been the end to administrative paper work.

By five o'clock she was convinced that she'd been swotting for a week, but there was no doubt about the fact that the desk looked better. In a few places, one could actually see the leather inlay.

Sylvia dialed John's number and spoke to his secretary.

"Hi, Janice. Sylvia here. Is John available?"

"Why, no. He hasn't been in all day. We thought he was sick since all his appointments were canceled."

Sylvia hung up in bewilderment. She called home but Jay told her that Daddy hadn't spent the day there either. All this was most unlike John. He was the soul of reliability, as he was fond of pointing out to her as a contrast to her own behavior. A stab of alarm hit her; she quickly brushed it away. Something must have come up early in the day. What could happen to a grown man in his own office building?

Nonetheless, she grabbed a couple of candy bars for the boys and hurried home as fast as rush hour would permit. Which wasn't very fast. A person had to be crazy to live like this.

Nothing had been heard from John. Sylvia pulled her housekeeper into the kitchen.

"Ingrid, have you spoken to John today?"

"No." Ingrid shook her head in disappointment. She was a small gray-haired, gray-clad woman of indeterminate age, wearing an air of perpetual disappointment. She'd never expected much from life and it hadn't handed her more. "No, he never called. But the man was around this afternoon looking for him."

"What man?"

"I don't know who he was. He never said."

"What did he say?"

"He just asked if Mr. West was in. I said he was at work, like usual, and he left very rudely. Didn't say good-bye, thank you, nothing."

"What did he look like?"

"I dunno." Ingrid was a very nice woman and the boys adored her, probably because she let them get away with murder. But trying to get information from her on even the simplest things was impossible. Sylvia pursued the matter, but Ingrid remained obstinately vague.

"Did either of the boys see him?" Sylvia tried one last time.

"No." Ingrid, presumably realizing that her employer wasn't entirely happy with the conversation, volunteered that they had been at school at the time.

Sylvia went out to the huge, child-ravaged backyard to spend some time with the boys. She played ball for a while but her heart wasn't in it and finally, after missing a catch for the umpteenth time, she called it quits. The boys were disgusted with her performance anyway and expressed no sorrow that she was leaving the game.

Sylvia paced around the living room for a few minutes, tripping over sports equipment every few feet.

"This room is a pigsty. Doesn't anyone ever clean it up?" She was muttering but unfortunately Ingrid was passing the doorway and heard. One of Ingrid's other faults was that she was not good at taking constructive criticism. With a moan, she rushed up to her room where she was likely to stay for several hours despite all blandishments and apologies.

"Goddamn it!" Sylvia had to take over dinner now, if she wanted to have one. And one of the myriad wifely duties she'd never had time to learn was cooking. Another failure that had not smoothed the path of her marriage.

The two kids crashed into the kitchen just as she was putting a rather underdone chicken on the plates with overdone vegetables.

"Yech!" the boys yelled with some justification, but overcome with famine, they attacked the meal and in short order dashed outside again.

"Come in when it gets dark," Sylvia called after them. She sat at the table a while longer gazing at the wall phone. Finally she picked it up. None of John's colleagues and acquaintances were able to offer assistance. They were unanimous in their surprise at his failure to appear.

Stuart Paliano took it worse than most. "I'm bloody mad about it. He was supposed to see a new client today. Supposedly a good account. And now the client's furious about John missing the appointment. When you find him, I want an explanation!"

Sylvia restrained her urge to scream like a fishwife and tried to smooth his ruffled feathers. The long and the short of it was that John had disappeared into thin air. The last anyone had seen of him was when she watched him enter the lobby of his office building.

Should she call the police?

The question echoed around in her mind while she sat at the table, munching her pills like candies.

It would be embarrassing if she did call them and John turned up with a perfectly good explanation. Not that one sprang to mind. She hated to make a fool of herself in front of the cops. It had taken years to get them to treat her seriously in the first place. She was still undecided after supervising the boys' baths and reading them a story. In the end, she followed them up to bed without picking up the phone again.

At seven o'clock the next morning Sylvia threw on her comfortingly bedraggled housecoat and grabbed the telephone. She had spent a sleepless night counting her marital sins rather than sheep. The list had filled a long night.

According to John's rigid standards, she hadn't been much of a wife. It had become apparent soon after the boys were born that she and John were mismatched, but neither had been willing to face up to that conclusion. They had pretended that the happiness of the first year continued to lurk around the corner.

When she had first met John, Sylvia thought he was the world's most handsome and clever man. She accepted his views of almost everything, including his didactic statements about her own shortcomings. She became convinced that their problems were her fault and she tried to remake herself in his image. She gave in to John on every point but one. The big one. Some atavistic instinct of self-preservation kept her working. As the uneasy truce disintegrated, there were times when only her work kept her sane. During the night, Sylvia had blamed herself bitterly for sticking her head in the sand, for refusing to deal with their problems. But reason told her that nothing short of succumbing completely, of staying home, would have satisfied John. There had been no acceptable compromise, so she'd given up without an attempt.

All this insight didn't help much at the moment.

"N.Y.P.D. Who do you want to speak to?"

Who indeed. Missing Persons Branch was the obvious choice but Sylvia was too worried now to care about her image. Someone who knew her might be more helpful than a faceless bureaucrat.

"Uh, Detective Masowski, please." Dave and she had worked together on several cases and they had developed a good relationship.

By some miracle, he was in his office.

"Dave, it's Sylvia West. I've got a problem."

He waited for her to go on, but now that she had him on the line, she was hesitant.

"Well, it's John. My husband. He's disappeared."

"What?"

"Yes, I left him off at his office yesterday morning and he never showed up. No one in his office knows where he is and he didn't come home last night."

"When did you speak to him last? Who spoke to him yesterday?" The officer was taken aback. Sylvia was the last person he could imagine involved with scandal.

"I guess I saw him last. His secretary said he didn't come in at all. Wait, she did say something about canceling his appointments for yesterday. Which is odd because . . ." Sylvia fell silent.

"Because what?"

"Uh, on our way to work yesterday morning, John mentioned he had a half dozen clients to see."

Masowski didn't say anything. Sylvia reached for an antacid tablet. She knew how it sounded.

"Dave, you've got to listen to me. You don't know John.

He wasn't the kind of man to run away. He was, he is, un-believably controlled. He's Swiss." As if that explained every-thing. "I mean, he always does the right thing. He built his life around duty. His practice, his sons. And me, of course," she added weakly. "He wouldn't leave just like that. Check with his friends, his partners. With anybody. Something must have happened to him."

Masowski was noncommittal. "This is really a Missing Persons case. Since I know you I'll start on it, but if he doesn't turn up really soon, I'll have to hand it over. They're pretty good on this kind of thing anyway. Right now, I'll need some information. Who are your husband's pals? What clubs does he belong to? What was he wearing yesterday? Is anything missing?"

The obvious things she'd checked out last night. Sylvia curbed her impatience and answered all the questions.

"Okay, Sylvia. I'll get on this and keep in touch. You'll be at home, I guess?"

"No, at the office. There's no point in sitting around here and worrying myself to death. Besides, that would scare the kids."

Masowski hung up. It was odd that a man would leave someone like Sylvia. Especially when she seemed to be in love with him. Lots of lawyers and policemen had made overtures to her over the years, but as far as he knew, she'd stayed on the straight and narrow.

Still, stranger things had happened. Like as not, the guy would be found in due course, shacked up with his girl friend.

The phone rang. It was Sylvia again. "I just remembered something. My housekeeper told me a man came around look-ing for John yesterday afternoon."

"Did he give a name? What did he want?"

"No name, and Ingrid couldn't remember a thing about him. He didn't leave a message. It seems strange. Why would any-one think he'd be at home at that time of day? And apparently the man was rude."

"Well," Masowski said slowly, "it is a bit unusual, but it could have been a client who found out he wasn't in his office."

"No way. His clients don't go to their lawyers' houses. Besides, a client or a friend would have left a name."

"Maybe I better speak to your housekeeper then. Will you tell her I'll be around sometime today?"

"Thanks." Sylvia paused. "John thought he'd be home last night."

Masowski perked up. "How do you know?"

"He mentioned that he'd take a taxi home because I thought I was going to be tied up with a trial." Silence. "He, uh, was a little upset that I wouldn't be home with the boys. He made a point of having to be there so they wouldn't feel like orphans. He loved them. He wouldn't have let them down."

From the way Dave said good-bye, Sylvia was under no illusions about his reaction to this tidbit. He was about as impressed with it as if she'd said she'd had a premonition.

The navy pants and striped blouse she'd worn the previous day were where she'd flung them. It seemed simpler to put them on again, particularly since John wasn't around to complain about a few wrinkles. Jay and Carl were noisily eating breakfast when she entered the kitchen.

"Is Daddy out of town?" Carl preferred to talk with his mouth full.

"Uh, yes. And stop eating like a pig!" Sylvia was angry with herself for snapping at him. "I'll bring home fried chicken tonight," she promised, to make up for her bad mood.

"Yay!!"

Sylvia hurriedly kissed them good-bye. She wasn't up to their high spirits. As she left the kitchen, she spoke to Ingrid who was still sulking but at least had emerged from her room.

"If you hear from John, please tell him to call me immediately."

As if he wouldn't know how frantic she'd be.

Sylvia had learned to control her emotions. Her mother, a full professor of Tudor history at Cornell, had constantly admonished her against publicly showing how she felt. Her parents had brought up their only child to aspire to a professional career, and in anticipation of it, they had not indulged any girlish tears. Later, Sylvia had had the lessons reinforced as a woman in a man's world. Male lawyers could yell and get red. It was called a tactic. Female lawyers who did the same thing were called emotional and were mistrusted. Sylvia had sometimes wondered if the price she'd paid for all this control was the loss of all emotion.

Today she didn't have to worry about that. The control refused to work. She couldn't concentrate on the simplest things and eventually she gave up. She and Bess spent most of the morning discussing the mystery, going over everything time and again.

By noon, every ashtray in the office was overflowing and the sheer bulk of the antacid tablets she'd swallowed was making Sylvia ill. She decided to call Janice.

"Sylvia speaking. Have you heard from John yet today?"

"No, we haven't. What's happening? The police came by to ask some questions and they said he's disappeared! We didn't want to disturb you but Mr. Paliano said if you called, he wanted to talk to you."

"I can't right now," Sylvia said hastily. "I'll call him back as soon as I can." The last thing she wanted to do was speak to Stuart. He was probably taking John's disappearance as a personal insult.

At three, Bess announced that Masowski was on the line.

"No luck so far, I'm afraid," he said. "I've been making some inquiries myself and I haven't come up with anything. If it's any consolation, he wasn't in an accident. At least not within fifty miles of the city."

"Dear God. What do we do now?"

Dave must have realized how close to breaking she was because his voice softened. "Listen," he said. "There's no point in doing this on the phone. I'll come over and see you. We've got to ask a lot more questions."

"We?"

"Yes, I had to call in Missing Persons when your husband didn't turn up after the preliminary investigation. A Captain Cameron is going to take the case over. Apparently he's the best they've got. In fact, he may come over with me, if that's all right."

Sylvia agreed. She got up to comb her hair and powder her nose in an effort to get a grip on herself. The mirror showed the wear and tear of centuries of hard living.

Bess came in. "What's happening?"

"Nothing. Dave's on his way. He's working on the case a bit longer."

"Good."

"Is there anything urgent?" Not that she was in shape to handle it if there was.

"Nothing I can't deal with. That mysterious Friedman called again and wouldn't leave his number. He wouldn't even say which case he was working on. Do you know him?"

"Never heard of him." Sylvia was indifferent to the small mysteries of life.

"Hi, Sylvia." Dave stood uncomfortably in the doorway. He was of average height and very thin except for a slight bulge where the beer had undoubtedly settled just above the beige jeans. He was by no stretch of the imagination handsome, but his was a nice face, sort of lived-in. It made Sylvia feel better just to see him.

"Come on in. Where's your friend?"

"Cameron? He'll be here later." Dave was curiously non-committal. "Listen, Sylvia, I'm sorry about this. I know how you must be feeling. But we need more information about your husband and it's either me or Cameron asking the questions."

She took a deep breath and lit a cigarette, motioning him to sit opposite her on the second sofa. "Okay. Let's get down to it."

"For a start, tell me something about his background."

"Well, he was born in Switzerland and came here in 1950 after his father died. He didn't get along too well with his mother and he was an only child, like me, so there wasn't anything to keep him in Europe."

"Where does his mother live now?"

"In Geneva. I've only met her once, when she came on a short visit about a year and a half, no, two years ago."

"When did you meet John?"

"I had a summer job with his firm after second-year law school. That would have been, let me see, 1966. We got married three years later."

"And you have two children?"

"Yes. Jay was born in 1970 and Carl in '72."

"How old is John?"

"Fifty-four."

Dave looked up in surprise.

"He's fifteen years older than I am, but he had to start a new life at age twenty-five, after all. He was a law student without a dime. He couldn't just settle down with a family right away." She was a little sensitive about the age difference, probably because Bess had made such a big deal out of it, and, for that matter, so had her family.

"Have you ever been separated?"

"No."

"Has he ever disappeared before?"

"No."

"Does he work late?"

"Rarely. He usually brings work home with him."

"Does he ever stay overnight in town?"

"Never. Look, Dave, I know what you're getting at but he's not a womanizer and never has been. He's a family man. He doesn't have a girl friend. I know that. You'll just have to take my word for it."

"Let's leave that for the moment." Dave was avoiding her eyes. "What about the kids, is he close to them?"

"In his own way, yes. He's very European, very formal by our standards. Manners are important to him. He's strict with the boys, very correct, but he loves them and they know it. They love him, too." Sylvia smiled. "He fought a losing battle, trying to teach them to stand up when an adult entered a room, to use the right fork, that kind of thing. It never made any difference," she added with a sigh.

"What about money?"

"No problem. We both make quite a bit and we've got money in the bank. Besides, John wasn't a big spender."

"Well, that brings us to the crunch. What about you? Was your marriage happy?"

Sylvia was saved for the moment by a knock on the door. Bess poked her head in and announced that a Captain Cameron was outside.

"Send him in," Sylvia instructed.

Cameron was clearly a policeman. Even without the uniform, he would never be taken for anything else. But he was not Sylvia's favorite kind of officer. He was one of the large, bull-like ones, a side of beef that hadn't been hanging very long. His face and neck were bright red and he wasn't blushing. His jacket was tight over the gut but it looked new, so Sylvia had to assume that he was in the process of quickly gaining a lot of weight. She'd have taken a bet that the weight came from too much booze. And that meant he was a mean drunk.

"Hello, Cameron." Dave was standing. "Sylvia West, Captain Cameron."

"I got some questions for you," the fat man grunted without so much as a nod. His style lacked a certain something in charm.

"Detective Masowski was just going over the facts—"

"Uh," Dave broke in apologetically, "uh, Sylvia, it's really

Captain Cameron's case." Captains, even uniformed ones, outranked plainclothes detectives. "He'll take the questioning from here. I'll give you my notes this far," he added, turning to the other man.

"Yeah. So, your husband's gone." Cameron sat down heavily on a protesting wing chair and pulled out his notebook. "Nine times outa ten, it's the same story. Money or a dame."

Sylvia noticed Dave wince. Cameron would be a great asset to the force's public relations department. Still, if he was good at his job, she could do without charisma.

"I gotta ask you to be frank with us. What was your husband's weakness?"

"Neither of the two you mentioned. John was a family man and he had more than enough money for his needs."

"The marriage was perfect, right?" Cameron looked at her pityingly.

Sylvia flushed. "No, I didn't say that. We disagreed about a lot of things. Like all married couples do. But that doesn't mean he had a reason for running away."

She got up and walked over to the window. "He wouldn't leave all his responsibilities without saying anything. He wouldn't have left his sons without a word." She looked out sadly. "Even if he'd have left me, he wouldn't have run away from them."

Cameron wasn't affected by the pathos in the air. "Any good fights lately?"

"No. We had, uh, ongoing disagreements but not really a fight." You had to talk to fight.

Sylvia crossed back to her desk. "Have you seen a picture of him?"

"No." Dave seemed interested, even if Cameron wasn't.

She handed Dave the family portrait that sat on her desk.

"Nice looking. What's the cake for?"

"It was our ninth anniversary. Last year. John organized a party."

"He was sentimental?"

"Yes, very. He never forgot, forgets, a birthday or an anniversary."

Cameron felt left out. "I'll take the picture," he barked.

"Very well, but you will give it back?"

"Yeah. Afterwards." Cameron was vague about the time frame. Sylvia had the feeling that if she pushed for more specificity, it could only further depress her.

"Let's go, Masowski." Cameron heaved himself up, no mean feat.

Dave started to the door with Cameron. "Oh, one more thing, Sylvia. We should get in touch with your mother-in-law. Maybe she's heard something."

"I don't have the address, I'm afraid."

"What?" Both men were looking at her strangely.

"Well, I never had anything to do with her. John didn't want to be close to her so I didn't push it. To be honest, once I met her, I understood why he felt that way. She was, to put it politely, formidable. And she didn't take to me so you'd notice either."

"Surely your husband had some contact with her?"

"She sends the boys presents from time to time, through John's office. That was about it."

"His secretary will probably have the address then. Okay, thanks, Sylvia."

She watched them leave, wondering why it had been so difficult to describe John. He was almost shadowy in her mind. She might have been asked to describe a stranger.

Dave parted from Cameron at the door of the office building. He walked along Forty-second Street, oblivious to the crowds and the raucous street vendors. Sylvia was an interesting woman. It wasn't his department, but he'd keep an eye on the case. He liked her. She was clearly badly hurt by the disappearance. But she was tough. She'd had to be, no doubt. A criminal lawyer, especially a woman, had to be tough. Or fail. The same rule seemed to apply to some marriages, like the one he'd left a year ago.

Sylvia decided to go home. She was all the boys had now, which meant she'd have to work harder at parenting. Small wonder Dave had been shocked about Mrs. West. What kind of a mother made no effort to keep in touch with her children's grandmother?

The parking garage attendant kept her waiting a good ten minutes. Sylvia spent them trying to recall the good times she and John had had. It wasn't easy; they were eclipsed by the horrors. Like her fifth wedding anniversary. John had gone to a lot of trouble to arrange a romantic weekend away. And she'd gotten a new client, a big tax evasion case, the kind a criminal lawyer lusts after. She'd had to cancel the weekend. Had to? Had chosen to. John had seldom been that angry and she had been furious that he wouldn't try to understand. No wonder the romance had disappeared. She opened her purse and took out another bottle of Riopan tablets.

FOUR

Sylvia was almost home when she remembered her promise to the boys to bring back fried chicken. Traffic was, as usual, terrible and the takeout restaurant meant retracing her route but she didn't like to imagine their reaction if she arrived empty-handed. Unenthusiastically, she turned the car around.

The frowsy waitress was behind the counter. As Sylvia waited in the hot, humid shop for her order, the woman broke her usual sullen silence.

"Isn't it your husband that's missing?"

Sylvia was so stunned by this apparent omniscience that she just stared.

The waitress responded to the unspoken question. "It was on the news, dearie. I recognized him from seeing him in here with you."

Sylvia hadn't thought of John's disappearance as news, and she certainly hadn't expected the media to pick it up. Which was foolish. Anything out of the ordinary was grist for their mill but it was sheer bad luck that they'd cottoned on so fast.

With a shock, she remembered the children. Ingrid often had the television on as she made supper or cleaned up. They might have seen the news! Sylvia turned and dashed out of the restaurant.

She drove home as fast as possible, breaking her record time as well as several bylaws.

Jay met her at the door. "Where's Daddy? The man on TV said he's gone away!"

Sylvia led Jay into the living room and called Carl who was sitting on the landing clutching his old stuffed tiger, something he did only when very upset. She hugged them to her and tried to explain the inexplicable. Not unreasonably, the boys weren't satisfied with her outline of the situation.

"But," Carl cried, "Daddy wouldn't go away without us!"

Jay tearfully agreed. "Daddy was going to take us to the ball game on Sunday, so he's got to come back."

Sylvia felt sick. These were the real victims. She rocked them for a few minutes.

"Why, Mummy? Why would Daddy go away?"

"We'll find out, darling," she promised grimly. She may have been so bad a wife that she didn't have an answer, but the children deserved one. And she'd make sure they got it.

After dinner, Sylvia wearily returned to Manhattan. She parked the car on the deserted street in front of John's office. His firm was a fair-sized one. Twelve partners and twenty-six associates, meaning overworked and underpaid junior lawyers. She was counting on someone working late because it was rare that juniors got to go home before nine or ten.

She wasn't mistaken. The offices were open and Glenn McEwan, a stocky, earnest young man, was still there. He was surprised to see her and more than a little embarrassed.

"I'd like to look through John's papers, if you don't mind."

"Uh, sure. Anything I can do to help?" His round face perked up when she refused.

John worked in a huge corner room, befitting a partner who billed as well as he did. The office was as different from Sylvia's as day from night. Where hers was comfortable and filled with color, his was functional and beige. The large spotless desk of chrome and glass faced four starkly modern chairs covered in pale leather. His bookcases were filled with law books and only one picture graced the cream walls, a severe pen and ink drawing by some minor Italian artist. If the room suggested anything about its occupant's personality, it was only that he might be a wee bit light in that department.

It struck Sylvia that in the room's decoration, as in almost every aspect of his life, John had been careful to avoid exposing his emotions and tastes. She may have deprived him of her time, but he had been stingy in other ways.

His daily diary was in the top drawer of his desk. Yesterday's entries were solely a list of the day's appointments, all apparently with clients. She continued to riffle through the desk.

She was opening the last drawer when the office door opened on a quiet knock.

"I'm going home now, Mrs. West. If, uh, you wouldn't mind making sure that the office is locked when you leave?" Glenn was a bit nervous about leaving a partner's wife alone in the place. Especially since the partner had gone AWOL.

"Certainly. I've locked up many times before, Glenn. And call me Sylvia." She smiled her most reassuring smile and ushered him out before he could change his mind.

Sylvia watched him walk down the dark corridor and let himself out through the heavy mahogany door. The air conditioning was working overtime and she was shivering slightly when she returned to John's desk.

She had found very little in the drawers. A few files, the ones he'd probably worked on last. An outline of his tax paper. Some notes on legislation in his field. Nothing personal. Not even the odds and ends that almost everyone squirrels away despite constant resolutions to stop. No matchbooks, no gum wrappers, bits of string, elastic bands.

Sylvia lit a cigarette, throwing a match into the wastepaper basket. John had no ashtray on his desk. He'd be complaining about her smoking if he were here to see it.

But he wasn't.

A noise in the corridor disturbed her thoughts.

"Glenn?" He must have been really uneasy about leaving her alone with God only knew what professional secrets. "Is that you?"

There was only a silence. Sylvia was suddenly quite certain that someone was standing silently outside the office door. The rhythm of the building's nocturnal quiet had changed. Sylvia's hands were cold and her heart was thudding. She stood up and very carefully made her way over to the door. It took forever to cross the room.

She flung the door open in one fast movement and peered out. She saw only a black, long hall. Empty. She had a subliminal feeling that she'd caught a tiny movement by the main door but the more she concentrated on the feeling, the less sure she became. Taking a deep breath, she raced down to the reception area and flipped on all the light switches, almost blinding herself with the garish fluorescent. There was no one around. She tried to laugh at her fears as she walked back to John's office but even to her own ears, her voice sounded slightly hollow.

She lit another cigarette and resolutely sat behind the desk again, picking up the diary. It had a page at the back for important dates on which John had methodically listed all the birthdays, anniversaries, clothes sizes, facts that she never had at her fingertips. The boys' sizes were in pencil so they could be easily altered as the children grew. Of course. Sylvia closed the book quickly.

There wasn't much of a chance that the answer to John's disappearance lay in his work. Corporate law didn't generally involve dramatic disappearances. Still, she'd have to go through all his files just in case a clue might spring out at her. She'd need a lot of help. First of all, she knew less than nothing about corporate law and secondly, God only knew how the filing system worked here. She'd have to wait for Janice's assistance in the morning.

The telephone rang. Sylvia hesitated and then thought that it might be Ingrid. She picked it up.

There was a long pause before a deep, accented voice spoke. "Is Mr. West there?"

"No, he's not. Who's speaking?" The caller didn't answer. "I'm Mrs. West. Can I help you?"

"When will Mr. West be in?"

"He's away for a while. Are you a client of his?"

"No." A deep chuckle. "I'm an old friend. Where is he?"

Sylvia was losing patience with this conversation. "Who is this?"

The line went dead.

She sat looking thoughtfully at the receiver in her hand. She suddenly recalled the visitor to the house. Should she phone Dave? She was just too tired to suffer through the cross-examination he'd put to her about the call. Tomorrow would do.

She took another look at the diary. It seemed that all six of yesterday's appointments were with clients because each name was followed by a brief note appearing to refer to a legal file. Still, it couldn't hurt to make sure. She walked out to Janice's desk. Sitting beside the duplicate appointment diary was a lengthy master list of clients.

All six of the names checked out. There was nothing to suggest that they were not clients of the most ordinary kind, all the more so since John had never bothered to mention any one of them to her.

The phone rang again.

This time it was Ingrid, plaintively asking when Sylvia would be home. Reporters were calling and knocking on the door and she didn't know how to answer their questions. Sylvia ordered her to say nothing and, in fact, not to answer the door or the telephone.

She was halfway home before she realized that she'd forgotten the diary in her rush to rescue Ingrid. It would have to wait to the next day.

Sure enough, the house was under siege. Many of the reporters covered the crime beat at the courts and she knew them well. With any luck, they'd go away if she talked to them briefly.

They were surprisingly tactful. Sylvia hadn't realized how well they liked her. After she'd outlined the situation and suggested that they ask their audiences to call the police if they'd seen John in the lobby the previous morning, they started to leave.

One guy she didn't know stopped at the road. "Hey, Mrs. West," he called. "Do the cops think there's any foul play involved?"

"Not at this stage. We don't have any theories at all yet." There was no point in asking for screaming headlines.

"Well, that just leaves the usual answer, doesn't it?" He leered.

"I don't know. You'll have to ask the police." She'd give him a miss next time she saw him coming.

"Sorry about that creep," a young woman murmured as she filed past Sylvia. "If there's anything I can do, please call."

Sylvia smiled her thanks. Maggie Brewster was one of the nicest reporters in town.

She closed the door behind her and turned to go to bed. The telephone rang. So far today, it had brought nothing but bad news.

Her luck wasn't changing. It was Stuart.

"What can I do for you?" Sylvia tried to disguise her lack of enthusiasm.

"Some stupid cop was around here today. He wanted to know if John had embezzled anyone's money. I told him that was ridiculous of course, but he made me promise to have an audit made. I've got no choice in the matter. I want you to know that it wasn't my idea and I'm absolutely confident in what it will show. But I did want to give you warning in case you heard about it."

Amazing. And here she'd always thought he was a boor. "Thanks. I appreciate your telling me."

"What do you think happened? It's obvious that he didn't have something on the side."

What a way with words. "No, I don't think so either."

"I don't mean this as an insult, but John was very ordinary. His life was ordinary. What could possibly have happened?"

"I don't know," Sylvia answered honestly, ignoring his assessment of John and peripherally of herself. "But something extraordinary happened to him. There's got to be an explanation somewhere. And I intend to find it."

Wearily she hung up the phone and went upstairs. She stopped in front of the children's rooms and opened the doors to watch them for a long minute. Whatever her own relationship with John, they loved him and they needed him. She went over to kiss their cool faces and finally got ready for bed.

FIVE

It was the last day of spring and the weather was perfect. Sylvia went straight to John's office, hardly noticing the uncharacteristically blue sky or the warm breeze. Janice was available to help her, albeit somewhat reluctant. For the first time, it occurred to Sylvia that John's secretary might well be in love with him. She certainly bristled at the notion of anyone going through his papers.

She took a closer look at the woman. Janice was ageless; she had probably looked exactly as she now did from the time she'd reached puberty. Which was not to say she appeared young. Janice was forty or so, but not the modern forty-year-old with the young, well-exercised body and the smooth, well-creamed face. She was nondescript, even dowdy, in her shapeless navy dresses, barren of makeup and charm, a plain woman who could have dyed her stringy brown hair blonde, layered on eyeshadow, and worn hot pants on her scrawny figure without being anything but nondescript. If Janice had harbored a passion for John, she had undoubtedly done so in secret. Sylvia assumed that somewhere there was an aging, hypochondriac mother who made endless claims on her defeated daughter.

Sylvia had always had a small twinge of pity when she dealt with the secretary, but today she had neither the time nor patience for Janice's grudgingness. She simply issued orders, starting with a request for all of John's current files.

Janice took her own time about it, but eventually she wheeled trolleys of files into the inner office.

"Good. And I'd like John's diary too."

"I don't have it. Mr. West keeps it in his desk," Janice said shortly.

Sylvia looked through all the drawers but couldn't find it.

"I left it on the desk last night."

"It wasn't here in the morning. I came in to clean up." Janice didn't specify the exact nature of her cleaning-up duties. "It wasn't lying around."

The woman spoke defensively as if Sylvia was somehow accusing her of theft. It didn't seem wise to pursue the matter with her. Sylvia combed every inch of the office but the diary was not to be found. It had disappeared into thin air like its owner.

That was ominous. Sylvia felt like kicking herself for leaving it behind. Not only had she not gone through its contents except to glance at the page for Monday, but she couldn't remember the names of the appointments for that one day.

She looked at the duplicate diary. It showed only five appointments for Monday.

Janice denied knowing that there had been a sixth booking. "I telephoned these five men when Mr. West didn't come in, but he'd already called them to cancel the meetings. As far as I knew, that took care of everything."

"Did John often do that, make appointments without telling you?"

Janice was unconcerned. "Not usually, but people do forget things."

She couldn't know John very well if she could say that.

Sylvia sighed. That left the files themselves. They looked as thick and as tedious as she'd feared. She hung up her jacket, rolled up her sleeves, and plunged in. She was looking for oddities but God only knew what was normal in a corporate file. At least she might come across and recognize the name of the sixth client.

In the middle of learning more about debentures than she'd ever wanted to know, an echo of Janice's voice startled her.

John had canceled the appointments himself.

The implications of that were staggering.

Most of the people she wanted were out, of course, and she had to leave messages for them to call her back. But two were able to take the phone.

The first was a Frenchman whose English left a little to be desired. "He call me yes, but I am not here so he speak to my aider."

Aider?

"But this is the person who aid me."

Sylvia talked with the assistant who fortunately commanded a better English. It seemed that John had called at eight in the morning to say that he couldn't make the appointment. He hadn't given a reason and the assistant hadn't asked.

Eight in the morning! John had been at home still, and she certainly hadn't seem him on the telephone. They left the house around then. It slowly came back to her that she'd waited outside for longer than usual that morning.

That was hard to take. If so, he had lied to her about his plans for the day. He must have known he was going somewhere. Which thus far she'd refused to accept.

Sylvia reluctantly called the last name on her list. George Sheppard was in. Yes, he'd spoken to John himself. He was always on the job early. John had apologized for his inability to make the meeting. They agreed to speak toward the end of the week and set up another appointment. There was nothing requiring urgent attention, so Sheppard hadn't minded the change in schedule.

Sylvia couldn't bear to hear any more. "Thank you."

"I was shocked to read about the, uh . . ."

"Yes."

"Maybe it's hindsight, but he didn't sound himself."

"What do you mean?"

"Oh, it was probably his cold."

"He had a cold? What gave you that impression?" Sylvia knew full well that John almost never had a cold, was impatient with people who got sick, and certainly had not had a cold when he disappeared.

"Oh, his voice was a bit thick and he coughed a few times. I think I even mentioned it to him. I figured he didn't feel well enough to go into the office and didn't want to admit it to me."

"Could you have recognized his voice without him identifying himself?" Sylvia crossed her fingers.

"No . . . maybe. I don't know," he ended apologetically. "It's hard to say, looking back. But I thought it was him, for whatever reason. I mean, who else could it have been?"

She didn't know. But in conjunction with the lost diary, it was odd. An idea struck her. She called the Frenchman's assistant again.

"Sorry to trouble you again. Did you notice anything unusual about my husband's voice?"

"No."

"How would you describe it?" Years of courtroom training held her back from asking leading questions.

"I don't know. There was the slight German accent, of course. I did not think it was unusual."

Sylvia's heart sank. "He didn't have a cold?" Courtroom

technique wasn't always applicable.

"Not that I could hear."

"I see. Well, thank you anyway. By the way, Mr. West is Swiss, not German. I'm surprised he never told you. He's fairly sensitive about it because he hates the Germans."

"Not unusual for a European. But I have not met him."

"You'd only talked to him over the phone?"

"Just that once. It is one week only, since I started my work here."

Sylvia hung up thoughtfully.

Dave Masowski was not impressed with her theories about the telephone calls. "Whoever called had to know who would recognize John's voice. Right?"

"I suppose," Sylvia admitted, knowing the bottom line.

"Well, that doesn't leave John out of the planning. Just means he couldn't count on making the calls in private. With his family all around."

"What about the missing diary and the call I got in his office last night?"

Dave was a little more interested in them. "Keep on looking through the files. Oh, and get his mother's address."

Sylvia hadn't found anything in the office to suggest that John had a mother, much less how to contact her.

"Janice," she called on the intercom, "would you look through John's address file and give me his mother's address?"

"I don't have it. I've never had any occasion to use it."

"Well, didn't the children's presents come here? Did they have a return address?"

"I never noticed one. They came by delivery service."

"Which company?"

"I don't remember." Silence. "I suppose I could call around and see if I can find out."

"Thank you."

There were a lot of delivery services in and around New York. Sylvia decided not to wait for results before calling Cameron. If he was desperate for Mrs. West's address, he could set a few of his men on it.

Cameron was in, but at first his flunkies wouldn't put Sylvia through. She threatened to come down to the station and camp out on their desks unless she got to speak to the great man himself. Apparently Cameron's minions weren't crazy to meet her because that did the trick instantly.

"Yeah?"

Sylvia bit her tongue. His manners hadn't improved over the past twenty-four hours. She quietly told Cameron about the new little mysteries.

"What about it?"

"What about what, Captain Cameron?"

"You lost a book, got a call from a friend of your husband, and found out he had a cold. Big deal. That why you called me?"

"Look, Captain, John had an appointment with someone the day he disappeared that might be relevant. At any rate, the only record of it has oddly vanished. And the other things are also out of the ordinary. The kind of thing one would expect to interest the investigating officer." Sylvia was still polite but it was getting dicey.

"Okay. I got the details. Anything else?"

"Yes. If it's not too much trouble, I would like to know how the investigation is going."

"It's not going anywhere. Your average joe who skips is gonna turn up real quick. But your husband's a smart guy. If he don't wanna get found, he's not gonna get found. Not till he makes a few mistakes. We've got bulletins out for him and when he makes his mistakes, we'll get him. Meantime, we check him out here and see why he took off. It takes time."

Cameron was ready to ring off but Sylvia was angry now.

"Captain, you hold on! You're assuming that my husband ran away. Which may turn out to be so though I doubt it. But right now there's as good a possibility that something happened to him because prominent lawyers with families they love and good jobs don't just leave on a whim. And when a man like that disappears, I expect the police to take it seriously! It's your job to find missing people. God knows that whatever you're paid is too much, but I expect you to try to earn it. The lousiest cop in the world, a title for which you're definitely in the running, knows enough to keep an open mind until the evidence is in! Now you listen to me and listen good. You'd better find him and fast! Otherwise, your job isn't going to be worth a tinker's damn. There are odd things happening and you'd better find out why. Now get off this phone and your ass and start making things move!"

Cameron was speechless for a good ten seconds. Sylvia found herself almost smiling. She certainly felt a whole lot better.

"I didn't say I wasn't going to check into things," Cameron blustered. "But you stay out of it. Your involvement just stirs everything up and makes it harder for us to find him. So leave it to the experts. Stay out of it and go back to work. Understand?"

"No, frankly I do not," Sylvia said coldly. "He is my husband and you can't do one goddamn thing to stop me from looking for him. There's more to this than meets the eye. And my eye will be, among other places, on you. So, if you like your job, remember what I've said." She slammed down the receiver.

Cameron had miscalculated. He'd forgotten that she'd been trained to excel in one situation that most people couldn't handle. Confrontation.

Sylvia returned to John's files with a vengeance. Two hours later, she was no further ahead. The only thing she was learning was that John was as unbelievably organized at work as he was at home.

The clients she'd left messages for called back. All had spoken to someone who said he was John, and either they didn't know his voice well enough to recognize it or he had appeared to have a cold.

Sylvia kept thinking about Dave's comments. Who, other than John himself, knew so much about his affairs? She started to buzz Janice. And stopped.

Janice would know everything about John's professional life. Everything.

It was ridiculous to suspect her. Paranoid.

Sylvia slowly removed her hand from the intercom and went back to the files.

An hour later, she'd learned only that she wouldn't recognize a corporate oddity if she fell across it. She was ready to give up in disgust when she found something. The file was delightfully thin to begin with and contained a note: "18th. 9 AM., V.S. & R." John had disappeared on Monday, June 18. Sylvia tried not to think about the fact that every month had an eighteenth. It was the first time she'd run into something that could, however tentatively, be classified as a "clue."

The client was a company incorporated under a number rather than a name. The file was so meager, it was clear that John hadn't had to work late on its behalf. Sylvia vaguely recalled that her corporation law professor had, from time to time, talked mysteriously about corporate searches. Common sense told her that the government must collect data on companies, as it did on plainer folks.

Glenn McEwan, fortunately, had a contact in the company's office. Sylvia spoke to a woman who actually seemed to want to help.

"I've found the file, Mrs. West. It's not very thick. Let's see, the objects of the corporation are charitable."

"Objects?"

"The purposes, what the corporation was intended to do." The woman tactfully refrained from sneering at Sylvia's ignorance. "It's supposed to act as some kind of charity but the phrases are too vague for me to figure out exactly what it does. The actual words are, uh, 'it shall fund research for educational, sociological, and humanitarian purposes.' Does that help?"

"Not a hell of a lot. The government keeps more information than that on us private citizens."

"That's for sure," the woman agreed cheerfully. "We have the head office address too, but no phone number."

Sylvia wrote down the information. "What about its directors? Do you have an up-to-date list?"

"Apparently they haven't changed since the company was incorporated in '72. All three were the first directors, D. V. Rogers, E.S. Castle, and J. Kellermann, with two *n*'s. We've never received a notification of change."

"Thanks. One more thing. Do you have a record of registered charities? The ones whose donors get a tax break?"

"No. That's another office. Let me give you a name you can call."

The details were pretty hazy in Sylvia's mind, but as she recalled, registered charities had a real advantage when it came to raising money. You got to deduct your donation from your tax. In return for the favor, the government undoubtedly kept pretty close tabs on the companies.

Number 693-088 was not a registered charitable institution. According to her source, it had never even applied for registration. Which was interesting. The company existed only for charitable purposes, vague though they were. Presumably it would need money to carry them out. Who would donate hard cash to a charity if it couldn't be deducted from income tax?

Sylvia drove over to the building housing 693-088. It was a small, rundown edifice on Broadway below Houston, crammed in among textile manufacturers displaying silver lamé plastics and look-like-leopardskin velvets in their grimy windows. Most of the suites on the building's eight floors were, according to the list in the minuscule lobby, unoccupied, and none of the four tenants were listed under a number. And none of them appeared to work overtime. She'd have to come back in the morning.

Her muscles were knotted up as badly as her stomach. The latest development in the continuing saga of the disintegration of her body was a mind-numbing headache. She couldn't face the children's questions in this state. She called them to say she'd be late but that she'd come into their bedrooms to kiss them goodnight when she got home.

In a moment of familial togetherness, she and John had joined the Avenue Fitness Club at Forty-third and Fifth, a fully equipped, lushly decorated, and wildly overstaffed establishment. Sylvia loathed it. She'd seldom been there but John's attendance record had more than justified the expenditure.

She borrowed a sweatsuit and ran for nearly half an hour. Her wind wasn't great, hardly surprising considering the amount she was smoking these days. But with the sweat pouring down her body and every inch protesting, she was able to clear her mind.

Afterwards, she rested on a bench collecting the strength for a shower.

"Hello, Sylvia."

"Oh, hi, Paul." Paul Firestone had been the closest thing to a friend that John had had. They'd played squash twice a week for five years.

"I was sorry to hear about John. Any word?"

"Nothing. But thanks."

Sylvia watched him walk down the hall. "Oh, Paul, have you got a minute?"

"Uh, sure."

He returned and sat down beside her.

"You knew John pretty well, didn't you?"

"Uh, I guess so." He didn't really want to discuss it with her. He looked excruciatingly uncomfortable.

"I'm trying to figure out the whole mess. I could use some help. Did John ever say anything to you that suggested he might be wanting to leave?"

"No, never."

"So you were surprised to hear about it?"

"Yes, of course I was."

"Did he ever mention problems in business? Or with money?"

"Not really. Sometimes we'd discuss the fine points of some legal question. That was about it. John didn't get specific about his cases."

"Did he discuss his family?"

"Sure, he was real proud of the boys. He talked about them quite a bit."

"And me?"

Paul squirmed and looked away. "Well, to be honest, he hasn't talked about you lately."

"How lately?"

"Oh, Sylvia, I don't know."

"Approximately."

"Not for a long time."

"I see."

They sat in silence for a while.

"Paul, leaving that aside, can you see him leaving the boys?"

"No, I can't. Not for good."

"So you expect him back?"

"Well, sure."

"It never occurred to you that something might have happened to him? That maybe he didn't run away from home?"

Paul didn't say anything.

"I'm not going to get hysterical, Paul. I just want your feelings. An objective view."

"Oh, hell. All right. No, it didn't occur to me." Something about the wall was fascinating him. At least he was staring fixedly at it.

"Didn't it at least surprise you that a man like John, conscientious to say the least, would desert us like that?"

"Uh, well, you've always been independent. It's not like you needed him."

The kiss of death.

Sylvia walked back to the car. It was unanimous. She was to blame. He'd left his very unnatural wife and that explained everything. Well, to hell with everybody. She and her children weren't going to take this lying down. She wasn't going to shoulder the blame until she'd learned a lot more. If no one else was going to look for him, she would.

Sylvia went back to the office to call her partners. They

could look after her practice for a while. Which was exactly what she'd always told John they couldn't do.

Four of the five were still working and the fifth agreed to participate in the meeting by telephone. "But how long will you be gone?" They were appalled at the thought of having to deal with her criminal clients.

"I don't know yet. As soon as I do, you'll be the first to hear." She smiled encouragingly. "My clients aren't that bad. Just don't let them sit on the white furniture."

Eventually it was agreed that one of the litigation partners would supervise Bess and a junior. Anything that could be adjourned until her return would be. And one of them would act in those cases that couldn't.

Sylvia left the meeting with some foreboding. Her clients were going to be none too happy. In fact, she'd be lucky if she still had any when she came back.

SIX

Rupert Thompson had been pleased to hear from Sylvia. He insisted that, despite the hour, she come right over to the Institute. She'd agreed, figuring that if he was there at ten, he might as well stick around until eleven.

The Wandling Institute was situated a few blocks from the UN in a gorgeous modern building of marble and glass. The Institute had obviously built the edifice, since its name was emblazoned in marble over the doorway, but the lower six stories were rented out to various government agencies and two establishment law firms.

Sylvia was expected by the guard at the door and she was immediately ushered into a private, silk-lined elevator. A few seconds later the doors opened to the twelfth floor, and Rupert was greeting her.

"I was so sorry to hear about John. What a horrible thing for you." He spoke soberly and without any inflection to indicate that he assumed she'd been left in the lurch by a dissatisfied husband. "Have the police come up with any leads yet?"

"No. Not a thing. That's one of the reasons I've come to you."

"I see. Well, let's go into my office. You look like you could use a good stiff drink and a comfortable chair. This way."

Sylvia followed him down several labyrinthine corridors, elegantly carpeted and beautifully hung with works of art. Wherever the Institute found its funds, it found plenty of them. Despite the hour, the halls were busy with scurrying secretaries and men wearing horn-rimmed glasses conferring earnestly.

She turned to her companion. "Is it always this active at night?"

"No. We're in the middle of a major project and the deadline for our report is coming up." Thompson himself looked very tired. Sylvia felt a twinge about adding to his problems.

"What is it, exactly, that you do here?"

"We, uh, think." Rupert laughed. "We get hired to work out solutions to problems. All kinds of problems, social, political, economic."

"By government?"

"Also by private enterprise. It's cheaper than keeping a huge think tank on your own premises." Rupert grinned. "Though not by much. The main advantage is that we're neutral. No political ax to grind. No interest in the commercial marketplace. So we're more likely to come up with an objective view and even to have somewhat original approaches. Besides, our conclusions carry more weight, especially to the political parties."

"You're not Republicans, so the Democrats will listen to you?"

"Exactly. Besides, our staff develops expertise in some areas that are not even touched by government or business. On rare occasions, we have to bring in someone but we always balance outside personnel with our own people so that our findings stay objective. We're constantly looking for people to steal. Here we are." He opened a door and ushered her inside.

His office, like the rest of the building, was spectacular. Big enough to hold a football game. The furniture was grouped in small arrangements so that one wasn't overwhelmed by it but every piece was a work of art. Not to mention the masterpieces on the walls.

Sylvia shook her head. "No wonder you work late. If I worked here, I'd move in permanently."

"I don't go home for other reasons."

Sylvia hastened to change the topic. "I feel bad taking up your time on my problem. I can see you've got a few of your own."

"My pleasure, my dear." Rupert was fussing at a marble table that supported a range of bottles that would be impressive at the Rainbow Room. "J&B, isn't it?"

She smiled.

"A double. Now drink up and tell me what's on your mind. Other than the obvious."

Sylvia recounted the events of the last two days, emphasizing that she didn't know what had happened but wasn't satisfied with the odds-on favorite theory. Thompson appeared very interested in the mysterious visitor and the phone call.

"Odd, very odd. I agree with you, they've got to be looked into." He listened in silence to the rest of Sylvia's account, occasionally making a note.

Twice during the monologue, the telephone rang. The first time, Rupert spoke for only a few seconds, telling the caller that he couldn't be disturbed at the moment. The second call was clearly more important.

"Please forgive me a moment, Sylvia. This is one man I must speak to."

"Would you like me to leave?"

"No, not at all." Thompson swung back to the phone. "Yes, Senator. Go ahead." There were long pauses broken by Thompson asking questions in a quick, decisive voice. "Right. All right, Senator. I've got the facts. We'll have to act fast on this. I agree with your analysis off the top, but I'd want to think about it for a few hours. I'll call you back first thing in the morning. By the way, I don't think you ought to discuss this with O'Neill right now." Thompson nodded at something and rang off.

"O'Neill? Tip O'Neill?"

"Yes." Thompson was pleasant but it was clear that he couldn't talk about the conversation so Sylvia returned to her story. When she finished, she leaned back, feeling for the first time some relief from the pressure that had been weighing her down. Rupert was pacing the office.

"Look, Sylvia. There are lots of people who can lend a hand. Did you want me to smarten up the police or did you want to leave them alone and take a stab at it yourself? I'm not clear on your plans."

"I would like the police to try to do their job, yes. But they seem so certain John has run away that I no longer believe it's possible for them to do an objective job. I'm going to stick my finger into it for whatever that's worth. But I need help."

"You've got it," Rupert answered instantly. "Whatever I can do for you is yours for the asking. To start with—"

A knock at the door interrupted him. Thompson sighed and crossed over to it. "Yes? Oh, Lorne. Hello. Come on in, there's an old friend of yours here."

A plump man with sandy hair dashed over. "Sylvia! It's been years since we've seen each other."

"You remember Lorne Reyes, Sylvia," Thompson interjected tactfully.

Actually, now that she saw him in the flesh, she did. Lorne

had been the sweatshirted slob she recalled from law school. But no longer. Today, he was a smooth, self-assured young man on the rise. He practically wore a sign to that effect.

"Congratulations, Lorne. I hear you're destined for great things."

"Thank you. I must say, I'm looking forward to the challenge of the Big Place." He sounded sincere about it and Sylvia smiled.

"When do you take up your new duties?"

"Monday. Formally. But I'm leaving tomorrow for some pre-briefing. I just came up to say good-bye for the time being to Rupert. It was all Rupert's doing, you know."

The two men smiled at each other. There seemed to be genuine affection between them.

"By the way, Sylvia," Lorne said, losing his smile, "I'm terribly sorry about your husband. Have you any idea where he is?"

"No." The double Scotch had made her very drowsy. Even polite conversation was too demanding. "Rupert, please forgive me, but I'm just dead. Thanks for hearing me out."

"Of course, Sylvia. Get a good night's rest. And remember, any help I can offer is yours. Here's my number. My direct number." He wrote it out on a business card. "Call me at any hour of the day or night. Whatever you want or need."

"Thank you. I'll keep in touch."

Rupert knew everyone worth knowing and his word was as good as gold. Better even, what with the gold market being what it was. If he said he'd help, he would. She wasn't alone anymore.

Sylvia woke up and immediately recollected her visit to Rupert's office. She was smiling as she got out of bed and even the sound of the boys squabbling noisily in the living room didn't faze her.

"Here, stop that, kids. What's the problem?"

"Carl won't let me read my books," Jay complained. "He won't stop bothering me."

"Okay, Carl, come with me." Sylvia led him in the direction of John's study. It had previously been sacrosanct; any little boys who dared to cross its portals faced an unspecified fate worse than death. Sylvia no longer cared about John's rules. She pushed open the door and gasped.

The room looked like a war zone. The contents of all the

shelves, all the drawers, were on the floor. The curtains had been ripped down and their linings removed. The leather on the top of the desk had been torn off. The old maps that had graced the walls were crumpled, hanging by corners or down on the floor. Even the wallpaper had been slashed away from the wall.

Carl immediately started to wail. "I didn't come in here!"

"Shh. Of course you didn't. Uh, why don't you go and play in your room?" Carl made no move, he was rooted to the spot. "Go on, to your room."

When he'd left, Sylvia collapsed against the door frame. The violence used on the study still hung in the air. It sickened and frightened her.

"Are you ready for breakfast?" Ingrid called from the kitchen.

Sylvia hastily closed the door. It wouldn't do for Ingrid to get nervous; she'd probably quit.

"I'll have it later," Sylvia said, trying to appear casual. "I'm going to make a few calls. By the way, I've spread out a few papers in John's study, so don't go in there. Okay?"

"I never go in there," Ingrid grumbled. "So there's no point in telling me not to. I never—"

"Good." Sylvia made her escape. Upstairs in her bedroom again, she instinctively dialed Dave's number.

He was appalled and promised to come right over.

Dave emerged from the room shaking his head. "A real professional job."

"How do you mean?" Sylvia was halfway through her fifth cigarette of the day. And still shaking.

"What went on in there is called a good search. What did John keep at home? Diamonds?"

"No. Nothing." Sylvia remembered something. "Well, just some money."

"Come again?"

"Money. John was European, remember? He didn't feel secure unless he had a fair amount of cash around. I hated to have it in the house, but he insisted."

"How much is a fair amount?"

"A couple of thousand. He also kept money at his office."

Dave was looking at her sternly.

"I know, I know. I should have told you before, but I figured that you would immediately assume he had planned to run away. But he's always kept money around. Even at the beginning when we were happy."

"Someone knew about it, obviously. I just don't understand why the study was the only room searched. The money was probably already gone."

"You see," Sylvia said accusingly. "You're assuming John took it with him. And he didn't. I may look like a fool but I'm not that dumb. I checked the money right after John vanished. It was still here. Two thousand of America's best."

"Where was it?"

"In a secret drawer of the desk." Sylvia led Dave in and pressed a button cleverly concealed inside the handle on one of the drawers. A small compartment popped up on the top. It was empty.

"Well, that explains it. Somebody knew that your husband was in the habit of keeping a large amount of cash on hand and figured that he'd most likely store it in the study. How many people knew about John's little fetish?"

"Quite a few," Sylvia admitted. "John felt safe about the hiding place so he used to joke about it."

"There is no place safe from a professional. Case closed."

Sylvia wasn't convinced. "It's an awful coincidence, isn't it? Right after John's disappearance?"

"That's not unusual. When a family gets publicity of any kind, it often becomes the target of a lot of criminal activity." Dave looked like he wanted to bite his tongue out.

"Swell."

"Sylvia, I'll make sure that a patrol car keeps a very close eye on your house. I promise. And we're not going to release this to the press. You'll be safe from now on. Meanwhile, I'm going to get the fingerprint guys in. It's just possible that the culprit is someone we know."

Sylvia nodded and left him to it. She had always resisted burglar alarms but this was definitely the moment for flexible principles. The best and noisiest alarm she could buy was going in just as soon as Bess could order it.

Bess was distraught about the incident. "Why don't you take the kids and Ingrid and stay at a hotel for a while? At least until the alarm is functioning?"

"I'm afraid of uprooting the children. They're upset enough now, what with their daddy disappearing. I'm sure we'll be fine."

Rupert agreed with Sylvia. "You'll be safe enough with the

police and a burglar alarm. Have Bess call my secretary. We can arrange to have it installed in a matter of hours."

"Wonderful!" Sylvia hadn't realized how nervous she was at the contemplation of another night without an alarm. "What do you make of the break-in?"

"Your policeman friend was probably right, Sylvia. The timing was unfortunate, but what could it have to do with John? If he had wanted to take something with him, he could have. Without destroying his study. And if he was spirited away, we'd have to assume he possessed something wildly valuable. A little incredible, surely?"

"I guess so." Sylvia changed the subject. "I'm going to check out my only clue. I'll let you know if anything comes of it."

There was no reception in the old building that was supposed to contain the head office of 693-088 so she walked into the office on the first floor.

"I'm looking for a company with this name." She showed the piece of paper with the number on it to the young woman behind the desk. "Do you know which floor it's on?"

"No," the clerk said slowly. "Are you sure it's in this building?"

"Yes, I am."

"Just a moment. I'll ask around and see if anyone here knows." The young woman disappeared into an inner office and came out with a tall black-haired woman in tow. The second woman looked at the number and nodded.

"Why, yes. I think that's the company on the sixth floor. It's usually called The Foundation, but the mailman once mentioned that some of the mail comes addressed to a number."

"Thank you," Sylvia said gratefully.

The elevator wasn't working so she climbed the stairs, cursing the bad luck that made the company choose this godforsaken location. The building, which wasn't exactly a Mies van der Rohe exhibit on the first floor, deteriorated badly as she ascended. The stairs were unventilated and poorly lit, which may have been a blessing in disguise because the walls, on closer inspection, turned out to be infected with some hideous form of mold.

She opened the door to the sixth floor and dropped her jaw. The decor was nothing short of magnificent. The carpet was a luxurious tan and so thick it damn near tickled her knees.

The walls were covered in an expensive-looking tan cloth and hung with pictures that looked to her eyes to be original impressionists and cubists. There even appeared to be a Picasso.

She stepped back and looked around to find the reception area. "Oh!" Sylvia jumped. A young, pleasant-looking man in a conservatively tailored flannel suit was at her elbow, regarding her quizzically.

"It is lovely, isn't it?" He jerked his red hair at the Picasso.

"Yes. Your collection's terrific. I'd like to have the time to go over it more carefully."

"I'm sure that can be arranged." He smiled, showing a broad mouth full of white teeth. "What can we do for you?"

Sylvia took the paper with the number written on it from her pocket. "I'm looking for this company and I've been told that this is the right address."

The man looked at the paper and cleared his throat. "What is your business?"

"Is this the right place?" Sylvia pursued.

"Yes." He remembered his manners. "I'm Leland Sterne. I work here."

"My name is Sylvia West. My husband is your lawyer, I believe."

It was as though she'd thrown cold water over him. "John West?"

"Yes. I'd like to talk to whoever's in charge."

"Please wait in here, Mrs. West." Sterne brusquely ushered her into a nearby office and excused himself.

Sylvia watched his disappearing back with some excitement. She'd certainly aroused a reaction from him. She looked around. While she was alone in the office, she might as well snoop a little. There was, unfortunately, precious little to see. The desk was clear of papers and it didn't look as though this office had an occupant. A noise at the door arrested her.

The most elegant man she'd ever seen stood beside Sterne. He was tall, as tall as John, slender, silver-haired, and dressed in a magnificently cut navy three-piece suit. The hair notwithstanding, Sylvia estimated his age at about forty-five. She found herself, despite her suspicions of the operation, regarding him with as much approval as he was presently conferring upon her person.

He broke the silence by advancing on her with hand outstretched. "My name is Johann von Schagg. I'm in charge here."

"How do you do, Mr. von Schagg. I'm sorry to trouble you but I have a problem that affects you and I thought I ought to come around to clear it up."

The younger man sucked in his breath. Von Schagg allowed a slight frown to cross his face before turning to Sterne. "I think Mrs. West will be more comfortable in my office. Thank you, my dear boy."

With this cavalier dismissal, von Schagg led Sylvia through the halls to a huge room. He motioned her to sit on an Empire sofa and offered her a sherry. The old stomach wasn't going to be very happy to receive it at this early hour, but Sylvia threw caution to the winds and accepted. She looked around at the antiques and pieces of art.

"You have an eye for beautiful things, Mr. von Schagg," she commented, sipping on the sherry. She opened her purse. "Do you mind if I smoke?"

"Not at all. Here's an ashtray. Yes, I enjoy having beauty around me. As I am here more than I am at home, I see no reason not to keep my favorite objects with me." Von Schagg carried a sculpture over to show Sylvia. "I obtained this just last week. It was done by a little-known French artist in the eighteenth century. Look at the carving around the base. And the expression on the milkmaid's face. Isn't it wonderful to see marble almost move with life?"

He was so delighted with the piece that he infected Sylvia with his enthusiasm, and for several minutes they discussed the history of his acquisition.

Finally, von Schagg recollected the purpose of Sylvia's visit. "I'm sorry to interrupt this with a mundane business matter, but I believe you wanted help of some sort?"

"Yes, in a way," Sylvia said. "My husband is unfortunately not available for his work right now, and I'm making sure that his most important clients are adequately taken care of until he returns to his office."

"Well, that is very good of you, but I'm afraid that we could not be considered one of his most important clients. He has done very little work for us and, in fact, he isn't doing any right now."

Sylvia smiled with what she hoped was a disarming air. "I was worried that you might have been inconvenienced by my husband's failure to keep his appointment with you on Monday."

Was it her imagination, or did he hesitate a moment?

"On Monday?"

"Yes. My husband tried to contact everyone he was supposed to see but I wasn't sure that he'd managed to speak to you. I hope you received the message?"

"I hate to keep correcting a woman as beautiful as yourself, but I didn't have a meeting scheduled with Mr. West. Where did you get the idea that I was to see him?"

Sylvia was nonplussed for a split second and then decided that honesty was the best policy for an apprentice liar. "My husband left a note of it. When I was going through his papers, I found it and as there was no indication that he'd reached you, I felt I ought to make sure, and apologize if he hadn't."

"I don't understand that because I wasn't aware of anything of the sort. In fact, I was planning to be away this week, but I had to cancel my plans at the last minute because something came up in the office. So I wouldn't have made an appointment for Monday."

He sounded sincere. Sylvia didn't know what more she could ask. "Well, I'm sorry to have troubled you," she murmured weakly.

"Not at all." He was very gallant. "Are you in practice with your husband?"

"No, I'm at another firm." Now, why would he assume that she was also a lawyer? It didn't seem right to complain about it in view of the fact that she was always attacking men for thinking she must be a secretary. But really, it was odd.

"Oh, isn't it more usual for other members of a firm to handle a partner's business when he's away?"

"Yes." Sylvia thought fast. "I'm protecting his interests, as it were, because I'm not sure when he'll be able to return. I'd like him to have something to come back to."

"I see. Very handy to have a second lawyer in the family. By the way, why isn't your husband at work? I trust he isn't ill?"

Surprising that he hadn't heard about John's disappearance. It had been on all the television stations and in the papers. She muttered something noncommittal and stood up.

Von Schagg walked her out. Sylvia started to turn back the way she'd come. "No, no. I suppose you walked up the stairs. What a shame. We have our own elevator at the back of the building."

She had not been able to picture the elegant von Schagg facing the filthy stairwells every morning.

They walked into a large reception area and von Schagg put out his hand. "Thank you for your concern, Mrs. West. There's nothing that needs attention at the moment. Anyway, our legal work is extremely routine. If Mr. West is not back to handle it, any one of the lawyers in his firm could certainly do so."

"I'm not familiar with your company. What is it that you do?" Sylvia asked, one hand holding the elevator doors open. It wasn't exactly a cunning question but she couldn't think of any other way to put it.

"We're a charitable organization. Very small, unfortunately, as so much needs to be done," he answered vaguely. "Good-bye and thank you again. I hope we run into each other another time."

Sylvia had no recourse but to leave after such a clear dismissal.

As she stepped out of the elevator into the alley, a group of four swarthy men made way for her. They were dressed in Savile Row suits, impeccable down to the last detail but the style wasn't designed for short, stocky figures. And one was missing an earlobe. Clothes didn't necessarily make the man.

She walked back to John's office, savoring the first really hot day of the year. Von Schagg had seemed natural enough and the note in the file had been ambiguous. Still, she'd come away with no more information than she'd arrived with. She pushed it out of her mind for the moment. The rest of the files were waiting.

She took a large, heavily iced Coke into the office with her and reached for the last pile. My God, John was organized. Unbelievably so.

She sat up sharply. No, it couldn't be. She tried to shake the notion out of her head but nobody was that well prepared. She remembered a few files that had surprised her, including the massive dossier on the Wandling Institute. She pulled it out again and as she'd thought, there were minutes and statements prepared for future weeks. Dated in the future. She glanced through two more folders.

Maybe most corporate lawyers worked ahead.

She swallowed an antacid tablet.

Finally she buzzed Glenn McEwan. He was happy to help and arrived in the office almost immediately.

"Glenn, take a look at these three files and tell me if anything strikes you as odd."

She paced the room, chain-smoking, while he immersed himself.

"Wow! Was he well prepared! It's going to be a cinch to take over these files. I've never seen a lawyer so far ahead!" He stopped abruptly, realizing what he'd said.

Sylvia stared at him but he couldn't meet her eyes. "It looks bad, doesn't it, Glenn?"

"I guess it does." He spoke almost inaudibly.

"He might have known that he was leaving, the way he cleaned up his cases, isn't that so?"

"I don't know. Maybe he always worked like that. Some people like to be ahead of the game. Maybe..." His voice trailed off.

"Thanks, Glenn."

Another pill. Another cigarette. Her hands were shaking and she couldn't get a match to it.

"Here." Glenn lit it for her. "Are you all right?"

"Yes. Would you...I'd like to be alone."

"Sure." He stopped at the door. "If there's anything I can do."

She nodded.

SEVEN

She couldn't desert the boys two nights in a row. She forced herself to go straight home and by the end of the long, dreary drive she was under control again.

She called for the children as soon as she turned off the car and stepped out, planning to have a game of catch with them before dinner.

It was not to be. The alarm system had been installed and Ingrid had been shown how it worked. She was to pass the information along to Sylvia and the heavy responsibility was weighing on her mind. Sylvia was hustled right down to the control box.

"I see. Uh huh." Sylvia was barely looking in the right direction. "Fine. Thanks."

"Oh," Ingrid recalled as she laboriously followed Sylvia up the basement stairs. "Your mother called."

Sylvia tensed. She had delayed informing her parents about the disappearance, hoping that they wouldn't hear about it at their secluded summer home and that she'd have something positive to say when she absolutely had to tell them.

She crossed her fingers and hoped that it had just been a routine call. "Hello, Mother. How are you?"

"Good. We're both busy marking papers. Your father says his students haven't learned the first thing about civil engineering but I'm glad to say that my class has turned in some first-rate work. How are you, darling?"

That was a toughie. "That brings us to the bad news. John's disappeared."

"What?"

"Disappeared."

"Oh, my! Are the boys all right?"

"Yes, they're fine, physically. They're very upset, of course."

"What happened?"

"We don't know. I dropped him off at work Monday and he just vanished."

"Oh, my poor dear. How are you coping?"

Maternal sympathy was exactly what she couldn't handle right now. Sylvia swallowed the lump in her throat. "Uh, it's a little rough."

"I can imagine. What's being done?"

"The police are looking for him in a half-assed way. I've been trying to ask around too. You know, it turns out that after all these years, I don't really know John. It's like I'm looking for a stranger."

"Mmm." Mother was no hypocrite. She hadn't wanted John as a son-in-law and she wasn't going to pretend differently. On the other hand, she was too tactful to say "I told you so."

"Why don't you and the boys come up north and spend some time with us, darling?"

"I can't. I want to keep an eye on the investigation. But I'll probably send the kids when school's over."

"Good. Now, what do you think happened?"

"The police are working on *cherchez la femme*. Naturally."

"Is there any possibility of that?"

"Mother! Certainly not. Well," Sylvia backed down, "I doubt it. The other theory is that he embezzled money."

"I don't believe that. John was not perfect, my dear, but he was too stuffy to do that sort of thing."

"Whatever the reason, I don't think he did either. But I don't have a better explanation. At first, I was absolutely certain that something must have happened to him. I couldn't believe he'd leave the boys. I still don't but it's getting harder to hold on to my faith. I've come up with a couple of things that suggest that someone in his office might be involved."

"His secretary, you mean?"

"I didn't say that. Anyway, I've got no proof."

"I never did like her. She's a cold woman. I wasn't surprised that she liked Geneva. It's a cold town."

"Geneva? What are you talking about?"

"John's secretary. What's her name?"

"Janice. What did you mean, she liked Geneva?"

"Well, that day when we met her at your place. You remember the Christmas party two years ago? She was talking about Europe."

"Go on, tell me what she said to you."

"Oh, she wasn't talking to me. She doesn't like women, that kind never does. I'm so glad you didn't turn out like that."

"Mother!"

"You don't have to shout. Let me see. It was just after you bought your pretty, suburban place." Mother hadn't pictured her daughter living on Long Island. "Some of John's clients were there. A lot of Europeans. She was talking to one of them, a German or Frenchman, I think. She was talking about the places she'd been and I remember her saying that she'd liked Geneva."

"Is that all you remember?"

"Well, it seemed she knew Geneva very well. And she had some friends there. Other than that, I can't remember anything. After all, I think it's quite remarkable that I recall a word she said. She's not particularly fascinating."

"True. Well, Mother, if you think of anything else, call me."

"Fine."

"I'll let you know when the boys are coming. Give my love to Dad."

Dinner was depressing because no one was in the mood to talk and Ingrid's cooking didn't provide much of a distraction. The boys had stopped asking about John but their very silence underlined their anxiety. Sylvia retired to the den with them to watch a moronic television program that the children apparently enjoyed. She tried to act cheerful and reassuring but when they were finally tucked in bed, she found that she was feeling more frightened and bereft than she had since John disappeared.

She headed for the liquor cabinet and discovered Ingrid lying in wait. Ingrid had, upon reflection, come to the conclusion that a house to which strangers were drawn to wreak havoc was not a house for her. It took an hour, but eventually Sylvia succeeded in calming her fears, throwing in for good measure a raise of ten dollars a week.

Sylvia went up to bed, clutching her glass and breathless with relief that the danger had been averted.

The telephone rang. It was Dave.

"Hi." Sylvia was too tired for enthusiasm.

"I'd have called today but it's been hectic down here." He misinterpreted her tone of voice.

"There would have been nothing to say." Sylvia considered

telling him about the mounting evidence that John had planned to skip. She sipped her drink instead; she didn't have the energy to go into it.

"I spoke to Cameron a few minutes ago. They haven't had any response to the APB."

"What else is new?"

"Not much. Uh, Cameron wasn't too happy to hear from me. In fact, he told me to stick to my own cases."

"That's rather touchy. Just because of a telephone call?"

"It is a bureaucracy. I'm messing up the flow charts. Anyway, it looks like Cameron's right after all, what with the money trouble."

"What money trouble?"

"Oh, God. I thought you'd have been told." Dave was embarrassed. "They should have told you." He paused. "Well, there's some possibility that the firm's trust account is a little short."

"Stuart Paliano said he was sure that there wasn't a problem."

"Now he's saying there is. I'm sorry, Sylvia."

"Yes." She hung up. She may not have known her husband as well as she'd thought, but she'd have staked her last dollar against him stealing money and deserting his children.

Despite her fatigue, it was a long time before she fell asleep.

She'd always hated the humid New York summers. To add to her misery, the first sticky weather had arrived with a vengeance. It was unbearable by eight o'clock in the morning. She threw on a sleeveless shell and a pair of cotton pants and left the boys just sitting down to breakfast. She went straight to John's office to wait for Stuart. When he appeared, it was evident that he had not expected to see her and was none too thrilled about his windfall.

"Good morning, my dear," he said. "I'm a little busy right now, but can we talk later?"

"No. I want to know what's going on, and I want to know now."

Stuart was intimidated enough by her tone of voice that he ushered her into his office. But he left the door open. Maybe he figured she was going to assault him.

"Now, Stuart," Sylvia began, "what's all this about missing money? When we talked on the phone the other day, you were dead certain that there was no problem like that. What's the deal?"

"Deal? There's no deal," he blustered. "I took a closer look at the books and it became obvious that something was wrong. My accountant, our accountant, says that he thinks there may be a shortage in the trust account. And John's disappeared two weeks before the annual audit. I'm sorry, Sylvia, but there it is."

"There what is?" Sylvia snapped. "You may or may not be missing money and it hasn't been traced, if it's gone at all, to John. When the audit's done and the checks signed by John turn up, then you'll have something." She was white with fury. "And you know just as well as I do that isn't John's style at all!"

He shrugged his shoulders.

"How much money does your accountant 'think' might be missing?" she asked scornfully.

"I don't know exactly."

"Give me a ballpark figure."

"I don't really know. I could call later, of course, and ask. I'll let you know."

"I'll wait." Sylvia settled herself in the chair, prepared to sit all day if necessary.

Stuart clearly liked that possibility least of all those available to him, so he reluctantly picked up the phone and dialed. He held a conversation with the accountant in hushed tones.

"He isn't sure. It could be as much as fifty. Thousand."

"Or . . ." Sylvia prompted.

"Maybe only a few thousand. He says there's money missing for sure."

That was a blow. Sylvia regrouped her forces. "You know as well as I do that John could have raised even fifty thousand and replaced it."

But both of them knew that that wasn't the point. You could be disbarred for misusing clients' trust money even if you later paid it back in full.

It didn't make sense. John could have taken money from their savings. He could have mortgaged the house or gone to the bank. He could have sold some stock. Of course, he could have done none of those things without Sylvia knowing about it and Stuart, who was no fool, was obviously thinking just that.

She got up with as much dignity as she could muster.

"I expect to hear from you as soon as the accountant has more information."

Bess was glad to see her. They took a break from the office and went out for coffee. Bess had only one practical solution. Sylvia should stop torturing herself and get back to work.

"I can't believe he'd do all these things, Bess. It's just incredible."

Her secretary stared at her.

"I know. I know. It doesn't look good. But it feels all wrong."

Bess dropped the subject. "To change the topic slightly, that guy who called before, Inspector Friedman, called again this morning. I tried to fob him off, but he wasn't having any. He said he couldn't tell me what his business with you was, but that you'd want to talk to him."

"Okay. We'll go upstairs and I'll call him."

"That's the oddest part. He wouldn't leave his number. He said he'd call back at three-thirty and you should be in your office. Some nerve, eh?"

"For sure. I suppose he's away from his desk for the day. Well, I might as well speak to him, I've got nothing better to do."

At three-thirty Sylvia was in her office waiting for the call. Sure enough, at exactly half past the hour, the phone rang.

Sylvia picked it up. "Mrs. West here."

"Inspector Friedman. I must offer my sympathy, Mrs. West. I know that these are difficult times for you."

"Thank you, Inspector. What can I do for you?"

"Well, the question's really what can I do for you. You see, I know that you don't subscribe to the police theory about your husband's disappearance. Very naturally. Of course, since you are his wife, you haven't been able to convince anyone else that he may have met with trouble."

"You aren't telling me anything I didn't know," Sylvia said drily.

"I, on the other hand," he went on, "do think you're right. For a reason of my own."

"And what is that?" This was the strangest conversation to be having with a cop.

"First, tell me, are you going to continue looking for your husband?"

"I don't know right now. There's a lot of evidence gathering that makes it seem a stupid idea."

"And, without a doubt, there will be more of that sort of evidence. I suggest you take it all with a grain of salt. In other words, be very leery of simple solutions to this problem."

"What are you talking about?"

"I have information that makes me think that the police are not right in assuming that your husband ran away for the usual reasons."

"Why are you telling me this? Why don't you talk to Missing Persons?"

"The force doesn't really want this kind of information."

"What information?"

"Well, briefly, I had an anonymous call suggesting that your husband was kidnapped."

"What?" Sylvia was shouting.

"The caller had no concrete information. Or at least he didn't give it to me. He just said that we should look into your husband's background because the answer to the mystery lay in the past."

The entire message seemed cryptic and ambiguous to Sylvia and she said so.

"I don't understand it either, but I think you should go on looking for him. Don't worry about what the police say. I'll keep in touch with you and give you a hand if I can."

"If you can? You're a policeman and this is certainly police business!"

"It would be if you came up with something specific. At the moment, the police can't do much. You may already have noticed that they don't give this kind of thing top priority."

"That's the understatement of the week. But how and why are you involved?"

"I'm not really because it's not my case. I wanted to encourage you. My informant is usually reliable."

"You said the call was anonymous." Sylvia was getting more and more wary of the caller.

"It was. But I know where the information came from."

Sylvia wanted to pursue the point but he interrupted her. "By the way, what exactly are you doing to find your husband?"

"I'm going through his files to see if anything out of the ordinary crops up. And I'm looking for an address for . . . Haven't you spoken to Captain Cameron? Or Dave Masowski? He's been helping me on this."

"No, I haven't. As I said, it's not my case."

"Are you in Missing Persons?"

"No," Friedman answered. "Whose address did you say you were looking for?"

Sylvia evaded the question. "What department are you in?"

"Never mind that for now. I'll call you back later." The line went dead.

Sylvia put the receiver down. On impulse, she picked it up again and dialed the central police number.

"Inspector Friedman, please."

"I don't have an Inspector Friedman listed," the operator stated after a few minutes. "There are a lot of Friedmans but they only go up to captain. What precinct is he in?"

"Uh, thanks anyway." Sylvia hung up.

The so-called inspector had had an accent. German or Austrian. Or Swiss, come to think of it. Sylvia suddenly remembered the visitor to the house.

Poor Ingrid was flustered at being hounded over her mysterious man. "I can't remember. No, I don't think he had an accent. Well, maybe he did. I don't know."

Sylvia was exasperated but it wouldn't do to upset Ingrid further. This would be a hell of a time to have to develop skills as a homemaker.

Rupert Thompson was as good as his word. The telephone number he'd given her was answered immediately and Sylvia, upon stating her name, was put right through. Rupert was intrigued by her account of the caller.

"Was he phoning long distance, do you know?"

"I couldn't tell. It was a good connection but you can have a terrific line to London and a dreadful one to Great Neck."

"True. Well, he sounds like a crank to me. Unfortunately, most people who get mentioned in the papers receive such calls. I wouldn't worry about it."

"I'm not worried, but if he has some information about John, I want to talk to him."

"I can understand that. Still, he's obviously lying about being an inspector of police. He quoted an informant who gave him virtually no information, nothing tangible anyway. He hangs up on you when you ask the simplest questions. I wish I could say otherwise, but he does have all the earmarks of a nut."

"He said he'll be contacting me again."

"Okay. This is what we'll do. Next time he calls, tell him you'll only talk face to face. He can pick the time and the place but if you can't meet with him, you won't talk to him. Be very firm. If he's on the level, he'll agree. Otherwise, hang up and forget him. If you do arrange a meeting, let me know. I'll have him followed so we can find out who he is."

"That sounds great. Thanks, Rupert."

"And Sylvia. Don't even think about meeting him without telling me. No matter what he says. We don't know anything about this guy and there are a lot of dangerous people out there."

EIGHT

Sylvia could not get Rupert's warning out of her mind. She found herself scrutinizing the neighborhood over the weekend, conscious of the ubiquitous joggers, the traffic, the strolling couples. She became uneasy when a tall black-haired jogger went by twice. A black sedan with diplomatic plates, clearly out for a drive on a beautiful Saturday morning, passed the house and then returned and Sylvia considered writing down the license number.

To get away from her burgeoning paranoia, she decided to take the boys out. In an excess of zeal, she let the children choose their destination. As a result, Sylvia was forced to sit through a local children's movie, a horror about an anthropomorphized computer that went to university.

They arrived home to find Bess waiting with bags of Chinese food. Sylvia gratefully sank into a large worn armchair in the living room, nursing a J&B on the rocks and listening to the boys recount the movie in horrible detail to a determinedly cheerful Bess.

"We're going out to play ball, Mom," Jay shouted from the kitchen.

"Be back by nine!"

Bess joined Sylvia. "Great kids."

"Yes, they've been good as gold all weekend. Before you got here, they hardly dared to speak. I think they're afraid that if they're bad, I'll leave them too."

"Any news?"

"Nothing. What do you think about that guy, Friedman?"

"It's weird," Bess said slowly. "I don't know what I believe, but there are a lot of possible explanations."

"Such as?"

Bess had obviously thought of something she didn't want to say.

"Come on, out with it, Bess."

"I just had a passing thought. Nothing much. It was just that Friedman could be a husband or boyfriend of, uh, a friend of John's. Trying to locate her. If you buy that theory. Personally, I don't," she added hastily at the sight of Sylvia's expression. "Or maybe a creditor."

It was possible. Sylvia got up to refill her glass.

"Let's see what's on TV." Bess wanted to change the subject.

The station she tuned to first was in the midst of a special announcement. Terrorists had struck at Charles de Gaulle Airport outside Paris. Sixteen people were dead and fifty-seven wounded. All ten of the marauders had been killed as well, shot by either El Al security forces or by French police. At the moment, each group was crediting the other with the sharpshooting.

"Oh, Christ! Not again!" Bess hit the sofa. "They're animals, the PLO maniacs! And they want us to give them a country twelve miles from Tel Aviv!"

The screen showed the red blood and the broken bodies lying in the midst of the devastated airport. It was hard to grasp the reality of the picture. Television had portrayed so much staged violence that it had lost the ability to communicate the truth.

"Let's turn it off, Bess. We'll read about it in the papers." Sylvia wanted to calm her friend who was white with anger and frustration.

"They won't be satisfied, you know, until the Jews are kicked out of Israel. They don't want peaceful coexistence," Bess said bitterly. "They've never said they do. It's been the rest of the world talking, saying that if only Israel would stop fighting and start trusting, peace could come to the Middle East." Bess's voice was uncharacteristically harsh. "We tried the trusting, suffer-in-silence tactic in Germany."

Sylvia put her arm around the other woman. Bess had arrived in New York as a young child in 1938, sent over by a worried mother and father in Germany after she'd been beaten up on the street by a gang of hoodlums in full view of numerous, unhelpful citizens. Her parents had intended to follow her as soon as they could sell enough of their possessions to pay the fares. Bess had never seen them again.

Fortunately the boys ran back in. Bess straightened her shoulders and forced a smile to her face. There was an impromptu parents and kids baseball game at the park and they had to provide two adult bodies. Sylvia and Bess didn't feel they could refuse.

The doorbell rang on Sunday night after Sylvia had set the alarm system and had retired at the unheard-of hour of ten o'clock. She cursed and ran down to throw the switch before the siren came on to wake the children and Ingrid.

Cameron was at the door with Dave and Bess. All three were wearing long faces.

"What's the matter?" Even as she spoke, Sylvia knew exactly what she would hear.

"Please sit down, Mrs. West." Cameron, for once, was being polite. "We have some bad news for you."

Bess sat beside Sylvia and Dave took up position behind her.

"We've found Mr. West." Cameron was a little flustered. This was not the kind of scene he did best. "It seems he drove down to Florida in a rented car. Uh, with a friend," he added without looking at Sylvia. "He had an accident. I'm afraid they're both dead."

Bess and Dave turned to her. She was in a trance and couldn't quite grasp what was being said. "John is dead?"

"Yes. I'm sorry, Sylvia." Dave was very distressed.

John had really run away and now he was dead. Sylvia closed her eyes. She knew she had to stay calm. There were matters to be attended to but she couldn't think what they were.

Bess was talking.

"I'm sorry?" Sylvia hadn't been listening.

"I assumed you'd want to go down to . . . to . . . claim him. His body." Bess was near tears. "I booked you flights. If you want."

"Yes. I suppose so," Sylvia said dully.

"You fly to Miami tonight and then, first thing in the morning, you take a local airline to Gainesville. You'll have to drive from there but Vesper City is only about forty miles east of Gainesville."

"Vesper City? Is that where . . . ?"

"Yes." Dave put his hand on her shoulder. "John is there now. Would you like someone to go with you?"

"No. I'll be all right. It's the boys. How . . . ?"

"You can break the news to them when you come back,"

Bess interrupted. "I'll stay with them until Mrs. Layton gets here."

"My mother?"

"I called her. She'll be here tomorrow sometime."

"You thought of everything." Sylvia tried to smile. "Could I be alone now, please?"

The three of them filed out silently, leaving Sylvia to come to grips with the fact that it was too late to repair anything. There wasn't going to be a second chance for her and John.

NINE

She arrived in Vesper City, population 500, shortly after noon.
It was as though she'd stepped into a B western. The main
street, called naturally Main Street, was a scorching dustbowl,
faced by wood-framed buildings and wooden-faced, straw-
chewing men. The stores bore the quaint names of a Gary
Cooper oldie, Luke's General Store, Robertson's Hardware
& Blacksmith, Lily's Ladies' Clothes. The raised board side-
walks had wooden railings, tied to which were a few old nags.
The faded cars and pickups lining the street did nothing to
modernize its look, with one exception. A huge, white, late-
model Cadillac sat outside the office marked with a star.

Sylvia parked her Rambler and headed in, trying to ignore
the insolent stares. The police office was very small, containing
two scratched desks, a bench, and, ominously, a barred gate
at the back beside a sign that announced that the cells were in
the rear of the building.

A grossly fat man in a sweaty tan uniform was lounging
behind one of the desks, his boots adding new scars to its
surface, his swollen hands clasped behind his head. Another
man in jeans and a T-shirt was standing nearby leaning against
the wall, arms crossed on his much thinner chest which was
covered in ashes from the cigarette dangling in best Western
style.

They stopped talking when she walked in and watched her
in hostile silence.

"I'm looking for the chief of police."

"You found him." The fat man spoke in a deep baritone
with a rasp that came from either chronic bronchitis or sneering.

"I'm Sylvia West. I understand that . . ."

"Oh. Yeah. We've been expecting you." The fat man didn't
sound thrilled that his wait was over. He made a cursory effort
to swing his legs off the desk.

"Please don't get up." Sylvia's comment was unnecessary.

"Well. You here alone?" It was hard to tell if the chief was pleased at the thought or scandalized at the notion of a lady traveling all this way unchaperoned.

"Yes. I want to find out what happened and arrange for the . . . the body," Sylvia tried not to gulp, "to be taken home."

"I guess you oughta make the arrangements with Len."

"Len?"

"The undertaker. He's got the remains." The chief scratched his hanging jowls reflectively. "I don't know how much you were told, up north." Implying that information received from Union officials couldn't be relied on.

"Very little. I know that my husband was in a rented car, that he," Sylvia turned her face to the wall, "he had an accident."

The two men exchanged a significant look. The fat man persisted and eventually was able to raise himself to a standing position.

"I'm just gonna call the little lady. I think you oughta have a woman friend."

Nothing Sylvia could say would change his mind. The buddy apparently didn't care for the idea of staying alone with her so she was left to gaze out the window while the two men disappeared down the street. A few hard-faced men had congregated around her Rambler. Since the car wouldn't excite attention even in Vesper City, Sylvia assumed they were talking about her. When she walked to the door of the sheriff's office the group melted away, giving her few looks and those oddly hostile.

She returned to her seat. It belatedly occurred to her that everyone's embarrassment could come from the fact that John had not died alone. Sylvia had not given this aspect of the matter much thought but it didn't seem to make her feel worse. She already felt about as bad as she could.

The sheriff returned with a woman who had to be his wife. She was almost as heavy as he, a grotesque woman in a voile housedress with a bosom that amply covered the territory from her double chin to what would, on a smaller person, have been a waist. Her hair was a vivid shade of yellow, teased into a terrifying beehive and wound around her head into a sequined comb. Despite her matronly figure, she wasn't motherly. Sylvia didn't warm up to her.

"Hi, honey." The woman put a saccharine smile on her face that didn't touch her small eyes. "I'm Ray's wife. Betty Hodgins."

"How do you do?" Sylvia turned to the chief. "I would like to talk to you about the accident."

"Betty'll take care of ya. There ain't much to know."

"Thank you, but before I leave, could you tell me how the accident happened?" Sylvia persisted.

"Just musta been drinking, I guess. The car was traveling at night, hit a tree, and that was it. It went up real fast. A couple of kids came by and tried to get the folks out but it was too late. They pulled your husband out, but he was, uh, gone." He gestured at his wife who put a heavy arm around Sylvia.

Hodgins tried to leave the office.

"Where was this, Chief?"

"Just outa town." Hodgins didn't want to talk about the accident. He shifted his weight. "Look, it ain't gonna do you any good, this stuff. Why don't you just have a good cry and get everything done so you can go on home?"

A simple formula. Sylvia wished she was that simple. "I will, as soon as I understand what happened."

"Take her to see Len, Betty." It was an order. The fat man was dismissing both of them.

"Come with me, honey." Mrs. Hodgins removed her arm and waited for Sylvia to get up. There was no point in not following. Sylvia went.

Len Morgan's Funeral Parlor was tastefully hidden around the corner from the saloon. It was another frame building, fronted with a fake set of pillars and a plastic imitation-walnut door.

Len was waiting for them, a funereal man with the measured sobriety of undertakers the world over.

"Mrs. West, allow me to offer you my condolences for the untimely departure of your beloved husband."

"Yes." Sylvia was short with him. She couldn't stand the style. "Where is the, uh," she paled, "my husband's body?"

Len and Betty exchanged another of the looks that Sylvia was getting used to provoking.

"I think we should go into my office and discuss a few things first," Len intoned solemnly.

Sylvia allowed herself to be led into the garishly appointed inner sanctum, wondering if she'd have to pay for the privilege of viewing John's body.

"Sit down there, Mrs. West." "There" was a heavily padded imitation of an Empire loveseat, covered in turquoise satin.

Sylvia eased herself down. "When can I see my husband?"

"Well, I want to prepare you. You see, he was in a very bad car accident. He was killed instantly, thank the Good Lord."

"Amen." Betty joined in.

Sylvia took a deep breath. "He is badly marked? I understand that." She could understand it but she didn't know if she could cope with it.

"Marked, yes. And, er, more than that." Len squirmed in his vinyl chair. "The car exploded into flames after it hit the tree. Ray told you that?"

"Chief Hodgins did." Betty was cold about the breach of protocol.

"Chief Hodgins, I mean," Len agreed quickly. "So there is damage from the fire. The fellows got him out before, er, before . . . Well, let me say that they got his body out first. The other body was left in the car and it burned completely."

"What are you trying to tell me?" Sylvia asked sickly.

"Your husband's body isn't just scarred. It's kind of badly burned too. I don't think you ought to see it. It isn't necessary and uh, it isn't very nice." Len spoke with pious conviction.

Dear God. She closed her eyes for a moment. "How was the identification made?"

"I heard it was done by the teeth. From dental records. The chief would know all about it."

Sylvia swallowed and stared at her feet. Somewhere inside this place was a blackened hulk of what used to be John's handsome body. The only thing that could be recognized were his teeth. She found herself trying to remember what his teeth looked like. Her eyes started to sting; it took every ounce of her strength to blink the tears back.

"Now, Mrs. West, about the arrangements. The chief tells me you want to get home as fast as possible. Naturally. So we better talk about the manner of casket."

"Casket?"

"Yes, it's usual to purchase the casket from the establishment closest to the remains. Then it can be buried in the normal manner from an establishment near your home."

"Usual?" Sylvia couldn't get over his gall. It was his job, she supposed, but even so.

"In this case, you'll want a closed casket." He hadn't noticed her distaste. "We couldn't, shall we say, improve the appearance of the remains. So the question is just the casket. Being as it's going to be closed, we don't have to concern ourselves with clothes, though naturally, we shall see that he is decently covered for his final resting place. Now the oak casket is the one I generally suggest for travel. It isn't too heavy, though it is a good weight, and it's lined with a truly superior silk. You'd hate to economize on your last expense for a loved one and...."

The bit about the last expense did it.

"Stop right there. You're not going to get away with playing on my emotions. My husband is dead and nothing is going to bring him back to life. I don't like your sales pitch and I'm not going to listen to any more of it. Come on, Mrs. Hodgins." Sylvia strode to the door. "I'll be in touch with you about my arrangements."

Betty trailed behind her in an appalled silence. Sylvia had gone too far, attacking the sacred American way of life. Of death, rather.

The fat man was in his favorite postion. He looked up with surprise and no pleasure as Sylvia marched in.

"I didn't see the body. I understand you had to identify him by dental records. How did you do that?"

"The car rental company gave us the names. Uh, the name. Your police force contacted his dentist." He spoke grudgingly.

"Without notifying me? When did the accident happen?"

"On Friday." The fat man spoke reasonably but with an inexplicable hostility. "We don't get in touch with anyone until we know for sure who it is. Why should we call you if it's not your husband? We let you know when I figured it was time."

Sylvia noticed without caring that the police chief was no longer talking like a hick.

"Is there another funeral parlor near here?"

"No, there isn't. And we haven't had any complaints about it. Before now." Betty's face was unattractively red. She was ready to elaborate on the theme until her husband curtly told her to sit down and shut up.

He swiveled slowly back to Sylvia and watched her from under half-shut eyelids. "He's the only game in town, Mrs. West, so you're going to have to use him." His voice carried a note she couldn't identify. "You better make up your mind about it. We want to make sure you get to go home as fast as possible. Pick a coffin, Mrs. West."

Sylvia wanted to leave as badly as he wanted to see her go but she didn't like the feeling of being pushed. "First, I'd like to talk to the boys who found the car. Who are they?"

"Just young kids. It was very unpleasant for them and they don't want to talk about it." He spoke flatly.

Sylvia thought about that. She didn't really have any pressing questions. She really just wanted to go home.

"All right," she caved in. "Could you find out how fast Morgan can get me a coffin? Nothing fancy. Just a coffin." The picture she was trying to keep out of her mind was persistent. A blackened shell of a man. Sylvia shivered.

"Get Mrs. West a cup of coffee. She's upset," Hodgins barked at his wife. He didn't sound sympathetic.

Betty hustled to it. "Just sit there, honey." She tried to paste the smile back on. It hadn't been compelling before and now it was distinctly off-putting.

The chief picked up the phone. "Len? Ray here. How fast can ya get a coffin for Mrs. West?" He listened to agitated talk for a while. Sylvia could hear the sibilants across the room. "I know, I know. Hold on to your pants. She wants one now. How fast?" He frowned. "You can do better than that. The lady wants to go home....I see." His voice got raspier. "I want better than that, Len. Understand me?...Right. I'll get back to ya."

He looked at Sylvia. "He can do it in two days. You can go on home and we'll send it up."

"Two days?" Sylvia ignored the suggestion. She wouldn't rely on Vesper City to mail a letter. "Surely he has something in stock?"

"It's a small place. Len runs a feed store too. Can't make a living on a parlor in a town this size. He doesn't keep anything in stock. In fact, he can only do it so fast if you pay for the best." His tiny eyes were malevolently amused.

"I see." Sylvia was disgusted but she couldn't see any alternative to the blackmail. Her little temper tantrum was costing her plenty. "Can I use your phone? I'll call collect."

He pushed it over.

The operator got Bess in record time. Sylvia filled her in briefly and added that she wouldn't be able to leave for two days.

"At least," Hodgins put in. "Unless you leave it to us."

"Two days at least," Sylvia amended her statement.

"I gather you're having a rough time with the red-necks?" Bess sympathized.

"You could say that. I don't have any options."

"Well, you could...no, never mind."

"What were you going to say?"

"Well, don't get upset. It's just a thought. You know, the Jews bury their dead immediately. Wherever they die."

"There isn't a Jewish funeral parlor here." Sylvia couldn't conceive of the social life an unfortunate Jewish family would have in this town.

"I know, but what I was getting at is that you could consider burying John there. Especially since he's . . . since you couldn't have an open casket. We could have a memorial service here. And then you could get back to the boys fast."

"What's the problem?"

"Ingrid didn't mean to, but they saw her crying and I'm afraid they know about it."

"Oh, my God!" Sylvia tried to figure out what to do. She hated the thought of going home without the body. "There's no point in having the burial here. I'd still have to wait two days for the coffin. At least."

"What about cremation?" Bess was braver now.

"Jews do that too?"

"No, in fact we're not allowed to. But you can."

It was a thought. Not without appeal. Sylvia would be able to get home much faster.

"I'll call you back." She had to think about it. "Chief Hodgins, I'm going for a walk, to sort of collect my thoughts. If you'll excuse me?"

"Sure. Betty!" he hollered. "Come on out here and take Mrs. West for a walk."

"Oh, I don't need help. I'm fine, really."

Hodgins didn't doubt it. And he didn't like it either. Grieving widows weren't supposed to act like this. He wasn't going to let her out alone, although he allowed that his wife could walk behind Sylvia to give her some privacy.

Sylvia gave in. From what she could tell, Mrs. Hodgins was as thrilled about the chief's edict as she, but neither of them could do anything about it.

As she paced Main Street, Sylvia had the feeling that dozens of hostile eyes were on her. Whenever she looked around, curtains swung as though someone had moved hastily away. Other passersby turned their heads quickly. Talk stopped as she walked by and started up again in whispers as soon as she passed. She turned back to the police station.

"I want my husband cremated. Tomorrow. With a simple prayer and no eulogy," she announced to the chief, expecting

stares of horror and protestations of disbelief. She got both
from Betty but the chief grabbed at her suggestion.

"That would probably be the fastest thing. I'll arrange it
with Len. Betty, take Mrs. West to Dorry's. She'll have a
room for her."

Dorry's turned out to be the saloon, upstairs of which were
a couple of crummy un-air-conditioned bedrooms and an old,
filthy bathroom shared by two women of dubious reputation
and the local drinkers.

Sylvia thanked Betty and sank down onto the bed. Its mattress had given out a long time ago, but mercifully she'd only
have to spend one night on it.

Sylvia tried to take a nap but her mind was racing too
quickly to permit her any healing unconsciousness. After a
fruitless hour, she stepped into the washroom and splashed
water on her face, trying to touch as few of the dirty surfaces
as possible.

She had changed her mind about questioning the boys who
had come upon the accident. Since she was here, she might
as well learn whatever she could. And since the chief was
clearly not going to help, she'd have to do some detecting on
her own.

As she descended, Dorry, a scrawny woman wearing too
much pancake makeup and too little clothing for her age,
stopped her.

"Hungry, honey?" Despite her words, Dorry was not the
proverbial hooker with the heart of gold. Her eyes were gray
ice.

"Not really. I thought I'd walk around a bit."

"Wait here. I'll call Betty Hodgins."

"No." Sylvia tried not to yell. "I'm fine by myself, thanks.
I'll just amble around. I won't get lost."

"I promised I'd call if you wanted to go out. Shouldn't be
alone at a time like this." Dorry didn't even try to sound
concerned for Sylvia's mental well-being.

"I want to be alone." Sylvia wanted to walk past the woman,
but without actually pushing her out of the way, she couldn't
get by.

"I'll call Betty." Dorry was turning ugly.

"Forget it." Sylvia turned to go upstairs and had another
idea. "I'll stay in, but I think I'd like a drink."

"I'll call Betty." The keeper of the hotel, if you could call it that, sounded like a broken record.

"No. I just want a drink. All by myself." Sylvia spoke firmly. Dorry hesitated and then apparently decided that she'd done all she could.

"What'll ya have?"

"J&B, on the rocks. Make it a double."

Sylvia followed Dorry into the saloon, a room not much cleaner than the toilet upstairs. It was decorated in styles consistent with the rest of the town, formica and plastic. The lights weren't on but enough illumination fought its way through the streaked windows to show that none of the many colors inside complemented each other. The total effect was not conducive to drinking, unless it was serious, get-unconscious-as-fast-as-possible drinking.

There were a number of men in the room, and the two women who presumably shared Sylvia's toilet. She perched on a soiled chair as far from the bar as possible. She didn't want Dorry poking her nose into any conversations she could strike up.

The drink appeared in a glass that didn't bear close scrutiny. Sylvia made a mental note to close her eyes when it came time to drain the bottom.

She took a sip, examining the other occupants without appearing to stare. Two of the men were clearly chronic alcoholics, bearing the same signs of permanence in the bar that the furniture did. A third now drinking with them wore a salesman's checked suit, carrying the loud material on a substantial frame. He prided himself on being a ladies' man, flirting with the two bored ladies at the bar who gave every indication of having heard those jokes from dozens if not hundreds of men, not to mention several times from him. Good-time Charlie had brightened up noticeably when Sylvia entered the room and if she played her cards right, he'd be over to wow her in a matter of minutes.

There was another group of men, five business types wearing baggy gray suits and string ties under button-down shirts, all talking earnestly. From time to time a word like "margin" or "equity" came wafting over.

"Hi, beautiful." Charlie had finally made it over, swaggering with glass casually in hand. Sylvia kept her eyes on it in case he started to spill it on her.

"Hi." She didn't want to sound too friendly, but she couldn't get information if no one would talk to her.

"When did you sail in? A gorgeous girl like you doesn't belong here."

Sylvia fervently hoped not. "I just arrived. This afternoon."

"My good luck," he said with what he probably thought was smooth charm.

"Mind if I sit down?" He suited his action to his words without waiting for the answer. "So, what's your business here?"

"Wonderful weather we're having."

"We don't have to talk business, if you don't want to."

"You're a perceptive man. What passes for entertainment in this place?"

"Just the good friends you make." He leered.

"Wonderful. I understand you had a little excitement the last few days?"

"Last few days? Oh, you mean the crash." He wiped the smile off for the requisite second. "Sad thing."

"Two people dead, I'm told."

"Who told you?"

"I don't know. I just heard it around," Sylvia said vaguely.

"'Cause most folks aren't talking about it. I know about it because I'm on the inside, know what I mean?" He winked.

Sylvia didn't have the foggiest but nodded knowingly. "What happened?"

"Car met tree." He cracked up at his own wit.

"Two local kids found it, eh?"

"Kids? Not exactly. Course, everything's relative. But to a young girl like you, they wouldn't be kids."

Sylvia managed a weakly appreciative smile. "Who were they?"

"Just locals. Wouldn't interest you none. How about you and me having dinner somewhere?"

A shadow fell over the table.

"Betty. I wouldn't have expected you to frequent a place like this," Sylvia said, trying not to sound annoyed.

"I heard you were having a drink. I thought I'd join you. Get lost, Ed." Betty sat without waiting to see the effect of her words.

Her confidence wasn't misplaced. Ed took off in a flash of checks. Sylvia supposed that when the wife of the police chief spoke, you had to jump.

Betty wasn't going anyplace until she saw Sylvia tucked in

for the night. Which made bedtime very early.

Sylvia tried to sleep but the images in her mind didn't help—a car hurtling against a tree, John's agonized face inside an inferno, two twisted, devoured bodies. She eventually took a couple of pills and knocked herself out.

Sylvia woke up disoriented. It was a few minutes before the memories came flooding back and before she realized where she was. She tried to concentrate on the good times with John but their last weekend together was the only vivid recollection. It had not been one of the good times.

Breakfast was a grim ordeal. Cold toast spread with margarine, tepid coffee with a skin of gray cream. Sylvia made a valiant effort and then pushed it away.

"I'm not hungry," she explained apologetically to Dorry, who didn't seem to care. There were a few men in the saloon, eating the meal with every evidence of enjoyment. From time to time, Sylvia caught one of them watching her. She couldn't quite make out the expressions on their faces but they weren't welcoming.

She left for the police station, thankful that Dorry wasn't trying to prevent her from leaving the hotel. Chief Hodgins was in his usual spot.

"My wife isn't with you?" He looked alarmed.

"No. I just had breakfast and thought I'd come talk to you for a moment."

"She'll be over soon."

"I can manage on my own today. But, uh, thank you."

"Wouldn't think of it." He spoke genially but there was a core of hardness in his voice.

Sylvia dropped the topic for the time being. "Was there an autopsy done?"

"What for? Cause of death was plain."

Terse but true. Sylvia winced. "Well, about the people who—"

"Hey. I nearly forgot," he interrupted. "The, uh, thing is set for two."

"Thing?"

"For your husband."

"Fine. At the funeral parlor?"

"Yeah." The fat man took out some chewing tobacco and started to put it in his mouth. "Oh, good. Hi, Betty."

Mrs. Hodgins looked a little taken aback, as well she might. She had probably not had such a friendly reception from her husband since their wedding night. "You take Mrs. West back to the hotel and stay with her. I got work to do."

Sylvia was hustled out before she could ask any questions. The morning did not pass quickly. Sylvia found that with very little effort, she could learn to loathe Betty Hodgins.

The woman wouldn't shut up or leave her alone and everything she said was either bigoted, malicious, or both. Sylvia restricted herself to bland nods. There was no point in trying to argue.

Eventually, after a lunch she couldn't eat, Sylvia suggested that it was time to go to the undertaker's establishment. At the very least, decorum would compel Betty to stop talking.

Len met them at the door again, this time with a much subdued air and no chitchat. "This way, Mrs. Mmmm." He wasn't going to give her the satisfaction of remembering her name. Sylvia had overcome worse things. She ignored him and walked in to sit with the covered body, hoping that the other two would do the decent thing and leave her alone.

They did. Sylvia tried to wipe her mind clear of Vesper City and its disturbing inhabitants. She wanted to say a personal goodbye to John but found she had little to say. She sat silently, sad for the marriage that had died unannounced, sad for her bereaved boys, sad for a man she'd loved who'd been so unhappy that he had come to die in this unspeakable place that he'd have detested. Most of all, sad for herself, for the feelings of anger she was trying to deny, for the humiliation at the hands of a woman she refused to ask about, for the guilt she'd carry with her much longer than anything else from the marriage.

"Excuse me, it's two o'clock." Len's habit of obsequiousness was reasserting itself. "This is Reverend Dubois. From Gainesville."

"How do you do?" Sylvia looked the plump, smug, white-collared man over.

"My deepest sympathies," he oozed in an unctuous voice. "I'll be reading the prayers and giving the eulogy. We ought to—"

"No eulogy. Whatever prayer you want." Sylvia looked at her watch. "Can we begin?"

She stared unblinkingly at the shoddy wooden box as it was pushed forward toward a hole in the wall between two faded black curtains, closing her mind to the rich, oily voice smearing prayers around the room. Eventually the box disappeared. Sylvia stood for a long time, staring at the curtains. She refused to sit down or to go to her room at the hotel.

She had buried John shabbily. The very least that she could do was to bear witness while the clay was consumed.

Len Morgan reappeared much later holding a small box.

"This contains the remains," he whispered reverently.

Sylvia nodded and took it from him. She walked out to his office and laid it down on his desk.

"I'll write the check now. How much?"

He was shocked at the crudity but eager to see her signature.

"Five hundred dollars. But you can write it later, if you would like to compose yourself."

"I'm quite composed. And I won't be here later." She handed it over contemptuously.

Chief Hodgins and his wife were waiting on the street.

"We weren't sure if you'd seen us inside. We were there, of course," Betty said piously.

"Thanks. I'd get going right now but there are a few more questions I'd like to ask."

"Well, it's a shame to keep you." Hodgins wasn't going to be heartbroken to say good-bye. "I'm sure your little boys need you. Why don't I give you a copy of the official police report? It's not usual, but I see no reason for you not to have it. If you don't understand anything, give me a call. Or your Captain Cameron can explain it," he added condescendingly.

Sylvia couldn't be bothered to point out that she'd read hundreds of such reports over the years. And understood all of them. "Yes, that would save me time."

"Hold on here, I'll get it." The chief lumbered away and was back with the report amazingly fast for a man of his size.

She made it to Gainesville in thirty minutes and by sheer luck slid onto a connection for Tampa that was almost on the runway as she drove up.

Sylvia kept the box with her on the plane. She wasn't sure what she could do with it, but perhaps it would help the boys to choose its final resting place.

TEN

She had a rough time with the boys, but with the combined help of her mother, Bess, and Rupert, who was around a surprising amount of the time, the kids eventually settled into a much-subdued but halfway normal routine.

Sylvia had put the police report away upon arriving home. She couldn't bear to read about the accident just yet. It was as much as she could do to cope with her grieving children and her own mixed-up feelings.

Bess fielded most of the zealous press inquiries and the equally zealous sympathy calls, leaving Sylvia free to spend every waking moment with Jay and Carl. They were as great a comfort to her as she was to them. The hardest hours were at night, when they had finally succumbed to the sleep denied Sylvia who paced the house, tortured by regrets and loneliness.

She decided to go back to work to preserve her sanity. "I'm taking over the Bailey trial," she told Rupert over lunch on Wednesday. "It's scheduled for Friday and I'll go crazy if I'm not busy."

"If you're sure you're up to it," Rupert commented dubiously. "Maybe you should take the kids and go up north for a few weeks."

"I'd have nothing to do but sit and brood."

Rupert nodded. His escape too was work, so he had no further arguments to offer. "By the way, if that nut calls again, let me know."

"What nut? Oh, Friedman. Why would he call now?"

"You never know. You've just had more publicity, don't forget, and that's probably what prompted him to call in the first place." Rupert looked like he wanted to add something.

"What were you going to say?"

"Don't get alarmed. After all, you've got the burglar alarm system now, but it is possible that Friedman was your unwanted visitor."

"The break-and-enter?" Sylvia thought about it. Friedman hadn't sounded like that kind of weirdo but she wasn't going to bet on her judgment of people for a while.

"Sylvia, Mr. Dutton is here." Bess had tried to keep visitors away, but he'd been insistent on seeing Sylvia.

— "Oh, send Herb in." Rupert flushed. "I'm sorry, Sylvia. I just assumed you'd want to see him."

"Sure."

"Hello, Sylvia. My deepest sympathies." Dutton was carrying a huge mum plant. "I can't tell you how we'll all miss John."

She nodded jerkily, hiding her face by taking the plant over to the window.

"Do you know exactly what happened, Sylvia?" Dutton hurried to rephrase his question. "I mean, how did the car go out of control?"

"I'm not sure." Sylvia didn't mention the report, still lying in a drawer in her bedroom. She couldn't face an afternoon going over the painful details.

"Were there any witnesses?"

"Apparently two people came by after the crash and pulled John out. It was too late to save him."

"Do you know their names?" Dutton ignored the appalled looks Bess and Rupert were giving him.

"I don't, no. It didn't seem important."

He smiled sympathetically. "I guess not. Well, the local police were certainly very efficient. They identified John as quickly as any big force could have done. I suppose they treated you well?"

"Mmm." Sylvia inclined her head noncommittally.

Bess had had it. "I'm sorry, Mr. Dutton, but Sylvia is looking tired. I'm going to throw you out so she can go to bed."

"I'm all right!" Sylvia protested.

"No, you're not." Bess spoke in a tone of voice that Sylvia knew well. Experience had taught her not to bother arguing with it.

"I'm sorry, Herb." She shrugged her shoulders. "You heard my keeper."

"Of course. By the way, please give my condolences to your mother."

"I'll pass the message along," Bess interjected, getting to her feet.

Dutton stood up too, smiling. "I'll keep in touch. If you need any help, please call me."

Sylvia shook her head when Bess returned from seeing him out, still hot under the collar.

"You're too protective," Sylvia said, amused. "Herb meant well. I'm going up to my room now." There was no point in mentioning that she intended to use the rest of the day to prepare for a trial.

It was the best thing she could have done. Before she knew it, Ingrid was at the door asking if she wanted dinner. Sylvia was exhausted, but for the first time since John had disappeared, she had had some hours of peace.

It rained on Thursday, a violent downpour that lashed away the oppressive heat of the past week. Sylvia and her mother went for a walk as soon as the sun reappeared, slowly meandering along the narrow roads of the village.

Sylvia felt strong enough, afterwards, to take out the police report. It was time to get that over with and start on the arduous job of reconstructing her life.

The report was a scant three pages, mainly full of technical details concerning the damage to the car. Sylvia skipped very quickly over the gory description of the bodies. Someone, no doubt Hodgins, had blacked out the name of the woman in the car. Probably from an overdeveloped sense of gentility.

The report concluded that, for whatever reason, the car had been going too fast, had slipped out of control on a sharp curve about ten miles east of town, and had rammed a very large tree. The writer recommended that a guard rail be erected on the curve. Apparently it was not the first fatality at the spot.

Altogether, not an extraordinary accident, except for the fact that one of the victims had been her husband. She started to put the report away and suddenly stiffened.

The writer had said that John had been behind the wheel.

John couldn't drive. He had never wanted to learn. He didn't like cars, period. In fact, Sylvia had been very surprised that John had undertaken such a long drive, even as a passenger.

She called Vesper City. Hodgins was less than pleased to hear from her and his tone was curt.

"It's no misprint. Your husband was pulled out from behind the wheel."

"My husband couldn't drive. He didn't even have a license and he didn't want to get one."

"Mrs. West. Your husband may never have driven before in his life. He sure wasn't very good at it. But he was driving when that car hit the tree. And he wouldn't have been allowed to rent the car in the first place if he didn't have a driver's license. Now, in my opinion, you should stop going over and over this thing. Your children need you and if you keep it up, you're gonna have a breakdown." He started to ring off.

Sylvia ignored the last comment. "Chief Hodgins, I want to talk to the people who found the car. Now you told me that they were youngsters but I've since heard otherwise."

"Where did you hear that?"

"It doesn't matter. What does matter is that I have a chance to ask them a couple of questions. Would you mind giving me their names?"

"I can't do that." He was drawling, almost enjoying the opportunity to be obstreperous.

Sylvia abandoned that point for the moment. "Okay, then let's move on to the identification. I want a copy of the dental reports."

"I can't do that either." He was defintely having a ball.

"Why not?" Sylvia had a dangerous edge to her voice now.

"'Cause I don't have them."

It was like pulling teeth. "Who does?"

"Your police do. I sent them up to your force."

"Fine. There is only one other thing. I want the name of the woman who died with my husband. It was covered up on my copy of the report."

"Yeah. I covered it. There's no point in stirring up her family. They've suffered enough for her mistake and I'm not gonna give you the chance to make it worse for them."

"I have no intention of causing a scandal or preaching to them about their fallen daughter. I simply want to find out a little about this so-called trip."

"I can't help you, ma'am." Hodgins chuckled and hung up.

Sylvia slammed down the receiver so hard that she half expected to see it crack. She paced her bedroom, thinking furiously. That odd creature, Friedman, had warned her against accepting simple solutions to the disappearance. There was a small possibility that he had been warning her against just such a solution as this one.

Dave wasn't in his office or at home. Sylvia left messages for him and reluctantly dialed Cameron's number.

He was bored by her new facts, so bored that he barely

managed to stay awake throughout the call.

"Mrs. West, your husband obviously could drive. He just didn't tell you. Most husbands don't tell their wives everything." Especially yours, his tone implied.

"That's one possible answer. The other is that there's something fishy about the accident. Could I see the dental reports tonight?"

"What reports?"

"The dental reports that identified John. Chief Hodgins said he sent them to you."

"I don't have them. Maybe they're in the mail." Cameron wasn't even trying to sound helpful.

Sylvia ended the conversation before she broke the law by conveying obscene suggestions over the line.

Bess answered the doorbell during dinner and returned with a disgusted expression on her face.

"It's Herb Dutton again. Shall I tell him you're not in any shape to see him?"

"No, Bess. Show him in." Sylvia wasn't wild about Herb either, but she couldn't start offending a senior official at State. Besides, he was a friend of Rupert's.

"Hi, Sylvia. I brought a few chocolates for the boys."

The two yelped and unceremoniously grabbed the bag out of his hand. Sylvia called for order but was too happy to see them respond with normal enthusiasm to scold.

"Let's go into the living room, Herb. I'm done with dinner anyway. We can have coffee there. Uh, kids, don't put more than five pieces into your mouths at once, okay?"

They settled themselves in front of the fireplace. Herb looked around the homey room with approval.

"What a comfortable place."

Sylvia liked him for that. He'd sounded sincere. Most people hinted that it was disgracefully scruffy.

"Rupert tells me that you're returning to normal life right away," Herb commented, puffing gently on his pipe. "As normal as possible. In a way, it must be a relief to clear everything up? Even if the answers are unpleasant."

"Yes, if it is all cleared up." It slipped out.

"What do you mean?" Herb spoke sharply.

"Oh, nothing really." Sylvia could see that she wasn't going to get away with that. "Just a few tiny discrepancies."

"Such as?"

"I didn't think John could drive, but he apparently was behind the wheel."

"John was an odd man," Dutton said ruminatively, changing the direction of the conversation slightly. "I was very fond of him, as you know, but we were on different wavelengths half the time. He often surprised me. Like when he turned down the chance to sit on the Securities' Regulation Commission."

Sylvia said nothing.

"Did he explain his refusal to you?"

"Well, he felt that publicity wouldn't do him any good with his clients." She made a face. "It was hard to swallow, now that I think of it."

Dutton sighed. "That's what he told me too. As you say, it's hard to accept. This commission was so blue-chip that it could only have added to his prestige." He turned to face her. "Sylvia, did you ever have any inkling about, well, about what happened?"

"I never considered for a minute that John would run off, if that's what you mean."

"Had you ever met Cass Harwood?"

"Who?"

"The, uh, other person in the car. I assumed the police must have told you." He had the grace to turn red.

"No, I never met her." Sylvia lit a cigarette to hide her elation at getting the name. "Amazing, isn't it? A man like John with a secret life."

Dutton looked very disturbed. "He hid a great deal from all of us."

"No." Sylvia felt driven to greater honesty. "The truth is that I was so busy with my own life that I wouldn't have had the time to listen. Much less to notice."

"Don't blame yourself, my dear. Well, I don't want to keep you from your family. I'll be in touch, Sylvia."

She closed the door behind him and leaned against it for a few minutes, thinking over the conversation. Dutton knew a lot about the accident. He had the contacts to find out anything he wanted to know, that was for sure. But that didn't explain why he wanted the information.

Of course, he had considered himself really close to John. He probably felt as betrayed as she did.

The phone rang.

"It's Cameron for you, Sylvia. You want to talk to him?"

Bess was standing in the doorway of the dining room with her hands on her hips. She was clearly watching for the slightest sign of fatigue.

"Sure, why not?" Sylvia bounced into the kitchen for Bess's benefit. She didn't want to go to bed.

"I've got some information for you, Mrs. West. Your husband could drive. A New York license was issued to him this past year and he used it to rent the car."

Sylvia didn't respond.

"I thought you'd be interested," Cameron said weakly.

She stayed silent.

"Anyway, we've cleared up that little mystery. Uh, if you have any more questions, just call."

"Good-bye, Captain."

Sylvia sat at the kitchen table, smoking incessantly and drinking endless cups of coffee. She added up the pieces a dozen times, never arriving twice at the same sum.

Dave called just before midnight. "Is it too late? I hope I didn't wake you?"

"No. I'm not sleeping a lot these days. Dave, I need your help." She filled him in on her latest discoveries. "If the accident is what it's starting to look like, then I've got to come to one of two conclusions. Either John's been murdered or it's a set-up and he's alive."

"Alive, but involved," Dave pointed out soberly. "Assuming you're right, but—"

Sylvia interrupted his doubts. "Could you do a search on Cass Harwood? According to the police report, she came from Manhattan. There has to be some record of her somewhere. And the other thing is this license. John hated cars, really detested them. There must be a few John Wests in New York and I don't think much of Cameron. He found what he wanted to find and it's very possible that he didn't ask the right questions."

"I don't much like him myself," Dave admitted, "but he's supposed to know his job."

"Maybe. You will look into it?"

"Okay. I hate to say it, but this time Cameron's probably right. John changed a lot of habits lately."

"A few too many for my taste, Dave. It doesn't smell. It stinks."

ELEVEN

Sylvia felt like she'd been away from the courtroom for months. It was reassuring to be back; the filthy, stuffy building was her home away from home. She was smiling as she pushed her way to the second floor past milling crowds of jeans-clad, dirty-haired youths flashing shallow bravado and bad teeth while awaiting their lawyers.

The court officers were already setting up for business in the dingy room where her trial was scheduled to take place. Both the clerk, a wizened old man who had been an antique a decade ago, and the cheerful court reporter knew and liked Sylvia. Their obvious sympathy for her loss was comforting.

Even the assistant district attorney checked his brusque march into the room to grunt something at her by way of condolence. He was somewhat embarrassed about forcing the trial on under the circumstances but he had witnesses who couldn't conveniently return another time.

"That's okay," Sylvia said easily. "It takes my mind off my own problems."

The other lawyer flushed. "I'll call you first on the trial list but I don't know when you'll be reached. There are a lot of adjournments and guilty pleas this morning."

Sylvia took her seat at the wooden counsel table in the front of the courtroom and set out her books and papers. The level of noise steadily increased as other lawyers, their clients and witnesses filtered in. Just before the hour, the slovenly police on courthouse duty arrived with the even more slovenly crew of handcuffed prisoners.

"All rise!" The judge, a curmudgeon known for his bad temper and uneven judgment, entered. He and the attorneys bowed hypocritically to each other and the day began.

The clerk called the cases for adjournment. A progression of hard-eyed men stood up with their lawyers to agree to reappear for trial on a subsequent date. Several of them had appeared in court six and seven times, and the judge began to harangue the unfortunate prosecutor.

"Why can't you arrange for trials to take place? This court-room is meant to be used for trials, not an endless series of adjournments. If you can't get your witnesses here on the day set for trial, I'll force you to go ahead without them! I'm getting tired of rubberstamping your inefficiencies!"

The lawyer stammered. "The court lists are too long, Your Honor. We don't have the time today to hear these cases. It's not a question of the State's witnesses."

The judge wouldn't allow reason and fact to placate him, and only after shouting for a few more minutes would he subside and permit the court to proceed.

"Really in a swell mood today," one of the other lawyers at counsel table whispered to Sylvia. "Now that he's had his fight with George, he'll want to take on one of us."

She nodded. She'd had many a fight with this judge and his mood did not bode well for her clients. She swiveled around to see that her clients, the Baileys, had arrived in time to hear the latter part of His Honor's charming diatribe. The spectators' seats were full and they were standing in the aisle, looking around helplessly. In a moment the judge would start to scream at them. Sylvia motioned the couple to follow her outside.

"Isn't he awful hard?" a pale Mrs. Bailey whispered.

"His bark is worse than his bite," Sylvia mendaciously re-assured her. She pointed them to a bench in the crowded cor-ridor that had just been vacated by a tearful Italian family, clutching unhappily at the son who undoubtedly was the reason for their presence in the place.

The Baileys calmed down as Sylvia reviewed their evidence. "And don't volunteer information," she instructed them for the fifth time. She interrupted herself suddenly and stood up to get a better view of the hallway.

A tall, silver-haired man was entering a courtroom at the rear of the building. Sylvia turned to her clients. "Just wait here." She hurriedly bullied her way through the mob to the last door in the corridor and peered inside. An unusually elegant spectator was seating himself.

She returned to the Baileys, deep in thought. "Uh, wait here until your case is called." She slipped back into her court and as soon as the prosecutor paused to allow a defense attorney to make submissions, she crossed to him.

"George, could you hold my case down? I've got to go to another court."

He nodded sourly. "Just don't expect to get on before lunch."

Sylvia returned to the chamber down the hall, quietly entering through a seldom-used door at the back.

The clerk called the last of the day's adjournments. The judge, a comparatively young member of the judiciary whose round cheeks and plump lips belied his jaundiced view of the world, disposed of it quickly.

"Di Angelo!" the clerk hollered.

A short dark man stood up. His lawyer, a boy fresh out of law school, stood beside him and tried to look jaded.

The prosecutor, hardly more seasoned than his adversary, was on his feet. "This is a sentence matter, Your Honor. This court convicted the accused last week on a charge of break and enter. Because of his lengthy record which his counsel has agreed to admit, I'm calling evidence as to sentence."

Di Angelo had to be a real baddie. The State rarely bothered to do more than make oral submissions on sentence though the defense frequently led evidence to mitigate it.

The witness, predictably, was a police officer who told the court about the conduct of the defendant when he'd been arrested. Di Angelo had apparently threatened to "wipe out" almost everyone involved in the criminal process and had been uncooperative and abusive throughout the investigation. Despite his name, Di Angelo had a long record of violent crime as well as an unbelievable string of property offense convictions. There didn't seem to be much any defense attorney could do.

Apparently, this one was going to try. He announced, when the officer had finished, that he had a character witness who would testify to the prisoner's attempts to go straight after his most recent release from jail.

The witness was the elegant man whom Sylvia had followed into the courtroom. It was none other than Johann von Schagg.

He took the witness stand as though he owned it. The judge beamed as von Schagg gave his name and occupation and swore to tell the truth. It was clear that His Honor regarded this witness as the sort he should be given more often.

The young defense lawyer stepped forward. "In your own words, sir, would you please tell the court what you know about the accused."

Sylvia winced. Only an inexperienced counsel would refer to his own client as an "accused" instead of investing him with some dignity by using a more polite title.

Von Schagg smiled charmingly at the judge. "I first met Mr. Di Angelo almost thirty-five years ago in Italy. He had just been demobilized and was badly injured. I too had fought in the war although I was, of course, too young to be drafted.

"In 1945, I was trying to leave Europe because the memories of my family, who had all died during the war, were too painful for me. But I was a young boy without money or friends. Mr. Di Angelo gave me help, money, and put me up with his family. Purely out of the goodness of his heart."

Sylvia took an incredulous look at the thug in the dock. It required an imagination better than hers to conceive of his having a heart, much less one with even a soupçon of goodness in it.

"As I mentioned, he was badly hurt, and in fact, before I managed to emigrate from Europe, he had the first of a series of operations designed to improve the strength of his right arm and leg. He had worked on his family's small farm before the war, but his injuries prevented him from returning to that occupation. The operations weren't an immediate success, and without a trade Mr. Di Angelo couldn't make a living. Especially in Italy after the war.

"So he came here. He had a rough time of it and fell in with bad company. After a few years, quite a few in fact, through sheer coincidence I ran into him and was able to return a small part of the help he'd given me.

"He left prison in 1977 and came to work for me. Things were going well but some of his old cronies unfortunately tracked him down and wouldn't leave him alone.

"He slipped again, but I assure the court that I have every confidence that his resolve is stronger now and that he will be able to resist temptation in the future. I will be more than happy to give him another job and to look out for him, perhaps a bit more carefully, when he is returned to society."

A heart-rending story. Sylvia, however, managed to restrain her tears. Von Schagg as a pure altruist was as fanciful a notion as his portrait of the greasy hood.

Von Schagg started to leave the witness box. The judge stopped him. "One moment, sir."

Sylvia caught the eye of another lawyer and they smiled at each other. The criminal court judges rarely used that form of address.

"The prosecutor may have some questions for you," the judge added politely.

The assistant D.A. was debating whether or not to cross-examine. Sylvia crossed her fingers and prayed fervently that he would. For one thing, he ought to remind the court for which side these two stalwarts had been fighting. The room could use some fresh air. And what kind of job did the dapper angel of mercy have in mind for the prisoner?

The prosecutor didn't have the nerve. "No, Your Honor. I have no questions."

The judge nodded approvingly and thanked von Schagg for his time. The witness smiled and walked over to the accused. They conversed in low tones for a moment.

The court took a brief recess, probably so that the judge who had yellow stains on his fingers could smoke a cigarette.

For which Sylvia was thankful. Hell was appearing in front of judges who didn't smoke and had strong bladders. She lit a cigarette and ran after von Schagg as he left the room. Seeing her did not appear to make his day but he quickly controlled himself and turned on the charm.

"Were you in the courtroom?" he asked. "I didn't see you but I was nervous about testifying and it was very crowded."

Not that nervous and not that crowded. "Yes, I was. I was very interested in your evidence. You've certainly led a fascinating life." Sylvia had a lot of questions to ask. Long experience in cross-examining witnesses had given her faith in her instincts. "Perhaps if you're staying around to see what sentence your friend is getting we could have lunch," she added.

"Oh, I am desolated but it is impossible. I have a terrible schedule today. As a matter of fact, only for old times' sake would I have made this hole in my day."

"It was extraordinarily kind of you," Sylvia commented. "He must have helped you a great deal. But I find it hard to imagine you destitute. You look so, well, so self-sufficient."

He laughed without humor. "No one was self-sufficient right after the war. Especially in Italy. There was no food, no fuel. Only the Americans had anything."

"Is that what made you decide to come to the States?"

"In a way." Von Schagg wanted out. "I must go now, but perhaps we will meet again when we have more time." He bowed to her and walked off.

Sylvia stared speculatively after him. It mightn't mean anything, but men like Di Angelo didn't usually get to hang around men like von Schagg. Not thirty-five years later. And Di Angelo's record didn't show much of a gap for going straight. Von Schagg said he'd employed him soon after he got out in 1977, but he'd been released in December of that year and the new offense was committed six months later. Maybe von Schagg was just a sentimental softy, but he could have fooled her.

The judge gave Di Angelo a low sentence. The prosecutor looked as though he'd been slapped, but after a moment he shrugged resignedly. He'd had worse things happen in court.

Sylvia's case was called after lunch. Bailey was arraigned on two charges of theft and one of resisting arrest. As the prosecution witnesses gave their evidence, part of her mind was fixed on Di Angelo. He'd left the dock happily, and no wonder. But it had seemed to her that he'd stared at her as he went.

Paranoia? Maybe.

The evidence against her client was very strong. Bailey wanted to give his version of the events, but after hearing almost half of the State's case, Sylvia decided she'd better plea bargain. If Bailey testified, he would obviously perjure himself and things would go very hard for him. She asked the assistant D.A. to agree to a brief recess which the judge reluctantly granted.

Bailey was truculent, but even he could see which way the wind was blowing. Eventually he agreed to plead guilty to one count of theft provided the prosecutor would withdraw the other two charges.

The judge wasn't very pleased by this development despite the fact that it ensured he'd have time to hear the rest of the cases on today's docket. He was one of the few who took such negotiations as a personal insult.

He got some solace by really hammering Bailey on the sentence, being clever enough to stay within the range that the appellate court wouldn't touch. Albeit on the extreme high end of it. And it was better than what Bailey would have obtained had all three counts been registered as convictions.

Sylvia shrugged at the other defense counsel and packed up. She decided to skip the office and drive straight home to the boys.

TWELVE

The pounding noise in her dream disturbed Sylvia. She twitched fretfully, trying to get away from the menacing nightmare rhythm that had overlaid her sleep. The thumpings became heavier, more ominous. She tossed and turned; the boys were in the dream, pursued by a danger. She didn't know what danger exactly, but it was coming closer and closer to them. She was rooted to the spot, unable to get to the children in time, screaming for them to listen to her and run. They didn't hear her and the danger came closer, casting its shapeless shadow over their pale heads.

Sylvia sat bolt upright. She was sweating, caught in the sheets that had become twisted into ropes around her legs. She took a deep breath. It had been a while since she'd dreamed at all, much less had a nightmare. Automatically, she reached for a cigarette. It was still very dark, couldn't be later than two or three.

Sylvia was bothered by something. She cast around for a match, trying to isolate her sense of uneasiness.

The thumping. It hadn't stopped!

Sylvia was in her housecoat and at the door of her room without consciously willing herself to move. She eased her door open, inch by inch. In the pitch blackness, the scraping of the hinges seemed to her to be horrendously loud. She stayed hidden behind the door, straining to catch any break in the blackness.

"Sylvia." It was a whisper, a sigh, a moan. Had she not been at the open door, she could never have heard the tiny sound.

She crept out into the hall, bare feet on the broadloom making no noise. The boys' rooms were at the other end of the second floor. And the sound had come from that direction.

"Oh!" Sylvia shoved her fist into her mouth to silence herself. She had stumbled into something lying on the rug. Something soft and warm. Like a person. She knelt and put her hand out, onto Ingrid's face.

"Ingrid?" Sylvia was whispering into her ear. "What is it? Are you all right?"

"The boys, they've . . ." Ingrid was gasping, still maintaining the conspiratorial hush. "They've got . . ." She couldn't finish the sentence.

Sylvia stood up, looking down the hall. Her heart was beating wildly. She started toward the children, then stopped because Ingrid hadn't moved. Sylvia turned to go back but her fear for her children took over. It propelled her along the corridor and it gave her courage. Some primal instinct made her pick up a heavy brass lamp sitting on a table beside a small window. A small, open window. Sylvia had not opened it. She caught her breath and discarded the lampshade.

The thumpings had started up again. Now that she was closer to the sound, she could make it out more clearly. It wasn't a real thumping. It was a dragging noise, the sort of noise made when a bundle was dragged over a rug.

Jay's door was open. Sylvia wasn't even breathing as she moved into the room, putting one foot silently in front of the other, willing them to shift her weight without disturbing even the air.

There was no one there. The child's bed was a mess, covers mainly on the floor, pillow tipped precariously over the edge, but no small body lying in its usual position.

Sylvia backed out, hardly daring to confront Carl's room for fear that it too would be barren. The door was still shut but even without the dragging sounds, Sylvia would have known that there were several people inside. Their breathing couldn't be heard as such through the thick, old-fashioned oak door but it broke the pattern of the night. Sylvia slid down to see if anything could be viewed through the keyhole. The blackness defeated her.

The dragging was coming toward the door. She moved away, terrified to consider the conclusion that could be drawn from the sound. The door opened smoothly on well-oiled hinges, slowly, interminably slowly.

A huge shape was in the hall, close enough to Sylvia that she could reach out and touch it. The shape moved down the corridor away from her and was followed by another, identical to the first, right down to the oddness of the silhouette bulging in front as if it had huge bosoms around its waist. Sylvia caught her breath, understanding that the bosoms were actually bundles and the bundles were her sons. She acted by instinct, screaming loudly to confuse the situation and to call for help, leaping at the nearest shape, wielding her heavy lamp like a caveman's club, trying to move quickly so that it would not be immediately obvious that she was alone.

The shapes shouted to each other in a tongue she had never heard. They rudely dropped the bundles and lashed out viciously, trying to identify and isolate the source of the painful blows.

Sylvia hurt one of them. She felt the crunch of bone, heard an agonized cry as he staggered against the wall, leaving the corridor clear for the other. He came at her, clad in black, terrifyingly faceless except for shining eyes glinting as he mouthed incomprehensible threats in a foreign language. He struck out and knocked the lamp down. Sylvia heard the thud as it hit the wall and then the ground. She was frozen to the spot for a split second and then running, faster than she'd ever run, grateful for her jogging, zigzagging through the house.

A shout came from behind her, different from the sounds that her pursuer had been making, a sound of pain. Sylvia skidded around a corner and peered back. A small figure was grimly pounding at the intruder with a poker.

Sylvia picked up the nearest lamp and threw herself back into the fray, shoulder to shoulder with her mother, both women unyielding in their drive to protect their children. The early light of morning was shyly slipping through the living room windows, lighting up the black shape, pointing out the flattened, grotesque face. The women were hurting him, but they were getting tired and their blows were lighter, slower.

There was a shout from the stairs. Their combatant answered it and suddenly struck out with both arms. Sylvia and her mother were thrown against a sofa, clutching their makeshift weapons.

The intruder spun around and disappeared.

"The boys! Quickly!" Sylvia was up the stairs, forgetting her fatigue, closely followed by the older woman. The bundles were lying where they'd been dropped, crying softly in terror.

A door opened in the house, the alarm sirens started.

Sylvia, clutching one of the children, ran to the window in time to see two figures sprinting down the road. She sank to the ground, tears pouring down her face.

"Carl! Are you all right? Speak to me! What happened?"

"They're fine, Sylvia. They're fine." Her mother had Jay in her lap and one arm around her own child. "They're fine. I'll watch them while you call the police."

Sylvia nodded, hearing the words but not taking in their meaning.

"The police, darling. Call the police. Or would you rather I did it?" Mrs. Layton paused for an answer. "Oh, wait a minute. I'll call Ingrid. She can—"

"Ingrid!" Sylvia almost screamed the name. She dumped Carl onto her mother and pounded toward her bedroom. The woman was still on the rug, lying in the same position.

"Ingrid?" Sylvia put her hand on the woman's shoulder. "It's all right now."

Sylvia got no answer.

"Are you all right, Ingrid? Ingrid?"

Sylvia's heart was in her mouth. She hurried over to the light switch.

In the sudden glare, it was immediately obvious why Ingrid wasn't talking. Sylvia stood beside the small body, looking at the gray-haired wig that had slipped sideways, the worn beige housecoat riding up on the hips, the protruding hilt of the knife jutting up from between the meager breasts.

Within a short time, the local officers, alerted by the burglar alarm, arrived in two cruisers. Dave arrived soon after, flanked by lots of comfortingly huge men who immediately set to work combing the house, the backyard, and the district. Cameron slid in last, called because of his recent involvement with the household.

Sylvia couldn't have too many policemen in the house. After they arrived, she gradually relaxed enough to leave the boys' side and answer questions.

She was making the third pot of coffee and trying to talk her mother into going to bed when the bell rang again.

"Rupert! How did you hear?"

"Are you all right? Are you hurt? How are you?" He was incoherent with concern.

"I'm fine. So are the boys and Mother. But," Sylvia's eyes welled up again, "but Ingrid's dead. They murdered her."

"Shhh." Rupert awkwardly patted her shoulder. "This is Chief Lorimer. He's one of the superchiefs, in charge of criminal investigations."

Sylvia had scarcely noticed the second man at the door. He

was a colorless chap who probably got overlooked often. At first. When he opened his mouth, it would be impossible to forget him. His voice was the richest, most authoritative speaking instrument Sylvia had ever heard.

"I'm just here to make sure that everything is handled right, Mrs. West. Rupert suggested that you haven't had the best time with us lately and I wanted to guarantee that you couldn't complain about our detective work again." He was a soothing presence. In another state, Sylvia might have minded the assumptions he was making about her emotional control but right now she was just delighted to have another tower of strength in the house.

"What happened, Sylvia?"

She led them into the kitchen, the only room at the moment that was not crammed to bursting point with hefty, serious men. They sipped coffee while she repeated the details, shivering slightly despite the heat. "Between us," she concluded with a weak smile, "we scared them off. It was just a case of two mothers protecting their babies. I had the boys and my mother had me."

The two men were regarding her with respect. "Did you get a look at the killers?" Lorimer asked.

"Yes, but it won't help much. They were dressed in black, all in black right down to the gloves and they had stocking masks on. Until I realized that, I almost thought we were fighting with monsters from another world."

"Those masks are frightening," the superchief agreed. "Did they say anything? Call each other by name or give any other information that might help?"

"No. They spoke in a language I don't know."

"What was it?"

"I don't even know that. I don't think I've ever heard it before."

"Well, we'll canvass the neighborhood. Maybe we'll come up with something." Lorimer's strong voice didn't hide his weak hopes.

Sylvia followed them out to the living room.

Rupert buttonholed one of the men from homicide. "How the hell did they get in without triggering off the alarms? Or were the locals so slow that they didn't get here until everything was all over?"

"No, sir." The officer had no idea who Rupert was, but he knew Lorimer by sight and he'd seen the two arrive together.

"The alarm went off as the two left. They came in a small window on the second floor. It was the only window that wasn't wired up in the whole house."

"I saw that it was open!" Sylvia had completely forgotten that detail. "But how could they have known it wasn't part of the burglar alarm system? And why wasn't it?"

"We'll find out." Rupert, Lorimer, and Dave looked equally grim. Cameron looked like he expected to find out that it was all Sylvia's fault.

Rupert stayed around as long as he could, but eventually he had to go to work. "Lorimer's promised me that you'll get round-the-clock protection. If you're unhappy with anything, and I mean anything or anyone, just call him. He's going to keep an eye on the investigation. Not on the day-to-day level, but he's making it known that he's taking a personal interest in this case. That," he added quietly, "should be enough to make sure that every man on it does his best."

"Thanks, Rupert. I appreciate your help."

"I'll call later. And I'll have my secretary call Bess. She should get in touch with that idiot alarm company. They have to come back today to fix up that one window."

Sylvia nodded listlessly. The old stable door.

"You've still got the two boys, Sylvia. You have to protect them, no matter how badly you feel about Ingrid."

Ingrid. Whom she'd persuaded to stay. The alarm system and the raise in pay hadn't been much of a bargain for poor Ingrid. "You're right, Rupert. Okay, we'll fix up the alarm."

Dave stayed at the house. He managed to amuse the boys over breakfast so that Sylvia and her mother could get some sleep. The boys were thrilled to have a real live cop to talk to, and the women were thrilled to have one guarding their slumbers.

Sylvia was just nodding off when she heard the police outside her door. They'd come for the body. It had been photographed, measured, poked, and fingerprinted. Now it was no more use to anyone.

THIRTEEN

Sylvia carefully avoided looking at the brown spots on the rug in the upstairs hall. Her mother was already up, having her late breakfast in an otherwise empty kitchen.

"Good morning, darling. Did you sleep?"

"Yes. You?"

"Fine. Now, Sylvia, I want you to hear me out before you say no."

"I was thinking that maybe you should take the boys up north with you."

"I want to take the children home with me and . . . oh."

They smiled.

"Very well, dear. I'll call Roger so he'll meet today's bus. Now what about you? Will you come too?"

"No, I can't. Far too much work to do and anyway, I want to be busy. It would be better for me not to have the time to think."

"Will you be safe?"

"Are you kidding? With Dave and Rupert watching over me like mother hens? I'll be fine." If only she could rid herself of the tension, the sudden starts at any unusual sounds.

Her mother must have noticed her reservations because she didn't look convinced. However, she didn't pursue the matter. She had never had any luck in changing Sylvia's mind. Sylvia had insisted on being independent from her earliest days. When her parents had attempted to restrict her activities or direct them, she had complained bitterly that she was no less a person simply by virtue of being short. The Laytons had taken some not inconsiderable pride in Sylvia's spirit and they had, accepting her argument, treated her as a tiny adult.

"Where is Dave, Mother? And the boys?"

"The children are in the backyard. Detective Masowski went to work as soon as I got up. He asked me to tell you that he saw the press earlier this morning and told them what he could, but they'll be back."

Sylvia sighed. "I bet that this time they'll want more than a brief interview."

"I'm afraid so." The older woman held up the *Times*. Ingrid had made the front page: "Dead Lawyer's Housekeeper Slain."

Sylvia read through the article and sighed again. She could just imagine how the tabloids were treating it. "Well, I suppose I have to give them one shot at me. But that's it."

She wandered out the back and watched the boys hiding their tension in a hard-fought baseball game. They'd been joined by two of the neighborhood kids, scions of the only family within quick walking distance.

Sylvia had liked the comparative isolation of the house. She still did in a way, but it had its drawbacks. She was very glad that the children wouldn't be spending any more nights at home until the break-in was solved.

She ambled around the house. It was a real summer's day, sultry and heavy under a hazy blue sky. In Manhattan it would be unbearable, but on Long Island the trees and bushes gave an illusion of some shade and respite. She flicked her cigarette into one of the parched flower beds. The place was looking scruffy, as well it might. No one had paid it the slightest attention for several weeks.

The promised patrol car was sitting squarely in front of the house. Two officers, a man and a woman, were in it chatting desultorily.

"Hi. I'm Sylvia West. How long have you two been out here?"

"An hour or so. We were called when Detective Masowski was ready to leave."

"Would you like some coffee?"

Sylvia straightened up during their enthusiastic assents to watch a long black sedan go by. She felt a slight twinge of uneasiness.

"Did you see that car?"

"The one with the diplomatic plates that just passed?"

"Yes." She paused. Oh, what the hell. They couldn't call her paranoid after last night. "Did you see the number, by any chance?"

"No, ma'am." The driver looked nervous.

"There's probably nothing to it, but I've seen that car a few times and I don't think it belongs around here. If it goes by again, would you take the number and check it out?"

"Sure thing." They brightened up. It wasn't a big deal but

it was concrete. The only concrete task they'd been set. Sylvia didn't lust after their jobs.

The press descended in force in the middle of the afternoon. Sylvia was prepared, thanks to her favorite reporter, Maggie Brewster, who had called to express her shock and to give warning of the impending invasion. It was quite an ordeal, grimmer by far than Sylvia had anticipated because she was unable, when talking about the break-in, to put any distance between herself and the vivid memory of Ingrid's broken body on the carpet in the hall.

She didn't have the strength to end the conference, but Maggie and her mother between them managed to do so. Eventually, the last flashbulb went off and the last question was posed. Her mother went upstairs to pack the boys' clothes while Sylvia sat alone in the kitchen trying to compose herself.

The bus left in the early evening. Dave had offered an escort, but it hardly seemed necessary in broad daylight in Manhattan. The boys were happy about the quickie hamburger and ice cream dinner and they were clearly looking forward to the cottage. Nonetheless, when faced by the open door of the bus, both clung to their mother. They'd lost the habit of casual good-byes. Too many of the people they loved had vanished without notice.

"Don't worry, darlings, I'll be up at the cottage very soon. And you can call me on the phone whenever you want."

It was hard to see them go. Sylvia watched the bus until it had turned the corner, two little hands waving desperately at the back window.

Her eyes were damp as she slowly walked back to the car. It was parked illegally of course. Short of driving into the terminal itself, Sylvia had had no option. She cursed at the piece of paper she saw on the windshield.

As she got closer, she noticed that the ticket, if that was what it was, was inside the car. She approached carefully. She could remember locking up. She always did in Manhattan and today she'd been even more scrupulous than usual.

The driver's door was unlocked and the window slightly rolled down. She made sure that the car was empty before getting in. The piece of paper was a note, printed in block letters: IF YOU'RE TOO NOSY, YOU AND YOUR SONS WILL BE REAL SORRY.

Sylvia got out quickly and looked around. No one appeared

to be paying her any special attention. There wasn't much point in asking if anyone had seen the mailman. It didn't pay to be too attentive down here and no one ever was.

Dusk was falling and the lights hadn't come on. Despite the temperature, Sylvia felt chilled. It was time to remove herself from the area. She didn't have to prove how brave she was, especially since she wasn't. She suddenly felt totally abandoned and very much in need of strong companionship.

She drove straight to the police station. Dave wasn't there but she knew where he lived.

His name was up in the lobby of the decaying upper West Side building. It wasn't much of a place, but a cop didn't have much of a salary.

She rang the bell, and then again when no one answered. Eventually, Dave's voice came over the intercom.

"I don't want any."

"Dave, it's me, Sylvia."

"Oh, shit. Sorry. Is it important?"

"Yes."

"Give me a minute and then come up. It's on the third floor."

The elevator wasn't working. She should try to break the habit of visiting buildings where the elevators were out.

Dave answered the door looking very rumpled. Sylvia understood better when she walked into the living room and found an attractive woman in a similar condition. The woman looked vaguely familiar. Sylvia suddenly recognized her as one of the female officers on the fraud squad. She nodded at the policewoman, feeling foolish and embarrassed.

The woman stood up. "I'll be getting along. See you, Dave. Mrs. West."

Sylvia turned to Dave. "I'm sorry. I don't know what to say."

"Forget it. What's the problem?"

She showed him the note and answered questions for the next twenty minutes.

Finally Dave exhausted his stock of queries. He picked up the note with tweezers and put it into a plastic bag. "I'll take this to the forensic lab tomorrow, not that they're likely to find anything."

"I know. Dave, what the hell's going on? Ever since the disappearance, strange things have been happening. And I can't believe it's just a coincidence. I'm frightened."

He smiled at her. "You've got round-the-clock protection. We'll find out who's hassling you, and meanwhile, you're in no danger."

"I'd feel better if you were in charge of the investigation. Everybody's so sure that John is dead. Even with Lorimer looking over their shoulders, I frankly don't have a lot of faith that they'll get to the bottom of it."

"Do you really think John masterminded the accident? A little while ago, you couldn't even bring yourself to admit that he might have run away."

"I don't know what to believe." Sylvia sank down into a large, soft chair. "I don't believe it was an accident but that's as far as logic takes me."

She lit a cigarette and took a few deep drags. "Dave, you've been great all along and I hate to do this, but I'm going to ask for a few more favors." She told him about her suspicions of von Schagg, The Foundation, and Janice. "Rupert Thompson offered help but you're the trained bloodhound."

He laughed.

"Oh, and there's von Schagg's sinister assistant. Sterne. Leland Sterne."

"Okay. I'll see what I can dig up. It's not likely that I'll be able to find out anything about Janice. I have no official way of getting into Immigration files and if I want to keep my job, I've got to stay unofficial in this case."

"How could I see those files?"

"Well, no legal way. I suppose, theoretically, if you knew a federal lawyer, you might be able to nose around. Theoretically."

"I see."

"Mind you, I wouldn't bet on the files containing useful information. It is the government, after all."

Sylvia smiled and accepted his offer of a glass of wine. She winced as he picked up the policewoman's glass on his way into the kitchen.

Dave brought out some cheese as well. If he wasn't harboring a grudge about his ruined evening, she might as well relax and enjoy herself too.

The room was very pleasant, done in various shades of beige and brown, brightened by lots of plants and colorful flowers. All of the chairs and the one large sofa were made for curling up in. There wasn't a *Playboy* or *Penthouse* in sight. There wasn't a book in view either. But on the whole, a comforting room.

And a comforting man. It had been a long time since she'd sat in companionable silence with a man. She and John had often been silent but not companionably. She felt less lonely now than she had in months, since even before John left. She realized with a shock that she was attracted to Dave.

He got up and put a record on the stereo. Sylvia appreciated the fact that it was jazz, rather than music to seduce her by. She moved over to the sofa to pour herself another glass of wine. She leaned toward Dave to refill his glass and as she raised the bottle, her hand brushed his knee.

Dave took the bottle out of her hand and replaced it on the table. He put his hands on her shoulders and turned her toward him.

She kissed him, at first tentatively and then more urgently. They fell together, down to the long soft warm couch, pulling each other's clothes off, coming together quickly as though each had desired the other for a long time without knowing it.

Afterwards, as they lay together sipping wine and softly touching, Sylvia tried not to remember how it had been with John. But the comparison was there, just below the surface of her mind.

They made love a second time, slower and with greater tenderness and patience. Sylvia held Dave's head against her breasts until he fell asleep.

FOURTEEN

The winding Long Island roads were deserted. Sylvia tried not to think about the blackness of the rural wastelands on either side and turned up the radio, humming along with the tedious disco music that was playing on every channel.

She had forgotten to turn on the floodlights when she'd left in the bright afternoon. It wasn't the first time that she'd approached the house in darkness, but it was the first time since they'd moved in that it was both unlit and empty. She sat in the car, telling herself that she was reluctant to face the deserted rooms and knowing that she was shrinking from the possibility that she mightn't be alone.

Sylvia tensed as another car pulled up. It was the patrol. She heaved a sigh of relief and asked the two delightfully bulky men to watch as she went inside. The house was filled with ghosts but none of them were corporeal.

It was a good thing that she'd sent the boys away. She needed all her strength just to worry about her own safety.

It hardly seemed worthwhile to undress for the little that remained of the night but after wandering through the spaces that had so recently been crammed with her family, unconsciousness was far more attractive than her thoughts.

The telephone woke her at nine. It was Dave.

"Good morning. Why did you go home?"

"I like to wake up in my own bed. How are you this morning?"

"Good, very good. What's on your schedule today?"

"Ingrid. I have to make arrangements for the funeral."

"That's grim. Can you handle it yourself?"

"Yes." Sylvia was tempted to add that she'd come over to his place later, but it wouldn't be fair. She wasn't likely to be very good company after spending a day immersed in death.

It was a grisly Sunday. The weather provided the gray skies and intermittent showers that pathetic fallacy demanded. Ingrid's closest relative was a nephew in New Orleans who hadn't

111

seen her in ten years. He left everything to Sylvia; it wasn't even certain that he'd make it up for the funeral. She sorted through Ingrid's few possessions, arranged with the undertaker to get the body from the morgue when the police were through with it, and spoke to the other two housekeepers nearby who had been friendly with Ingrid.

Sylvia tried to keep busy, but her tasks weren't exactly designed to alleviate the spasms of loneliness that hit her as she moved through the house. The kitchen had retained signs of Ingrid, dish towels strung through the handles of cupboard doors, teacups upside down beside the sink. The living room was still strewn with childish toys. Her own bedroom was no improvement. Her eyes kept returning to John's closet, the chair he had used for his late-night reading. Just when she could have used a strengthening dose of hostility, forgotten sweet moments sprung to mind. It did very little good to remind herself that those moments belonged to history, most of them to antiquity.

To make matters worse, the press had come back to torture her a little more; she couldn't leave her house to go for even a short walk. She stayed in, lowering the level in the bottle of J&B until she was sufficiently anaesthetized to sleep.

Sylvia arrived at the office to find Florence Nightingale disguised as Bess waiting with a pot of steaming coffee and two toasted bagels.

"You didn't have breakfast, did you?"

Sylvia admitted the crime, cheerfully eating the food put in front of her.

Her mouth was full when the phone rang.

"That's probably Dave again. He called earlier." Bess, who missed nothing, avoided Sylvia's eye and picked up the receiver. Sylvia shook her head, wondering not for the first time how her secretary's grapevine worked. It would be the envy of *The New York Times*.

"Can you speak to him?"

"Who?"

It was the wrong thing to say. Bess smiled triumphantly, her suspicions confirmed. "Detective David Masowski."

Sylvia nodded wryly and took the phone, laughing as Bess ostentatiously left the office.

"What's so funny?"

"What did you say to Bess when you called earlier?"

"Nothing. Well," Sylvia could picture him blushing. "Well, I asked for you by your first name."

"You often do." She thought for a moment. "And then you corrected yourself, right?"

"How did you know?"

"Fine. As long as I know she's not a witch. Okay, shoot."

"I've got a couple of things for you. Shall I give them to you over the phone?"

"Unless you're going to confess to a crime."

"John did have a license issued to him. Right description, right address, right age."

"Couldn't anyone get a license just by describing someone and saying they're picking it up for him?"

"The description would have to match the guy taking the driver's test. But, given that tall, blond men aren't that uncommon, sure. If a guy who's six four or so, fair, blue-eyed, went for a test, he could get a license. If he also had identification in that name. It's a little far-fetched, Sylvia."

"When was it issued?"

"Uh, well, that's the only thing. Now don't get carried away, but the date was a little smudged. Either May nineteenth or June nineteenth."

"Dave! That distinction's pretty relevant since he disappeared on June eighteenth! When did he supposedly rent the car?"

"On the same day he disappeared."

"Thanks. Thanks a million, Dave."

"I've got more. Cass Harwood had a police blotter."

"What?!"

"Yeah. I ran a computer check just to be on the safe side and I turned up quite a record."

"Stop sounding so smug and give me the lowdown."

"Lowdown is the word for it. She was a hooker."

"Come off it."

"No, really. She was a pro and had been for most of her life. She's originally from Idaho but she's been in the Big Apple, taking bites, for over thirty years."

"How old is she? Was she?"

"I don't have an exact date of birth but in the vicinity of forty-five. Not a spring chicken."

"Watch it." Six years passed like nothing.

"In that business, she was old. Really old. It ages the women like you wouldn't believe. I've got some names for you. Her most recent parole officer, a few friends. All on the track themselves, I'm afraid."

"Dave, I won't keel over. I've been in criminal law for a decade. Besides, I haven't found the street folk to be any more dishonest than the commuters. Can we get right down to it? I'd like to talk to all of them today."

"I can't go with you. My captain called for a meeting at eleven, but I'll give you the details and you can handle it. Would you like a plainclothes date?"

"Not necessary."

Hannah van der Tole was a nice motherly woman. She had a ready smile for everyone and there was just nothing that one could do to earn her enmity. Lovely for a favorite aunt or even a grandmother. But as a parole officer, she terrified Sylvia. Out there on the streets were animals looking for prey whose entire duty to society consisted of visiting with Hannah twice a month.

Sylvia hid her cynicism for the forty minutes or so she spent listening to the social worker burble on about rehabilitation and destructive environments. All of it true but useless.

"Back to Cass, if you wouldn't mind. This is fascinating," Sylvia lied straight-faced, "but I do have a tight schedule today."

"Of course, of course. Poor Cass. A lovely woman, you know. And she had gone straight about a year ago. Such a shame." Hannah had tears in her eyes.

Sylvia had no bones to pick with Hannah's view of Cass's personality. She had nothing against prostitutes and had always been repulsed by the law's organized harassment of them. On the other hand, she had difficulty reconciling Cass's two convictions this past year with going straight.

Hannah was genuinely shocked. Somehow, the court records hadn't reached her and she had no idea that Cass had been turning tricks again. "Well, you know, it's very hard for someone like Cass to start all over again. I feel so badly."

Sylvia looked up at the ceiling. She counted cracks while Hannah berated herself for Cass's lousy environment.

"We failed her. We all failed her."

"No doubt." It was very true, but Sylvia had to be ruthless. Forty minutes was all she had to give this woman. "Had you seen her recently?"

"No, not for a while. A few months. I was almost at the point of having to report her for breaching her parole although I hated to."

Hannah was certainly not your average parole officer. "How often was she supposed to report to you?"

"Once a month. But it was hard for her to get here."

The parole officer ought to consider relocating to Times Square. So much more convenient for the clientele. Sylvia made a thankful escape.

Times Square was seamy even in the early afternoon. The ground was covered with the debris of countless litterers, faded wrappers of chocolate bars and hotdogs, fliers advocating new churches and adult flicks, used tissues and sunflower seed shells, the odd condom. Police marched in groups of three and four, hands never far from their weapons, rubbing shoulders with the local players. Everyone knew everyone else. It was almost a family, but that wouldn't stop any of them from playing out the tedious game.

The street people were already hustling. To make a living, the regulars had to work long hours. You could get anything you wanted and the price would be almost as low as the quality.

Sylvia scanned the women leaning against dirty plate-glass windows of so-called bookstores. The high-class hookers, even the middle-class ones, wouldn't have been caught dead here. For one thing, dead was a not-unusual state in the neighborhood. She walked over to one of the more worn, a woman in black ripped fishnet stockings and a short tight black skirt. The uniform of the *putain*.

"I'm looking for Deirdre."

"Don't know her." The voice was nasal and very un-French.

"How about Toffee? Or Suzie?"

"Not them either. I'm busy. If you don't want to talk business, go away."

"Hey, baby!" A particularly well-dressed man, if somewhat flamboyant, strutted by.

His effect on the woman was electric. "Get outa here! I gotta work."

"I'll pay for your time."

The woman looked her over suspiciously. Sylvia seemed to make her nervous. "You can't afford me."

Sylvia shrugged and walked to the next corner. She'd repeated her requests without success to several working ladies when the same picturesque man she'd noticed earlier approached her.

"You lookin' for something?"

Sylvia ignored his rude tone. She rhymed off the names again, expecting the usual brush-off.

"What for?"

"I want to talk to anyone who knew Cass. Cass Harwood."

"Cass? Why don't you just talk to her? Since you're so nosy about her."

Sylvia stared at him. "Cass is here?"

He slowly turned to survey the track. "Not right now. She'll be by later, lady. What's it your business?"

"Just that. My business. What time does she usually come out?"

"Whenever her money's low."

"Does she have a man?"

He sneered. "Not me."

"Where does she live?"

"You can get hurt asking so many questions."

"Look, I'm sort of a friend of hers. I can find her through her parole officer, but I'd rather not go to the authorities and let them know she's back on the job."

Sylvia opened her purse and fiddled with a bill. "I'll make it worth your while to point out one of her friends."

"Friends!" He giggled unpleasantly. "The broads don't got time for friends." He watched Sylvia close her purse. "Hey! Baby!" He whistled at the woman in the black net stockings.

"Deirdre's comin' over. It's up to you." He held out his hand. She put ten dollars into it.

"Yeah, man? What's up?"

"Friend of Cass." He pointed casually to Sylvia. "Lady'll have to pay for your time if she wants to use it."

"You know Cass? Where is she?" Deirdre seemed to care.

"She hasn't been around lately? Your, uh, friend seems to think she's been working as usual."

"You seen her?" Deirdre questioned the man intently. "When d'ya see her?"

"Who knows?" He shrugged and flicked her hand off his impeccable lapel. "Don't touch. You ain't clean."

"Let's go for a coffee, Deirdre. Pick a place." Sylvia wanted to dump their audience but she certainly didn't need an ugly scene. Fortunately, he'd noticed one of his girls window-shopping as though she was a purchaser rather than the goods. He hustled over to remind her.

The greasy spoon was filled with hookers. It appeared to be off limits to the Johns, a spot where working women could take a short break undisturbed. Except by their men who from time to time came in to abuse them and send them back out to the job.

Sylvia was cased thoroughly. One of the waitresses, a ravaged, aging ex-prostitute, curled her lip. "We got the hoity-toity comin' in now, girls."

The atmosphere wasn't friendly until Deirdre spoke up. "She's got news about Cass."

The women clustered around, voices raised shrilly. "Where is she? Is she all right? Is the new John really rich?"

Sylvia put her hand up. "I've got bad news."

They quieted down, many returning to their stools.

"Cass was in a car accident. She's... she's dead."

Most of the hookers took it philosophically. Even callously. Life was hard enough without caring too much about other people.

Deirdre hadn't learned to be as tough. Her eyes filled with tears. "I knew something was wrong."

"When did you see her last?"

"A coupla weeks ago." Deirdre took one of Sylvia's cigarettes. "I knew she was dead. She'd'a come around otherwise."

"What's this about a new John?"

"What's it to you?" Deirdre's sorrow was turning into belligerence. "Who are you, anyway?"

The camaraderie of a minute ago was fast slipping away. Sylvia came to a quick decision.

She leaned forward and spoke confidentially. "Look, what I've got to say is just between us for now. Understand?"

The woman didn't look up.

"I think she was set up to die."

"What?" Sylvia now had Deirdre's entire attention.

"I can't..."

Sylvia stopped talking while the grisly waitress brought them coffee and two Danish. The restaurant was no more than a hole in the wall and a dirty one at that, but the coffee smelled terrific and the plates were, if not clean, at least better than they'd been at Dorry's in Vesper City.

"I can't prove anything yet," Sylvia continued, "but I'm working on it. The car accident stank. Which means that Cass was a pigeon." She spoke a great deal more positively than she felt. There was no way she'd get information unless the players wanted to help her find Cass's killer.

Deirdre wasn't educated but she wasn't stupid. She bit her lip while she considered Sylvia's' words. "What do ya wanna know?"

"When did you first notice that Cass was missing?"

"I dunno exactly. You see, she'd just left the corner. It didn't mean nothing. It happens the same way all the time."

Sylvia didn't grasp her meaning.

"Look." Deirdre was patient. "A girl meets a guy, right? She falls for his line and they're talking love. So she leaves her corner and disappears with him. Happens all the time. The guy is crazy about her, doesn't want her to walk the streets. He pays for everything. Then the money's gone. He's spent every dime on the dame and he's stone cold. So she hits the streets again to make money for him. Now he's not so down on it." She shrugged. "We all know that's the way it works. It's happened to all of us. Still, we keep goin' for it, whenever the guy's good-looking enough."

"What about you? Do you fall for it too?" Sylvia was genuinely interested.

"Sure." Her face told the whole story. There was so little pleasure in the world that you took what you could find even if you knew it was fool's gold.

"And Cass fell in love?"

"I figured. But when she didn't show up again, I got worried."

"How long does it usually take?"

"A week. Maybe ten days. No more. So she wasn't here this week and I got a bit scared."

"Did you check at her residence?"

Deirdre laughed. "We don't got residences around here. We got holes. Nobody knows anything. Ain't no use to go around the rooming houses. If we don't know on the streets, nobody does."

"Did you think maybe she was back in jail?"

"Nah. We always know who's in the slammer."

Sylvia sighed resignedly. "So we're at a dead end."

"Sorta." Deirdre took another cigarette.

"No one knows who the new John was? Or even if there was one?"

"Sweetie heard her making the date."

"Sweetie?"

Deirdre eyed her cynically. "You don't know Sweetie. You'll like her." She was enjoying her private joke. "Hey, girls, where's Sweetie?"

"Back on the track." The waitress knew everyone's movements. Now that she'd gone straight because she had no trade, she participated vicariously in what she evidently perceived as the good life.

"Come on." Deirdre pushed herself up and out the door. Sylvia threw a couple of dollars down on the table and hurried after her.

Times Square was getting crowded but Deirdre knew every inch of it. To the regulars, it was as staked out into individual turfs as the map of Europe.

"Hey, Sweetie!" Deirdre slapped hands with a big, buxom woman standing under a movie marquee. The woman had a badly pockmarked face and wore unusually modest clothing. As Sylvia got nearer, she saw that the pockmarks went down the neck, disappearing into the red jumpsuit.

"Friend of mine." Deirdre indicated Sylvia. "We're lookin' for Cass. You seen her?"

"Not since I told ya."

"Wanna tell my friend about her date?"

"Hey, what's in it for me? I'm busy today."

"I'll pay for your time," Sylvia interjected. "You heard Cass making a date with a man?"

"Not with the John. With some dame. This dame comes up to me first, see, and looks me over. I'm not her type." Sweetie started to laugh. "There's those that can't live without me, so I'm not too upset."

"Why weren't you her type?" Sylvia felt left out since both women were grinning.

Sweetie pushed up the long sleeves of her jumpsuit. Her arms were scarred from hand to shoulder. Thick, red weals that almost doubled the circumference of the limb. Sylvia glanced down at the legs. The tight outfit hid the marks but the bulges left no doubt that the legs were, if anything, worse.

Sylvia looked up to see Sweetie watching her for any sign of repulsion. She swallowed and kept her face impassive.

She must have passed the test because Sweetie went on. "Whips wasn't her thing. Cass was just over there," pointing to the next window, "and the dame heads over. I start talking to a John and don't hear what they say. After a while, the dame leaves and Cass comes over to tell me about it. She's real excited, stupid cunt."

"Go on," Sylvia urged. Sweetie had stopped to return the ogle of a mean-looking fat man on the sidewalk. "I'll pay you for lost business. Go on."

"Okay. Later, sweetheart." The man slumped off, disappointed.

"Cass told me she had a date with a rich John who'd seen her on the track and had fallen for her. He was too embarrassed to come around himself so he sent the dame. She thought good luck was right around the corner." Sweetie's expression suggested that she'd been around that corner and it didn't offer anything.

"Wasn't that unusual? A woman making the date?"

"Nah." Deirdre answered her. "Lots of guys don't wanna be seen around here. They send their secretaries, wives. Even their daughters."

"What did the woman look like?"

Sweetie thought about it. "Not bad. Not my type, a little thin, but I don't think she was bad-looking. I can't really remember. I think she had dark hair. Long, dark hair."

"Can you remember the day she came?"

"It was at night. Two weeks ago or so. I think it was a Friday or maybe a Saturday." Sweetie scratched her left breast for a while and shook her head. "I can't do better than that."

"You didn't believe Cass's story? About the rich man?"

"I guess that's what the woman said. But I figured it was a dame trying to get a hooker for her old man and didn't want anything too gorgeous." Sweetie didn't speak with malice. She just told it like it was.

"What was Cass like? I mean, her looks?"

The two women shrugged.

"Ordinary."

"Getting on." Deirdre was at least thirty and coming up fast, but she still clung to the illusion of being young.

"Did she have a regular man?"

"You mean a pimp?" Deirdre shook her head. "Naw, she was between pimps."

"I thought it was rare for an independent to work Times Square."

"I'm independent," Sweetie pointed out. "And any man who wants to mess with me is gonna be sorry."

"Cass felt that way too?"

"No. She wasn't tough enough, but her last man got knifed so she was kinda at loose ends. She was lookin' for someone nice. Ain't we all." Deirdre spoke bitterly. Speaking of pimps reminded her. "Hey, I gotta get back to work or my old man'll tan me good."

Sylvia tried to give her some money, but Deirdre refused it. "I ain't so low yet that I'll take money for helping a pal. See ya."

Sweetie kept her eyes on the bills. She wasn't so finicky. Sylvia held on to them tightly. "Were there any other players around who might have seen the dark-haired woman?"

"Might've been."

"Would you ask around?"

"What's this all about?" Now that Deirdre was gone, Sylvia had lost a little of her acceptability to Sweetie.

"Cass is dead."

"Oh, hey." Sweetie popped a stick of gum in her mouth. Chewing substituted for tears. "How did it happen?"

"A car accident. But I have my suspicions about it so I want to know who hired her to get into the car. I want to find this lady who made the date and I need your help. I'll pay for it."

The combination of regret for Cass's passing and greed did the trick. "Sure thing. Let me have a number."

"Here's my card. And ten dollars to start."

Sylvia started to walk away. Sweetie whistled after her. "Yes?"

"She was okay, you know?"

Sylvia understood perfectly. "We'll find out who got her. I promise you that."

FIFTEEN

"It's a good thing you're back," Bess observed with a grin on her face.

"Oh, why's that?"

"As your engagement secretary, I'm running out of ways to stall your boyfriends."

"What boyfriends?"

"Well, let's see. Dave called, Rupert called, Herb called and, uh, let me see. Oh yes, a Roger Hechman called."

"Who's the last one?"

"Another of your cops. Patrolman Roger Hechman. Going for the babies now?"

"Bess, it's business. You remember business. Give me his number."

Hechman turned out to be the young officer who'd been guarding her house the morning after the murder.

"That car came by again, Mrs. West."

"Car?"

"The one with the diplomatic plates."

"Oh, yes." She'd almost forgotten about it.

"Not to worry, Mrs. West. I traced the number and it's registered to Haffad Hassir. He's a minor attaché with the Syrian embassy. I, uh, understand that he has a girl friend on Long Island."

"Who?"

"I don't know. I didn't think you'd care. It's kind of hush-hush because there's a Mrs. Hassir and three little Hassirs."

Sylvia thanked him and rang off. Before she could think it through, Rupert called back.

"You're going to dinner with me tonight and I won't take no for an answer."

"That's very nice of you, but I know how busy you are, Rupert. I'm okay, honestly."

"I'm not asking out of pity. Can you meet me here at six-thirty?"

She smiled at the receiver and began to get ready to leave the office.

The restaurant was newly opened, an elegant Italian place on East Forty-fourth Street. She'd read good reviews of it, and besides, Rupert had excellent taste. She was salivating before they'd arrived.

"This way, Mr. Thompson." The maitre d'hotel was fawning all over him. Sylvia looked away. She had always hated the New York style of service. You were either a nobody and treated abominably or a someone, to be obsequiously pandered to.

"Rupert!" A table of prosperous-looking couples was in front of them, and one of the men at it was on his feet. "I'm glad to see you. I've been meaning to give you a call."

"Jack, how are you?" Rupert smiled and made as if to move on.

"Have you got a second?" The man ignored Sylvia as if she weren't there. He didn't mean to insult her. In his book, women weren't quite real. "Did Harris get in touch with you? About the nomination?"

"Yes, yesterday."

"Good. What do you think of the suggestion?"

"I'm of two minds about him. Not bad, but not quite as good as Stenning, don't you agree?"

"You may be right, Rupert. What about Herb, how does he feel?"

"You know he can't express a view. He's a civil servant, after all."

"Yeah, yeah. Come on, have you talked to Dutton about it?"

"I can only say that I've considered the matter fully, using all available sources of information, and I'm more inclined to Stenning."

The other man laughed. "Gotcha."

Rupert smiled again and excused himself.

When they were seated at an intimate table for two tucked away in a corner of the room, Sylvia turned to him curiously. "What nomination were they talking about?"

"In confidence?"

"Of course."

"The next election may not go well for the White House. There's reason to think that the present man isn't suited for the job."

"Are you talking about the President?"

Rupert nodded. "I've heard some disturbing things about him that might leak out before the election. If so, the Republicans stand a good chance of getting their candidate in."

"That's incredible. I mean, the President's very popular with people."

"For the moment." Rupert looked as though he'd like to say more but couldn't.

"They mentioned Herb. Does he agree with you?"

"Off the record, I'm afraid so. He can't get involved officially since he's with the government, but we've talked about it extensively."

"I didn't know you were a Republican."

"I'm not. I'm not attached to either party. I'm only concerned that the best man gets in, whatever his colors. And I'm not sure that the present one is the best. That's Herb's position as well, by the way. Party politics don't appeal to either of us. Maybe that's why we get asked for our opinions."

"Those men think a lot of you and Herb, that's for sure. Are they Republicans?"

"Yes, they're the men who basically will decide who the next candidate will be."

Sylvia smiled. It had seemed to her that Rupert and Herb would have a hell of a lot to do with it, not that they would ever be so immodest as to say so.

"I recommend the tortellini. They're out of this world." Rupert licked his lips.

"Fine with me. And a salad to start."

They ate happily, chatting about inconsequential matters until the zabaglione arrived.

"Sylvia, seriously, how are you doing?"

"Fine, really."

"Any news about the break-in?"

"No. Ingrid's funeral is on Saturday, by the way."

"I'll be there. How are the boys?"

"Okay. I've sent them away with my mother. I don't need the additional worry while I've got so much on my mind."

"Good idea. You need time alone to adjust to John's death."

"It's not that. I mean, I'm not sure he's dead. Or if he is, that the car crash was an accident."

"I don't understand."

"The issuance of the license is screwy. The date's illegible and it might have been issued after he disappeared. And if that wasn't enough, the woman in the car was nice enough from all accounts, but she happened to be an aging hooker. Not exactly fastidious John's type."

Rupert avoided her eyes.

"You think I'm crazy?"

"No, Sylvia. But maybe a little quick to jump to conclusions. A kidnapped, murdered corporate lawyer? It's slightly incredible. Who would want to kill him? And, uh, men have some very strange tastes in women."

Sylvia thought about Sweetie's specialty. "I know. But you can't deny that at least one attempted kidnapping and one murder have taken place."

Rupert nodded reluctantly. "Do you have any theories about it?"

"None at all. I've been going through John's papers and the only even slightly unusual client is this charity called The Foundation. It's run by a couple of odd characters, a von Schagg and his assistant named Sterne. I've been wanting to ask you if you knew either of them?"

"No, but I'll check around."

"Thanks. Look, it's possible that John set up a phony accident to account for his disappearance and then hired goons to snatch the kids. I can't believe that he'd go so far as to arrange the deaths of two people, but I suppose that if I wasn't his wife, I wouldn't rule it out. But I wouldn't be sure that it was the answer either. I'm hoping that I can get somewhere with my few leads. With your assistance and I've also got a friend on the force chipping in."

Rupert wasn't convinced but she would take all the help she could get, however skeptical.

"Do the police think you're in danger?"

"Oh, no way. They're giving me super protection just in case, but no one figures I'm a target." This was not the moment to mention the threatening note. If Rupert thought there was someone menacing her, he'd want her to get out of town. Which she couldn't do. Until this whole mess was cleared up, she'd live in fear for her children. "No, nothing like that at all. Could I have another coffee, Rupert?"

SIXTEEN

Bess called early the next morning. Two men from the Bar Association were sitting in Sylvia's office poring over her books.

They were still there when she breathlessly arrived, one behind the desk and the other lounging on the sofa.

"I'm Sylvia West. What can I do for you?"

The man behind the desk looked up coldly and briefly. "We'll be ready to question you in a few minutes."

"That's not what I asked. I asked what you were doing here and I want answers or I'm calling the cops to eject you." Sylvia had run into similar creatures when she had represented lawyers charged by the Bar Association with various misdeeds. They were hired guns, accountants and general investigators who did the Association's dirty work when complaints were made against an attorney. They had all the charm and compassion of cobras. There was no polite dealing with them; there was no dealing with them, period.

"We have authority to examine the books and records of all New York State attorneys when directed to do so by—"

"Yes, yes. I know the Act. What I want to know is what complaint made this necessary."

"We will be ready to question you in a few minutes."

Sylvia threw up her hands and went out to sit with Bess.

"What are you going to do, Sylvia?"

"Nothing. They've got the law on their side and I've got nothing to hide. When they find out there's nothing to the complaint, whatever it is, I'll make a hell of a stink about their tactics. It probably won't do any good but at least I'll get an apology."

"Well, I may as well give you your messages. Herb Dutton has phoned a few times. He's driving me nuts with his questions about, uh, what you're doing."

"I think he's very upset and embarrassed that he was so wrong about John. Don't forget that Herb really promoted him.

126

He wants to get to the bottom of this, like we all do."

"Well, I think he's sleazy."

"He's too well respected and too important to be sleazy, Bess. Besides, I like Rupert and Rupert likes Herb. What other calls?"

"Mrs. West!" An authoritative voice from her office interrupted them. "Mrs. West!"

"Excuse me, Bess, I must go. The Lords and Masters beckon. Bess!" Sylvia shook her head at Bess's obscene gesture. "Tacky, and besides, it could get me in trouble."

"Sit down." The man behind the desk, a gaunt character with caved-in, acne-scarred cheeks, stayed put. Sylvia considered pointing out that he had her chair but decided not to make a fuss about the little things. She sat down beside the second hired gun, closer than made him comfortable. Which had been her intention.

"What money don't you put through the books?"

"I beg your pardon?" Sylvia was thunderstruck.

"What money do you keep off the records?"

"None! I obey the law and beyond that, I wouldn't cheat my partners. And hold on for a moment. Before we go any further with this, I want your names and I want to know the complaint. I won't answer questions blind, any more than I'd let a client do so."

"My name is Donald Benjamin and this is Brendan Mansfield." They flashed their I.D. cards in unison.

"And what is the complaint?"

"We do not have to tell you that at this point."

"Fine. Then will you please get out of my office. I don't have to answer your questions either."

Benjamin put the tips of his long bony fingers together and pursed his lips. Mansfield, a plumper younger version and obviously a sidekick, tried to follow suit but his fingers were a lot thicker and his lips too full to carry it off.

"Very well." Benjamin acted like he was conferring a great favor on her. "It has come to our attention that you accepted money from a client on the basis that you would use it for the purpose of bribing a judge. That in itself, naturally, is an offense. The client also complained that the money was not used in this way, and as a result he received a very heavy sentence."

"What's the complaint? That I did bribe a judge or that I didn't?"

Sylvia's attempt at levity did not go down well but it did go down in their notebooks.

"That was a joke, boys." She shook her head. "I don't believe this. There is no way that I ever even indirectly suggested to anyone that I could fix a judge or that anyone could. Moreover, I have never taken money from a client for anything other than fees and disbursements and all the money is shown on the firm's books. Have I covered everything?"

Benjamin didn't look impressed. Naturally, Mansfield didn't either. "We want to see your other bank books."

"For my personal accounts? Strictly speaking, you'd need a search warrant for that but I have no interest in being difficult. I want this cleared up as fast as possible." She stood with her purse in her hand. "Who was this client?"

Benjamin pursed his lips again. Apparently it was his alternative to thought. "Very well. If you show me the bank books, I will give you the name."

Sylvia looked down on him contemptuously. "I don't go back on my word." She threw the purse on the desk. "The books are in there."

Benjamin took them out and flipped through quickly.

"Well, Mr. Benjamin, how about your word? Who is the client?"

"A Mr. Walter Bailey."

"What?" Sylvia's mouth dropped open. "Are you serious?"

"We are always serious."

That was undoubtedly the truth. Sylvia stood up and started to pace. "The allegation is ridiculous, laughable!"

"Not so amusing, Mrs. West. Mr. Bailey has witnesses who say that he told them that you promised to fix the judge. We have a money order made out to you for two thousand dollars. Over and above your fee which we note was paid by ordinary check. Mrs. Bailey says she bought the order on her husband's instructions and gave it to him. He says he then handed it over to you and it was endorsed with your name, in your handwriting."

"I never saw that money order, much less endorsed it!"

"We'll have to leave that up to the handwriting experts. It certainly looks like your signature."

Sylvia sat down heavily. "It's a lie. The whole thing."

"Is that your only answer?"

"It's enough because it happens to be the truth."

Mansfield stood up quickly when Benjamin did. They sneered and left.

Bess came to the door looking anxious. "What was it about?"

"Wow. You wouldn't believe it. I've got quite a problem." She repeated the allegations to her friend.

"Why would Bailey say that?"

Sylvia lit a cigarette and took a slow drag. "That's an interesting question. Why would he? And why at this particular time?"

They contemplated the timing in silence.

"You'd think that one of the lawyers on the discipline committee would have called to ask you about this! Instead of just sending in the dogs. You're the most ethical criminal lawyer in town and everyone knows it."

"Not quite everyone apparently. Bess, would you get Mrs. Bailey on the phone?"

Sylvia sat at her desk in deep thought. She had always considered herself more than usually cynical. She could see that until now she had only begun to plumb the depths.

"Sylvia, I can't find her. Their phone is out of order and the gas company says that the house has been vacated."

"Oh, Christ."

"But I did get hold of Bailey's new lawyer's name."

"How?"

"Through the secretary at the Bar Association. We have lunch occasionally and she thinks a lot of you."

Sylvia smiled wryly. "Well, at least I've got one friend left. Two," she amended, looking fondly at Bess. "Who is it?"

"Charlie Seabridge."

"You're kidding!" Bess wasn't. Seabridge was one of the sleazier young lawyers around. He scooped other attorneys' cases, paid off jail guards to call him when undefended people were brought in, pleaded clients with a possible defense guilty to make a fast buck. Sylvia had never had to deal with him, a situation she had hoped to prolong indefinitely.

Seabridge's secretary was reluctant to put her through. It took a great deal of persuasion and a veiled threat before she got him on the line.

"Sylvia West here. I understand you now represent Walter Bailey."

"Yeah. He needed a good lawyer."

She let that pass. "I want to speak to him and his wife about the allegations they've made against me. His wife has moved and it wouldn't be right to go to the jail to see him without your permission."

"Damn right. Though I'm surprised you're worrying about ethics. When did that start?"

Sylvia closed her eyes. "Look, let's not argue the case now. I want the wife's phone number."

"Forget it, babe. You aren't going near either of my clients. I told Mrs. Bailey to move so you couldn't harass her. You'll have a chance to talk to them at the hearing. Not that it'll do you any good. You blew it this time, lady."

"The name is Mrs. West," Sylvia snapped. "And nothing's been proved yet. Your duty to your clients doesn't preclude you from allowing me adequate discovery."

"Go to hell. You're not seeing either of them. I'm making it my business to see that you never practice law again in this State."

The line went dead.

Sylvia gripped the receiver for a good two minutes before replacing it very carefully.

"Well?" Bess was at the door.

"You better call my partners in here. This is something that they should know about."

The five men were almost hysterical about the allegations. Sylvia wasn't able to allay their fears very well. She had too many of her own.

The consensus was that any firm who allowed a member to practice general criminal law got what was coming to it. Their idea of acceptable criminal practice encompassed the odd impaired driving charge and white collar crime. Price-fixing, insider trading. Respectable activities.

The meeting ground to a helpless halt when Bess called her out to take the phone.

"How did yesterday go?" Dave asked.

"Yesterday? Oh, Cass. Okay. I have a lead. What happened with the captain?"

"Ah, yes. My meeting. It seems that Cameron has been complaining about my interference in his case. I've been given the word to stick to my own files. I'm not supposed to be involved with the murder investigation or anything else that arises out of the disappearance."

"So you'll be careful." Sylvia couldn't worry about Dave's job right now.

"Sylvia, I hate to bring it up but you ought to know."

"What is it?"

"About John. Uh, have you checked your bank accounts lately?"

"Yes. The day after the disappearance. I may be a wife but I'm not a fool. Nothing was missing."

"Well, I think you should keep in touch with the bank-manager," Dave muttered.

"Why?" She tried not to comprehend. "What have you found out?"

He told her.

"No, it's not possible."

"I'm afraid it is. If you were religious, you'd say that the car accident was God's way of slapping John's wrist. I'm sorry, Sylvia."

She rang off and started to leave for the bank.

"Sylvia! Friedman is on the phone!" Bess was very excited.

"Oh, hell. All right, I'll take it. Hello, Inspector Friedman."

"I want to talk to you," he announced firmly as though it had been Sylvia who had been unreachable. "I can be in New York by nine tonight. Can you meet me for dinner?"

"Are you from out of town?"

"Yes, of course. You surely must have found out by now that there's no Inspector Friedman in New York?"

"Well, yes," Sylvia admitted sheepishly.

"I'll tell you more about myself at dinner. I don't like the telephone."

They agreed to meet at a downtown steakhouse at nine-thirty.

"Oh, Mrs. West!" The assistant manager had always liked her. "How nice to see you. Come over to Mr. Whitehead's office. I'm sure he'll be delighted you're here."

He didn't act it.

"Mrs. West. Yes. Um. Please sit down." He waved vaguely at the Danish modern chairs across from the teak desk.

Sylvia smiled charmingly. "I hope I haven't taken you away from a crisis, but I need some information. Has anything gone out of our accounts? My husband's and mine?"

"No, your joint accounts are exactly as they were when you

came in just after the, er, uh, event."

She was on her feet, jubilantly ready to go give Dave hell when she recalled that John had had another account. He'd used it from time to time, usually for presents to her so that she wouldn't know what they cost. She'd thought it an outdated but rather sweet notion.

The manager hemmed and hawed. Finally he broke down. "I'm not supposed to do this. The Banker's Code is quite specific, but since I've known you so long, I'll say this. There has been some movement in Mr. West's personal account."

Sylvia felt like she'd been plowed in the solar plexus. "How much movement?"

"I can't tell you that."

"When did it happen?"

"I can't tell you that either."

"Why the hell not?" Sylvia was shouting.

"The police have asked me not to release any information."

"They didn't mean to me, Mr. Whitehead. I'm his wife."

"They, er, most specifically meant you." He was anguished, as evidenced by the thin stream of perspiration running down his vacuous face and onto his shiny navy suit. "They said I wasn't to give you any information unless they gave me the go-ahead."

"Well, call them and get the go-ahead." Sylvia stared relentlessly at the little man until he took up the telephone.

Whitehead mopped at his forehead throughout his conversation with Cameron. "I'm very happy that I can give you some details," he gasped as he hung up. He was sincere. He hated trouble. "Mr. West's account was cleaned out by means of a bank draft on the twenty-first."

Three days after John had disappeared.

"How much money did it contain?"

"Over forty thousand dollars. Forty-two, to be precise."

She couldn't believe her ears. "Forty-two thousand dollars?"

"Yes. I, uh, won't transfer funds out of your joint account without calling you. It's not strictly proper for me to do so, but, well, I want to be fair."

"Good of you. The problem isn't likely to arise now, is it?"

Whitehead paled. He had forgotten about the accident. "Quite, quite."

"What bank did the draft come from?"

"I, uh, can't tell you that."

"Now don't start that again. I know the worst and I didn't

get hysterical. I can handle all the details."

"It was the captain himself who told me to keep that information secret." As if to cheer her up, he added, "I, heh, heh, can't imagine you hysterical, as you call it." His expression left some doubt as to whether this was a compliment.

Sylvia stood up. Further pushing would send Whitehead into a heart attack. He was a stupid man but this wasn't really his fault. "All right. I'll speak to the police about it."

She left, both she and the manager stating with considerable untruth that they were at each other's service.

She went directly back to the office and called Dave. "I've just been to my bank. The manager said that the police, specifically Cameron, the bastard, told him I was not to be informed where the bank draft originated. Does that make any sense to you?"

"No. I guess he just wants to keep you out of the investigation. Or, who knows, maybe he suspects that you're involved with the embezzlement."

"It hasn't been proved yet that there was an embezzlement. Much less that John did it. Can you find out where the draft came from?"

"Um, well, it could mean trouble. After all, I was just told to keep away."

Sylvia was silent. She had no intention of letting him off the hook. She didn't have enough ammunition to be ladylike about how she used it.

"Okay, I can try," Dave sighed.

The other line had been engaged while she spoke with Dave. Sylvia buzzed for the message.

Bess came in to deliver it in person.

"Why the long face?" Sylvia asked.

"Brace yourself. Stuart Paliano phoned. The auditors have found that forty-two thousand dollars are missing. And they've found the checks. They were signed by John."

Sylvia sat absolutely still for a long moment.

Then she grabbed her purse and walked out of the office. She went home to sit in her bedroom, with a brand-new bottle of Scotch. She fell asleep at about six.

The telephone woke her four hours later. It was Friedman, none too happy at being stood up.

"I'm sorry. I've had a bad day and I took the coward's way out. Could we leave it to tomorrow?" There wasn't much point in seeing him anyway. It was time to accept the unpalatable facts and stop torturing herself with fanciful theories.

"No. I'll come over now and bring dinner."

After hanging up, Sylvia realized that she had never given him the address. On the other hand, she hadn't given him the number either and it was unlisted to save the household from midnight calls from her clients.

Standing up was a big mistake. The top of her head fell off. She decided to refrain from drunkenness in the future. If life got too awful, there were pleasanter forms of suicide.

SEVENTEEN

The door opened to a handsome man with dark hair and eyes. He stood only about five feet nine, but his wiry build was in perfect proportion to his height. For some reason, she hadn't expected him to be attractive.

Friedman was surprised at her too. "Wow! You didn't sound that tall on the phone."

"Come on in," Sylvia said, unnecessarily since he'd already walked in and dumped his suit jacket. He appraised her carefully and seeing that she wasn't in great shape, took over. Before she knew what was happening, he'd found the dishes and cutlery, set the table and put out steaks, baked potatoes, and a salad.

"Where did you get all that?"

"I convinced the steakhouse to prepare a meal for me to take out. I told them my wife was eight months pregnant and had a burning desire for steak."

The man was clearly crazy. The food smelled good, however, so she sat down to it and found that she was ravenous. Friedman had brought a bottle of wine too but the mere sight of it made her wince; he polished it off by himself.

Neither said much until the table was pretty well clean.

"You look better," Friedman observed. "Why don't you make coffee? I take mine black."

She brought two steaming mugs into the living room and found Friedman prowling around, looking into drawers and through papers. She stood still for a moment, belatedly remembering that she'd promised to let Rupert know if Friedman contacted her again. In case he was dangerous. Experience was teaching her that she wasn't the best judge of men but for what it was worth, she didn't feel threatened by Friedman. Just curious.

"I can tell you're shy," she said drily as she walked in.

He wasn't at all embarrassed. "I like to know who I'm dealing with."

He took a mug and settled himself in John's favorite chair. "Take yourself, for example. You're much younger than your husband. You're good-looking on the large economy-size scale. You make good money and I'm told you have a good personality. Now why would a man leave you?"

Sylvia closed her mouth which had dropped open. "You aren't the subtle type, are you?"

"Why did you marry your husband?"

"I met him, fell in love, and married. It's a common enough story."

"Not so. He was European, older than you, hardly the man your family would have chosen, isn't that true?"

She stared and shook her head. "You've got a lot of nerve! Who the hell are you? And what do you want with me?"

"I promise that I'll answer all your questions in a minute. First, just tell me what your husband told you about his background, his family."

That seemed innocuous enough. "Not much. He didn't like to talk about the past and I didn't push him. Most of his family was dead, including his father whom he cared for very much. He isn't, wasn't, close to his mother."

"Have you ever met her?"

"Once. She came for a visit a couple of years ago. I haven't had any other dealings with her, as strange as it sounds. She communicated with John and I left it to him."

"Have you talked to her since your husband's, uh, sudden departure?"

"No. The police wanted to but I don't know exactly where she lives."

"Oh, that's the address you were looking for?"

"You don't miss much. Yes, that was it."

"Any luck?"

"No. The police are supposedly in touch with the Swiss authorities but I haven't heard anything."

"The Swiss authorities?"

"That's where John's family comes from. I think his mother still lives somewhere in Geneva."

"Oh." Friedman paused. "What—"

"Hold on. John's dead now. Why are you asking all these questions?"

"Ah, yes. The accident." He looked quizzically at her. "What do you think about The Accident?" He capitalized the words.

"I don't know what you mean."

"I think you do. A very convenient ending, isn't it? Dead in Florida. Burned to an unidentifiable crisp."

Sylvia winced.

"Except for a few problems. The man couldn't drive. And he had a beautiful wife plus lots of opportunity to meet other gorgeous women but he chose to run away with an old whore. His identification is just about the only thing that didn't burn. How fortuitous."

"What? Where did you get that idea? They identified him by dental evidence."

"What?"

Sylvia repeated what she'd been told.

"No way, absolutely not. That tears it."

"What?"

"That takes time. Either the dental examination was very sloppily done or, and this is what I think, it wasn't done at all. Have you seen the reports?"

"No," she admitted slowly, "but why would anyone want to fake it? Assuming that John didn't set it up himself."

Friedman didn't comment on the assumption. "It's too bad the body isn't still around, isn't it?" He was staring at her. "Such a shame."

She dropped her eyes. "When I ordered the cremation, I had no idea that there was any problem with the identification."

"But why did you want him cremated? An old family custom?"

"No, I—I wanted to be with my children. And it wouldn't have done John any good to have a big funeral. He was dead. Or so I thought."

"Why not ship the remains home?"

"It was going to take too long and my children needed me here. Look, I made a mistake. I admit it." You'd think she was the suspicious figure in the room.

Friedman was still staring at her.

"And anyway, who the hell are you? You're cross-examining me as though you've got some interest in the case! What is it?"

"My curiosity. I get an odd call about a vanished man and I love a mystery."

"You either talk or get out of my house. I'm not giving you any more information until I get some answers from you. You're obviously desperately interested in John's whereabouts.

That's as mysterious as anything else about the whole thing and I bet the police would be fascinated too."

"What else do you know about your husband's background?"

Sylvia would not be drawn. She stood up, indicating that the interview was over.

"Hm. Well, I do have a reason for wanting to find him but it's very confidential. Does anyone know I've contacted you?"

"Only my secretary." There was no reason to bandy Rupert's name around.

"How long have you known her?"

"A long time. She's my oldest friend and I trust her absolutely."

"Yes, but then you also trusted your husband."

She couldn't argue with that.

"Well, I'm going to take a chance but I want your promise that you won't repeat what I'm about to tell you to anyone."

"I can't promise that, and if you really are a policeman, you know I can't. If you're involved with the disappearance I won't protect you. And I'll be the judge of it."

"Other than that, you won't talk about me?"

"I'll see." Sylvia stared back at him until he dropped his eyes.

"I am a police officer, from out of town obviously. For the moment, I can't tell you where. My force is investigating a large fraud and extortion ring. Your husband is involved with it. He may be a victim or he may be less innocent, but we won't know which until we talk to him. It's a huge rip-off, millions of dollars and hundreds of patsies. I've been given orders not to bring any other police force into it, especially New York's. It's an undercover investigation and it looks as if the fraud originated here. With, I might add, the willing cooperation of some of your cops. So we have to keep it under wraps. I can't risk blowing it by talking to the wrong guys."

Sylvia stood up and walked around the room, ignoring the trail of cigarette ashes. Friedman's tale was pat, too pat. But assuming that John had really embezzled money to make a fast getaway, it was barely possible that he had been mixed up in something illegal that was on the verge of coming home to roost. Friedman's explanation didn't have the ring of truth but there was something about him she liked. And was she in a position to turn down any answers, however implausible? Or turn away a figure like Friedman who might lead her, even unintentionally, to the solution?

"I'll tell you what," she said finally. "I'll accept your story for the moment. But I'm not wild about it."

"Remember, you've got to keep it to yourself."

"For the moment," Sylvia repeated noncommittally. "Now, what do you want from me?"

"Same thing you want from me. Help in finding out what happened. What have you been doing?"

Sylvia told him, keeping her suspicions about von Schagg to herself. It never hurt to have something up your sleeve.

"The diary could be the key!" Friedman was excited. "Does his secretary remember the appointment?"

"No. She said she didn't even know there was a sixth client coming in. On the other hand . . ."

"Yes?"

"I may be doing her a great injustice but someone who knew a lot about that office could have arranged for the calls to John's clients. Janice, that's her name, fits the bill. On the other hand, John could have arranged it all by himself. And Janice has been with him a long time. She seems devoted to him; I can't believe she'd help someone hurt him."

"But she'd help him disappear, if that's what he wanted."

"I guess she might. I don't see John taking her into his confidence and hiding it from me." She hadn't seen a lot of things. "Well, maybe so."

"Would you take him back?"

"He may be dead!"

"If not, would you take him back?"

"I don't know," Sylvia said slowly. "My life seems very empty now. I'm not sure that I like being alone, that I want to raise the children alone. But I've learned things about my marriage that I'd ignored for years. I loved John when I married him but it wasn't enough then. Well, I have even less now."

Friedman got up. "That reminds me. About the children, any leads on the kidnappers?"

Something about the way he said "kidnappers" caught Sylvia's attention. It was as though he didn't believe it had happened.

"Not yet. The funeral for my housekeeper is this weekend, if you're interested."

"Not really. Why would anyone want to snatch your kids? Are you that loaded?"

"No," Sylvia smiled. "Far from it. I don't know why, except..." She looked at her feet.

"Except maybe your husband wants them?"

"Who knows?" she asked helplessly. "But I've got to get to the bottom of all this. No one is going to try that again!"

Friedman continued to watch her impassively for a moment. "Well," he said, moving to the door, "it's late and I'm tired. And you've got children to feed in the morning."

"Oh, Jay and Carl aren't here. I've sent them to... I've sent them away. Where they'll be safe for the time being."

"Jay and Carl?"

"Yes, my two boys."

Friedman had a strange smile on his face. It wasn't pleasant.

"What is it?" Sylvia asked.

"Never mind. I suppose your husband chose their names?"

"Yes, actually he did. After some friends of his."

"Dead friends. See you. I'll be in touch."

EIGHTEEN

The peaceful breakfasts that she'd dreamed of ever since Jay was born were turning out to be merely lonely. She was actually pleased when a knock on the kitchen door interrupted her.

"Mr. Friedman. What's the problem?"

"Oh, there are a few things I want to go over again." He took a chair and one of Sylvia's pieces of toast. "By the way, is that car out front a permanent fixture?"

"The patrol car? For a while. Didn't you see it last night?"

"It wasn't there."

Sylvia frowned. "Are you sure? Well, maybe they drove around the block or something. Anyway, it's there to protect me until the murder is solved. Is that why you came to the back door?"

Friedman took a cup of coffee without answering.

She dropped the issue and ate the remaining piece of toast.

"Good coffee, Sylvia."

"Since we're on first-name terms, what's yours?"

"I'm usually just called Friedman. No 'Mister.'"

"Yes, but what do your friends call you?" she persisted.

"I don't have many friends. You can call me anything you like."

"It's usual to use the name you were given." He was impossible. He wouldn't give a straight answer to anything.

"No. You pick a name for me." His tone was jocular but he made no bones about the fact that he had no intention of revealing his given name.

Sylvia gave up. "What did you want from me today?"

"Let's go over the whole thing again. Tell me everything that's happened, everything, since the morning of the day your husband disappeared."

She repeated much of what she'd told him the previous night. Again, she found herself avoiding the topic of The Foundation.

"You've got a lot of friends," he commented.

"Yes. They've been a big help."

"Don't trust any of them."

"What?"

"Don't trust a living soul."

"If I followed your advice, you wouldn't be here," she pointed out drily.

"You don't know me and you really shouldn't have taken this gamble. You were lucky, as it happens, because I'm on your side. At least, I'm not against you. But don't trust anyone else." Friedman looked at her soberly. "Your life may depend on it."

"Friedman, what's going on? What do you know that I should know too?"

"Nothing. I arrived in town to talk to your husband just in time to find out that he's vanished and I'm a few days too late." Friedman wasn't looking at her.

"Please. You've warned me about some danger. You obviously know more about it than I do. Don't you feel any responsibility, if I really am in danger, to give me ammunition so that I can protect myself?"

Friedman looked like he was about to say something. The moment passed.

"Hell, if I knew something, I wouldn't be here quizzing you. Now, let's get back to your husband."

"Stop calling him 'your husband'! He had a name. John West," Sylvia snapped. "Use it."

"Mmm. Now, let's go through his papers here at the house."

"I'm not the idiot you take me for. I've gone through everything. There's nothing here, at least not since the break-and-enter when his study was ripped apart. And I'm tired of information flowing in only one direction."

"Nothing in the house? Odd man, your husband."

Sylvia controlled herself. Friedman had a remarkable ability to make her want to scream like a fishwife.

He stood up.

"Where are you going?"

"To run a few checks on your husband."

"How?"

"Credit company files. The usual skip-tracing techniques. I'll see you later."

Sylvia watched helplessly as he left by the back door. She hadn't exactly come out ahead on this exchange.

* * *

She was walking into the office when something occurred to her.

"Bess! When did Friedman first call?"

The secretary flipped through a steno pad. "I've got it somewhere. Let me see."

Sylvia paced impatiently around the secretarial desk.

"Here it is!" Bess looked up in dawning bewilderment. "On the eighteenth. In the morning. But that was—"

"Yes. That's right." Friedman had not arrived a few days too late. He had called before John disappeared or at least before anyone could have known about it.

"Sylvia, I've got a lead on Mrs. Bailey. Remember she once mentioned she had a sister?"

"No."

"She did, in an interview with you. It's in my notes. The sister's name is Rose Matulak. She lives in Queens."

Sylvia grabbed the address and dashed out.

The street was a dingy lower-middle-class strip. Each house was as carefully tended as increasing inflation and decreasing pensions could manage but the overall effect was one of desperation.

The bell at number thirty-six rang a couple of times without answer. Sylvia persisted until she finally heard steps approaching the door.

"Yes? Who is it?" It was the voice of an elderly woman who had read a lot about young punks ringing doorbells and mugging the unwary homeowner.

"Mrs. West. Sylvia West. Could I talk to you?"

"Who?" The woman was still suspicious but she felt better on hearing that her visitor was a woman.

"Sylvia West. I was the lawyer for your brother-in-law."

"Oh. Oh my." Mrs. Matulak was very embarrassed. "Oh dear. What do you want here?"

"I want to speak to you. It will only take a few minutes. May I come in?"

"I . . . I don't think so. I'm not supposed to talk to you."

"It would be better if I came inside. You don't really want me standing on the doorstep where all the neighbors can hear."

Sylvia was counting on the fact that this kind of neighborhood was dedicated to maintaining the very thin line that divided the respectable poor from the riffraff.

"Oh, oh dear. I guess so." Mrs. Matulak unlocked the wooden door and unhooked the aluminum screen door with its fancy curlicues of fake wrought iron. "Come in."

She was a faded woman, probably not past sixty but looking much older, who had never been pretty and wasn't about to start. The hall of the house had a lot in common with its mistress. Sylvia could barely see ten feet in the gloom.

"Mrs. Matulak, I must speak with your sister. I don't know what pressures have been put on her, but she's been making false allegations that could land her in a great deal of trouble, even put her in jail."

Which was the truth, although at the moment Sylvia had a far better chance of experiencing first-hand the State's premises.

The threat was enough to cause Mrs. Matulak to gasp, clutch at her heart, and sag into a chair. "Jail?"

"I'm afraid so. I've made some inquiries and I have reason to believe that you're harboring her." It sounded like a dreadful crime and it was effective.

"Not harboring, no. She's staying with me, but I'm not harboring her! I had no idea that she was in trouble herself. I mean, that no-good husband of hers is always in trouble, but it's not a woman's fault what her man does, is it? I mean, we don't have any control over them, do we?"

Sylvia cut into the babbling. "Could I see her, please." She didn't make it a question.

"Just a minute." Mrs. Matulak got up wearily and went down the corridor.

A woman, looking from a distance like the twin of Mrs. Matulak, slopped up in fuzzy, hot pink slippers. "Excuse my feet. I've been having a bad time with my arthritis. I can't wear shoes for very long, I've tried a lot of medicines but they don't do any good at all." She couldn't look Sylvia in the eye.

"Mrs. Bailey, please relax. It will be all right. Come on, let's go into the living room."

Sylvia jockeyed her into the drab room and urged her to sit down. "Now, tell me what's happened. I suppose you must have been under terrible pressure to say those things? I can only help you if you tell me all about it." She made her voice sympathetic which wasn't very difficult in the face of the pathetic creature beside her.

"Oh, I didn't want to, Mrs. West. I haven't had a wink of sleep in the last week, I feel so bad. I didn't want to get you in trouble; you were the only person who cared about us at all. I feel so ashamed." Mrs. Bailey started to cry.

Sylvia made soothing noises. "We'll get it all straightened out. Just tell me what happened."

"We've got no money. None at all. And I can't work, not with this arthritis and all. Walter's been real worried about me and he said this was the only way. He didn't want to do it either but he couldn't think of any other way to make some money. I mean, he makes a little inside, but it's not enough to live on. And Rose can't keep me here forever. We don't really get on that well together. We never did. I told him I could go for welfare but he got real upset at that. We've never been on welfare."

Sylvia tried not to smile. Considering that Walter had spent a fair amount of his adult life residing in institutions that provided both room and board, his scruples were rather surprising.

"Of course it would have been a temptation. Who offered the money?"

"I don't know. Walter'd be the one to talk to, Mrs. West. He was asked about it inside. Someone came up to him and said they'd take care of me while Walter was inside if he'd just say you took the money. He didn't want to do it but he was that worried about me."

"Of course. Have you been paid yet?"

"Not yet. We weren't going to get paid until we'd given evidence about it. I was terribly scared. I didn't want to lie but Walter told me I had to. All I had to say was that I bought the money order and gave it to Walter."

Sylvia lit a cigarette without noticing that there were no ashtrays in the room.

"I'll get one," Mrs. Bailey said, scurrying out to the kitchen. Sylvia could hear the two women whispering. She joined them to avoid giving Mrs. Bailey a chance to renege. She needn't have worried. Mrs. Matulak was giving her sister hell.

"I certainly can't blame Mrs. Bailey," Sylvia interjected. "Not under the circumstances. And it took courage to admit the whole thing to me. I think I can protect her from any trouble provided she tells the truth now."

"Oh, I will! I promise!" Mrs. Bailey grabbed Sylvia's arm frantically. "But Walter won't get into no more trouble, will he?"

"No, I'll see to that." Sylvia was feeling good enough to promise immunity to Jack the Ripper.

"My sister won't go to jail?" Mrs. Matulak was still worrying about that word.

"Not if she tells the truth. Mrs. Bailey, can you be in my office tomorrow morning at ten-thirty? I'll have the investigators there and you can repeat what you just told me. That should end the entire affair."

"I'll . . . I'll be there," the woman whispered.

"I'll see to that," her sister promised grimly.

Margo Whitten was in her office at Justice when Sylvia called.

"Oh, Sylvia, I've been meaning to write you. I'm so sorry about John. I don't know quite what to say."

"Thank you. Listen, I called to ask you to lunch. Are you free today?"

"Are you kidding? I never say no to a free meal."

Sylvia laughed. Margo had always disparaged her own appeal to men but she was actually adorable and very popular. She'd never married, claiming that she hadn't met anyone she could kiss before breakfast, but Sylvia knew that a not inconsiderable number of guys had tried to change her mind.

Sylvia arrived early at Les Couscousiers, a Moroccan restaurant just around the corner from Grand Central Station. Vast swathes of heavily embroidered material converted the room into a Moroccan sheik's tent. Huge sweeps of Oriental rugs in shades of burgundy and blue covered the floor and walls, surrounding the groupings of knee-height brass tables and low pillow-strewn couches with intimacy and warmth.

Lounging on a tapestried cushion and sipping a drink handed to her by what appeared to be a genuine Bedouin, Sylvia could almost believe that when she stepped outside the tent she would find herself in the desert. Her guest's arrival shattered the illusion. Margo was a tiny blonde with short-cropped hair and massive blue eyes who couldn't have seemed more alien to the mid-Eastern ambience if she'd worn a space suit.

In fact, she was wearing a tailored raw silk pantsuit and shirt. She looked, as always, smashing. Sylvia had perennially envied Margo's clothes but what was designed in size five did not get made in extra-large, not that Sylvia would have given up an inch of her height in exchange for beautiful clothing. She would have loathed Margo's lifetime of looking up at people.

The two women chatted easily until the menu had been deciphered and their orders placed.

"Margo," Sylvia said, breaking into their reminiscences,

"I called because I need help."

Her friend leaned forward in concern. "Anything I can do, just ask. Is it money?"

"No, John's disappearance has disrupted my life but not in that way." She took a deep breath. "I hardly know where to begin. Now don't start thinking I'm paranoid, but the vanishing act has set off a string of frightening events that aren't over yet."

"I read about your housekeeper," Margo put in seriously. "I couldn't get over your bad luck. First John and then that."

"Luck may have very little to do with it." Sylvia started to tell Margo about her suspicions. She stopped abruptly, remembering that Pat Dutton had mentioned at Stuart's dinner party how fond both she and Herb were of Margo. And how Herb frequently called on Margo for assistance. Not that Sylvia believed for a moment that Bess's dislike of the man was well founded. There was no way that Herb could be even remotely involved in whatever was going on.

Still, there was no point in blabbing everything.

Sylvia turned her pause into a moment of sipping wine and went on with her summary, omitting any reference to The Foundation or Friedman. "I need information, Margo. I know next to nothing about John."

"Aren't the police investigating?"

"Not anymore. They figure he's dead which is not, in my book, a certainty. Oh, I guess they'd like to find the forty-two G's but they're not knocking themselves out for it." She fell silent as the waiter approached with the couscous.

"Sylvia, what do you want from me? With friends like Rupert Thompson and Herb Dutton, you don't need a little fish like me." Margo laughed. "I should be the one asking for the favor. A job with the Wandling Institute is the stuff dreams are made of."

Here was the crunch. Sylvia crossed her fingers and plunged in. "I think the answer to everything lies with John. Whether someone wanted him dead or whether he wanted to disappear. I can't find any explanation in the present so I've got to look to the past."

Light was slowly dawning in Margo's eyes. "I see," she said reluctantly. "You want me to find out what the government has on file about him?"

"Even if I could just get his mother's address in Switzerland. It's possible that he contacted her for money, if nothing else.

Forty-two thousand doesn't last forever. Assuming he's alive,"
she added quickly for credibility's sake. So far, only two people
would entertain even the possibility that he was, and one of
them, namely herself, had grave doubts.

"You really never dealt with Mommy?" Margo was still
having trouble with that point.

"Amazing, eh?"

"My, weren't you the perfect fool? What a hell of a mess."
Margo looked at her uneasily. "I'm sympathetic, Sylvia, but
I swore an oath not to reveal anything in government files.
You know that."

"Yes, but I don't have anywhere else to go. What can I
do?"

Margo said nothing for a few minutes, toying with her food.
Finally she came to a decision. "I'm not even sure that I can
get hold of the immigration file. I'll do this much. I'll try to
look at it and I don't promise that I'll be successful. But if I
am, I'll look for an irregularity. If there isn't one, I'll have no
recourse but to put the file back. But if there is something
wrong, I'll start an immigration inquiry and what the investigating officers choose to tell you in the course of their duties
is up to them. That's the best I can do."

"Thank you. Whatever you can manage. Uh, there is one
more thing." Sylvia was almost afraid to breathe.

"Yes?"

"John had a secretary for twelve years. She wasn't born
here either. I know it's a long shot but since some of John's
papers have been disappearing, there's a chance she's involved."

"I can't start pulling files on people who haven't called
attention to themselves in some way!"

Sylvia backtracked fast. She didn't want to push Margo to
the point where she'd do nothing at all. "I just mention her so
that if for some reason you see her name in John's file, you'll
recognize it. Janice Wagoner."

Margo didn't respond.

NINETEEN

Bess was having a whale of a time with Sweetie. The two of them shared a somewhat sardonic view of male sexuality and Sylvia hated to break it up.

"I came to give you a picture of Cass." Sweetie was fumbling through a large shoulder bag. "I talked to some of the girls about her and one of them had a picture."

Sylvia scrutinized it carefully with Bess hanging over her shoulder. It was a Polaroid shot, poorly lit, but it did convey the impression of a tired woman trying to look alert and young. Cass had been slightly overweight and more than slightly overblown, a blonde who proved that not all fair-haired women have more fun.

"She was not bad when she first came to town," Sweetie said. "I was already working the track and I met her a few days after she got off the bus."

"What brought her here?" Sylvia was dying to ask what had induced Cass to take up her profession but she was afraid Sweetie would take the question badly.

"The usual story, as I remember. Knocked up by her father or stepfather. Or maybe it was the brother. I don't know exactly. I've heard the same shit a thousand times. Anyway, she got picked up by one of the big pimps. Big Marvin. He was really something if you dig men," Sweetie mused.

"Is he still around?"

"Nah, he's dead. Stiffed by another pimp because Big Marvin's girls kind of had the habit of poaching on turf. Some of the girls got wiped out too but Cass was somewhere else at the time. She's been through a few pimps since. And a lot of bad numbers."

"Like what?"

"Dope, for a while. I think her last pimp made her give it up. You gotta work hard in this business and you can't if you're shooting. She drank a lot, but then, who doesn't? Look, lady, hooking doesn't make you any younger." Sweetie looked down at her own body in disgust.

"Did any of the women you talked to get a good look at the woman who arranged Cass's last date?"

"Not a real good look. Once we talked about her though, I remembered more. She was about ten years older than me."

Sylvia had no idea what that would make her. She wondered how to ask delicately.

Sweetie saw her hesitate. "I'm thirty-two. Yeah, unbeliev-able, isn't it?" she added to Bess who hadn't been able to stifle a gasp. "This broad, she wasn't on the track, that's for sure. But something aged her. She was the most dried-up piece of ass I've seen in a long time. Long straight hair. The color of shit. Dark shit. She dressed like a scared virgin, though with her looks she didn't have a thing to be scared about. Dark blue dress with no shape to it. It even had one of them little white collars! Like schoolteachers used to wear in the movies."

"This is terrific, Sweetie. Was there anything else?"

"Yeah, me and the girls remembered glasses. Thick, big ones like that." She pointed to a tortoiseshell cigarette case lying on the coffee table. "And her complexion was bad, really bad for a straight dame."

"Would you recognize her if you saw her again?"

"Might."

Sylvia gave her twenty dollars and said she'd keep in touch.

"Bess," she said when Sweetie had left for work, "does that description remind you of anybody?"

"Millions of people. But only one of them was close to John."

Stuart was so overwhelmingly vain that making up to him was a simple matter. Once she'd flattered him and eaten a small amount of crow, he was putty in her hands.

"I need your advice, Stuart."

"Surely, my dear. Just tell me what the problem is."

"I want to find out as much as I can about what John was involved in before he left. I must find out if the attack on my babies had anything to do with him."

"How could it? Er, he was already, you know, when it happened."

"Yes, I know. But it was such a coincidence in timing that I wondered if John mightn't have had something to do with it and then when he died, no one canceled the order."

"Aha." Stuart, who had never been closer to a criminal than a newspaper, nodded knowingly. "Aha."

"It occurred to me that a man's secretary knows an awful lot about him."

"Good thinking," he said generously with no more than a hint of surprise. "I wouldn't be telling tales out of school if I said that was true." Clearly Stuart didn't recall, if he'd ever believed, that she had a secretary too.

"I want to ask Janice some questions, but it would be helpful to look at her personnel file first." Hopefully, he wouldn't analyze the dubious syllogism.

"Certainly, my dear. I'll have my girl get it for you."

Sylvia winced. "Uh, Stuart, do you think that there's the tiniest chance that she might mention it to Janice?"

"True. They're all friends. I'll tell you what, let's go get the file ourselves!"

"Good idea," she gushed.

The personnel file was thin. Janice was the same age as Sylvia, thirty-nine. She'd been born in Australia and had come to the States twelve years ago. She'd started working for John almost immediately. Apparently she'd been a legal secretary in Australia too, but there was a two-year gap between her departure from Down Under and her arrival here. Otherwise, she couldn't have been more ordinary.

"Never been married," Stuart pointed out in his inimical manner of pursuing the obvious. "Not that I think there was anything between her and John," he added pompously.

"Of course not," Sylvia agreed. It didn't seem likely but at this point, she wouldn't have taken a bet that John was not a multiple rapist.

Janice wasn't unattractive, or she wouldn't have been if she made the slightest effort. But she had the soul of frozen fish fillets. Sylvia couldn't have worked with her for a week. On the other hand, both she and John were so impersonal, they'd probably got along just fine.

Janice wasn't at her station. She was behind John's desk.

"Oh, Mrs. West. I was just looking for Mr. West's notes for the tax seminar. I'll look later."

"I wouldn't dream of disturbing your work. Go on. I'll sit here and wait." To make her point clearer, Sylvia plopped down on one of the clients' chairs.

Janice had no option but to continue, and sure enough she came up with the tax material in a moment. "Why, here it is. Thank you. I'll get out of your way."

"Just a second, Janice. I'd like to talk to you."

With bad grace, the secretary sat down.

"You've been with my husband for twelve years now. Isn't that right?"

"Yes."

"I guess the two of us saw more of him than anyone. We should be able to figure out what happened."

"We know what happened. Mr. West is dead."

"Maybe."

Janice's head shot up. "What do you mean? Is he alive?"

"I'm not sure. That's one of the reasons I wanted to talk to you. When we understand why he left, and the circumstances of his leaving, we'll be in a better position to decide if he was in that car or not."

"I have no ideas. I was just his secretary and I really have no idea what went on in his life, other than his work."

"Of course, Janice. I understand that." Anyone would if they saw her now, sullen face framed by not-quite-clean hair. "Still, since he spent so much of his life at work, that amounts to a fair insight. Now I have great difficulty believing that my husband would have stolen money from this firm."

"I would have also, but it looks like he did."

"Yes, it looks that way. On the other hand, it looks like he's dead too and I wouldn't stake my life on that." Sylvia paused for a moment, wondering if that wasn't exactly what she was doing. She pushed the sense of menace away. "I have a great deal of trouble accepting that he ran away from his family."

Janice stayed quiet. Sylvia controlled her spasm of dislike.

"At any rate, I've got to find out what did happen, if only to explain it to the boys."

Janice looked away. She turned back suddenly as if an idea had struck her. "Do the police think he might be alive?"

"I doubt it. Frankly, I am not particularly interested in what the police think. By the way, Janice, where are you from?" It was awkwardly inserted into the conversation but she hadn't been able to think of a better introduction.

"I'm from Australia."

Silence.

"Did you work as a secretary there?"

"Yes."

Chatty, wasn't she? "After all these years, you'd think we'd know more about each other, wouldn't you? So you were a secretary there too. For a lawyer?"

"Yes." After another pause, even Janice could recognize that more was expected. "His name was George Streicher."

"He must have been sorry to lose you. I know you're a fabulous secretary."

"He died."

"Oh. Did you take the boat from Australia to the States? I hear it's a lovely voyage."

"No, I traveled around first."

"How interesting! Where did you go?"

"Through Europe. Really, Mrs. West, I can't see what help this can be and I've got work to do."

"Sorry, I just got sidetracked. Back to John. How did you come to work for him?"

"The usual way. I answered an ad in the paper, I think. It's hard to remember now. Maybe I heard about the job on the grapevine. At any rate, he interviewed and hired me."

"Did he ask you about your background? I'm trying to find out what was important to him, you see. Anything could be helpful." Janice was no fool. Another question like that one and she'd be gone.

"Not that I remember. I imagine he just looked at my references."

"Did John have any friends that visited him here?"

"No. He was very businesslike. I don't think he ever did anything personal in the office."

"Did you meet his mother when she was here?"

"Yes, I did once."

"I gather you haven't had any luck finding the delivery service she used for the boys' presents?"

"None at all. I called all of them in Manhattan. I didn't have time to try more. I have work to do."

"Did John ever write her? Or vice versa?"

"I don't know. I never saw any letters, but then Mr. West wouldn't have wanted to dictate letters to his mother, would he?"

"Maybe not."

"I really must go back to work." Janice didn't appear to think they'd be great chums. In fact, she was torn between boredom and hostility. Sylvia let her go and tried to figure out if anything useful had been said.

Not that she could see. Except that Janice didn't seem like the type of woman who'd enjoy traveling around for two years. She didn't seem the type to enjoy enjoying.

Her musings were interrupted.

"Mrs. West, your secretary's on the line."

"Hi, Sylvia. Your mystery man wants to see you tonight."

"Where?"

"He wouldn't tell me. He just said you'd know the steakhouse and he would wait thirty minutes for you. Period." Bess sighed. "I wonder where he heard that women love masterful men."

"Do we?"

"I do. Of course, I love quiet men too. And mean men. And nice men. And short men. And..."

"See you."

Sylvia dashed out, remembering Rupert only after she'd stepped into the elevator. She called Bess from the lobby and instructed her to let Rupert know about the meeting.

Friedman had just sat down to eat when she arrived and was studying the menu as if his life depended on it. Not what you'd call a poor eater.

"How did your day go?"

He looked up as if he hadn't heard her join him. "Not bad. Yours?"

"You first. I'm not saying another goddamn thing until we get a little mutuality into this relationship."

"My contacts say that there's no evidence that before all this started your husband gambled, took dope, or ran with fast women."

"Terrific. You're way ahead of me. I could never have found that out without you."

"You were his wife, lady. Not an objective witness."

"Okay, okay. And what else did you find out?"

"First, I want to know about this burglar alarm system. Odd that it missed one window, isn't it?"

"I thought so."

"And odd that the so-called kidnappers found that very window."

"What are you getting at?"

Friedman didn't answer directly. "Did you give the security company instructions about that window?"

"Yes. I was tired of the boys and I didn't want to go through the paperwork involved in putting them up for adoption," Sylvia snapped. "How did you guess?"

This was getting them nowhere.

"Look, Friedman, let's not waste time attacking each other.

Tell me what else you found out," she repeated.

He either didn't know or wasn't saying.

Fine. She could play her cards close to her chest too.

They had a pained dinner. After a fast coffee, Friedman turned to her. "I'm going home tonight. I'll keep in touch."

"Are you going to go hog-wild and tell me where home is?"

"No." He said it flatly.

Sylvia got up. "Don't bother calling. I've had it with your mysterious presence. I'm going to find out what the truth is with or without your help, and frankly, I'd rather do it without."

She strode out, stopping at the door to speak to the maitre d'hotel who knew her. "Don't let the gentleman pay. I'll cover it, bill me."

"Yes, madame."

That would piss him off. The tiny guys couldn't stand women paying for them.

A familiar-looking man was standing across the road. As she got into her car, she thought for a moment that he was watching her but no doubt that was pure fantasy. She couldn't think who he was, but he was very attractive.

Sylvia sipped on a cup of tea, lounging on the chair beside the bed with her feet up on the rumpled blankets. John would have a fit if he saw the state of the house.

She had to stop thinking about that kind of "if." John wasn't here and he wasn't likely to return. She drank up, trying to pretend that the bedroom didn't feel empty.

A noise outside the house startled her. Without thinking, she was on her feet and at the window, peering cautiously between the curtains. Every muscle was taut; the fear she'd been pushing away the past few days was still close to the surface.

She tried to laugh at herself. It was time to stop acting like a nervous nellie and go to bed. The backyard was a favored playground for at least half of Long Island's substantial raccoon population and sometimes they were very rambunctious.

She started to drop the edge of the curtain. The movement of a shadow near the peach tree alerted her again. She strained at it and then hurried to extinguish the dim lamp she'd been drinking beside. She stayed at the window until she saw the shadow move out from the base of the tree toward the house.

It was far too large to be a raccoon, and anyway she was no wildlife expert but the raccoons she knew didn't walk on two legs. Sylvia gasped and ran to the front bedroom, intending to signal the patrol car.

The road was empty.

She forced herself to take a deep breath and think about the situation. The house was far too remote to expect help within a few minutes of calling for it. She was on her own.

She pounded back to her bedroom and threw on the clothes she'd just discarded. With her purse clutched to her chest, she slipped down the stairs to the front door.

She was about to open it when it occurred to her that she might be walking right into the arms of the prowler. She moved noiselessly into the kitchen from where she could survey most of the backyard. She cursed. In that part that was visible, she could detect no two-legged large shadow.

She had to gamble.

She closed her eyes for a moment, crossed her fingers, and returned to the front. The door opened almost silently. For once, Sylvia was grateful for John's attention to small details like oiling door hinges.

The street was black and still. Nothing appeared to be moving. And still no patrol car.

She had no choice. Sylvia sprinted as quietly as possible to the garage. The door was open since she'd stopped closing it the moment John had ceased to be around to complain. She dropped to her hands and knees and crawled to the car, slipping into it without slamming the door shut. The key went in as she prayed for it to start immediately. The motor turned over but didn't catch. She desperately pressed down twice on the accelerator and tried again. This time, the car started.

She shot out of the garage in reverse, turning on the lights only when she reached the road. As she backed out in a curve so that she could gun the car forward, the headlights caught a frozen figure on her lawn. It was the man she'd seen outside the restaurant this evening.

She now remembered where she'd first seen him. She'd been rapturously gazing at a Picasso oil at the time. It was Leland Sterne, von Schagg's assistant.

TWENTY

Sylvia told Dave only that the police cruiser hadn't been keeping watch so she'd decided against staying at the house. He called the station in fury. An apologetic officer explained that the two patrols who should have overlapped had made a mistake. It wouldn't happen again.

Sylvia nodded. "That's for damn sure because I'm not sleeping there until the dust has settled."

"Fine by me," Dave grinned. "This hotel is known for its service. Clean sheets, good breakfasts, and affectionate staff."

She smiled weakly. Sooner or later, she'd have to explain that while she liked him a lot, this relationship wasn't going to develop into anything more. On the other hand, she wouldn't feel safe at a hotel so this did not strike her as the opportune moment.

Bess wasn't at her desk when Sylvia arrived in the office. It was only eight-thirty but her secretary was an early riser and Sylvia could count on the fingers of one hand the number of times she'd beat Bess to work.

When Bess finally did turn up, she strode into Sylvia's office and startled her by throwing a newspaper down on the desk. "Get a load of this!"

It was a small daily from a Connecticut town. Bess had circled a letter to the editor which commented on a book entitled *The Conspiracy Among Us*.

"Where have I heard that title?" Sylvia frowned in an effort to remember.

"It's been in the news. The book's a piece of filth that drags up old slanders about the international Jewish conspiracy," Bess said bitterly. "It's based on *The Protocols of the Elders of Zion* which was a disgusting bit of hate literature that pretended to be the Jewish master plan for taking over the world.

It's been proved a fraud and a fake dozens of times but it keeps on popping up. The thesis of this rehash is that the plot has malevolently succeeded in Washington."

"Oh, I remember now. Some creep was using it as a text in a school, isn't that it? And then angry citizens got into the act?"

"Right. A lot of school boards and libraries won't even put it on the shelves."

The letter to the editor was from a Vernon Rogers and the gist of it was that the book was a fine piece of scholarly writing that explained brilliantly the dollar's decline, the increase in pornography, the malaise of the churches and, in general, every social evil short of tooth decay. He was careful, in his letter, not to identify the conspiracy but having whetted the readers' curiosity, Rogers included an address from which the book could be ordered.

Sylvia read in horrified silence.

"That's not the only letter of its type." Bess slammed her fist against the desk. "There's a flood of them, to almost every paper in the country. Not all editors are printing them, but those who don't get harassed by lots more mail along the same line."

"Can't somebody get an injunction or something?" Sylvia was vague out of necessity. She knew nothing about noncriminal remedies.

"Against who?" Bess laughed shortly and picked up the newspaper. "Well, I feel better just getting that off my chest. Back to business. Shall I show Mrs. Bailey in as soon as she gets here?"

"Yes, please. Say, did Rupert manage to put a tail on Friedman last night?"

"No, because I couldn't reach him."

Sylvia sagged in her chair dejectedly. She was making a hell of a detective. No clues at all and every opportunity to develop one was scrupulously avoided.

The two investigators from the Bar Association blew in at ten-thirty on a cloud of skepticism to hear Sylvia's surprise witness. Bess kept them waiting outside, enjoying to the full the thought of their discomfort when Mrs. Bailey walked in.

She didn't.

Sylvia saw Benjamin and Mansfield out and then took the next elevator down herself.

Mrs. Matulak's mood had changed. "She doesn't want to

see you," she announced harshly. "So don't bother coming around again. If you don't leave us alone, I'll call the cops."

Sylvia was learning. She accepted the dismissal with apparent grace and retreated down the street. She parked her car around the corner and waited.

Within half an hour, two dowdy women walked slowly by. Sylvia leaped out of her car and confronted them. Mrs. Matulak was indignant. With one arm around her sister, she berated Sylvia and repeated her threat of calling in the authorities.

Sylvia wasn't listening. She was taking a good look at Mrs. Bailey. She hadn't been a beauty the previous day but in retrospective comparison, she'd looked swell. The woman was wearing sunglasses but they failed to hide the bruised, swollen eyes, far less the puffy black-and-blue marks on the rest of her face.

"What happened?" Sylvia had the sinking feeling that she already knew.

"Don't talk to her, dearie," Mrs. Matulak advised her sister. "Now, get away from us. Right now!" Her voice was getting shrill.

"It's all right, Rose." Mrs. Bailey's subdued words were hard to hear. "It's all right."

"What happened?" Sylvia repeated.

"I . . . they . . ." Mrs. Bailey started to sob. She was hoarse from what had clearly been hours of sobbing.

"Take your time," Sylvia said softly. "Who hurt you?"

"The same people as will hurt you, if you don't watch out." Mrs. Bailey was hiccupping. "I can't talk to you. Please. Leave me alone or they'll come back."

"That's why you didn't come to my office this morning. I see. Well," Sylvia hardly knew what to say. "Well, how did they know you talked to me?"

"I saw Walter yesterday. I had to tell him I wasn't going to lie no more. I had to, he's my husband."

"Walter did this?"

"No! No, he never hurt me." The notion wasn't foreign to Mrs. Bailey, but she seemed sincere enough that this time her bruises couldn't be laid at his feet. "No, but he must've told them we weren't going to go through with it."

"I can arrange protection for you, Mrs. Bailey. I feel sick that I didn't think of it yesterday. We'll protect both you and your husband."

Mrs. Bailey began to laugh. It was partly hysterical and

partly sardonic. It was in no way humorous. "You'll protect us! You haven't any idea what these people are like! You don't know who you're dealing with! I don't know what they've got against you and I don't want to know, but if they want to get you, they'll get you. You can't protect us. You can't even protect yourself!" She was now alternately laughing and crying. "Please, please, just leave us alone! If you're smart you'll do whatever it is they want. Please go away! You don't know them."

Sylvia watched the two women make their sad way back to the little house. Mrs. Bailey was right, she didn't know much. But she knew one thing. That the woman had been genuinely terrified.

Fortunately, Sylvia knew the guard at the door of the jail. She had spent a good part of the past ten years going in and out of the premises and it didn't take much to get admitted. She asked to see Bailey, representing herself as his lawyer without actually saying so in as many words.

Bailey walked into the consulting room. He wasn't expecting to see his former counsel.

"Oh, my God! It's you!" He stood stock-still. "Get out, I've got nothing to say to you."

"I just saw your wife, Mr. Bailey, and if you want to make sure that she's never beaten again, you'll talk to me."

"Get out!"

"Not until you've answered some questions."

"Guard! Guard!" Bailey was shouting at the top of his voice. "Help! Guard!"

The uniformed man opened the door. "What's going on in here?"

"This woman isn't my lawyer. She used to be but she's a crook. I told the cops about her and now she's threatening me and my wife. Get me out of here!"

Sylvia watched the scene in horror. "Mr. Bailey, what are you saying?"

"Look, lady, I have to take him back to his cell, if that's what he wants." The guard didn't need to ascertain the truth. He didn't care, it wasn't his job. He nodded impersonally at Sylvia and led Bailey out.

Sylvia sat still for a few minutes, trying to figure out another way of getting to speak to Bailey. She came up with nothing. Except the certain knowledge that her problem had been compounded.

* * *

"Sylvia, you've got to do something! You could be disbarred!"

"I know, Bess." She grimaced. "I know. But do you have any suggestions?"

"Just one." Bess paused. "Do you have a funny feeling about the Bailey case?"

"You mean its timing?"

"Yes." Bess looked significantly at her friend. "I have the distinct feeling that the Bailey problem would vanish overnight if you shut up about John's disappearance."

"You might be right."

"Well?"

"Well what?"

"Sylvia, if you get disbarred, you might just as well shoot yourself! You love being a lawyer!"

"True. I also love being alive."

"So do it! Do whatever they want."

"Who's 'they'?"

"I don't know but it sure isn't worth finding out. Don't be a fool, Sylvia. There's no future in being brave," Bess pleaded.

All that was unarguably the case. The only difficulty was the niggling worry at the back of her mind. That they, whoever that was, weren't through with her and her children no matter what she did. That she'd gone too far to back down.

Sylvia smoked cigarette after cigarette and considered her options. She eventually reached a conclusion. She wouldn't give in to the blackmail. But she wouldn't continue to play the lone wolf. She stubbed out the butt and reached for a pad of paper.

She wrote for a long time. The result was a great deal more impressive than she'd expected, not that it amounted to a single provable piece of evidence.

"Bess, please make copies of this. I'm going to mail them right now."

"Sure, but what is it?" Bess looked at the pages in her hand.

"A summary of everything that's happened since John vamoosed. And it's also got all my suspicions, all the things that don't add up. I'm going to send it to a lot of important friends with a letter saying that if anything happens to me, anything at all, it should be opened and acted upon."

Bess lifted her eyebrows. "Is this really going to make a difference? No one's listening to your theories now."

"Aha, a vote of confidence. Maybe you're right, but whoever's behind all this has been going to a fair amount of trouble to shut me up. They can't want even the risk of influential people asking questions."

"Oh, terrific. That would be a big consolation to you up in The Big Courtroom in the Sky." Bess gave Sylvia a dirty look and left to do the Xeroxing. The effect of her dignified exit was somewhat marred when she stuck her head back in. "How many copies?"

"Uh, let's see. Margo, Rupert, Herb, Maggie Brewster at the *Times*. And, um, a couple of judges. Your choice, pick a few I've appeared before. You can mail them out right away."

Sylvia was on the telephone to a lawyer in the district attorney's office when Rupert called to invite her to a late lunch. She was delighted to have an excuse to cut her conversation short. It was doubly nice that the young attorney was wildly impressed that she knew the great Rupert Thompson.

Rupert was sitting at a table for three in Lutèce.

"Who's joining us?"

"Herb called as I was on my way out. He actually invited himself because I was selfishly looking forward to having you all to myself."

"Umm." Sylvia's life was already too complicated to pursue that topic. "How are you?"

"Fine. I got a message that Bess called last night. What was it about? I'm sorry I wasn't available but I just returned from Washington about two hours ago."

"You're entitled to your own life," Sylvia said generously. "Bess was calling to tell you that I had a meeting with Friedman. Remember, the—"

"Of course I remember! You didn't go without some protection? I warned you that he could be dangerous." Thompson was pale.

"I met him in a very public restaurant and I arrived and left on my own. I wasn't running any risks. I'd still love to find out who he is." Sylvia gave Rupert the bare bones of Friedman's explanation for his interest in John.

"Very credible," he snorted. "Is he still in town?"

"Not so far as I know. He said he was leaving and that he'd call. I don't think he's going to. Rupert, he's not a nut. I think he's genuinely interested in whether John is alive or dead."

"Maybe."

"Anyway, more dangerous things have been going on. No, hold on, Rupert. Not dangerous that way. Dangerous to my future at the bar."

Rupert was horrified at Bailey's allegations. "What can I do? Would you like me to call Simon Heller? He's on the discipline committee and I've worked with him a great deal."

"No. I don't think it would help. It would mean that he'd have to disqualify himself from adjudicating my case. It would be more useful if you appeared as a character witness for me at the hearing."

"Of course!" Rupert toyed with his fork. "Sylvia, excuse me for suggesting it, but have you considered getting out of detective work? I still think it's unlikely that everything's connected, but if you're right, your adversaries are pretty formidable."

"You sound like Bess."

"Bess sounds sensible. Why don't you—"

"Hi, Herb!" Sylvia was more than usually friendly.

Rupert subsided and the conversation became very general while they placed their orders.

"I heard about the trust fund, Sylvia." Herb believed in coming right to the point. "I've had as hard a time as you, accepting that John did all these things. I thought I knew him. Otherwise, I would hardly have recommended him for so many appointments. But the trust fund about tears it, doesn't it? I'm sorry."

Sylvia frowned. "Maybe."

"What maybe?"

"I've still got a few cards up my sleeves, boys, and I'm not going to shut up until they're played out."

"What cards?" Rupert was trying not to be condescending. He just couldn't understand how she could continue to ignore the mounting evidence in favor of the simple explanation.

"The hooker in the car with John. I've got someone who saw Cass being hired by a woman for what appears to have been her last date. My witness thinks she could recognize the woman. In fact, my witness is another one of the Times Square ladies and she was approached by this dame before Cass was. She was apparently not suitable, probably because she's an S&M specialist and badly scarred."

"Do you have a lead on the woman who hired Cass?" Herb asked.

"I don't want to say until I'm sure. I'll know tomorrow."

The paté arrived and for the rest of the meal, both Herb and Rupert tried to keep the conversation general and cheerful.

They left the restaurant, happily glutted. Dutton tactfully discovered a call he had to make that very moment, leaving Sylvia and Rupert alone.

"By the way, Sylvia, you asked me to make some inquiries about The Foundation."

"Yes, did you find something?"

"Not really. It is a charity, or at least it acts like one. It funds a few community groups, apparently specializing in youth groups. Educational programs, nature studies, that kind of thing. Pretty innocuous."

"Did you get the feeling it was also pretty secretive?"

"Yes. And that was the only odd thing I could find out about it. Otherwise, it's run of the mill."

"Keep on it?"

"Sure. If you think it might help." Rupert smiled at her with affection but she had no doubts about his skepticism.

The postman arrived at the office as Sylvia did. The mail was less than fascinating except for one piece.

"Hey, Bess! Get in here!"

"What is it? What's wrong?"

"I'm invited for dinner next Monday evening. With no less an eminence than Johann von Schagg! How about that?"

"Hey, hey, hey. You're turning into a regular femme fatale." Bess ran a finger down the heavy embossed notepaper. "Real class that one. It would be a shame if he turned out to be a villain."

Sylvia grinned. She hadn't had so many men around her since high school days. And then she'd had the distinction of being a cheerleader which everyone knew drove upper-classmen mad. She got up and peered into the mirror. She'd have trouble quavering a cheer nowadays. She had trouble putting on a credible makeup job.

The police were keeping her as informed as usual. She decided not to bother with the niceties and went straight to Lorimer himself.

"I've just received a report, Mrs. West. I'm surprised you haven't been notified." He paused, evidently unwilling to be the messenger under the circumstances. "The news isn't good."

"Please go on."

"Well, I'm afraid that we're at a dead end. The van that was apparently used by the men who broke in was found a few streets away from your house. It was stolen. A high school principal reported the theft earlier that same day and he's clean. Which was also the state of the van. No hairs, no prints, no papers. Nothing."

"Do your records show any similar MOs?"

"No pattern came up from the computer room. We have very little to go on. Because of the masks, all we know is their approximate heights and coloring. That simply isn't enough. And we went over your house with a fine tooth comb. They never took their gloves off. No prints there either."

"So now what?"

"Not a great deal. We've got feelers out. Our informants are asking around the streets to see if they can pick up anything, but these guys seem to be professionals. And professional kidnappers don't go around shooting their mouths off to stoolies."

Sylvia sighed.

"Sooner or later, Mrs. West, we'll come up with something. We always do."

"What about my husband's disappearance? This could be linked to it in some way."

"We considered that. I was informed that that was your belief. But since he's, uh, passed away, it isn't easy to see how. If you come up with anything concrete, I'll be more than happy to hear about it."

Sylvia didn't want to make another enemy on the force. She kept her voice pleasant. "One more thing. I understand that my husband withdrew over forty thousand dollars from his bank on a bank draft. I would like to know where the draft came from but my manager told me that he was specifically instructed by your men not to tell me."

"That's curious. He must have misunderstood. I'll get on that right away and find out for you," he promised. "I'm terribly sorry."

Terribly sorry about the dead end. Terribly sorry about John. Terribly sorry about Cameron. That and fifty cents would get her a cup of coffee.

She didn't want to hang around Times Square after dark. There would be time enough for that if she got disbarred. The light was already fading when she arrived but dusk did nothing to hide the dreariness of it. Business was brisk, the dinnertime trade apparently. Sylvia wondered how many steaks were being overcooked in suburban kitchens because the man of the house had missed his train.

Sweetie wasn't on her corner but presumably she did have some business from time to time. Sylvia walked around the square, browsing in the few reputable bookstores and politely refusing offers of gainful employment.

After an hour, she approached two of the women who worked near Sweetie. They recognized her name.

"Oh, yeah. Sweetie said you was lookin' for Cass."

There was no problem finding Cass but Sylvia didn't remind them. "I'm looking for Sweetie now. How long has she been gone?"

"Since this afternoon, honey. I was real busy so I didn't see her go." The speaker, a brassy redhead with incredible lungs, moved off to speak to a man.

Sylvia turned to the other woman. A more unlikely-looking hooker couldn't be imagined. This woman was puny, dowdy, and at least forty-five. She looked exactly like everyone's wife in the Bronx and her accent matched. She hadn't seen Sweetie since the afternoon either.

"She'll be back tonight. A rich broad, she ain't. Come back later."

"Can I leave a message with you for her?"

"Why not?"

Sylvia wrote down the address of John's firm on a piece of paper and handed it over. "Please ask her to meet me there tomorrow morning at ten. Oh, and I'll pay for her time, naturally."

"So she'll naturally be there," the woman mimicked.

Sylvia got into her car feeling very grubby. She'd worn the same clothes for two days now and she decided to go back to the house before going to Dave's. The prospect of all that driving was nauseating but then, so was the thought of putting on her present costume tomorrow morning.

Two miles from her house, she saw a car parked on the other side of the road. She slowed down when she noticed a figure standing beside the raised hood. It was a woman, waving her arms desperately.

Sylvia rolled down her window. "What is it?"

"Oh, thank God you stopped! Nobody uses this goddamned road and anyone who does won't stop! My stupid car won't start!"

"How long have you been standing here?"

"At least thirty minutes. I parked to take my jacket off and then my car died. And nobody stopped. I was so afraid I'd have to spend the night here!" She started to cry.

Sylvia pulled over. She couldn't leave a woman alone on a deserted road at this hour. Besides, she couldn't be more than eighteen.

Sylvia got out of her car and walked over to comfort the girl. A noise behind her made her stop in her tracks. Hands grabbed her shoulders, preventing her from turning around. She felt a sharp pain in her head and then felt nothing more.

She recovered consciousness to find herself lying uncomfortably on her stomach. She was aware of something digging into her diaphragm, making it hard to breathe. It was a few seconds before she oriented herself sufficiently to realize that she was lying on the floor of the back seat of a car. For a moment she was terrified that she'd been blinded because she could see only inky darkness. She twisted her head and became aware of a pressure around it. She was wearing a blindfold and her legs and arms were tightly bound.

"She's moving. Hello, you awake?"

Sylvia didn't answer the man's voice.

She was prodded and shoved as someone else got into the back seat.

"Are you conscious, Mrs. West?"

She stayed mute.

"We are friends. Don't worry, we won't hurt you. We had to knock you out and blindfold you for your own protection. It will be better for you if you don't know who we are. But I assure you, we won't hurt you."

The voice was low-pitched and soothing.

"Who the hell are you?" Sylvia found that anger chased fear away.

"I can't tell you that. We don't want you to be able to identify us. Please accept that these precautions are necessary."

Sylvia couldn't hold on to her anger. The smoothness of his voice terrified her. So might a spider sound, approaching the struggling insect in the middle of the sticky web.

"You've caused a great deal of trouble, Mrs. West. Ah now, don't do that." Sylvia had tried to kick him. He placed a heavy foot very firmly on her upper thighs. It hurt.

"You've caused a great deal of trouble."

"What do you want from me?" she gasped. It was getting

harder to breathe because his foot had moved up to press on her back.

"Please don't interrupt me, Mrs. West. I'm giving you a warning. You are going to get hurt if you don't stop asking questions about things that don't concern you. Already, several people are dead because you have stirred up so much trouble. There is much evil around you but you are not the person to handle it. Believe me, you haven't got a chance. Let those who are experienced in such matters take care of it."

"Who are you?"

"Don't interrupt, Mrs. West." His foot pushed her face to the floor. "I don't want to have to gag you. We are friends, giving you a friendly warning. You are in much danger and there is no point to it. You can't do any good, so leave the investigation to the professionals."

"Yes, sure, like the cops?" She tried to laugh contemptuously but succeeded only in moaning.

"Don't you worry about who. There are people who will take care of everything. You must go away and take care that nothing happens to you or your children. What would they do without you? What would you do without them?"

Sylvia was chilled right through. "Don't you threaten my boys! They aren't a danger to anyone. Leave them alone! Leave them alone, goddamn you!"

"I told you, we are your friends." The silken voice was imperturbable. "I'm telling you this because I don't want anything to happen to you."

"Why were my boys attacked? Why did you try to steal my children?"

"I personally have no interest in your boys." His tone was patient, dispassionate. He might have been speaking to a particularly slow child. "But if you want to protect them, you will stop asking questions."

"How do I know that someone won't try again to grab them? How do I know that?"

"You are not important to them. If you stop asking questions about your husband, they won't bother you."

"Who are 'they'?"

"Just listen to me. Don't trust anyone, including your friends. You have some dangerous friends. Say nothing more to anyone and go away with your children. Make it very clear that you have finished with this nonsense. Don't risk another attack on your family. The next one will be a great deal worse than the last."

The back door of the car was opened and the speaker started to leave. "Oh, one more thing, Mrs. West. Have you had any contact with politicians or diplomats? Have any approached you?"

A picture of the Syrian's black sedan flashed into her mind. "No, none at all. Why do you ask?"

"Mrs. West, I would like to be sure that nothing will happen to you," he repeated in his honeyed, persuasive tones. "Act wisely."

She was pulled out of the car and placed on a hard, bumpy surface. She heard the automobile pull away and felt the fumes from the exhaust on her face.

At first she lay very still, trying to calm the shaking and the tears that had appeared as soon as the sound of the engine had died away. It occurred to her that she might have been left in the middle of a road, just waiting for the next car to come by. In the dead of night, there was no way she'd be visible to a driver.

She wriggled her arms and legs, trying desperately to slip out of the ropes around her wrists and ankles. One of the arms came free. It took a few minutes to get her hand under control; the circulation had all but ceased. Eventually, she was able by using her free hand to undo the other binds and finally to remove the blindfold.

She was lying on the shoulder of the Long Island road she'd been driving on earlier. Her own car was neatly parked across from where she lay, apparently in good order.

Sylvia looked around her. It was very still and very black. Even the crickets were hushed. She had never felt so alone.

She started to run to her car, ignoring the tears and trembling that had come on again.

TWENTY-ONE

Dave greeted her at the door of his apartment.

"I thought you were going to bring some clothes with you?"

"I decided to get them in the morning." Sylvia had been warned twice now to trust no one. She couldn't help trusting Dave and relying on him to lessen her loneliness and fear, but since he was hamstrung by his orders to stay out of the case she might as well work on the need-to-know principle. It was rather melodramatic but it had been tested by the best people. Who was she to demur?

Dave took that to mean that she hadn't wanted to lose any part of their evening together.

The next morning, after going home and picking up fresh clothes, she drove directly to John's office. Bess called to tell her that Benjamin had been in touch.

The butterflies in Sylvia's stomach recommenced their passionately intricate dance. "What did he say?"

"The hearing's set for Wednesday and if you try to see either of the Baileys again, actually his word was 'intimidate,' he'll take you into custody."

"Swell," Sylvia said, hanging up.

By ten-thirty, Sweetie hadn't shown up. Which was just as well since Janice had called in with a sick headache. Sylvia paced up and down, finally stopping in front of Janice's desk.

It was spotlessly neat, everything in carefully marked boxes or file folders, making the search less than challenging. Sylvia didn't really expect to find anything interesting but to her surprise, Janice kept her personal papers in a file scrupulously flagged for the intruder.

Sylvia removed the whole file to the inner office.

Janice had been born in January 1940 to Marlene and Kurt Wagoner in Sydney, Australia. Her parents were apparently naturalized citizens of that country but the file didn't indicate their original home nor their year of immigration.

Janice had left Australia in 1965 and had arrived in the

States two years later. She became an American citizen in 1972. Oddly enough, she'd kept her old Australian passport. According to the official stamps, Janice hadn't traveled around a great deal in 1965 or 1966. There was a Swiss entry stamp for February 1965, and a final exit stamp from late 1966. In the interim, except for a Christmas trip in 1965 to Germany, France, and Belgium, Janice had apparently stayed put in Switzerland.

The personnel file that Stuart had shown her had included only one reference, from the now-dead Australian employer. There had been no indication that she'd worked during her two years in Switzerland. Sylvia had to assume that either Janice had saved a hell of a lot of money in Australia, because Switzerland was one of the most expensive places on earth, or she'd had a job she didn't want to talk about.

Well, for damn sure she hadn't been a kept woman during that period. Sylvia replaced the file. Her mother may have been right. Whatever Janice had been doing during those two years, she may have done it in Geneva. Two years was more than enough time to learn a city well and to meet people in it. Was it just a coincidence that John was Swiss? Or that his mother had ties to Geneva?

Sylvia looked at her watch. She didn't have time to pursue the thought. She had agreed to meet Dave for a late lunch.

It was a beautiful day. The sun was out and a mild breeze had brushed away the usually oppressive humidity. Large numbers of sun worshipers had taken to the streets to bake their skins and clean out their wallets. The boutiques and stores along Fifth Avenue were doing a land-office business. Despite the horrendous prices, most of the shoppers were laden with parcels. If there was any truth to the rumor that the country was in the midst of a recession, someone had neglected to inform the locals.

With the peculiar calendar of the fashion world, the stores were already having sales of summer clothing and a few windows were displaying winter gear. Sylvia stopped in front of one that beckoned with a tweed fall jacket surrounded by heathery sweaters and trim wool pants. The shop was very glamorous, flashing a sign on the inside of the glass that boasted "New York, Paris, Geneva." It would be nice to be able to walk right in and try on clothes. Unfortunately, only the stores for tall "girls" thought to order her size and they never ordered anything remotely resembling the chic styles in the window.

Dave was loitering outside the sandwich bar, unable to bring himself to leave the sunshine.

"Why don't we go for a walk instead?" Sylvia suggested, taking his arm. "What did you come up with?"

They strolled along the sidewalk, trying to avoid the crush of shopping enthusiasts who were waving their parcels around in a homicidal manner.

"Oh, the information on The Foundation is very skimpy. I asked around and nobody seemed to know anything about it. Even the government records are thin."

"I know that," Sylvia interrupted, "but have they ever been involved with the law?"

"I checked with the fraud squad. Oddly enough, they did get a complaint about The Foundation recently. It was checked out and apparently the company came up smelling like roses."

"What was the complaint?"

"I don't know yet. The officer who handled it was out of the office today. I should know tomorrow."

"And von Schagg?"

"Nothing concrete. He has no criminal record, not that you'd expect to find a criminal running a charity."

"Unless it's a phony charity. Besides, by the same token, you wouldn't expect the head of a charity to be chummy with a convicted felon."

"Yeah. Well, he's clean. At least in the States. He's been here for twelve years and—"

"Twelve?"

"Uh huh."

"Where did he come from? He testified that he left Europe after the war."

"I dunno. But he's only been here since 1967."

Immigration had been heavy in 1967.

"Sorry, go on, Dave."

"Well, von Schagg has been running The Foundation for a few years but it only started four or five years ago. Before that, he worked for another numbered company."

"What was that one? Let me guess."

"Right. Another charity of some kind. No one knew exactly why it folded, but it did. And then almost immediately, he was managing The Foundation."

"Did you look at the letters patent of the earlier company?"

"No. I don't have its number yet. But one of the boys I was talking to thought he remembered something about it. A complaint or scandal of some sort. I asked him to try to dig it up but our files aren't exactly the best once they're closed."

"I'll try to work on it too. What else do you know about our mystery man?"

"He's single, seems wealthy, and has no other job that we can see. He lives in a large and very posh apartment on Park Avenue no less, drives a big Mercedes. Not the cheap one, the thirty-eight-thousand-dollar number. But that's all we know. Now it's your turn."

"I didn't come up with much. Janice really is Australian, like she said. She became an American citizen in 1972. Oh, by the way, when did von Schagg take out his papers? They must have a file on him in the citizenship bureau."

"There's no record that he ever did."

Sylvia pondered that for a few minutes, while Dave watched the people relaxing in front of the Forty-second Street library steps. The small kids were playing their incomprehensible games near their basking parents, oblivious to the couples lounging nearby, playing at somewhat more sophisticated activities.

"Anything else on Janice, Sylvia?"

"Not really. Except that she spent two years, more or less, in Switzerland before coming here. Which happened," Sylvia paused significantly, "twelve years ago."

"Twelve? Well, I don't know if we can make a big deal out of it. I'm sure a lot of folks came here twelve years ago. Still, it is interesting."

Sylvia smiled. "Very interesting."

"Speaking of Switzerland," Dave continued.

"Yes?"

"The Foundation has other offices. In Europe."

Sylvia leaped up. "And I bet I know where one of them is! Dave, I have a feeling about this company. We've got to find out where it gets its money and where it spends it. What it really does, in other words. Which reminds me, what about John's bank draft? Where did it come from?"

"I hope you won't be too upset, Sylvia, but I couldn't find out. When I tried, some creep in Cameron's office got onto me. I, uh, kind of got called up on the carpet. One more interference and I'm on suspension."

Sylvia hid her disappointment. "Well, we'll have to make sure you don't mess with anything that's directly related to the disappearance."

She sighed. Now where could she get another inside man?

"How about a movie and dinner later?" Dave suggested.

"Sure. I'll meet you at your place."

Sylvia phoned Bess for her messages.

"Nothing important. Except that Herb Dutton called twice. He wants you to get back to him before four."

Sylvia called him.

"Are you free for dinner tomorrow night, Sylvia? My wife and I are having a few people over. Just very casual." Herb made his voice absolutely colorless. "Rupert will be coming. It seems he and his wife have separated so I guess he'll be coming alone."

Rupert obviously trusted Herb. Sylvia could see why. "Oh, I'd love to come. Thanks."

She walked along Forty-second Street to Broadway. Sweetie was still nowhere in sight but the Bronx beauty was flashing her wares.

"Could Sweetie have been around while you were, uh, absent?" Sylvia asked.

The woman snickered. "I wasn't absent for long, doll. I'm known as the Fifteen-second Finish. And I came out at eleven. She's turning into a regular lady of leisure."

Sylvia thanked her and walked slowly away with an uncomfortable feeling of déjà vu.

TWENTY-TWO

The house looked idyllic as they drove up in the morning, its walls caressed by the shadows of gently dancing trees, the gardens blooming yellow marigolds, red and purple petunias, white masses of impatiens.

Sylvia found herself loathing every inch.

"Do you want me to come inside with you?" Dave asked, eyeing a bright patch of sunlight covetously.

"No, thanks. Have a cigarette with the constable on patrol. He looks bored enough to scream."

Her footsteps echoed in the halls. Despite the light pouring in, the house seemed almost dank. Sylvia shivered. She would never be happy living here again. She hurried to her bedroom and started to throw a few things into a suitcase. She suddenly whirled around. No one was in the room, but she had the distinct feeling of being watched.

"Dave? Are you there?"

There was no answer. Sylvia pulled out her one black dress, telling herself that it was ten o'clock in the morning and that two strong cops were sitting just outside on the lawn. The feeling of not being alone persisted.

To hell with this. She could buy more clothes if she needed them. Jamming a few last items into the suitcase, she stomped downstairs, stopping only to grab the last few days' mail.

The sun caught her at the front door. She closed it firmly behind her and relaxed in the warmth.

"Ready?" Dave was surprised. "That was fast."

"Let's go." Sylvia nodded to the patrol and started to the car. "Just a minute, Dave. I feel dumb but I'd like you two guys to come with me."

They obediently trooped after her into the house.

"Please search this place."

"Sure, Sylvia, but would you like to tell us what we're looking for?" Dave was bewildered.

Sylvia tried to think of a good answer. There wasn't one. She plunged ahead with the truth. "I had a weird feeling that someone else was in the house with me."

The two whipped out their guns and motioned her to stand well behind them. They used the best police procedures, crashing through doorways and canvassing cupboards with outstretched guns. It looked foolish, and by the end they appeared to feel foolish. Which was nothing to the way Sylvia felt.

"All clear," Dave reported unnecessarily.

"Oh, good." Sylvia nodded sheepishly, avoiding his eye. "Thanks."

Sylvia was unusually quiet on the drive back to the city. Dave tactfully left her alone, attributing it to Ingrid's funeral which was to be held that afternoon.

He came into the bedroom as she was changing.

"I just got some dope over the phone on that company that von Schagg used to run. Apparently there was a complaint made to us at about the time it folded up and crept away. We've got a card on it but no file. We lose half our files in Archives," he added, shaking his head.

"What was the scandal that finished it off?"

"All I've got is what was on the card and what Jake remembers."

"Who?"

"Oh, sorry. Jake Neszinsky. He worked on the case. The company's number was 271-160 and it carried on business as the Guardian Society, whatever that means. Its head office was the same as The Foundation's. You might also be interested in the fact that Jake remembers them having another office. In Switzerland."

"Swell. But what about the scandal?"

"You're going to have to get the details elsewhere. All Jake recalls is that there was some sort of brouhaha at a meeting of the Society. Some of its employees assaulted members of the public. Jake is almost positive that it was a private company so I'm not clear why it had a public meeting."

"That's why it was closed down?"

"We didn't close it. We didn't find anything to go on. Jake said that the file was closed within a matter of days as not being a criminal case. Maybe it was just a coincidence. Or maybe its donors didn't want to contribute to a charity that got into trouble. I don't know. Anyway, it all happened in the spring of 1974."

"Do you have the date?"

"No. I might add that Jake wasn't wild about your pal, von Schagg."

Sylvia resolutely ignored the last comment. "Okay, I should be able to dig up more. What about the complaint against The Foundation?"

"I haven't seen the file yet. They're still digging for it. It's something about an old lady who's screaming that her husband was cheated into bequeathing it money. She's saying that it isn't a real charity. The informed opinion is that it's just another ugly fight over a will."

"When you get the details, let me know. I'm in the market for information that proves The Foundation's a phony."

The funeral was extremely depressing. All Ingrid had to show for her fifty years was a tepid eulogy from a bored minister who had never met her and didn't care and a handful of mourners who were outnumbered by the undertaker's staff.

Sylvia and Bess retired to the office afterwards. They helped themselves liberally to the stock in the boardroom's bar. Sylvia drank down hers and called Maggie Brewster at the *Times*.

"Maggie, Sylvia West here."

"Oh, hello. How are you doing? Back to your regular life, I hope."

"Well, the case isn't closed yet."

"Really?" Sylvia could almost hear the notebook being whipped out.

"I could use some information from you. Information that might be in a newspaper morgue."

"What is it?"

"I wonder if maybe you could come to my office. I don't want to talk over the phone and I think it would be only fair to give you some background. Off the record for the moment."

"Of course. I'll be right there." Maggie was clearly interested in a potential story, particularly if she could get in on the ground floor.

She was as good as her word. Sylvia poured another Scotch and the three women settled down conveniently close to the bottle.

Sylvia gave Maggie a carefully edited summary of the facts, suggesting that this was only one of a number of clients she was investigating to see if any bore animus for John.

"It's a long shot, of course," she concluded, "but I want to know what the scandal was that finished off the Guardian Society. Maybe, just maybe, it has some sort of bearing on the things that have been happening."

"Sure, glad to poke around," Maggie said enthusiastically.

"One more thing, Maggie. You're going to get a rather strange letter from me. I'm surprised it hasn't already arrived. It's basically a summary of what I've just told you. In my covering letter, I ask that you don't read it or act upon it unless something, uh, sort of happens to me. So keep all this under your hat, will you?"

Maggie shot her a probing look. "I don't get it, but okay. Speak to you soon."

Sylvia and Bess left the building a few minutes later.

"Can I drop you off, Bess?"

"Nope, I'm going shopping."

Sylvia was looking forward to a perfectly quiet, even dull hour or two. She let herself in with Dave's key and found him glued to the television.

"What is—"

"Shh!" Dave pointed to the screen.

Sylvia poured herself a drink and listened with a growing sense of disbelief to an announcer telling her that terrorists had struck a couple of hours ago at Kennedy Airport. Two El Al clerks had been killed and seven bystanders wounded, three critically, when a bomb in a suitcase meant for an El Al flight went off prematurely.

"Habash is taking credit for this, if you can believe it," Dave told her without removing his eyes from the set.

"Credit!" Sylvia laughed rudely. "Incompetent in the first place, thank God, and unbelievably barbaric in the second. Credit!"

"All four terrorists have been killed in today's cross fire at Kennedy Airport," the announcer intoned, "and we have just learned that one of the wounded bystanders has died. That brings the death toll to seven."

The cameras panned to the numb faces in the crowd standing around the devastated baggage room. The announcer's voice cut through the tumult, repeating the few facts that were known.

Sylvia noticed that her hands were shaking. She put the drink down. Dave was white-faced with fury. "Those bloody bastards!"

The camera was now showing snapshots of the terrorists, presumably from C.I.A. files. Sylvia and Dave gazed silently upon the very ordinary-looking visages that had brought so much grief to the country.

"Oh, my God!" Sylvia pointed to the screen. "Did you see that one?"

"Yes, what about it?"

"I've seen that man. The one with the missing earlobe!" Sylvia gasped. "When I was leaving von Schagg's office, a group of men, Arabs, were approaching the elevator. He was one of them!"

"Are you sure, Sylvia? All of them look pretty much alike to me, small, swarthy. You know how frail identification evidence is. How can you be certain?"

As she thought about it, she became less and less sure. They did all bear a great resemblance to each other and missing earlobes weren't all that uncommon. When she tried to recreate the face of the man she'd seen behind von Schagg's building, she found that she really had only a vague impression of him.

"I guess I'm not positive. But for a moment there . . . well, I thought it was him. But now . . ."

"NBC brings you an on-the-spot interview with Davidson Raleigh from the Secretary of State's office."

The camera faded and another picture replaced it. A very serious reporter was talking to a bland-faced man in horn-rimmed glasses and a slightly baggy gray wool suit.

"Mr. Raleigh, terrorism has usually been something that hit other countries. Now that it's coming here, to American soil, what can the American government do to protect ordinary people?"

Raleigh mouthed platitudes about better security, stricter immigration controls, tighter gun laws. He ended with an almost frantic reassurance that the government hadn't been caught napping but in fact was in the middle of working out strong counter-measures to terrorism.

"I understand, sir, that an international anti-terrorist conference is soon to be held somewhere in Europe and that the United States will be attending. Can you comment on this?"

"Oh, well, several suggestions for this kind of conference have been made in recent years. Naturally, if one does get off the ground, we'd participate."

"It is not true then that there are plans for an imminent conference on this topic?"

"As I said before, there has been a lot of discussion about it and I'm not free to say any more."

"Mr. Raleigh, surely there are no security reasons that would prevent us from talking about this kind of conference on a theoretical level?"

"All I can say is that, obviously, if anything was to develop along the lines of such a conference, the security surrounding it would have to be the tightest ever known."

"To protect the conference from terrorist attacks, I presume."

Raleigh was sweating only slightly under the hot lights. His urbanity and bureaucratese were more than up to this reporter. "That, and another consideration. The participants would have to inform each other of their present security arrangements. That information is, of course, highly classified, as any agreement worked out would be."

The camera returned to the anchorman at Kennedy Airport. "That was Davidson Raleigh at the Secretary of State's office. And—"

Another reporter's voice came over the air. "Larry, before we return to the site of today's tragedy, I'd like to add that the problem of terrorism has been concerning our government for a while now. The White House, for example, has in its hands a major, hush-hush paper on the topic developed by the Wandling Institute."

Larry thanked him and returned to the blood and guts at the airport. Sylvia and Dave stayed in front of the television, unable to turn if off in case further information came to light.

The phone rang. Dave reluctantly answered it.

"Sylvia, it's for you. Bess."

"Hi, Bess. Have you heard?"

"Yes, I'm watching now. Listen, the reason I'm calling is that Herb Dutton phoned me. He couldn't get hold of you so he figured I'd know how to reach you. He has to cancel the dinner party tonight. His wife isn't feeling well."

"Thanks. It wouldn't have been very lively anyway, not after this. Are you alone?" Sylvia was recalling how deeply upset Bess had been, watching the last terrorist strike at De Gaulle Airport.

"Yes, but I'm fine. Really. If I wasn't, I'd tell you."

Dave was very pleased to hear that Sylvia was now free for the evening. He proposed a toast. "To Mrs. Dutton. May her frail health get no worse. And no better."

Sylvia laughed. At the back of her mind was a strong suspicion that if today's incident hadn't occurred, Pat Dutton would be as healthy as a horse.

TWENTY-THREE

The Wandling Institute was as frenetic on Sunday afternoon as it had been the evening Sylvia first visited it. It took quite a while to get clearance because Rupert hadn't known she was coming and so hadn't been able to smooth her path.

"Sylvia! What a nice surprise!" Rupert took both her hands in his as she stepped into his office. "Come in. I was just talking to Lorne."

She greeted the second man and turned back to Rupert. "Am I interrupting anything? If so, I'll say a quick hello and good-bye."

"Not at all. We were just discussing yesterday's event."

"I couldn't believe it," Sylvia sighed, shaking her head. "I guess I'm like most Americans. Terrorism is something that happens in the rest of the world."

"Not anymore," Rupert commented drily. "We better get off our butts and step up our counter-terrorist planning."

"It's time for us to start showing the way," Lorne added.

Sylvia didn't point out that the rest of the world probably didn't share the American egocentric view that until the United States took over the reins of leadership, all that could be expected was bungled and inexpert fumbling.

"There was talk on the television about an international conference," she mentioned. "Is there going to be one?"

"Let's just say that the western democracies have been developing plans of attack for some time. So it is only to be expected that they will, in some fashion, communicate their ideas to each other."

Sylvia closed her eyes briefly. Lorne was fitting right into the White House. When she opened them, Rupert was watching her with an amused expression.

"Anyway, Rupert," Lorne concluded, "I've got to get going. I've got a meeting tonight in Washington and there's a lot of preparation still to be done."

They both looked duly impressed and waved him off.

Sylvia turned to Rupert. "Does high office have that effect invariably?"

He laughed. "Oh, the pompousness will wear off. He'll soon find out how little he knows and how much work there is to do. It takes many new men that way at first."

Thompson called his secretary and told her not to put any but the most important calls through. "Now, Sylvia. I received a letter from you. I was kind of puzzled by it."

She felt very foolish. "Uh, well, I wanted protection and I figured that the only way I could get it was to make my death undesirable to them."

"Who's them?" Rupert asked.

"I don't know. That's the problem." Sylvia resolutely kept going. "I sent out summaries of my suspicions to several people. Friends who carry a fair amount of weight. That way, I can't just disappear the way John did."

"You're still sure that John didn't run away?"

"No, I'm not sure. But I don't believe in coincidences and there have been too many strange things happening since he left. Or was taken," Sylvia added simply.

"Shouldn't you try to protect yourself in a more concrete way?" Thompson came over to sit beside her. "If you're in danger, you should get out of town. Until the heat dies down. I'd hate to think, well, what I mean to say is that if anything happened to you . . ."

Sylvia leaped in. "I appreciate your concern. Really I do. You and Bess are on the same wavelength. You're great friends, but I can't do it that way." She was terrified that he was going to make some sort of emotional declaration.

Thompson sat back and watched her. His eyes were understanding. "Relax, Sylvia. I'm not going to push you into anything."

Sylvia lit a cigarette to cover her discomfiture and carried on. "I've written an update to my summary. I'm going to send it out too. And from time to time, I'll send out new bulletins. But what I said in the letter goes for all of them. I don't want you to read them unless, well, you know."

"Okay. You're the boss. Who else have you sent it to?"

"Lawyers and reporters, mostly. I wanted to arouse the curiosity of the most tough-minded people I know."

"Like your friend, what's her name, at the . . . oh, hell." The buzzer on the intercom was going.

Rupert answered it. "Yes? Oh, I suppose so. Excuse me a

minute, Sylvia." He picked up the receiver. "Hello. Uh huh. Oh, Jesus!"

Sylvia watched him for a few minutes. It was clear that this was an important call and one that would last awhile. She stood up and motioned that she had to leave.

"Just a second, please." Rupert covered the mouthpiece. "Don't go. I'll be a few minutes more, but I want to talk to you."

"No, no. I've got a few things to do anyway," Sylvia insisted. She'd intended to ask for help in investigating Guardian Society but Rupert's obvious involvement with her meant that he'd give her concerns priority over his own. And he was just too harassed right now. She couldn't bring herself to add to his burdens.

She walked back to her car, thinking about Dave and Rupert. It never rained but it poured. She was enjoying her relationship with Dave; she needed it. It wasn't only a matter of a good time. She cared about him and his stability was important in her otherwise shifting life. But it was becoming evident that Dave had started to get deeply involved with her, more than either of them had anticipated. She wasn't in love with him nor was she likely to be. It wasn't the right time and he wasn't the right man, but at the moment his companionship was exactly what she desperately needed. The future would have to take care of itself.

Dave took her to a movie near Times Square. They checked Sweetie's corner both before and after the flick but she wasn't around. According to her neighbor on the track, she hadn't been seen since Thursday.

"Do you want me to report it to Missing Persons?" Dave could see that Sylvia was worried. "You know it's not unusual for the women to disappear from time to time. There could be a lot of reasons."

"There could be," Sylvia agreed. But in this case, she had a feeling that there weren't. "Yes, make out a report. Not that it will do the slightest good. If they didn't care about John, they're not likely to break their backs over Sweetie."

Bess called during breakfast. "You'd better come into the office right away. There's been some trouble."

"What kind of trouble?"

"A break-in. The place is a disaster zone!"

"I'll be right there."

Sylvia had to push her way through the milling crowd of secretaries and policemen. "I'm Sylvia West, one of the partners. What's going on?"

"Sylvia! I'm glad you're here." Gerry Oxley grabbed her arm and led her into his office.

"Hi, guys." Sylvia nodded to the four men already seated. None of her partners responded effusively. "What the hell happened?"

All heads swiveled to the senior partner, George Brogan. He gazed out the window as he spoke. "We had a break-in sometime over the weekend. The police can't say exactly when. The files are all over the place, both in our offices and in the storage room. I've never seen anything like it for wanton destruction."

"It had to have occurred later than Saturday afternoon. I was here and nothing was disturbed," Sylvia commented. "What's missing?"

"Who can tell?" Gerry spluttered. "A herd of stenos couldn't find a single goddamn thing out there!"

"Why would anyone want to take our office apart?" Sylvia mused.

"That's a good question. None of us does anything the slightest bit controversial. No one could possibly be interested in our files," George pontificated.

Sylvia had to admit that that was the God's truth. Not one of her partners did exciting work. Real estate and incorporations seldom aroused frenzied passion.

"Then what . . . ?" Sylvia stopped. "Oh, I see." She looked at the impassive faces. "It's my clients who do this kind of thing."

She paced the office, pondering the possibility. She shook her head. "I don't think so. In the first place, I'm on their side. They don't attack their lawyers. And anyway, the files belong to the clients. They could simply have asked for them." She sat down again. "No, that's not the answer."

The faces hadn't cheered up. Her partners were definitely avoiding her gaze. "Besides, if it was one of my clients, why would he go to the trouble of messing up your files too?"

There was still no response.

It slowly dawned on her that the break-in was being laid at her door because it was an odd thing and odd things had been happening to her lately. Moreover, odd things didn't come into the lives of reputable lawyers, ergo . . .

She started to protest but caught herself. What could she say to convince them that it had nothing to do with her? What could she say to convince herself?

She muttered something noncommittal and wandered out to survey the damage. It was mind-blowing. Files, papers, torn pages from books lay everywhere. It would take at least a month to get the office back into shape.

Bess was roaming the halls aimlessly with the other secretaries. She came over as soon as she saw Sylvia. "This is incredible! It looks like someone wanted very badly to either see something or destroy it. It's too bad he didn't understand our filing system so he wouldn't have had to total the place."

It did seem that the search-and-destroy squad hadn't known where to check first. Or else had wanted to leave that impression.

"I'm getting nailed with this, Bess. You should see the gloom in the partnership meeting."

"How can it be your fault? Every office was invaded." Bess suddenly stiffened. "Unless this was all a cover. I haven't been inside your office yet, the cops insisted I wait for you."

She hurried into Sylvia's office and started to laugh. Sylvia joined in after a stunned moment. They would never know if anything was gone. It looked as though every paper in the place had been through a shredder. There wasn't enough Scotch tape in the world to remedy matters.

The phone rang. Bess picked it up. "It's Margo," she whispered, holding the receiver to her chest. "Do you want me to tell her you'll call back?"

"No. I'll take it. I've got nothing else to do. Hi, Margo."

"Hello. I've seen the file." When Sylvia didn't respond instantly, the other lawyer paused. "Is anything wrong?"

"The firm was broken into over the weekend and my own office is unbelievable. Everything's completely ruined."

"It was a busy couple of days for the criminal element." Margo was bemused. "We had one too."

"You're kidding!"

"No, someone came in and threw all the files around. Nothing's ruined though. It's just a mess."

"Is anything missing?"

"We won't know that for a couple of weeks at the very least."

"Did you get a letter from me? Is it there?"

Margo didn't answer for a few moments. When she did,

her voice had lost its warmth. "It's at home." She came abruptly to the point as though she couldn't wait to get off the phone and out of Sylvia's life. "All the papers in the immigration file are in order."

"I see. Well, I sort of expected that."

"And there's no record of living relatives. So there are no addresses."

"You mean, except for his mother."

"No. No relatives listed as living. Period."

"That's odd. Did the form ask what had happened to his family?"

"Yes. He wrote down that they were all dead of natural causes."

"All dead?" Sylvia was nonplussed. "Uh, did he give a previous address in Europe?"

Margo was silent. Sylvia kept quiet too, pleading under her breath with Margo to break a rule, just this once.

"2034 Rue des Ormes."

Sylvia hazarded a guess. "Geneva?"

"Yes."

"Thank you. Thank you very much. Anything I can do . . ."
Margo interrupted her to ring off precipitously.

Minus one friend. Sylvia felt sick but there was no time to think about Margo now. When this was over, she'd gather up her losses and mourn them together.

Janice was at her desk.

"I'm glad to see your headache's better," Sylvia said pleasantly.

"I find that if I'm not here, things don't stay in order," she answered coolly.

Did that refer to the search of her desk? But how could she know? Sylvia decided that guilt was making her overly sensitive.

Dave might have the name of the woman who was complaining about The Foundation. Sylvia started to dial his number and then remembered that he'd been bitching over breakfast that he had to go to court today. She replaced the receiver.

The light on the telephone console remained on for a moment.

Sylvia stared at it thoughtfully. This was no place from which to base her detective work.

Sylvia sent Janice over to the courthouse for some bulletins on courtroom procedure that she already had. It sounded simple enough, but the bulletins came from the most notoriously inefficient desk in the city. If the assignment didn't keep Janice away for ages, she was brilliant.

The storeroom that housed the old dead files was filthy. Sylvia rolled up her sleeves and plunged in. The card index showed that there had been a file opened in the name of Guardian Society. John had apparently acted for it since 1955, just after he'd joined the firm as an associate. The file had gone inactive in 1974. She took down the number of the folder and crawled around on her hands and knees.

"A16-456 . . . A16-458." It was missing. There wasn't even a gap to indicate that it had ever sat on the shelf. Sylvia canvassed the nearby rows but came up empty-handed. She noticed only one disturbing thing. The files in and around the relevant shelves were clean. Well, not clean, but much cleaner than the more recent racks.

She left the storeroom, thinking about the conclusions she could jump to.

Sylvia hurriedly cleaned herself up and made Xeroxed copies of all the documents in The Foundation's file. When Janice returned, she was back in John's office sitting demurely in front of a stack of innocuous documents.

The secretary slapped the sheaf of papers on the desk with ill-disguised bad temper. "I hope these are what you wanted." She obviously hoped nothing of the kind. "Your instructions weren't clear and the clerk couldn't figure them out."

"Yes, these look right," Sylvia answered innocently. "Thank you. I'm going back to my office now. By the way, do you have a list of the delivery services you called when you were helping me look for my mother-in-law's address?"

"No. I simply ran down the names in the yellow pages. It was a waste of time," Janice added sourly.

Which was no surprise. Perhaps Bess would have better luck.

She dragged the suitcase crammed with Xeroxed pages into her wreck of an office and cleared a space for herself by shoving the newly made streamers into a corner. She dialed Glenn McEwan's contact in the company's office. "Sylvia West here. I've got another company I'd like to check out."

"Oh, yes. Is it a numbered one too?"

What a memory. "Yes. Number 271-160."

The woman put her on hold. Five minutes later, Sylvia was still holding.

"Mrs. West? I'm sorry to keep you waiting but the darn file isn't where it should be. I'll have to put a search on it. Can I get back to you?"

"Of course." Call her a cynic, but she'd bet that the file wouldn't turn up until hell froze over. "Before I let you go, does the number itself tell you anything?"

"Not really. The companies are numbered consecutively, give or take a few errors. The only thing I can say is that it was incorporated a long time ago. Probably in the forties. Sorry."

She'd have to work with what she had. She lined up a few more calls. Two of The Foundation's directors were easily found. Castle owned a couple of businesses, including one with the nauseating name Ye Flower Bower. Rogers was a sales manager for the Federal Associated Insurance Group. She arranged appointments with both by asking about flower arrangements and life insurance respectively, playing the demanding rich bitch who insisted on seeing only the top men.

The third director was named Kellermann. According to the original application for incorporation, he'd been a schoolteacher but his former employers said he'd quit and dropped from sight. The present owners of what had been his house had no idea of his whereabouts. For all anybody knew, he wasn't even alive.

Chief Lorimer wasn't in his office.

"He'll call you back the moment he arrives," the breathless assistant assured her.

Bess popped in. "I'm going to do the banking. Do you want me to cash a check for you?"

"Yes. No, on second thought, I'll do the banking today. I want to make another stab at getting some information."

She was waiting for a teller when Whitehead went by. He tried not to notice her but wasn't successful.

"Ah, Mrs. West. Um. Yes. Actually, if you have a moment when you're through here, I'd like to speak with you."

Sylvia instantly abandoned her post. "I'm free now."

He managed to control his enthusiasm and led her into his office. "Er. Uh. Actually, I wanted to talk to you about your line of credit."

"Yes? What is it?"

"You're a little overdrawn right now."

"Yes." Sylvia couldn't figure out what he was getting at. Her credit rating had always been excellent. Over the years, she had developed a mutually agreeable arrangement with the bank. Her income was substantial but cash flow, from time to time, could be a problem. Particularly these days. Since she'd been doing little work, Sylvia had tried to pull very little out of the firm. "The money's available, as always, Mr. White-head."

"Um. Uh. Well, when will you pay the bank back?"

"I beg your pardon?"

"When will you reimburse us for the money we're lending you?"

"I don't understand. There has never been any difficulty about money before. I haven't had a single problem in ten years with you."

"You've never been in trouble with the Bar Association." Mr. Whitehead delivered his line in a single agonized gasp.

"I see. You had a visit from Mr. Benjamin, did you?"

"This morning."

"Well, you don't have to worry about the money. Nor about the Bar Association. That will all be cleared up."

"Perhaps. I mean, I hope so." Mr. Whitehead was very pale. "But I can't authorize a line of credit to you under the circumstances. How would I justify it to Head Office? What with this investigation going on, I just can't allow it," he bleated.

"You'll get your money tomorrow morning. And that will be the end of my dealings with this bank."

Whitehead was tickled pink about the promise of repayment. His elation wasn't the slightest bit tempered by the other announcement.

For this she had given up her place in line?

Sylvia returned to her vigil, mentally computing her financial position. What with John's defection, not to mention his theft which she felt she ought to repay, she'd better start earning again. Very soon.

"Hi, Mrs. West." The pretty young teller had often served Sylvia in the past.

"Hello, Mary. How are you today?"

"Fine." Mary flicked through the deposit book in record time.

Sylvia gazed at her thoughtfully. "Oh, Mary, I suppose you heard about my husband?"

"Yes. I'm terribly sorry. What a terrible tragedy."

"Yes. Before he, uh, passed away, a bank draft went through his account. I'm trying to balance the books for the estate and I think there may have been an error in your records. Could you get me the exact amount of the draft?"

"Oh, sure." Mary bounced off, eager to help one of her favorite customers. She returned to her station in a couple of minutes.

"Exactly forty-two thousand dollars." She held out a debit memo for Sylvia's scrutiny.

"Thank you. It must be my error." Sylvia smiled sheepishly and moved off. The draft had come from the Paris branch of the First Chicago Bank.

Bess was cradling the phone as she typed. "Oh, wait a minute. She just walked in. Sylvia, it's Dave."

"Are we on for dinner tonight, gorgeous?"

"No, I'm afraid not. I see von Schagg tonight."

"Where are you going?"

"I'm meeting him at his office. I don't know where he's taking me to eat."

"I hate to lose an evening with you because of that crook," Dave complained bitterly.

"It is a shame," Sylvia commented tactfully. Dave would like it a whole lot less if he knew how good-looking von Schagg was. Or how suspicious a character. She had to be very firm before Dave would drop the subject.

"Have you found out anything more on the charities?"

"Oh, yes." He was proud of himself. "The old lady who's bitching is named Laura Wilkinson. She lives out on Long Island in a big old house that they used to show on house tours as the best of the Victorian worst. It's apparently a real monstrosity, covered in turrets and heavy carved gargoyles. Anyway, according to my source, her old man made a fortune out of scrap metal during the war and willed most of it to The Foundation. She's screaming that she's going to sue the world. She was left a comfortable cushion of cash, so God only knows why she cares so much. Just loves the green stuff, I guess. Anyway, it isn't the sort of thing the department gets involved in. If you want to see her, no one is going to get hot about it."

"I certainly do. In fact, I'll probably go there first thing tomorrow. Give me the address."

Bess was standing in the doorway pointing to her watch.

"Oh, yes. I've got to run, Dave."

She went to the mirror to brush her hair and apply a touch of lipstick. She felt like the room looked. She was almost out the door when the phone rang again. It was Lorimer.

"Thanks for returning my call. This is what I call service." Sylvia was about to add that she'd found out about the draft all by herself when he forestalled her.

"That bank draft your husband sent? It came from a small bank in Chicago. I haven't got the name yet."

Sylvia was speechless. That bastard Cameron was even lying to his superior. Unless Lorimer had made a mistake. She didn't have time to get into it now and it would be wise to think out her response before hurling accusations around. "Er, thanks very much. I'm in a bit of a hurry at the moment."

"Sure thing. I'll keep you informed."

TWENTY-FOUR

Sylvia walked out of the elevator into Sterne's arms. She tried to control her instinctive flinch, hiding behind the polite platitudes that covered a variety of social sins.

"Good afternoon, Mrs. West." He at least was perfectly self-assured and unembarrassed. "Please come this way. Mr. von Schagg is waiting for you in his office."

Von Schagg stood up at his desk. "How nice to see you again! Thank you, Leland," he added, dismissing the younger man as cavalierly as ever.

Sylvia accepted a glass of sherry and wandered around the room. As they had the last time she'd been in the office, they spent some time talking about his objets d'art. Finally, Sylvia put her glass down and turned to her host.

"I don't want to seem rude, but I haven't eaten lunch today and I'm starving."

He laughed. "I like people who speak their minds. I'm hungry too. Let's go."

The huge silver-gray Mercedes was soporifically luxurious. He drove very fast and well to a Spanish restaurant called Fernando's in the Village. The captain obviously knew von Schagg and showed them to the best table in a secluded alcove overlooking a charming formal garden in the back. The room was decorated in heavy Spanish furniture, complete with leather-covered high-backed chairs and pictures of famous matadors.

It was not Sylvia's sort of decor but she could overlook it because of the heavenly garlic perfume wafting out from the kitchen. No one would want to spend time with her tomorrow.

Von Schagg was his charming self over the drinks and hors d'oeuvres. He seemed to have nothing on his mind but dinner with a woman he considered lovely and desirable. Sylvia found herself responding to his old world charm, just as thirteen years ago she'd responded to John's. But this time she was conscious of the effort and technique. And technical it was. About as

192

natural as the color on her cheeks. She might be just the thing for Dave and even Rupert, but she had no illusions about a man like this. His companion of choice would undoubtedly be at least ten years younger and considerably dumber. As John's choice had been a long time ago.

Von Schagg stood up as the waiter brought the gazpacho. "Please excuse me for a minute," he apologized. "I'm very rude, I know, but I must make an important call."

"Quite all right," Sylvia assured him.

He returned in short order, looking a bit grim.

"Not bad news, I hope?" she probed.

"Not really." With a smile, the call was forgotten and he devoted himself to her again. It seemed churlish to interrupt such a performance with suspicious questions. Finally, as dessert was being served, von Schagg himself interrupted the small talk.

"My young associate saw you downtown the other evening."

Sylvia gave herself time to control her reaction by lighting a cigarette. "Yes, I thought I recognized him."

"Leland tells me it's a very good steakhouse."

"Yes, I like it. Have you never been there?"

"Not yet, but I intend to try it now." And then casually, "Leland thought he recognized your dinner companion."

Who hadn't entered or left the restaurant with her. "Oh, isn't it a small world?" Sylvia commented fatuously.

"I suppose you were working on a criminal case?"

"In a manner of speaking."

"Do you do much out-of-town work?"

"Not much."

He wasn't getting discouraged by her monosyllabic answers but he sure was blowing his cover.

Sylvia decided to take the offensive. "How do you know him?"

"Oh, I don't myself. Leland does. He isn't too fond of Mr. Friedman because of some run-in they had a few years back. It seems Mr. Friedman isn't the most trustworthy policeman in Denver."

This was turning out to be a profitable evening after all.

"What made Mr. Sterne come to that conclusion?"

"Leland had some business in Denver. Mr. Friedman told him that his business associate had a long history of shady activity. Naturally, Leland didn't go ahead with the deal. All in all, Mr. Friedman ruined what might have turned out to be a very profitable venture simply because he had a personal grudge against the man for refusing to play the'Denver rules.'"

"The Denver rules?"

"Graft, in other words. This man wouldn't pay his protection money, I think they call it, so Mr. Friedman and two of his fellow officers intervened in his life until he changed his mind."

"Oh, my. Did Mr. Sterne report them to their superiors?"

"No. There's no point in doing that. Police protect their own and it's wise not to accuse them of corruption without a courtroom full of witnesses. Good witnesses like Supreme Court justices." He smiled ruefully and changed the subject. "How long have you been practicing law?"

Sylvia accepted another cup of coffee and answered briefly. She tried to turn the conversation back to Friedman but having completed his character assassination, von Schagg would only talk about more cultural matters and without being grossly obvious, there wasn't anything she could do about it.

Von Schagg checked his watch. Before he could suggest leaving, Sylvia asked about Di Angelo.

"Oh, there's nothing to add to what I said in court. He's a sad case, really. The war finished him, as it did so many others."

"You said you fought in it. But surely you were too young?"

"Yes, when it started. But by the end, everyone who could hold a stick or a gun was recruited into the civilian defense force. We were supposed to protect German cities. With hammers, against your air force." He still sounded bitter.

"What made you leave?"

"My family was dead. The country was entirely ravaged. There wasn't any reason to stay."

"Did you come directly here?"

"Not directly." Von Schagg called for the bill.

She was dying to know where he'd gone first, but there was a good chance that that would be the last question she'd get to ask. "Germany has recuperated very well. Do you ever think of going home?"

"I have a new home now. I wouldn't want to leave this wonderful country. We who came to it out of need," he added sincerely, "love it no less than you who were fortunate enough to be born here."

But not enough to take out citizenship. "I suppose you've run into some prejudice here because you fought for the Nazis?"

"Some at first, but not any longer. Most people realize that the Nazis are the bad guys because they lost. That's the way of the world. The winners are right."

"Well, I think that there's some opinion that the Nazis committed a few crimes other than just losing." Sylvia was too appalled for tact.

"Oh, yes. I myself disapproved of their excesses. Most Germans did. But it was wartime and a patriot cannot divide his country with civil war when enemies from outside are threatening its very existence."

A curious way of describing the Allies' reluctant war against Hitler.

"But," von Schagg added as though she might mistake his meaning, "I was firmly opposed to Hitler's incidental goals. Any civilized person was. In fact, my disillusionment after the war, when we found out for the first time what had been going on, made it easier to leave Germany." He looked again at his watch. "It is late and I have an early meeting. I don't like to end this wonderful evening but I'm afraid I must."

Sylvia insisted that he let her get home under her own steam. He was not what she'd call intransigent about it.

It would be tacky to go to Dave's after dinner with another man. Sylvia drove out to Long Island, pulling into the driveway that she'd love never to see again. The house was dark and, at least to her eyes, charmless. She considered going to a hotel but the police cruiser was outside so she was probably safe enough.

The young patrolman got out of his car and came over to her.

"Everything all right, ma'am?"

"Yes, fine." He was a lovely sight, enormous and heavily armed. "I'm glad you're here. This part of Long Island is awfully deserted."

"You're getting better protection than anyone I remember, ma'am. Chief Lorimer's been insistent about it."

"Very kind of him. I forgot my front door key, Officer. Would you mind coming around the back with me?"

The door was unlocked. And she'd definitely locked it on her last visit. Sylvia glanced around the dark backyard. The watch on the front door was dandy but it hadn't taken Sterne very long to discover that suburban backyards were well hidden and vulnerable.

"I'll go through the house, Mrs. West. You wait here."

She laughed nervously and refused to stay further than two feet away from him.

Whoever had come had gone. There were unmistakable signs of a search. If she was uncharitably minded, she would wonder about von Schagg's telephone call at dinner.

"All clear. You lock the door behind me," the young man ordered protectively. "Don't worry about a thing. I'll be right outside all night."

She poured herself a stiff Scotch.

The telephone bell startled her into spilling some of her drink.

"Hello?"

The caller was silent.

"Who is this?"

No answer. Sylvia hung up without another word. With any luck, it was just a sex pervert. Nonetheless, she was shaking like a leaf. She ran to the doors and checked again that they were securely locked. And the windows.

The telephone rang again. She considered ignoring it. But then the caller would know she was afraid. She walked slowly over to it, finally picking it up gingerly. "Hello?"

"You've received a lot of warnings. Don't push us any further. This is the last warning." The line went dead. The caller's voice had been odd, thick and almost indistinct. As if it had been muffled by something.

Sylvia contemplated calling Dave. But there wasn't anything he could do right now. And the police officer was still in front of the house. The call had been just a threat, anyway. Nothing would happen tonight.

But if she didn't stop, what then? She finished her Dutch courage and went upstairs.

TWENTY-FIVE

She wolfed down what she firmly intended to be her last breakfast in the house and set off to see Laura Wilkinson.

The house was at the top of a crescent-shaped street in a pocket of Old Money and Respectability. All of the houses were substantial, if ugly as only Victoriana can be, but the area had not worn well. There was an air of desperate gentility along the tree-lined road and upon close inspection, it could be seen that every second house needed a good coat of paint. The gardens were still tended carefully but their lawns were sparse, the earth showing through in patches like the scalp of an old woman's head. The next step down was the irreversible decline into rooming houses.

The Wilkinson house was as grotesque as Dave had predicted. Sylvia shuddered at its fussiness and focused on the long flight of stone steps to the front door. The house was one of the few that showed attention and care within the last decade. But here too, the garden was tired and the grass was losing its unenthusiastic fight with encroaching weeds.

Sylvia rang the bell. She didn't hear anything inside and had just reached up to ring again when the door opened on its chain. A small woman with gray hair and pearl earrings looked out.

"Yes?"

"My name is Sylvia West. Are you Laura Wilkinson?"

"Yes, I am. What do you want?"

"I want to talk to you about a so-called charity by the name of The Foundation. I know that you're having some trouble with it and so am I. I thought we might be able to help each other."

The woman looked Sylvia up and down. "Are you alone?"

"Yes."

The woman continued to stare at her for a few minutes. Eventually, the chain was removed and the door was opened widely.

Sylvia stepped into a marble-tiled foyer large enough to take all her living room furniture and then some. Mrs. Wilkinson led her through it into a small room at the back of the house.

As they settled themselves in a cozy den filled with cheerful chintz-covered furniture and walls of books, Sylvia took a good look at her hostess. Mrs. Wilkinson was probably seventy-five, but like the inside of her house she had weathered well. She was dressed in a smart black cotton pantsuit which she still had the figure to carry off, topped by a beautiful brooch and the pearl earrings Sylvia had noticed at the door. If the garden looked distressed, it was only for want of interest, not for lack of means.

"What are your difficulties with The Foundation?" Mrs. Wilkinson didn't believe in beating around the bush.

For some reason, Sylvia was loath to mention her husband's mysterious disappearance. It was just as well, because it soon became apparent that Mrs. Wilkinson mistrusted anyone with even a slight connection to The Foundation.

"The charity is involved with a business associate who has run into financial trouble. I'm trying to find out what it does and how it's financed. There's some suggestion that it's as phony as a three-dollar bill." The widow was nodding earnestly. "I understand that your late husband bequeathed it some money?"

"Yes. You're a lawyer, aren't you?"

"Why, yes. How did you know?"

"Your language. I've dealt with so many lawyers in my life that I can pick them out at fifty paces." It didn't sound as though this skill had contributed much to her enjoyment of life.

"It's in my professional capacity that I'm investigating The Foundation. A colleague on the police force suggested, off the record, that I talk to you. If you know something about the people involved in The Foundation, it could help me substantially. And any information I can dig up can only help you too."

"Yes, that's true. But how do I know that you're not from them, sent to find out what I know?" She was a cagey old woman. Or crazy.

"Would you like to call the police to check me out?"

"I don't care to speak to them again. They are not the slightest bit concerned about this kind of thing."

"Some of them are, you know. Detective Masowski mentioned to me that the department hadn't been able to come up with much, but your complaint worried him."

"Is he in the fraud squad, I think they call it?"

"No. Something close. He's in daily contact with the squad." Almost true. He played squash with Davies of the fraud squad a few times a week.

"Well, I suppose there's no harm in talking to you for a bit." Mrs. Wilkinson was wavering. "Would you like some tea?"

"Yes, please." Sylvia curled up in her comfortable chair. This had the smell of a real break.

Mrs. Wilkinson returned to the den with a tray of tea things, including some terrific jam cookies, the kind Sylvia's grandmother used to bake. Sylvia made the appropriate noises and then the two women settled down to serious matters.

"My husband was a bit of a fool," Mrs. Wilkinson said bitterly. "I married him when I was very young and didn't know any better. He was far from rich then. He made his money in the thirties when anyone with a few dollars and any luck at all could make a fortune. Particularly when the war started. Then, after the war, he sold out his company and looked around to spend his money on whatever foolishness he could find. He became friendly with a man named Laforge, a schoolteacher, and they joined a group that I thought was just a fishing club or that sort of thing. It was very secret, you know, the kind of club that men love. The members swore not to tell anyone what went on, not even their wives.

"Usually those groups are too boring for anyone to want to know about them, so I paid no attention and was just glad that Hubbard didn't spend his money on chorus girls. I could never stand Laforge or any of the others I met, but I didn't see them very often. It wasn't until the last few years that I realized something bad was going on."

She fell silent.

Sylvia watched her quietly. Mrs. Wilkinson was taking this hard. Her eyes had filled with tears and she didn't look like a money-grubber.

"Please go on," Sylvia urged gently.

"Yes. Well, in the late forties, Hubbard wasn't doing too much with his old cronies. I thought maybe he'd tired of them. I certainly wasn't sorry.

"I was wrong. His group was just lying low. Later, he went back to his weekly meetings and he became even more secretive about it. Every year, from about 1952 or '53 on, he went away in the early summer for two weeks. I don't know where he went, but I always suspected it was overseas because he took to hiding his passport from me.

"Laforge died in 1967 and I went to his funeral with Hubbard. The other men there all knew each other and there were a lot of them. Maybe three or four hundred. My husband wouldn't say too much but he did admit that they were all part of the mysterious club. I remember I asked about it then. He told me it was none of my business, that politics were a man's affair.

"I guess that was the first I understood that the group had some political purpose, but I still didn't know what that was. I still don't for that matter. The group was incorporated a few years ago. My husband paid the legal bills. I came across them once when I was cleaning his study but I knew by then not to say anything to him.

"He left this company they formed a lot of money. Most of his money. I don't care about that for its own sake. He left me plenty too. But I don't like the dangerous people he was dealing with."

The woman was really worked up about it.

"How do you know it's sinister?" Sylvia asked.

"I don't have any real proof. I just have a very strong suspicion. If they didn't have something to hide, why would they be so secretive? Besides, my husband was afraid of them, after a while. I think he'd have liked to get out but he wasn't allowed to. That's sinister if anything is."

True enough, if the facts were right. "How do you know that?"

"Because he said as much before he died. We hadn't been that close. I was a disappointment to him because I didn't have children, and I guess he was a disappointment to me too, for other reasons. Anyway, in the end, we got closer. He said to me, a few weeks before he went, that he had naturally made provision for me but he was also making some bequests that might surprise me. He knew I didn't like his cronies and he must have figured that I'd make trouble for them. He warned me not to. He said I wouldn't be safe if I made a fuss over the will. He almost begged me not to.

"Of course I promised I wouldn't. I didn't want to upset him. But I can't just sit here and see his money go to a bunch of overgrown schoolboys who frightened him!"

The old woman was spunky. If the story was true and not

a figment of the imagination of a widow with God only knew what regrets and guilt, these fellows were more than wrinkled schoolboys.

"Did you know any of the men, other than Laforge?"

"Many of them by sight but I was seldom introduced to them by name. Laforge was some sort of leader, at least at first. He was Hubbard's closest friend. I think others took it over after a while, even before Laforge died. I'm only guessing now, but it seemed to me that Hubbard felt out of his depth by the end. There was one man at Laforge's funeral that the others seemed to fawn over. He may have been the new leader, I don't know."

"What was his name?"

"I wasn't told. He was a remarkably handsome young man."

"Have you seen any of the men who run The Foundation? Von Schagg, Sterne?"

"No, I've never met them."

"Do you remember any names at all?"

"They mostly called themselves Smith, Brown, Jones. They didn't even try to pretend that those were their real names. They were just like children playing at spy games. I did know a few names, though. Let me see. Well, there was a McEnery and a Lawson. Kellermann. And Cassels or Castel, something like that."

Sylvia decided not to push her for the moment. "Never mind about that. What about your impressions of the men?"

"They were all different. Fair, dark, young, old. The young ones tended to be the real tough types. Thugs. But the old ones were more frightening in a way. They were very smooth. Menacing. I guess that's why I was always a bit nervous about them. Hubbard was their bankroll. He paid for things. He wasn't the only one. I know he once felt that they should stop expecting him to foot so many bills but he went right on paying."

"Did he tell you that?"

"No. I overheard an argument. Well, not an argument exactly. One time, when some of them brought him home from a meeting, I heard them talking outside. One of them told Hubbard that all of the contributors would be repaid many times afterwards."

"After what?"

"He didn't say."

Sylvia didn't like the implications of the statement. Neither did her hostess. They were silent for a moment.

"You've had no contact with them since your husband died?"

"No. Well, I haven't seen any of them, but I have heard from them."

Sylvia knew instinctively what kind of communication Mrs. Wilkinson had received. She pulled the copy she'd made of her threatening note from her purse and handed it over.

Mrs. Wilkinson gasped. "Where did you get this?"

"In my car. A few days ago."

Mrs. Wilkinson was white. "Are they following you?"

"Not so far as I know. But it might be a good idea for you to come into town with me. You shouldn't be staying out here all by yourself. I know some police officers you can trust and they'll make sure you're safe."

"No. I'm not going outside. Please leave now. Please go!" Sylvia was almost pushed out the door. Before she could say good-bye, the bolt was shot home. She walked to her car with a sense of foreboding. There was no one around that she could see, but the estate and the street afforded lots of cover. If privacy was what Laura and Hubbard had aspired to, they'd been all too successful. This was no place for the widow.

Sylvia drove out past the overgrown shrubs onto the street. There were no cars loitering suspiciously nearby, no assassins furtively trying to conceal guns. All the same, she intended to arrange protection for Mrs. Wilkinson whether she wanted it or not.

Dave was neither in his office nor at home. Sylvia left messages for him and tried to put the worry out of her mind. She was almost late for her appointment with Rogers.

The insurance company's offices were modern and hideous. Instead of floor-to-ceiling partitions setting off each cubicle from its neighbor, the inmates were forced to sit behind curved, free-standing barriers that supposedly cut down on noise, established territorial prerogatives and still reflected wide open spaces. The panels were covered in purple and hot-pink cottons which somewhat undermined the free-floating feeling.

"Mr. Rogers?" She peered around the divider that had been pointed out to her. A soft-looking middle-aged man was fussing at some papers on a desk. "I'm Mrs. Johnson."

"Oh, yes. Come in and have a seat." He tried to look impressively busy as she settled herself on a molded plastic chair that was touted as being a great deal more comfortable than it looked. It wasn't. "I'll be right with you." He eventually gave a phony sigh and ostentatiously pushed a pile of documents away from him.

They discussed life insurance for housewives, Sylvia having donned that disguise in the belief that few men were wary of housewives. She asked cretinous questions and allowed the flabby little man to expand his chest and self-esteem on her naiveté.

"Tell me, Mr. Rogers." He was calling her Sylvia now but this was not the moment to insist on feminist equality. "I suppose I ought to have a will too?"

"Yes, certainly. I won't bother your pretty little head with all the complicated reasons, but everyone should have a will." There was nothing he wasn't an expert on.

"Yes, I thought so. My husband is making one right now but we're having some trouble. My husband believes that everyone should leave a little something to charity but he isn't happy with his lawyer's ideas. He's an idealist, you know." Said proudly as though she'd heard the word used but wasn't sure if it was a third political party or an obscure religion.

"There are always the churches." Rogers wasn't interested in their ethical deliberations.

"Yes, but he's looking for something else. He's very unhappy with most charities. I don't know anything about it myself, but he's always talking about the country going to the dogs. Everyone on welfare and so on." She batted her eyelashes. "It isn't as though he's a poor man. Georgie wants to be sure that he leaves his money where it will do the most good."

Rogers bit. "Well, this isn't something my company handles. I can only talk off the record." He looked around nervously and lowered his voice to a conspiratorial hiss. "As a friend, so to speak."

"Please do. I can tell you're the sort of man my husband admires."

Rogers warmed up to the topic. "There are a lot of men who feel the way your husband does. I, myself, do for one. Perhaps your husband would be interested in meeting some of my friends? Here's my card. I'll just write my home number on the back. If your husband wants to talk to me, have him call."

She cast around for a way to keep him talking. "I'm interested in politics too. I'm very unhappy with the way things are going. Like my husband."

Rogers stiffened. She was striking the wrong note.

"I mean, if the world is falling apart, we aren't looking after our children very well, are we?" Sylvia added hastily. It would be a hell of a lot easier to appeal to his politics if she knew what they were.

Rogers could understand even a woman worrying about the state of society when it developed out of her inescapable biological obsession. "True," he approved, relaxing and moving his chair closer. Despite the topic of saintly motherhood, Rogers was more than a little randy. "True. We must leave our children a world that's fit for them. The superior people are outnumbered. The weak rule today and in a few generations, the strong will be bred out!"

Well, she'd wanted a hint.

Rogers recollected his purpose. "I wouldn't forgive myself if I made you worry about these things. Why don't you have your husband call me? Now, have you decided which policy you want?"

"Uh, it's so difficult."

The phone on Rogers' desk shrilled. He answered it. Sylvia was fascinated to watch his face disintegrate as he nodded. "I'll be right out." Rogers took his handkerchief and wiped the sweat off his forehead. "I have to step outside for a moment."

"Certainly." Sylvia was being gracious to an empty space. She stood up and pretended an interest in a large artificial rubber tree at the corner of Rogers' free-standing office. Through the gaps between the dividers, she could watch Rogers and his companion walking toward her. The second man was plump like the insurance agent but there the resemblance ended. He was completely hairless and almost entirely colorless. His lips were drained of blood and scarcely darker than his pale skin. His eyes lacked lashes and the pupils were a washed-out beige. They were also ice-cold. Sylvia couldn't take her eyes off his.

He had been watching her too. He brusquely interrupted Rogers' agitated speech as they approached. "I have interrupted you."

"What? Oh, no. Quite all right. No problem." The little man was moving his hands around in an ineffectual attempt to placate everyone. "Oh, yes. Mr. Castle. Mrs. Johnson."

Sylvia forced herself to nod blankly through the smoke of

her cigarette. This put paid to her appointment with the second director this afternoon.

"Mrs. Johnson," Rogers explained to the second man, "is interested in insurance."

"I assumed something of the sort." Castle was barely polite.

"Mr. Rogers has been so helpful." What Sylvia didn't want was for Rogers to start talking about the mythical Mr. Johnson's interest in political organizations. "Do you work here too?"

"Oh no. Mr. Castle owns his own company," Rogers answered brightly. "It's a florist shop called Ye Flower Bower. Isn't that cute?"

Sylvia smiled bravely. "Very cute." She shuddered at the joyless grimace that Castle undoubtedly intended as joviality. "I can't imagine anything nicer than being surrounded by flowers all day."

Castle nodded impassively. His imagination was clearly better than hers. He turned to Rogers. "I would like to complete our conversation and I have only a few minutes." He inclined his head toward Sylvia. "You will excuse us." It wasn't a question.

Castle's voice didn't travel well. Sylvia could make out the odd word by straining at the very edge of the room divider.

". . . don't like . . . no time . . . dangerous chances . . ."

Rogers was a little shrill. "I didn't let on to anything! I was very careful!"

Castle interrupted him. "Shh!" They carried on an inaudible exchange for another few seconds.

"Very well." Rogers was no longer attempting to make a point. His voice was unmistakably craven. "I'll look after that. See you overseas."

Rogers returned to his office, trying to regain his lost sense of dignity. "Where were we?"

"I was just thinking about insurance. I can't make up my mind," Sylvia cooed. "I'd never understood it before but you make it so easy. I'll have to think about it and let you know."

"Of course."

"I'll call next week, if that's all right. My husband won't be home for another ten days." Don't want him fretting when he doesn't hear from either Mr. or Mrs. Johnson.

"I'll be away for two weeks but my assistant, Mrs. Irvine, will be available."

"You're going on a vacation?" Sylvia fiddled with her gloves and purse.

"More or less." Rogers couldn't pass up the chance to be mysterious.

"How lovely. Where are you going?"

"To a lodge in Europe."

"Fabulous! Where in Europe?" She kept her voice light and casual. It would have been rude to ignore such an innocent question.

"In Switzerland."

Sylvia stepped out of the office and tried to swallow a small yelp. Castle was standing within earshot against the magenta panel. She couldn't tell if he'd been there long or if he'd just returned to add something to his chat with Rogers. She smiled at him and kept on going, pretending that she hadn't seen the narrowed eyes and flared nostrils.

TWENTY-SIX

Maggie was in the office, waiting for her. She was clearly excited and as soon as Sylvia walked through the door, the reporter pulled her into the inner office, ignoring the chaos.

"I've been working on your case all day! Guardian Society was definitely weird! Definitely! It was a private company with supposedly charitable purposes, but I don't know how it could possibly have raised a dime for its charities, whatever they were, because it was the most secretive outfit I've ever run into!"

"Maybe it was privately endowed."

"Nope. Well, maybe, but if so, it was done on the Q.T. Nothing was ever reported to the IRS. I found no explanation for its money at all. If it had any. A few reporters tried to do stories on it at the time but they never got anywhere."

"Maggie, slow down and give it to me in order," Sylvia commanded.

"Right. Sorry. Well, like I said, it was a private company. My information is really skimpy before March 14, 1974. That's the date the trouble started.

"The thing is, they held some kind of meeting on that date. It wasn't meant to be public at all, but one of the reporters on the *News* got wind of it for some reason. He snuck into the meeting and so did someone else. A guy called Irving Gibson. This Gibson started asking questions about the various causes that the Society supported financially and without asking him politely to leave, without answering anything, some thug dumped Gibson outside and roughed him up a bit.

"Then they started checking on who else was there. There were maybe a couple of hundred people in the room, but they went around to everyone. The notes aren't clear, but the reporter wrote up a news story saying that there seemed to be some kind of magic password. Naturally, he didn't know it, and when they got to him, they turfed him out too.

"First, though, they asked him a few questions. He pretended to be a stray who made a practice of crashing corporate shareholder meetings and saw that there was one going on. Apparently, there are people who do go to these meetings, for the refreshments I guess. I don't know. Anyway, they believed him and they weren't rough with him. They just told him that it wasn't a public meeting and he had to leave. He left.

"This is where it gets interesting. He tried to find Gibson, but he wasn't able to. So he wrote a cute little story about this uncharitable charity."

"What's the reporter's name? It might be a good idea to talk to him," Sylvia interrupted.

"Yeah. I thought of that, but he's dead."

"How did he die?"

"Car crash, soon after. The file on Naylor, that was his name, showed his obit on April third."

"What happened after the article appeared?"

"Well, the company folded up. But that's not what I'm getting at. Gibson did turn up. He came around to the newsroom to see Naylor. What they talked about isn't clear. Naylor's notes show that he had one meeting with Gibson and that he figured he was onto something big. He had another meeting scheduled with Gibson. That's it. There aren't any notes about that one at all. Or about what the big story was."

"The company shut its doors right after some light was shed on it? That's interesting."

"Yes. And it's interesting that there aren't any records of Naylor's meetings with Gibson. Naylor was a very organized guy. He had notes on every goddamn thing you could think of."

"Can we find Gibson?" Sylvia asked.

"Yes. But it won't do you any good. He's in an institution. He's a vegetable."

"How did that happen?"

"Care for a coincidence? In a car crash. At around the same time as Naylor's. The day before, in fact. Except Gibson survived, if you call what he's doing surviving."

"I see. You did a hell of a job, Maggie."

"There's one more thing. Some dame came around the newsroom looking for Naylor right after the story appeared. And then again on the morning he died. A reporter talked to her. He was a cub reporter then and after Naylor bought it, he tried to do a follow-up on the story. Figured it might lead to something. He couldn't find her. Naylor's notes don't indicate whether he met with her or not."

"Did the reporter know her name?"

"No. Said she was not so young and not so pretty. He remembers that she had some kind of English accent. He might recognize her again, he said, by her temperature. Apparently below freezing. And this guy's a hot number with the ladies according to him."

Maggie's tone of voice suggested that she wouldn't have known had he not told her. Sylvia laughed.

"As he recalls, she asked about Gibson too. Whether he'd been around to see Naylor and where he could be found. Norris, that's the reporter, gave her Naylor's home number but he thinks he told her that the two men had been meeting."

"Have you seen Gibson yourself? Maybe he's not entirely uncommunicative."

"He's in a hospital in Philadelphia. I had a friend check him out. Forget Gibson. He doesn't even know his own name. He only knows his number and that's because it's on his wrist. He's regressed to the age of four or five."

"What number?"

"Well, I shouldn't be flip. He was a survivor of Belsen. He has the tattoo on his arm, you know the one."

"Yes. Is there anything else?"

"Nope."

"I guess we know why the Society went out of business. Was there ever any mention about a replacement company being formed?"

"Not a word. Do you want me to see if there was?"

"I know there was. But you wouldn't find out a thing about them. If they'd received honorable mention in the news, they wouldn't be around either. These guys are either very humble Good Samaritans or very camera-shy."

"Keep in touch, Sylvia."

"I will. It's your story when the time comes to unwrap it. Not that we've come up with anything that proves it ties into John's disappearance."

Maggie wasn't going to swallow the disclaimer but she had better manners than to say so.

"Bess, have you tried to get hold of Dave lately?" Sylvia asked over the intercom.

"No, but he's easy to reach. He's about three feet away from me at the moment."

Sylvia rushed out. "Dave! Thank goodness you're here." She told him about Mrs. Wilkinson. "I'm afraid for her. Can you arrange protection?"

He looked uncomfortable. "I can try. My standing isn't that high in the department at the moment, so I can't promise."

"You've got to try."

"You have no reason to think that The Foundation hires killers. There's nothing linking them to the break-in artists who knifed Ingrid."

"I can't pin Ingrid on them, but I have cause to worry about their immortal souls." She told him about Naylor and Gibson.

"Both in car accidents? What rotten luck!"

"If it is luck."

"You seriously think that the crashes weren't accidents? Sylvia, you're going off the deep end."

"Maybe." She'd arrange protection for the widow if she had to pay for it herself. "I've got work to do, Dave. See you later."

"Okay. Actually, I came over to tell you that I may be going out of town on Monday."

"For what?"

"I've been assigned to an extradition case in Seattle. I tried to get out of it because it looks like it's going to be a long one, but I don't think I'll be successful."

The arguments in favor of planning a trip for herself were increasing tenfold.

Bess spent the afternoon trying to get a lead on Kellermann, the third director of The Foundation. By six, she'd had it. The only stroke of luck was in finding a neighbor who'd lived beside him for six years. According to him, Kellermann had once mentioned something about moving to Europe.

Sylvia had an idea where. Whoever said all roads lead to Rome had been about four hundred and fifty miles off.

"Bess, it's time for you to go home."

"No, I'm still calling delivery services. By the way, tomorrow is your mother's birthday. Do you want me to send her flowers?"

"No, I'll pick up something for her and a treat for the kids. I could use the exercise."

She ambled over to Fifth Avenue. The walk past the spectacular windows was one of her favorite routes although she seldom ventured beyond their portals. The boys were easy; she went straight to their favorite candy store and made a huge purchase, resolutely ignoring the thought of future dentist bills. As she continued to walk through the almost impenetrable crowds on the sidewalk, she kept her eyes peeled for gifts for her mother. She was ready to give up and turn around when she noticed the boutique, Chic, whose window had caught her attention last week. It was still displaying the lovely tweed jacket. Sized for a midget.

She stopped abruptly, staring at the sign in the window. It was a dumb idea but it was the only one she had. She walked into the store. A tiny brunette saleswoman crossed to her, dubiously eyeing her height. Sylvia asked to see the owner. The woman floated into the back and returned with a pretty, plump woman in her late fifties.

"Hello. I'm the manager. Can I help you?" Her accent was charmingly French.

"I feel very foolish, but I noticed that your store has a branch in Geneva. I was wondering if you're familiar with the city?"

"Oh, yes. I lived there for thirty years."

"I'm asking because I want to locate someone. I had a friend who went to live in Geneva a few years ago and we've lost touch. I'm going to be there on a vacation and I wondered how one went about finding someone in Switzerland. I know she won't have a listed phone number."

"Well, the government keeps records of all foreigners living and working in the country. They are required to register with the authorities. The government would almost certainly know where she is."

"Would they give out that kind of information?" Sylvia asked doubtfully.

"Maybe not," the woman admitted. "Let me think about it. But first, why don't you join me in a cup of tea in the back? I was just pouring it when you came in."

Sylvia protested that she was a nuisance, but Michele Tessier, as she introduced herself, insisted that she'd be delighted to have company.

They settled themselves on smart, modern stools at the dressmaker's table in the rear. Sylvia was enchanted with Michele's unquestioning friendliness to a total stranger with a crazy request.

"Let me think," Michele continued. "We have the store

there, as you noticed. The owner of these stores lives there and she knows almost everyone so she could probably steer you to the right place. Her name is Regina Forrester. She's American herself."

Michele wrote the name on a card that showed the addresses of all the branches. "It's downtown, right near the good hotels, and Regina does know absolutely everyone. Geneva's really a very small town."

"I don't know how to thank you," Sylvia said. "I'm overwhelmed by your kindness. I know how silly this sounded but I don't know a soul in Switzerland and I got this crazy notion of asking someone who'd lived there how to get around."

"I'm only sorry I don't have more ideas," Michele smiled. "Oh," she exclaimed, struck by a sudden thought, "how stupid of me! My son-in-law works for the city of Geneva. The city council. He might be able to help you find your friend. Here, take this too." She wrote a second name on the card. "I don't have his number at work but it's easily found. And here's his home number."

Sylvia looked at the card. His name was Franz Jung. "Thank you again."

She firmly intended to call Michele when everything was sorted out. There were too few terrific people around to let one of them pass you by.

Bess noticed that Sylvia was carrying only a candy box. She smiled to herself and made a note to send flowers to Mrs. Layton in her daughter's name.

Sylvia dialed Mrs. Wilkinson. She let it ring for five minutes but there was no answer. Clearly the old woman had decided to leave the house. After all, Sylvia herself had pointed out that it was far too isolated under the circumstances. Or else the widow wasn't in the mood to talk to anyone. Either was a logical explanation. Sylvia gave up trying to talk herself into logic. She'd drive out there.

Bess walked in and handed over two sheets of paper. "Here are my notes on the delivery services. No one I've called so far remembers taking parcels to John's office. Can you read this or should I type it out?"

"No, after all these years, I've learned to decipher your chickenscratch," Sylvia answered absently, running her eyes down the pages. "Hey! What's this?"

"I told you I should type it."

"No, no. I can read it. What's this 'Flower Bower Delivery Service'?"

"It's a company that has a florist shop too. I guess most of its deliveries are flowers."

"Don't bother making any more calls. I've got what I needed."

TWENTY-SEVEN

It was dark when Sylvia arrived at the Wilkinson house. The street lights had come on but they served only to cast unnerving shifty shadows through the trees onto the road.

She parked the car down the street, responding to an innate sense of caution that she didn't know she had. From the end of the driveway she couldn't see even the outline of the house. She mustered her courage and sauntered up the gravel path, trying to look like a curious sightseer. As soon as she was within sight of the mansion's front door, she dove into the blackness of the trees on the lawn and waited for her night vision to improve.

There were no lights showing at the front of the house. Sylvia circled it, hiding behind shrubs and trees as if her life depended on it. No lights at all were on.

Surely Mrs. Wilkinson wouldn't be sitting in the dark? Sylvia wanted very much to go away and assume that the widow had taken her advice to leave the house.

Her conscience wouldn't let her. She reluctantly crept up to the back door and tried the knob.

It was open!

Something very definitely was wrong. Mrs. Wilkinson was not the type to forget to lock up her house. Sylvia removed her shoes and very slowly walked in. A search of the kitchen and back wing, originally intended for non-unionized servants and not substantially improved since then, revealed nothing. She was crossing the enormous front hall to enter the main rooms when she stopped short.

Was that a sound from upstairs? Sylvia listened intently and it came again. Almost a moan. She forced herself not to dash out the front door. She grabbed the banister and tiptoed up the vast wooden stairway. The sound came again and then stopped.

She didn't know her way around the house so it was impossible to tell where the noise had originated. She peered into one large inky bedroom after another but found nothing. By

214

now, she was sweating heavily. Not that it was hot. She came to a huge sitting room, off of which was another bedroom. She looked in and was about to leave when she detected the sound of someone breathing.

On the far side of the massive four-poster bed in which several generations of Wilkinsons had obviously been born and died, she found the last of them bleeding to death.

Someone had bludgeoned Laura Wilkinson so savagely that her features were virtually unrecognizable. The body was garbed in the black suit that Sylvia had admired earlier in the day.

She knelt down and whispered to the woman. "It's Sylvia West, Mrs. Wilkinson. Don't talk, I'll call an ambulance and we'll get you to a hospital immediately."

The body shuddered. "No. Wait."

The sound was so faint that Sylvia had to put her ear almost on top of the woman's mouth to hear.

"What?"

"Too late . . . call no one. . . . Get out. Get out!" Mrs. Wilkinson's agitation was using up her little remaining strength.

"Don't talk. You're going to be fine. Just wait here for the ambulance." Not that the poor woman was going anywhere.

"No!" Mrs. Wilkinson reached out a bloody thing that might once have been a hand. "Listen! Please listen!"

Sylvia returned to her knees and smiled gently at the woman. "I'm here. But you shouldn't talk. I won't go far away and I'll be back as soon as I call for help."

"Too late. It's them. Don't keep on . . . don't . . ." She could hardly speak. "They'll kill you too. Go away!"

"Was it someone you recognized? Someone you knew?"

Mrs. Wilkinson gave no sign of having heard. Sylvia felt for her pulse and it was gone. The poor old woman had been right and no one had listened to her. Now she was dead.

Sylvia stood up in a cold fury. She cleaned her hands and tried to wipe off any surfaces she might have touched. She left silently, the way she'd come. This was no time to stick around. She, for one, would follow Mrs. Wilkinson's advice. It would be far better for her that the group didn't find out she knew the widow. Unless they knew already.

Sylvia drove to Dave's as fast as she could manage, given the usual horrendous traffic.

"Hi. You look pale. You must be working too hard. Let's eat here tonight."

Sylvia readily agreed. The less exposure she had, the better. She was quiet during the evening but Dave attributed it to her tension over the case. Which, in a way, was true. She didn't propose to enlighten him with the details. Once a cop, always a cop. And cops generally took a surprisingly narrow-minded view of citizens who found dead bodies and didn't report them. She couldn't help Mrs. Wilkinson now and it might be the most unhealthy statement she had ever made. This was an opportune time for travel.

Over breakfast, she told him that she was going to Europe. Specifically, to Geneva. He was less than taken with the idea. "Why? You don't know anyone over there and if you get into trouble, you're on your own."

Eventually, Dave agreed to accompany her to her house while she packed. And he agreed not to let on to anyone where she'd gone. With any luck, his promise would make him hesitate to mention her when Mrs. Wilkinson's body was discovered.

They drove over to the house in Dave's car. As they turned down her street, she noticed a long black sedan parked across from her driveway.

"Keep going! Don't even slow down!" He was a well-trained police officer with good reflexes. As he continued on at the same pace, Sylvia slid down in her seat.

He drove back to the apartment building without a word. Once they were in his underground parking space, he turned to her.

"Okay. I've been very patient. Now I want to know what's going on."

"Fair enough. I owe it to you," Sylvia said sincerely. "I've had another threat. I got a phone call when I got home from dinner with von Schagg. And someone had been in and searched the house."

"What was the threat?"

"Just someone telling me to leave well enough alone. It was a disguised voice. I think he had something over his mouth when he talked. It could even have been a deep-voiced woman speaking."

"Is that why you're going to Geneva all by yourself?"

"I can't stop now, Dave. And with all due respect, if I leave it to you guys, I'll be dead before anybody even believes that a criminal conspiracy is being played out."

"Why did you refuse to go into your own house?"

"That was the last straw. There was a car parked outside, across the street, with a man in it."

"You know the car?"

Sylvia paused. She remembered the need-to-know principle. "No. But you don't get stray cars in that area."

"What did the man look like?"

"You may have noticed that I didn't exactly stare out the window. I couldn't see much from my position on the car's floor."

Dave kicked himself for not taking a closer look, at least to get the license number.

"Never mind, Dave. I should have told you that I thought I might be watched. Can I use your phone?"

"Yeah. Let's go up."

She hated to cut into Bess's weekend but this could certainly be classified as an emergency. "Can you meet me in the office in twenty minutes?"

"Sure thing."

Sylvia kissed Dave good-bye. "If I get anywhere, or if I need help, I'll call you. Believe me."

The taxi let her off a block from the office. She got into another cab and circled the block a few times. There was no one making it obvious that he was watching the building. She entered through the service door in the rear.

Bess was already waiting for her.

"Did you see anyone hanging around, Bess?"

"No. But there are quite a few people in the building today. I might have missed someone suspicious." Bess acted as though this was a normal way to start a conversation.

Sylvia told Bess most of what had been going on. She didn't mention the dead woman. There was no need to make Bess an accessory to her crime of failing to report it.

"So," she concluded, "I'm off to Paris this afternoon. I need some more clothes and cash. Have we got any here?"

"Not much. I've got some and there's a bit in petty cash. Let me forage around."

Sylvia found her passport and made a few telephone calls, including one to Stuart.

"I'm all in, Stuart, and I'm going to take your advice and have a rest. I think I'll be away for a week or two. Maybe longer. I thought I might drive down to California. Thanks for all your help."

"Quite all right, my dear. You just relax and cheer up.

We'll take care of everything while you're away. You're making a wise decision."

Bess brought in a few hundred dollars.

"Where did you find this?" Sylvia was amazed.

"I don't think you want to know."

"In that case, don't tell me," she said hastily. "Here's a list of everything else I need. I'd go myself but I want to stay undercover until the last possible moment."

Rupert was in his office as usual. It had belatedly occurred to Sylvia that if she needed help, Rupert would have friends in Europe. She scratched the California story.

He was so delighted to hear that she was getting away from the investigation that she didn't have the heart to tell him the real purpose of her jaunt. Or that Maggie and Bess would be pursuing the investigation at home.

"That's quite a coincidence," he said happily. "I leave for England the day after tomorrow."

"Will you be coming to the continent? Because if you are, give me your itinerary and maybe we can get together."

"Mmm. I'll be at the Savoy in London for about a week. Try to call me there before I leave the U.K. I'll be in touch with Bess if I don't hear from you."

"Okay. By the way, have you managed to learn anything about The Foundation?"

"Not yet. I'll keep trying, if you like."

"I would like."

Sylvia spent the next hour developing theories, all of which accounted for some of the facts but none of which accounted for all.

Bess returned with a suitcase full of clothes and some food.

"You've got to eat. Airplane meals are disgusting." Her tone was firm. From time to time, Bess lapsed into inflexible Jewish motherhood.

Sylvia munched obediently as she gave her friend last instructions. "My car's in the underground garage at Dave's. I think we should leave it there. And if anyone asks, except for Rupert, I'm on a motoring vacation and can't be reached. I'll keep in touch with my mother and I'm sure you can handle everything else."

The two women embraced and Sylvia walked out with a suitcase in one hand and the ubiquitous briefcase in the other.

"Hold it," Bess called after her. "No self-respecting tourist carries a briefcase."

"Oh, right. Well, let's put my papers into the suitcase."

"You might lose them. Here, my purse is large enough. Let's trade."

Sylvia transferred bags and strode off again, this time without mishap.

TWENTY-EIGHT

The plane to Paris loaded only twenty minutes late, presumably because not a single union had walked off the job that day. An oversight, no doubt.

Sylvia sat in a window seat in the nonsmoking section, hoping to have the row to herself. The smoking seats were always the first to fill up and there was a good chance of privacy in the rest of the plane. Well worth the deprivation.

Fifteen minutes later the static of the public announcement system stemmed the complaints of the restive passengers.

"Good afternoon. This is Clive Sandler, your head steward. I want to welcome you aboard and thank you for flying on our airline. We apologize for the delay but we've been waiting for the arrival of a connecting flight from Atlanta that has just landed. We will be ready for takeoff in the next few minutes. Thank you for your patience."

Sylvia had heard of planes waiting for people but she'd certainly never been the lucky beneficiary of such good manners. Some bigwigs must be due to join them. Sylvia returned to her novel.

A few minutes later a stir at the front of the compartment caught her attention. The latecomers, to the evident relief of the rest of the would-be travelers, had arrived. There were five men, apparently unconnected to each other. Three seated themselves near the entrance door so she couldn't get a good look at them. Neither of the two who made their separate ways toward the rear looked like the reason for the aeronautical courtesy. A thin, pale European man with an elegant goatee and exquisite tailoring glided by. He had the air of an aesthete, a man of privilege but no particular power. The second was a young man in the swinger's obligatory leisure suit. Although there were plenty of empty rows, to Sylvia's horror he swung in beside her with a quick "do you mind?"

Sylvia did, but one couldn't say that. She reopened her novel and tried to read it, ignoring the persistent stares of her unwanted new friend.

"Are you staying in Paris long?" he asked.

"No." She resolutely didn't look up and continued to study the printed page. Not that it was easy to read with Romeo there hanging on to your bra strap.

"Have you traveled to Europe often?"

"Mm."

"I'm from Cincinnati, myself."

Naturally.

"Would you like a drink, honey?"

"No."

"C'mon. Try one. They have good wine on board, even champagne."

Enough was enough. "Listen, I said no and I meant no. I don't want to talk to you. It's nothing personal, you understand. I just don't happen to need another friend right now."

He got up and moved down the aisle. Sylvia grinned to herself. It had been a lot harder to be rude ten years ago. There was something to be said for the passage of time.

A stewardess approached as she was eating the cardboard steak dinner. "Mrs. West?"

"Yes?"

"I have a note from another passenger for you."

Probably hate mail from the swinger. Sylvia took the envelope. It was thick, luxurious cream-colored stationery, quite out of keeping with Cincinnati. Someone called Count de Veutrier begged her pardon for intruding on her privacy, but he desired her company for dinner the evening of their arrival in Paris. This was the sort of come-on Sylvia liked.

She called the stewardess back. "How did the gentleman know my name?"

"He didn't, madame. I had to look it up for him."

"I see. Well, give him this, please." Mrs. West would be delighted to dine with the Count. She enclosed the name of her hotel.

The stewardess was biting her lip. "Did I make a mistake? I wouldn't have given him your name if I hadn't thought that he was so, well, so classy."

"No, that's quite all right."

Sylvia was dead-tired when she stepped off the plane but the adrenaline started to flow again as soon as the taxi hit the city proper. She'd been in Paris once before, the summer following her college graduation. She'd been making the Grand

Tour student-style. She hadn't had the money for the famous Parisian restaurants; in fact she'd eaten most of her meals in the parks. She'd stayed at a cheap hotel near the Bastille that had been the only one on the block to rent rooms by the entire night and not by the hour. She'd used the Metro and her feet no matter how exhausted she got because taxis were out of the question. But she'd fallen in love with the city and had dreamed of her return. John had consistently refused to come to Paris. He'd never wanted to travel to Europe at all. He hadn't wanted to go anywhere, for that matter. Ironic, when one thought about it.

She arrived at the George V at six in the morning. The lobby was a masterpiece of marble and gilt. In fact, a visitor who stood too long in one spot might be in some danger of being gilded. The concierge had a record of her hasty reservation, and she was shown immediately to a large room furnished elegantly with Louis XVI furniture and a huge bed covered with what looked like a real silk bedspread. Sylvia didn't bother to undress. She lay down after leaving word that she should be called at nine and was instantly asleep.

The bell was strident. She swung her legs out of bed and surveyed the damage in the ornate, full-length mirror. Her suit looked like it felt. As though she'd slept in it. The housemaid came in as she was stepping out of her bath. In her schoolgirl French, Sylvia attempted to ask that the suit be pressed. The young woman nodded vigorously and removed the offending garment.

Sylvia tried to remember her lessons. She had either asked that the suit be ironed or that it be eaten. She shrugged. It was hardly likely to be tasty but on the other hand, it didn't look like it could be made chic either.

Parisian breakfasts of croissants and sweet butter and strong hot coffee were the feast she remembered. Eventually she forced herself to get moving. Otherwise, she wouldn't be able to stuff herself again at lunch and at dinner.

The First Chicago Bank was not far from the hotel.

"It will be Monsieur Armand Druot that you will have need of." The young man at the reception had taken quite a lot of trouble to find out who was in charge of foreign drafts.

His office was on the next floor up. It was guarded by a woman whose sole function in life was to maintain the dignity

of Monsieur Druot's position. She was outraged that Sylvia
expected to see him on the day of her first request.

"I will inquire, and then if it is possible for him to see you,"
the dragon snapped in a voice suggesting that this was as
farfetched a fantasy as she'd ever heard, "I will make an appointment. It will not be possible that that could be this week."

Sylvia employed the bullying techniques she'd found helpful
with recalcitrant witnesses and eventually managed to make
an appointment for the following day.

She was none too pleased about the delay, but it appeared
that even that was a miracle of no mean proportion in France.

She headed over to the Bastille area called Le Marais and
stopped in at the hotel she'd stayed at so many years ago. Of
course it had long since been sold and no longer rented rooms
by the entire night, but she was illogically disappointed not to
find Monsieur Champille behind the counter, smoking his ri-
diculously large pipe filled with what had smelled like seaweed.

The new concierge was a snazzy number with a brilliantined
head of dyed black hair and an obsequious smile. Really more
of a leer. Only with great difficulty did Sylvia succeed in
convincing him that she wasn't a customer with unusual tastes.
She got out speedily.

She walked through the market with the old Jewish butcher
shops and bakeries into the Place des Vosges. The arcaded
buildings looked shabby, but the surrounding streets were now
inhabited by the chic and rich. Somehow, she'd liked it better
when the place had been somewhat rundown and seedy, reminiscent of a bygone age of elegance and privilege. It was
harder to imagine the king's carriage driving through the streets
on its way to the royal mistress when expensive limousines sat
waiting for their owners to descend and carefully groomed
poodles pranced affectedly along the roads.

Sylvia returned to the main thoroughfare and walked along
to the Pont Sully to the Left Bank. It was still haunted by the
eternally long-haired students, each indistinguishable from the
next and all of them looking rather American as though America held the copyright on the hip look. She had a *croque-
monsieur* at a sidewalk cafe and browsed among the bookstalls
and art stands beside the Seine. One of the merchants had a
few out-of-print books she'd wanted for some time. Sylvia was
waiting for a couple of volumes to be wrapped when she noticed
a pile of newish hardcover books in a garish blue-and-green
jacket. It was called *The Conspirators Among Us*. Sylvia had

heard the title before though she couldn't recall where.

"Voici, madame. Vos livres." The peddler thrust the parcel at her.

"Oh, thanks. Uh, *merci*. And this too. *Ce livre aussi,"* she stammered. According to the texts, half of speaking another language was not being embarrassed to try. The other half was remembering vocabulary and grammar. It was the latter half that held her back. "Oh, taxi!" Sylvia grabbed it from under the nose of a real Parisienne and proudly sank back in fatigue. As she got out at the hotel, it occurred to her that she'd promised to have dinner tonight with the Count. All she really wanted to do was order dinner to her room.

Sylvia crossed her fingers and asked at the desk if anyone had called. Unfortunately, the Count was as adventurous on the ground as in the air. He would pick her up at eight-thirty.

She dressed leisurely and was in the bar sipping an aperitif when he arrived. The Count was the late arrival on the plane, the aesthete with the charming goatee. Sylvia didn't like goatees but when she saw the long limousine with the honest-to-God chauffeur, she figured she could learn to appreciate facial hair if only she gave it a chance.

"I have promised this evening to attend a small party for just a few minutes. There will be a man there I would like to meet. A countryman of yours, Mrs. West. If you don't mind, we could go first to this affair?"

"Of course. And call me Sylvia."

The small party was about twice the size of your average Long Island bar mitzvah. Sylvia couldn't follow any of the conversations which, not unnaturally, were conducted in French, so she sipped at her glass of white wine and watched the glitter. It seemed that everyone who was anyone in France was here.

"Aha? Over there is the man I wish to meet." Roland, for so he told her he'd been named, took her elbow and steered her carefully across the room.

Sylvia's countryman was a very tall Southerner, a massive man with a booming voice that was incongruous against its relaxed Dixie drawl.

"Senator Stenning and his wife, Juliana. This is Count Roland de Veutrier." The man doing the honors appeared to be their host.

"I am very pleased to finally make your acquaintance, Senator. May I present Mrs. Sylvia West?"

"Howdy." The tall man took a good look at her and smiled broadly. "Another Yankee?"

"I didn't think there was a single Southerner in the States who would admit to being a Yankee." Sylvia grinned. So this was the man Rupert favored as the next Republican presidential candidate.

"Ah'll deny it if anyone here quotes me." Everyone laughed. There was no denying the man's charisma. He had not done anything to focus attention upon himself but a large crowd had just naturally congregated around him.

"I had hoped to meet you on my last trip to New York," the Count murmured to Stenning. "I represent a few minor trade interests in France that would like to talk to your commerce committee. A mutual friend told me that you were away from Washington last week."

"Yes, Ah've heard about you, Count. Perhaps we can set up a meeting. Are you going to be back in the States?"

"Whenever it is convenient. I go quite frequently. I have business concerns of my own."

Stenning took out a notebook and made a notation. "Ah'll have mah office get in touch with you."

Sylvia made casual conversation with Mrs. Stenning. The woman obviously adored her husband, and from time to time they caught each other's eye and smiled affectionately. It made a pretty picture and Americans love a pretty picture. Richard Stenning's political future was clearly something to keep an eye on. Trust Rupert to pick the best.

The crowd around the Senator became claustrophobic. Sylvia was relieved when her date suggested a move toward the door.

"Quite an impressive man, isn't he?" She motioned back toward the mob.

"He certainly is. He has a wonderful reputation in your country. I have even heard rumors that he might go higher than the Senate."

"I know he's got backing for the presidency but I'm surprised that the rumors have spread all the way across the Atlantic."

"It seems they have. He is certainly being treated royally everywhere he goes. But I heard about him in New York from some of the businessmen I deal with."

"What is he doing here?"

The Count handed her into the limousine with great care.

"Lasserre, *s'il vous plaît*. I imagine that he is establishing credibility on the international scene."

"For a presidency race?"

The Frenchman shrugged expressively. "It is certainly as an international figure that the incumbent has always the great advantage. If a new man can contest that, there is no telling what he can do in an election. Some of his backers, I am told, are unusually influential."

The limousine pulled up outside Lasserre. The doorman held the door and greeted de Veutrier with much bowing and scraping.

"*Bonsoir,* Henri. Have you eaten here before, Sylvia?"

She laughed, thinking about the little hole in the wall that she'd patronized on her previous visit when she felt like splurging. "No. But I've certainly heard of it."

The elevator left them off on the second floor in a room filled with wafting odors that made Sylvia want to run to the kitchen for immediate oral gratification. They were seated at their table against a wall, surrounded by padding waiters and busboys, before Sylvia noticed that the roof was missing.

"Ah, yes. On nice nights Lasserre opens its ceiling so that one can eat beneath the stars." Roland enjoyed her wide-eyed appreciation.

In the magical atmosphere of the restaurant, de Veutrier's charm was almost irresistible. Almost, because of a corner of her mind that registered the fact that he was very curious about her intentions in Europe.

"We've done nothing but talk about me," she cooed when the coffee arrived. "It's your turn. What business are you in?"

"My family has a manufacturing plant. More coffee?"

"No, thanks. Where is it? Your business?"

"Oh, south of Paris. Now, how would you like to go for a drive around Paris at night?"

"Lovely. What did you say you were doing in the States?"

"I was over on business. Far too mundane to talk about on a night such as this."

"Not at all. Everything about you is fascinating." She smiled sweetly and gazed directly into his eyes. "You mentioned that you had friends in New York. Perhaps I know them."

"Not friends really. Just business acquaintances. Let us go to the car. I would like to show you the most romantic city in the world."

The Count was now uneasy. Sylvia's attack had not uncovered any useful information about him, but it did at least have the desirable side effect of ending his cross-examination.

Sylvia was returned to the George V at midnight. Much earlier than she suspected the Count had intended, but his Gallic gallantry had not obscured the fact that he was no longer entirely delighted with her company. So few men liked inquisitive women.

There was a strong smell of a Gauloise cigarette in her room. Unless the chambermaid had smoked it, unlikely in such a hotel, she had had a visitor.

Sure enough, the room had been searched. She could see clearly that her clothes were not as she'd left them.

Someone was making a habit of searching her living quarters whenever she had dinner with sophisticated European men. It was enough to make a girl want to stick to farmers. Fortunately, the papers she'd brought with her had been in her purse. Ugly though it was, she'd carried it to dinner because she had no other bag.

This group didn't miss much. Sylvia fantasized flitting around Europe to throw them off her scent but she reluctantly came to the conclusion that she didn't stand much of a chance of eluding them on their turf. She checked the lock on her door and for good measure, put a chair under the knob.

Monsieur Druot was enchanted to see her. True, he gulped when he greeted her at the door of his office and found that there was at least eight inches difference in their heights. But except for insisting that she sit down immediately, he took it with good grace.

"To what do I owe this great pleasure, Madame West?" He was now perched on his desk so that his head was considerably higher than hers.

Sylvia explained very briefly that she was tracing a cousin by means of a bank draft.

"The bank at home said it came from you. It would assist me enormously if I could find out what address was given for the purchaser."

"You are looking for the address of your cousin?"

"Yes, precisely."

"If your, er, cousin does not wish to be found, he can have given a false address, madame. We do not require proof of address."

"Well, it's worth a try."

"Eh bien, give me the details and I will attempt to determine this address."

Sylvia did so. "How long will it take for you to look it up?"

"Oh, it would be several days at the very least. I will require my staff to act with the utmost expedition and it may be that the file will be in my office by early next week. Where may I reach you?"

"I'll be moving around. Will you permit me to give you a call next week?"

"But of course, if that is the easiest course for you."

"Thank you for your time." Sylvia got up to leave. "How long are those records kept?"

"Ten years or more. Do not worry yourself, madame. We will still have the file."

He was kindness itself, but now that the American giantess was standing again, he did want her to leave.

TWENTY-NINE

Geneva's airport was surprisingly small, although it ran with big-time efficiency. Sylvia had heard that the Swiss were the most efficient nation in the world. It hadn't been meant as a compliment.

She could see from her drive into the city that it was clean if not quaint. The most striking thing about the town on first glance was the abundance of gendarmerie. Every second car was a police patrol and it was the rare block that lacked an officer walking a beat.

Her hotel was great. It overlooked Lake Geneva, which the French insisted was more properly called Lac Léman, and both the lobby and her room were beautifully, if heavily, furnished. It went without saying that both were scrupulously clean.

Sylvia ordered coffee in her room and drank it at her window, looking down at the neat rows of people crossing the streets, taking care to stay within the white lines on the pavement. John had lived the first half of his life here. Would Switzerland give her insight into him? Into her marriage?

John had been much like the city. Neat, ordered, precise. It wouldn't surprise her to learn that eating crackers in bed was illegal in Geneva. She was at home in the raucous, almost slovenly, marketplaces of the Mediterranean countries. And she wasn't, as the kids would say, getting good vibes from Heidi's birthplace.

She lay down on the bed and tried to empty her mind. Just as she fell into a deep sleep, the phone rang. She awoke disoriented. It took a moment or two before she realized that she was holding a dead receiver. The switchboard didn't keep records of incoming calls. The equipment was automatic and all the supervisor knew was that the hotel's lines were in perfect condition. If the line had gone dead it was because the caller had hung up.

Not even Bess knew where she was.

Sylvia lit a cigarette and paced the room. It no longer seemed a terrific idea to wander around without notifying someone of her presence. She could disappear right this moment without anyone raising a ruckus for a week.

The American embassy had a branch here. Sylvia threw on a suit jacket and went out. She sat in the bleakly furnished waiting room without seeing a soul for thirty minutes. Eventually, a young man skipped through, clearly intent on avoiding eye contact with her.

Sylvia interposed her body between the door and him. "I'm waiting to see someone. My name is Sylvia West." She handed over a business card. "It's crucial that I speak to someone this afternoon. Can you help me?"

"Who did you want to see?"

"I have no idea. The receptionist mentioned something about telling a Mr. Rosslin that I was here."

"Oh. Mr. Rosslin is an assistant to the assistant ambassador. He's usually terribly busy. Maybe you could make an appointment to see him on Monday."

"No. I won't leave this building today until I've spoken to someone in authority."

The young man flushed. "I can't help you much, Mrs., er, Mrs. West. I'm just a junior aide in the lost passport division. I can ask the receptionist to tell Mr. Rosslin that you're still waiting."

Sylvia took a deep breath. "Look, could you go and see this Rosslin fellow yourself? Tell him that I must see him about a matter of life and death."

The aide blanched. "Yes. Sure. Of course. Life and death." He sidled out without taking his eyes off her for a second. He didn't want to be attacked by a wild crazy lady.

Almost immediately the receptionist came in to lead her upstairs.

"Mrs. West is here, sir."

"Thank you. Come in, Mrs. West." Rosslin stood up behind his desk and gestured toward two upholstered chairs. "Take your pick."

Sylvia sat down, wondering if he'd just tested her. Would a true nut be unable to decide between the chairs? "I'm sorry to push my way in here on a Friday afternoon, Mr. Rosslin, but the matter is very important. At least it is to me."

"Yes, so I understand."

They looked at each other for a moment. Rosslin turned out to be young, probably no more than thirty or thirty-two. He was as tall as she, with strikingly blond hair and fair skin. His blue eyes were becomingly framed by his pale blue suit. Not that the net result was one of good fashion. Rosslin was the messiest-looking man she'd seen in a long while. His suit had clearly been slept in. To achieve its present state, it would have had to be methodically slept in, under varying weather conditions, for some considerable period of time. His shirt was frayed at the collar and cuffs. His tie was askew.

He was adorable.

"Mr. Rosslin, I imagine that you are trying to decide whether I'm really serious or whether I'm a lunatic. I'm afraid that when you hear what I have to say, you're going to opt for the latter. Please hear me out before you make up your mind." Sylvia ran through her story as concisely as possible.

Rosslin listened quietly. When she had finished, he stood up and walked to the window. "Let me see if I have it straight. Your husband has disappeared. You have been threatened and your children were almost abducted. The authorities are unanimously either obstructionist for some unknown reason or stupid beyond belief. So you're here on your own, tracking down dangerous killers." He turned to her. "Is that a fair recap?"

She cleared her throat. "Well, it's accurate. I'm not sure I'd call it fair."

"What do you want from us?"

"Some protection. If no one knows I'm here, I could vanish conveniently with no one the wiser. At least if the embassy keeps track of me, I'm less of a sitting duck."

"I see. Okay. I know you're here. Now what? You know that we don't have the resources to help you investigate it. Whatever it is. You can certainly call me on a regular basis and I promise to ask questions if you disappear. More than that I can't do."

"That's something. Especially if I make it obvious that we're in regular contact. I'm sure I'm being watched so I expect that whoever's behind this whole mess knows I'm with you right now."

Rosslin smiled weakly.

"You don't believe me, do you?" Sylvia wasn't terribly upset by his lack of faith; she just wanted to know.

"Uh, well, to be truthful, I have some difficulty with it. Still, my generation believes in conspiracies, particularly conspiracies in high places. So I'd like to believe you. Let's just say that I'm willing to go along."

"Since going along involves taking a brief phone call from me from time to time, you'll appreciate that I don't feel overwhelmingly grateful." Sylvia grimaced. She hadn't meant to sound so bitchy. "Sorry. It's just that I'm afraid. I've been afraid for some time now so you'd think I'd be getting used to it but I'm not. Thanks for seeing me. How about if I call you every morning at nine? I won't miss a day without telling you ahead of time so if I don't call, get in touch with the cops."

"Sure."

"And call my secretary. She'll start the ball rolling at home. Here's her number."

"Okay."

Sylvia stood up.

"Oh, Mrs. West. One warning."

"Yes?"

"Geneva's a very stuffy town and the authorities are even stuffier. Don't alarm them by causing trouble because if you do, they'll personally escort you to the airport. So keep your nose clean."

"I'll certainly try, Mr. Rosslin, but you'll excuse me if I spend more time worrying about keeping it breathing."

Bess was delighted to hear from her.

"It's a good thing I didn't know where you were this afternoon."

"Why?"

"Because I'm a lousy liar. However, worry not. I'm getting better which is not surprising considering the practice I'm having."

"Bess, you're not making the slightest sense. What are you talking about?"

"The Bar Association. You remember the Bar?"

"Oh, my God! The hearing!"

"That's right, the hearing that was. On Wednesday, to be specific."

"What happened?"

"They were very cranky when you didn't show up. They called me in. I had to tell them that I didn't know where you could be reached and that I didn't know when you'd be back."

"Well, that was almost true."

"Yeah. Anyway, I didn't want to say that you'd gone to Europe because you were so careful to tell everyone that you'd gone on a rest cure. So I just played dumb. The result was they adjourned it and suspended you. You can't practice law until the hearing is reconvened. Which will happen whenever you return from wherever it is that you are, at which time they hope to disbar you. And if you're not heard from within the month, they'll disbar you without benefit of a hearing."

"Okay. I'll be back by then. If you hear from them in the meantime, just act confident that I'll have an explanation for everything."

"I can't wait to hear it."

"Me too."

Sylvia spent the weekend playing the tourist with a vengeance. With any luck, her normalcy was boring her pursuers beyond endurance. It was certainly boring her.

Geneva wasn't interesting enough to take her mind off the immediate problem. Not that the buildings weren't beautiful, some of them, but it was people that intrigued her and those in Geneva were all monotonously similar. Although the civil servants in town had been sent from countries all over the world, they were a new international breed of senior bureaucrat that might have been cloned from the same cell. They looked alike, despite their many colors, spoke the same jargon in their various tongues, approved of the same things and disapproved similarly. The city was full of them. The glamor that others appeared to find in Geneva eluded her. The only good thing about the place was that everyone spoke several languages, usually including English.

To add to its disadvantages, Geneva was really very small. Sylvia had exhausted its scenic and historic possibilities by Sunday evening. She sat in the park by the lake, aimlessly flipping through her well-thumbed guidebook and debating the merits of another day's pretense. A Swiss family was relaxing nearby, father, mother, and two well-dressed model kiddies. The children were playing peacefully while their parents watched benevolently. A sharp vision of Carl and Jay made her suddenly very homesick.

The sound of drum rolls penetrated her consciousness at the same moment that the two children rushed excitedly to the road. A small parade was making its way toward them. Out of nowhere, a crowd materialized in the park.

As they said, everyone loves a parade.

Sylvia collected her belongings, intending to get away from

the mob but she was too late to cross the avenue in front of the marchers. She sighed and lit another cigarette while she waited it out.

A few hundred teenagers strutted past, wearing the lederhosen and felt hats of the Swiss storybooks. Their hands and legs moved in unison, despite what looked like very heavy packs on their backs.

"Excuse me, do you speak English?" Sylvia leaned over to a woman beside her.

"Yes."

"What is this? Who are the children?"

"It is the, how would you say it, the nature club. These boys and girls go into the mountains for learning how to live in the hills. To not be soft, you understand."

"I see. Thanks." A laudable purpose, sort of like the Scouts and Girl Guides. One could not fail to be impressed with the uniformly flushed faces, the determined set of the jaws, the precisely measured strides in perfect time to the drumbeats. None of the marchers looked to the right or the left, eyes firmly fixed ahead of them as though on a future goal invisible to all but themselves.

The crowd dispersed when the parade disappeared over the Pont de Mont Blanc. Sylvia crossed to her hotel, wondering why the youngsters had left her slightly chilled, uneasily longing for good old American sloppy jeans.

She curled up with one of the books she'd bought in Paris. It took only two pages of *The Conspirators Among Us* to remind her of the nasty letter to the editor that Bess had brought to her attention. This was the slimy piece of innuendo that pretended to prove that the Jews were set on destroying western society. A few minutes of it were all that she could take. She called for a drink to take the bad taste out of her mouth.

She was almost asleep when a sudden thought caused her to sit bolt upright in bed. The parade tonight had had martial overtones. That was what had disturbed her. That and the fact that the watching crowd had been ominously silent as the kids stepped past.

THIRTY

She woke up early, still with a bad taste in her mouth. A couple of cigarettes took care of that. Sylvia had never subscribed to the theory that smokers' mouths were as appealing as dirty ashtrays. Coffee arrived with the morning's international edition of the *Herald Tribune*. The lead editorial was about the much-vaunted anti-terrorist conference that everyone knew was going ahead at some unknown place and time. The *Herald* 's editorial board was in favor of requiring all participating countries to undertake never to deal with the terrorists regardless of the individual threats. It argued, with some justice, that it would take only a few bloodbaths before the terrorists realized that there was no point in further hostage-taking incidents.

Sylvia was still shaking her head over the callousness inherent in breezing past a "few" bloodbaths as she dialed Rosslin.

"Oh, good. Mrs. West, can you come in to see me this morning?"

"Sure. What about?"

"I'd rather talk about it in person."

Sylvia found him in the same blue suit, looking as though he'd worn it straight through the weekend. He motioned toward the chairs again and offered a cup of coffee.

"Thanks. Black. Now, what's the problem?"

"Shirley, two coffees please. One black. Well," Rosslin stood up and faced her, "I suppose I should tell you straight off that I've had instructions to encourage you to go home."

"What?"

"Over the weekend the embassy received a note from Washington about you."

"Saying I'm crazy and should be sent home?" Shirley brought in the coffee. "Thanks."

"Something like that. To be more specific, it said that you had been thrown off balance by the tragic circumstances of your husband's death and that you hadn't been able to accept the, uh, entire situation. As a result, you were wandering around maintaining that he was still alive."

"So I should be sent home to see a shrink?"

"Not exactly. The government doesn't care about your mental health. It wants to be sure that you won't cause an international incident. I'm supposed to watch you very carefully and send you home, by force if necessary, at the first sign of trouble."

Sylvia nodded sourly. "What are you going to do about it, Mr. Rosslin?"

"I'm naturally going to encourage you to go home. I like my job."

Sylvia stood up. "Well, thanks for the coffee. See you around."

"Hold on!" Rosslin was smiling. "I said I was going to encourage you. Not force you. It isn't my fault if you won't go."

"What are you trying to get at?"

"I have no grounds to require you to leave Switzerland. In fact, only the Swiss can compel you to go. And I don't have any direct orders to ask them to. So I've passed on the message which, as I see it, takes care of my duty."

Sylvia scrutinized him. "You sound a lot friendlier than you did on Friday."

He grinned. "I'm just a sucker for the underdog."

"You believe me!" Sylvia was thunderstruck. "You believe me now."

"Yes, I guess I do. I've never seen a note from home like this before. It seems weird if you know what I mean."

Sylvia sat down again and offered him a cigarette.

"No, thanks. I don't smoke. But Mrs. West, I'm really sticking my neck out. If you make waves, I'm in a lot of trouble." Rosslin smiled. "But keep your nose breathing, no matter what that does to my chances for a post to Addis Ababa."

Sylvia chuckled. "It's pleasant there, if you like it warm. Mr. Rosslin," she continued more soberly, "I can't tell you how important it is to me that you're willing to take this risk. If it's any consolation, I've got a friend at the State Department. Herb Dutton's pretty senior and I think he can protect you from Ethiopia. If it comes to that."

"That's good news," Rosslin agreed cheerfully. "Especially since, just between us, we're expecting another visit from Mr.

Dutton in the near future. What are your immediate game plans?"

Of course a man like Herb would come to Geneva frequently! She should have thought of that right away. "Oh, sorry." The wonderful notion of friendly reinforcements had made her forget the question. "Uh, my plans? Well, I've got to trace my mother-in-law and I want to see what I can dig up about my husband's secretary. She spent some time here about a decade ago."

"Wow. You've got a lot to go on."

Sylvia shrugged. "Can you give me any concrete help?"

"Not with either of those two items. I can't get into that kind of information."

"Can you see if there's any record of John entering Switzerland?"

"I can try. But I doubt it."

"Fine. And I'll keep calling at nine in the morning." Sylvia crossed to the door. "And thanks. You're the first nice thing that's happened in a while."

Sylvia walked into the boutique Chic and asked for Regina Forrester. She looked around at the designer clothes, bitterly wishing that for once a buyer would come to grips with the fact that some women couldn't fit into size ten.

Ms. Forrester was a stunning woman with flaming red hair that suited her pale complexion even if the two hadn't been born together. She was made up strikingly, wearing huge jet-black eyelashes that would have been laughable on a lesser mortal but looked great on her. She was probably in her fifties, but not what Sylvia would have called grandmotherly. Ms. Forrester weighed in at no more than one hundred and ten and stood at least five feet eight even without her five-inch heels.

The total effect was dazzling. Sylvia wasn't sure that she'd be up to eating breakfast with Ms. Forrester, but by lunchtime she'd be a lot of fun.

"I'm from New York, Ms. Forrester. Michele Tessier suggested I come to see you."

"Ah, come in! How is darling Michele?"

"Very well. Missing you. And Geneva, of course." Sylvia could improvise with the best of them.

"But of course. There is nowhere else to live." Sylvia was less than convinced but she nodded amiably and followed the woman into the rear of the shop. "Are you here for any particular purpose?"

"No, I'm just a tourist. By the way, my name is Sylvia West. I'll only be here a few more days, but I did promise Michele that I'd see you."

"Oh, I am thrilled that you did! I am from the United States originally, myself." She looked at Sylvia for confirmation of the fact that it couldn't have been guessed. "But you know," she continued, "an older woman who is considered to be in her prime in Europe is just a hag there. I love the attitude of European men. I won't go back, even for a vacation. I felt twenty years older whenever I visited. I have family still in New York but they must come here if they wish to see me."

Sylvia was taken aback at this wealth of information but she found herself smiling as she wondered how to go about pumping Regina. It wouldn't do to confide in her. As kind as she undoubtedly was, giving her information would be tantamount to publishing it over an international wire service.

"How long have you lived in Geneva, Regina? If I may call you that?"

"Of course you must call me Regina! Oh, many years."

"Michele tells me you know everyone here?"

"I do, yes," Regina said proudly. "No one would have a party without me. If they did, I would make sure that all the women turned up wearing the same outfit!" She laughed.

"I had a friend here," Sylvia said slowly. "She came years ago. We lost touch unfortunately, but I suppose she's moved on."

"Who is she? Perhaps I know her?"

"Her name was, is, Janice Wagoner."

"Wagoner?" Sylvia had a fleeting impression that Regina reacted to the name. "No, I did know a Wagner, but her first name was Leonie. Or Cheryl? At any rate, I don't know a Janice."

"Well, she was a nice woman but hardly glamorous. I wouldn't expect a woman like you to know her, much less to remember her. She wasn't particularly good-looking and she was a bit prim. Not a lot of fun with men, you understand."

"Perfectly. But she was a friend of yours?" Regina suggested flatteringly that such a woman had nothing in common with Sylvia.

"We, uh, grew up together. She was here in 1965 and she stayed at least until '67. That's a long time ago now. I guess she's moved on. It was just a thought."

"Well, if I can't help you find your friend, perhaps you will do me the pleasure of coming for a drink to my apartment this evening? And joining a few friends and myself for dinner?"

"Why, that would be lovely." Sylvia was actually looking forward to socializing. She'd started to feel quite lonely.

The city's restaurants reflected the polyglot nature of its temporary inhabitants. Over the last few days, Sylvia had eaten Italian, Chinese, French, American, and German food. A few blocks away from Chic she found a slightly seedy mid-Eastern cafe. She looked in the window and decided to throw caution to the wind.

The waiter was very helpful. Since the menu bore no resemblance to that of Les Couscousiers, she was at a loss and agreed with his suggestion that she leave it to him. The resulting meal was fabulous. After an eggplant salad and a few strange mixtures that apparently, if she'd understood him correctly, originated from the lowly chick-pea, Sylvia barely had room to cram down the lamb.

"Dessert?"

"Oh, no." Sylvia blanched at the thought. "No, just coffee."

A group of men came into the tiny room and sat down at the only table large enough for six. It happened to be immediately behind Sylvia. She tried to ignore their insolent stares but the restaurant was too tiny to carry it off with aplomb. She conceded them the turf and called for the bill.

As she was counting out the Swiss francs, she caught a bit of the conversation behind her. "Waiter, what language are those men speaking?"

"Why, Arabic, of course."

"Thank you." She paid and left.

She had heard that language spoken once before. By the men who had tried to kidnap her children.

It was a balmy day. Sylvia walked along the lake, still with the feeling of being followed although she tried to tell herself that it was probably her imagination working overtime. Unfortunately, she'd always been sure that lawyers didn't own imaginations.

She was running over the meager list of clues as she meandered through the tiny park by the *jet d'eau* and into the shopping district. The street narrowed and the crowds thickened. In front of her, a woman was walking a highly decorated poodle. Both dog and owner looked overfed and bad-tempered. Sylvia had often remarked on the strong resemblances between pets and their keepers. Did someone choose a dog because it was reminiscent of him or did the two just grow to look alike?

She noticed a couple, up the street, that looked oddly familiar. They could almost be her mother-in-law and von Schagg. Sylvia froze. More than almost.

Running up to take a closer look did not seem wise. She could at least follow them while she made up her mind what to do.

The couple continued to walk away from the Jardin Anglais for several blocks, immersed in a conversation that apparently engrossed them enough to make them ignore their surroundings. Their concentration was so complete that at one point the woman stepped off a curb into the path of a careening sports car. She leaped back, raising her fist at the rapidly disappearing vehicle. Sylvia got a clear view of her profile. It was Mrs. West, wearing a vicious snarl that Sylvia had not seen on her face before.

The man stopped in front of a small building. He stood very close to the woman and said something quickly, then ran up the stairs. The woman continued on.

Sylvia hurried up to the doorway and discovered from a small, highly polished brass plaque on the wall that it was a private club, undoubtedly a men's club from the look of the horrified doorman. She smiled wickedly at the outraged sentinel and followed Mrs. West. They walked for quite a while into the modern section of Geneva frequented by the international community, particularly the Americans.

The Budé, as the area was called, was overpriced and filled with glass and pale stone edifices containing apartment and office accommodations. Mrs. West stopped in front of a huge building, an apartment block with a complicated security system involving several keys. Mrs. West had a complete set.

Sylvia waited a few minutes and then stepped up to the first glass door. Every one of the hundreds of units appeared to be rented but her mother-in-law's name was not among those listed on the directory.

She called the Hotel de Ville. Franz Jung was away from his office but his secretary promised to give him Sylvia's number with the message that Madame Tessier had asked her to call.

Wearing her one and only dress to Regina's was a mistake. Or in the alternative, having worn it she should have taken a cab. It had turned chilly and by the time Sylvia arrived at her hostess's, she was ready for a warm drink and a cozy apartment.

Regina's apartment was what she ought to have expected. It was definitely not cozy. Oddly shaped artifacts in the middle of the living room turned out to be chairs. The walls and ceilings were covered in enormous erotic paintings that left the squeamish with nowhere to gaze. Sylvia was comfortable only with the thick oatmeal-colored carpet, but she lost her taste for that too after Regina recounted a few events that occurred on it.

Regina herself, however, more than made up for the setting. She fixed Sylvia a generous drink and then amused her with tales of doings at supposedly staid local parties that made Sylvia's hair curl.

The dinner guests began to dribble in. A "few friends" turned out to mean more than thirty, all of whom spent most of their time and, unless they were very wealthy, all of their money on their appearance. Sylvia felt dowdy in the extreme, but as the social set in town was so limited, the new face among them guaranteed her a great deal of attention. She found herself having a nice time with the crazy people and the evening passed quickly.

The crowd began to drift off after the coffee and liqueur, or, more accurately, liqueurs. Sylvia, too, made to leave.

"My dear!" Regina called from across the room. "I simply must have a chance to talk to you and I haven't had time all evening!"

Sylvia walked over to her. "I'm tired now, Regina. Will you allow me to take you to lunch tomorrow?"

"Oh, how wonderful! Come to my little shop at one, and I'll show you the most perfectly fabulous restaurant in Geneva!"

THIRTY-ONE

Sylvia had no sooner hung up from reporting in to Rosslin in the morning when the phone rang. It was Franz Jung, the city clerk, speaking an almost-perfect English.

"My mother-in-law wrote that you might call, Mrs. West. I am delighted that you did so. What can I do for you?"

Some people actually had a relationship with their mothers-in-law. Amazing. "I think it might be better if I could speak to you in person, Mr. Jung. Could I perhaps come around to your office?"

"Well, I have meetings all day. Could you come to my office at five o'clock and allow me to buy you a drink?"

"I'd love to," Sylvia accepted gratefully.

It took a while, but eventually the French telephone operator acceded to her pitiful begging and condescended to connect her to Paris.

"Monsieur Druot? It's Sylvia West calling. I hope I haven't disturbed you?"

"Not at all, madame. I was waiting for your call."

"Were you able to obtain any information about the draft?"

"Well, there is a problem." He paused. The giving of bad news was generally the province of a junior member of the staff.

"What is it?"

"Ah, well, unfortunately, my people have not found the right file."

"Oh, I see. Well, how long will it take?"

"It is not a question of time, alas."

Sylvia still didn't grasp the point.

"Madame, it is the first time that I can recall such a thing occurring. We are most scrupulous about our records. This is an outrage and will not occur again, I assure you. But I quite understand that this is not your concern. My punishments for the guilty parties cannot assist you."

"Do you mean that the file is lost?" Sylvia asked stupidly.

"Yes, it is simply not where it should be. There is the envelope in which it should be filed. But the envelope is empty.

I am desolate and most embarrassed."

"Please don't blame yourself. I imagine you must have hundreds of bank drafts going through your bank daily."

"Yes, but nonetheless, we have records of all of them. All but this one."

What rotten luck. Sylvia cursed French inefficiency and was then struck by another thought. Inefficiency? Or just the opposite?

It was raining at lunchtime, despite which the hotel doorman was able to find her a taxi. Regina was waiting for her and as she came out of the store, the cabbie rushed out in the rain to open the door. He hadn't done that for Sylvia. No wonder Regina liked Geneva so well.

"Creux de Genthod, please," Regina instructed the driver with a coquettish smile. "You'll absolutely adore this place, Sylvia. It is on the lake and it has the best fillet of perch in Europe!"

The sun was fighting valiantly to recover center stage, and by the time the taxi drew up it had won.

"It smells rather nice," Sylvia admitted, ravenous as soon as the odors of the kitchen hit her.

They had a good table, close to the water, due apparently to the fact that Regina was a local celebrity of sorts. The waiter took their orders for drinks while Sylvia looked around at the parties of beautiful people.

"I wouldn't have imagined that I'd feel so unfashionable in Geneva!"

"Geneva is a very chic town!" Regina was appalled at Sylvia's slur against her world. "The best-dressed women in the world live here. There's so much money in Geneva!"

"I'm sorry," Sylvia apologized. "I just don't travel much. As you can see, I've neglected my clothes too. You must take me in hand and outfit me."

"Oh, you look very nice." Regina was mollified. "You should always dress simply because of your height. But I do have one evening dress that is absolutely perfect for you. It is perhaps a bit risqué but you will carry it off."

That would be another hurdle to face. It was awesome to contemplate what a dress must be like for Regina to consider it risqué.

They ordered their meals and chatted about their backgrounds until the coffee came. Regina had had a typically American upbringing in a small Midwestern town. She'd married a man who did very well as a breadwinner and less well as a husband. As soon as her children went off to college, Regina gathered her reserves of strength, mustered up from God only knew where, and left home. She went to New York City to get a job and when she and her ex-husband came to a financial settlement, she gambled it all on a dress shop. The rest was history.

"I don't know why I ever married him," Regina confided. "I never found him sexy. Not that I knew much about sex at eighteen. And he was such a pill. Can you imagine, he kept a notebook so that he could jot down everything that I or the children did wrong! He used to discuss it once a week. For years, I hated him for that! Still, I suppose it wasn't such a sin. I should never have married him, that's all."

Sylvia could understand Regina's feelings. It suddenly came to her that she not only didn't miss John, she was relieved to be alone. There, it was thought. She was relieved at not being constantly criticized, at not being perpetually uneasy about the way she did things. She had been feeling guilty since John left, but it wasn't really guilt for her conduct during the marriage. It was guilt because she didn't miss him.

Sylvia came to with a start. Fortunately, Regina was still talking. "... and I decided to stay here."

Sylvia smiled. No one could accuse Regina of being secretive.

Regina, on the other hand, had not learned much about Sylvia. She was not, as was evident from her life story, a stupid woman. When coffee came, she turned to Sylvia.

"I know that you're not really a tourist, my dear. You're here for some specific reason, and I get the feeling that things aren't going well. Do you want to talk about it? I do know my way around this place. Maybe if I knew what you were really after, I could help."

Sylvia was touched. She studied Regina for a moment and then smiled. She had to trust someone; her adversaries were on her heels and it wasn't very sensible to keep her cover story alive at the expense of assistance.

"You're right, of course. And very kind. I do need help. In a nutshell, my husband disappeared from home in New York a few weeks ago. I wasn't happy with the way the police were handling the case so I started to look for him myself. I won't bore you with the details, but the disappearance seems to be connected with a lot of other scary occurrences and it all ties in to a political organization here in Geneva. I don't even know its name, but I do know that it's right wing and very dangerous. It may even have me under surveillance this very moment."

Regina drew back in alarm. Sylvia put her hand on the other woman's wrist. "Please don't look like we're talking about anything important. If you like, I'll shut up right now."

"No, no. I have a special reason for concern but it doesn't have anything to do with you. Go on."

"I have the Geneva address of this group but that's not very helpful on its own. My mother-in-law also lives here, or at any rate, she's here now. And she seems to have something to do with the case. And to top it all off, my husband's secretary who may be involved too used to live here."

"In 1965 or so?"

"No flies on you."

They laughed, both grateful for the break in the tension.

"I don't have much of a chance to get into the records I need to see, but I'm trying. The worst of it is that I think I have to work fast. They're on my back and I get the distinct feeling that I don't have a lot of time.

"I have so little to go on. I don't even know the extent of my husband's involvement. For all I know, he's one of their keenest members. Or he might have been abducted and murdered."

"Maybe I can help you." Regina was frowning in concentration. "I don't know anything myself, but there's an old woman who used to be part of the underground in France during the war. She's kept in touch with things for old time's sake and she might be able to put you in touch with a good private eye. Her name is at the shop."

Sylvia looked at her watch. It was after three. "Oh, my goodness! I'm really keeping you from your work. Let's go back."

She successfully wrestled Regina for the bill and they left.

The store was busy and Regina was corralled by several customers when she entered. Sylvia tried on a few things and decided to buy a nightgown and a silk shirt which would enliven what pathetically passed for her wardrobe. Besides, its sleeves were only an inch or two too short, something of a record fit for a French shirt.

Regina took her money at the cash register, passing the receipt along with a second piece of paper. "Someone has been watching you," she hissed under her breath. "Don't look now, but it's the woman in the red suit at the scarves." She looked up and smiled. "Good-bye. Give Michele my love when you get home!"

Sylvia smiled into the dramatically drawn eyes. "I certainly will. Good-bye, Regina." She waved airily and was gone, giving the woman in red a quick once-over as she left the store.

She had never seen the woman before but that didn't mean a thing. Sylvia walked quickly to the hotel, not pausing until she'd closed the door to her room behind her. She dumped the parcels on the bed and pulled out the paper she'd been clutching tightly all the way back.

The name was Françoise Mathieu. There was an address too, apparently out of town. No phone number. Regina had unsuspected reserves of discretion after all.

Mr. Jung, a clean-cut fastidious man in his thirties, met her at the door of the city offices. He kissed her hand politely after assuring himself that it was indeed she. They stood in the square by the cannon making the usual numbing conversation until Jung suggested retiring to the café.

"Have you been enjoying your visit to Geneva?" he asked as they walked down the street, both of them pretending that she wasn't towering over him.

He seemed assured that she would answer yes, as in fact she did, amused all the while by the smug attitude the locals had to what was, after all, not one of the great metropolises of the world.

"Ah, here we are." He ushered her into a pretty café decorated with hundreds of flowers and green plants. She ordered a Cinzano as he did and looked around her. These were not the beautiful people. The habitués here were clearly more ordinary folk, secretaries and low-level civil servants, though evidencing inordinate concern with outward show.

"Is my mother-in-law well?" He smiled, showing a mouthful of the whitest teeth she'd seen except on television toothpaste ads.

"Very well, the last time I saw her. Missing Geneva, of course." Sylvia was getting very good at this. "I hope you don't mind your mother-in-law giving me your name?" She felt it would be just as well to remind him of his filial duty before she asked him to break the law.

"No, no. Whatever help I can give you is yours," he replied gallantly.

"Well, all right, but please don't hesitate to tell me that it can't be done if it's too difficult," Sylvia cautioned hypocritically. "My mother-in-law lives in Geneva. Unfortunately, my husband has been estranged from her for years and I know she's no longer a young woman. I want to find her and make peace with her before she dies."

"You are quite right. Such a thing will bring her much happiness in her last years," Jung said sympathetically. "Why do you not approach her?"

"Well, that's the problem. I can't get her address from my husband since he won't talk about her at all. So I don't know where she lives."

"Is she not in the telephone directory?"

"No. I think she must be living with a friend or else she doesn't have a telephone."

"I see."

"Your mother-in-law said that records are kept of all residents of Switzerland." Sylvia looked down at the table. "I know how difficult it would be to find her. If you can't do it, please just tell me."

She held her breath.

As she'd hoped, Jung, like most European males, couldn't bring himself to admit to a woman that his abilities were in any way limited. "No, it can be done. With great difficulty," he added grimly. He forestalled her protests. "You must allow me to see if I can help you. No, I insist."

"Well, if you insist." She hesitated. "There's one other thing."

"Yes?"

"There was an Australian woman working here in 1965 and 1966. She knew all about the trouble between my husband and his mother. I know almost nothing about it, he'd never give me the whole story. So it would help a lot if I could find her and talk to her."

Sylvia gazed at him sincerely.

Jung swallowed the whole thing. "I don't know if we keep the work cards so long, but I can try to find out."

"Her name is Janice Wagoner. I wouldn't be surprised to learn that she'd emigrated since, but it's worth a try." She gave him the few details she had about Mrs. West and then took her leave. Jung promised to call her in a day or two with whatever information he could dig up.

She returned to her room and ordered a quick meal, unwilling to hazard out into the harsh cold world of women in red. She tried to read with the radio on and the curtains securely drawn but found it impossible to concentrate. She went to the window and pulled back the drapes. Geneva's lake lay before her, obstinately placid and ordinary. The figures in the street appeared malevolent; any of them could be an enemy. She shivered and closed the drapes.

The telephone startled her.

"Hi, Sylvia. It's Herb Dutton."

"Herb! Where are you calling from?"

"I'm here, in Geneva. I'd love to see a friendly face. Have you had dinner yet?"

"Yes, I just ate. But I could do with a coffee."

"Great. I'll meet you at the hotel and you can watch me munch."

Herb arrived at the table shortly after Sylvia had received her first refill. He was patently delighted to see her and was unaccustomedly effusive.

"Sylvia! You look wonderful! How are things going? What are you doing here?"

"I'm pursuing John." She sighed. "Assuming he's alive."

"What?"

"The car accident was a phony, Herb. We're supposed to believe that John learned to drive and ran away with a not-very-young hooker."

"Hmm. I see. So you figure that he arranged for the crash?"

"Or else someone else did and he's been murdered. Either way, I'm hoping that I can learn enough about him, here in his native land as they say, to give the boys a picture of their dad."

"And?"

"And no luck. About all I've achieved is to come up with more questions. No answers, just questions."

Herb put his hand over hers. "You sound tired."

"I am." She pulled herself together. "Enough about my depressing life. Let's talk about you. What are you doing here?"

"Government business. Very top-secret so my presence here isn't supposed to be known by any but a very privileged few. If anyone else thinks she saw me, I'll deny it."

She laughed. "How long aren't you here for?"

"Only a few more days."

"Then where?"

"Then I'm not going to be in London."

"Aha, with Rupert. Give him my best, will you?"

Herb was eating ravenously. Sylvia watched in silence until he appeared to have quelled the worst of his hunger pangs.

"How ever did you track me down, Herb?"

"Ah," he smiled mysteriously. "I have spies everywhere. Actually, I spoke to Rupert yesterday. He said he's kept in touch with your office and suggested I give you a call. Which I was delighted to do, of course."

Sylvia smiled fondly at the thought of Rupert's solicitude. "Is he coming to town, by any chance?"

"What for?"

"I don't know. He said he was coming to the continent."

"In confidence, we will be back here but not for a while, not until the very end of the month. And then it will be a hush-hush visit. I don't think either of us will be able to contact you."

"Damn. I was hoping to get some help from Rupert. I need information and I have almost no way of getting it."

"I know government people," he offered.

Sylvia thought about the embassy's interest in returning her to the States. There was no point in involving Herb in that unless she had to. "No, I'd rather stay away from official circles."

He pondered the problem. "Hey! I know one place that might help. There's a research institute here that's very cozy with Wandling. I imagine Rupert's stock is pretty high there."

"What's this place called?"

"Anvers et Companie."

"I think I've heard of it." Sylvia searched her memory. "I've got it! There was an article on the Common Market in the last *Time* or *Newsweek*. Anvers was quoted."

"Could be. They do a lot of research for the E.E.C. Unfortunately, I don't know anyone there particularly well, but if you mention Rupert's name, you're bound to get red carpet treatment."

As he left her at the elevator, Sylvia smiled. "I hope we'll have a chance to get together again soon."

"I'm afraid that's doubtful, Sylvia, much as I'd like to. Both Rupert and I will be going what the police call undercover very soon. Security on this project is extremely tight."

Sylvia tried to be optimistic about Anvers et Companie. It

would probably prove as fruitless a lead as all the others so far, but it would be easier to sleep tonight if she went to bed with a little hope.

Or with something warm and breathing.

She took a cold shower and pushed the thought out of her mind.

THIRTY-TWO

The morning was sunny and warm, perfect for a trip into the country. She started to get into a taxi in front of the hotel and then thought better of it.

The doorman directed her to the nearest department store, only a block away. She had to kill a few minutes waiting for it to open, but fortunately Swiss women did their shopping early and within fifteen minutes it was jammed.

Sylvia wandered around, apparently aimlessly, and eventually ended up in a dressing room in the women's fashion department. She tried on a hideous black dress with a silver lamé jacket that the saleswoman, with the mendacity of her kind the world over, assured her was absolutely her. If Sylvia had really thought so, she'd have shot herself. She succeeded in repressing a shudder and asked the woman to wait in the dressing room while she went out to see herself in the large mirror on the floor.

No one seemed to be unduly interested in her, except for a few well-dressed matrons who were fascinated in a horrible kind of way by the dress. Sylvia sheepishly avoided their eyes and meandered around as if to see the monstrosity from a number of angles. She noticed an exit sign near another entrance to the fitting rooms.

After telling the saleswoman that yes, it was amazing, this outfit, but she really had no need of it at the moment, she changed back into her clothes and headed for the rear stairs. She slipped out, unobserved, by the back door.

There were plenty of taxis on the Rue de Rhône. She flagged the third one.

"Do you know this address?" she asked.

"Oh, yes. It is possible to go there, but it is a drive of a long distance," the driver informed her in a heavily accented English.

"I would want you to wait for me and bring me back. How much would it cost me to hire you for the morning?"

He named a figure that was only twice an outrageous amount. Sylvia countered with a much smaller number that would still pay for his family's weekend on the Riviera. They agreed on a midpoint.

The driver proceeded slowly through the city, continuing to crawl on the quiet streets outside the main core. He noticed her impatience. "The police have a machine, an electric eye, on the roads. They are always around. If you speed in Switzerland, you will most certainly spend much time talking with the police."

Sylvia was increasingly unappreciative of the neatness and regulation of the, albeit clean, city. It was cheering to leave it for the wilder hills and then the mountains. The drive became quite exciting on the two-lane mountain roads with their hairpin curves and heart-stopping drops.

She forced herself to concentrate on the scenery instead of the road. The countryside was tamer than the American and Canadian Rockies; no doubt the Swiss had regulations concerning the permissible height of peaks. But on a scale of one to ten, it still ranked high. She counted no less than forty shades of green in twenty minutes, and hardly fewer of gray. As they rose, the valleys fell away beneath them, revealing voluptuous contours and subtleties of light and color that made the earth look as soft as velvet. The valleys were linked to the violently blue sky by the harsh vertical lines of the Alps.

Sylvia opened her compact a few times, ostensibly to check her makeup. The road behind them was clear.

The cab turned off the paved road onto a private lane that ran through a thick wood filled with wild flowers and birds. Sylvia had the illusion of driving straight into the heart of the mountain; in reality, the path twisted up around crags and boulders to a flat, tiny plateau overlooking the many hollows beneath the foothills.

"The house is up there," the cabbie announced, pointing vaguely off to one side. "I can take you further in the car."

"Thank you. Just wait here, please."

"Yes. If Madame Mathieu will see you, I'll be waiting near the house. If you return in the next few minutes, I will be here still. She does not see everyone."

"How did you know who lives here? Oh, the name was on the paper with the address," she added.

"Ah, everyone who fought in the last war knows Madame Mathieu. She is a great lady. She saved many lives. But she knows too much about the so-called heroes of the French resistance. So," he shrugged cynically, she cannot go back to her own land. Even Switzerland is afraid to take too much notice of her. So she lives here, alone like a nun with her servant. Bah! It is a disgrace."

"Why is she ignored in this country? I thought Switzerland was neutral during the war."

"Yes, as a country it was. But many of us have family in France. We could not stand by and see them suffer at the hands of the Boches! Many individuals fought."

Sylvia was fascinated. "Did Madame Mathieu organize the Swiss volunteers? Is that how you all came to know her?"

A mistake. A direct personal question didn't go over well in Europe, especially with a man such as this one. It was not unlikely that a fair amount of his life wouldn't bear scrutiny. Sylvia apologized for her lack of tact. It was like speaking to one of the granite faces of the mountain. She trudged up the hill to the front door.

Madame Mathieu may have been penalized in some ways by her past, but she certainly lived in a setting fit for a hero. The house was built into the hill. Every room opened onto a terrace with a view similar to that probably enjoyed on Olympus. The road couldn't be seen from the windows and it seemed, thus nestled into the forest, as though one was the last human being in the world.

Sylvia rang the bell. After a long time, a gnarled hand appeared, opening the door a meager inch. A cracked voice asked her business.

"My name is Sylvia West. I was sent to Madame Mathieu by Regina Forrester in Geneva. I don't know if Madame Mathieu actually knows Ms. Forrester, but I needed help with some inquiries I'm making and I was told that Madame Mathieu could assist me."

"Madame Mathieu is not a reference library. She cannot help you." The door started to close.

"Please! I'm desperate! My husband disappeared from our home in the United States a few weeks ago and I'm trying to find him. His children have the right to know what happened to their father. Somehow, he's mixed up with a right-wing political group in Geneva and I think they're dangerous people. I was told that Madame Mathieu was interested in such things." Sylvia put every ounce of emotion she possessed into her plea. "Please help me!"

"Wait here." The voice was rough and rude. The door shut, leaving Sylvia with the awful feeling that she could stand there for ten days and it wouldn't open again.

It was a very long time before anything happened. Then the door opened very slowly and very grudgingly.

"She says she'll see you. I don't know why." The voice belonged to an ancient hag, wrinkled as a newborn baby. She was frowning horribly at Sylvia. If she'd had her way, Sylvia would have starved to death waiting for entry.

"I'm very grateful," Sylvia ventured. A startlingly loud sniff put an end to the conversation.

She was led through a long hall to a vast room at the other end of the house. Straight ahead was a wall entirely made of glass, looking out onto a vertiginous panorama of blue sky and far below, tiny dots of green and brown. Sylvia instinctively reached for the nearest wall to avoid falling off the end of the world. She recollected herself and looked around at the room itself. It was paneled in limed oak, the golden tones contrasting peacefully with the dark shining hardwood floor. Despite the temperature outside, a fire was burning intensely in an enormous stone fireplace.

"Please excuse the heat," the occupant of a rocking chair in front of the fire, a second very old woman, whispered. "I have a heart condition and I suffer from the cold."

"It's very good of you to see me," Sylvia thanked her, dismissing the temperature with a wave of her damp hand. "I'm an American. I don't know how much your companion told you, but I'm—"

"You're looking for your husband, Mrs. West. Yes, Otile told me that much. Sit down, my dear, and have some tea."

Sylvia helped herself. It was a fragrant mint variety, exquisite in taste.

The woman turned to Otile. "You may leave us now."

"You are not to get tired," the crone threatened. "I'll leave you one of these days, the way you ignore my advice." She left the room reluctantly, muttering and casting black glances at Sylvia who was hard put to pretend not to see them.

"A wonderful woman. A bit difficult at times, perhaps, but very loyal and competent. She's been with me since I was fifteen. Can you imagine me fifteen?"

Despite her present great age, it actually wasn't difficult to picture Madame Mathieu as a young girl. She still had a beautiful olive complexion, large black eyes, and an expressive full mouth. She was sitting down but she was obviously beautifully proportioned, and Sylvia could see the long neck and the graceful, finely tapered hands.

"Well, let us go on. I do tire very quickly so you'd better tell me about your search right away."

Sylvia told her story. She found herself including every detail, something she hadn't done with anyone else. There was a great deal to tell when she put it all together; it took almost forty minutes.

"You are a very enterprising young woman," Madame Mathieu observed approvingly. "But," she added in a grave voice. "I do not think you realize what you are getting into. You do not have the background for this that we in Europe do. You cannot understand the power, the violence of these people. You have never lived with them. You fought them yes, but not on your own land, in your own homes."

"I'm beginning to understand," Sylvia answered evenly. "I started out to look for my husband. I still want to find him but there's more at stake than my marriage. Something evil is happening. I can feel it. These people, whoever they are, have resources. Lots of them. Not just here, but in the States, and no one is prepared to do anything about it. That's what I can't understand. No one knows or cares which makes it all the more important that I find out whatever I can. Someone will have to use my information if only I can get it."

"Oh, my dear. People do know. Do you really think that such groups could continue to grow without the governments of the world knowing about them? Oh, that is not to say that the United States approves, but these creatures must have friends in high places to survive. And survive they do. Friends in the government, in the armies, the police forces, in business. That is why nothing is done."

"If that's the case, what should I do? Is there any point in even trying to find them? Must they win?"

"No, of course not. This kind of scum can't live in bright daylight. Like all slugs and worms, they hide in the dark. Knowledge is a powerful weapon against them.

"Don't forget, they have been fought successfully. We fought them here in Europe and we won. But they are patient, they husband their resources, they make new friends or buy them, and then, when everyone is looking the other way, they try again. Our vigilance must be unflagging. And most of you young people don't worry enough."

"Well, I'm learning to. But you need to tell me how to proceed."

"That is difficult to say." The old woman was clearly not enthusiastic about Sylvia's determination to persist. "What do you know at the moment? You know that your husband had a client that fronted for a political organization. You know that this organization was probably right wing. You know that it has an office in Geneva and that it is highly secretive. You don't know if your husband's disappearance is connected to this organization. You don't even know if he's dead or alive."

Sylvia remained silent.

Madame Mathieu sighed. "You would have to start by finding out more about this organization. And that would be very dangerous."

"I'm afraid. Don't get me wrong, madame. I'm terrified. But it has gone too far now for me to try to step out. Too far for me and for the children. We're in danger no matter what I do. I also have the feeling that something important is just about to happen." Sylvia laughed hollowly. "But don't think I'm not absolutely terrified."

"Well, that is something I suppose. If you are really afraid, there is a chance for you." She looked at Sylvia in silence for a long while and then raised her eyebrows. "Very well. It will be necessary to find this lodge that they are going to. I am unable to move around myself, as you can see, but other people are now my eyes. I will see what I can find out. But you must be very careful. It appears, if you are right, that they have killed more than once. It becomes easier to kill each time."

"I was very careful not to be followed up here," Sylvia interjected.

"Good. Of course they know of me. Everyone here does. But it is very important for your safety that they do not know you have seen me. They will assume that on your own you cannot find out very much. But with my resources..." She moved her hands expressively.

"You speak as if you know them."

The old woman didn't answer immediately. Eventually she came to some sort of decision and turned to Sylvia. "Yes. I think I know of these people. At least, I know about some of their friends. But I had not heard that anything important was ready and I had not suspected that their reach stretched across the ocean."

She paused again and fixed Sylvia with her dark eyes, compelling her to take seriously what she was about to say.

"There are dangerous people in Europe. The last war taught many of us how to kill. We too became animals. It was the only way to fight them; maybe it still is. We have always said that we, at least, became like that in a good cause, but it is probably fortunate that we are dying because we might, in the end, become exactly the same as they are.

"This is not the battlefield for a nice American. You believe in justice and equality and the presumption of innocence. You have no idea what is really going on under the flat stones, in the dark of night, behind black corners.

"I can give you some help, but not a great deal. I will try to obtain information about this lodge. I may not be able to get it and what I get may not be correct. But I will give you what I find out. I can do no more than that. The information I get is bought with the blood of my people. It is not that I do not trust your sincerity. But I cannot trust the lives of my people to your naïveté."

In the deeply shadowed eyes of the old woman, Sylvia caught a blood-chilling glimpse of the ghosts of war-torn Europe that still paraded on the graves of dead heroes. "I can only thank you for what you're willing to do. You've been very kind, hearing me out. A stranger who has come to interfere in your business."

The Frenchwoman appeared to have changed her mind. "No, my dear. I was wrong a minute ago. It is not only the affair of Europe. It was, perhaps, thirty-five years ago. Now, from what you say, it is yours too. America got off lightly in the last war. You were not disillusioned the way we were and you do not live openly with the hatreds as we do. But you won't escape again. It has crossed the sea now, and I suppose it is as good a time as any for you to learn too."

Sylvia gave her a card with the hotel's number written on it. Otile came into the room so promptly she must have been listening outside the door.

Sylvia got up to leave and remembered something. "Oh, yes. I think it would be helpful to have von Schagg followed. Do you know a reliable private investigator? I can afford to pay for his time."

"You will be contacted. Whoever comes from me will tell you that it is very cold outside. Don't listen to anyone else. And on no account, go anywhere with anyone else. One more thing. If someone tells you that I want to see you, don't believe them even if they tell you how cold it is. It is a common trick. I will contact you myself in some way, if I must. But I will not want you to come out here again. It would be far too dangerous. For both of us. We do not want them to think that you may be on the right track."

"Am I?"

"I can't tell you anything more, my dear. Good-bye."

Otile showed her out silently. Sylvia turned to thank her too, but the door shut soundlessly before she could get a word out.

The taxi driver was waiting for her in the car.

"You were very fortunate, madame. She sees almost no one these days and no one for so much time. How is she?"

"Old, very old. How would you expect someone that old to be?"

"She is sixty." He started the car and returned to the road.

Sylvia couldn't believe her ears. "Sixty? That's not possible!"

The driver wasn't talking anymore.

She couldn't bear to imagine what would age a person so.

The hotel looked mighty inviting. She would start with a double Scotch and go on from there. She pulled out her wallet to pay the driver and waited for him to pull up in front of the hotel. He kept on driving.

"Hey! That's my hotel! What are you doing?"

"Yes, that is why you would not want to get out there. Most people who visit Madame Mathieu do not want anyone to know that fact. Is that not so?"

"Yes."

"Well, if someone is watching for you, they could very easily find me again. I would not refuse to give them the information they want. I have a family. I will take you back to where I picked you up."

Sylvia sat back with a wry smile. She had a lot to learn and very little time in which to learn it. Madame Mathieu was right to refuse her unlimited help. She'd be lucky to get out of this in one piece, let alone with the information she wanted.

She returned to the department store. Only two and a half hours had passed. A manic shopper might well spend that much time in a big store. She herself would personally expect to be carried out if she attempted it, but who was to know that?

She bought a few inexpensive but bulky items and left by

the main door, heavily laden and trying to strike the right note midway between euphoria and prostration.

Someone had been in her room again. This time, he'd left a calling card. A butted-out Gauloise cigarette in the ashtray.

Sylvia put her parcels down slowly. This was no game that they were playing. It was for keeps and she had only one weapon. Her wits.

A real tourist would be outraged.

She called the desk and asked for her chambermaid. Sylvia unhappily bawled her out in the hallway, making sure that her voice was audible throughout the floor.

She felt terrible for the poor young woman who was in tears as she protested her undoubted innocence. But the young woman would certainly survive the inquisition to complain about the American bitch. The American's future was much less assured.

THIRTY-THREE

"By my calculations, it's eight-thirty in Geneva. Am I right?"

"Bess! It's good to hear your voice! How are you?"

"Okay. My news isn't great, though."

"Oh, shit. Well, in that case I might as well break it to you that it's six-thirty here. I didn't want to make you feel bad."

"Six-thirty. Jeez, that's awfully early for what I've got to tell you."

"Plunge ahead."

Bess hesitated. "Okay. To start with, we haven't come up with a thing on The Foundation's financial affairs. They've got lots of the green stuff but we can't find out where it comes from or where it goes."

"You said that was to start with. Is there more bad news?"

"Uh, yes."

"Out with it."

"Maggie isn't feeling too well."

"What's wrong with her?"

"She's in the hospital."

"What?"

"In the hospital. She got mugged last night."

"Who mugged her?"

"Two guys near her apartment. It can happen. There have been a few muggings in her neighborhood, so it might not have anything to do with the case."

"How is she?"

"She'll be fine. A lot of bruises and a few stitches. She won't have scars that would be visible to anyone but a very close friend."

"Did she get a good look at the men?"

"No. It was night and the whole thing happened very fast. They didn't say anything, just roughed her up and grabbed her purse. Fortunately, she wasn't carrying her briefcase with all her notes."

"How long will she be in hospital?"

"Oh, it's hard to say."

"If she isn't hurt badly, it shouldn't be hard to say. Bess, you're holding something back."

No response.

"Bess. I want to know." Sylvia spoke in an ominously quiet voice.

"All right. She has a couple of broken bones."

"They broke some bones?"

"Her arms. The doctors say that they'll be as good as new when the casts come off."

"Okay, Bess, listen and listen carefully. I want both of you to stop your detective work immediately. No more poking around into The Foundation. You understand me?"

"You're jumping to conclusions. There's no reason to think that it's connected to John's disappearance."

"Don't argue with me. I don't want to discuss it. I'm ordering you to just lay off. Got it?"

"Got it."

Sylvia didn't trust Bess when she caved in that quickly. She started to repeat her warnings but got nowhere, since Bess kept pointing out with injured innocence that she'd already agreed to stay out of trouble.

Sylvia couldn't get back to sleep so she had a protracted breakfast in her room. Regina called as she was draining her third pot of coffee.

"How about joining a few friends for the theater tonight?"

In her present mood, that was the last thing in the world Sylvia wanted to do but she wasn't sure how to go about refusing.

"Come on," Regina pressed when she sensed Sylvia's hesitation. "You'll enjoy it and there's no point in spending the night alone."

"Well, thanks." Sylvia sighed. Hell had to be one round of compulsory socializing after another.

They agreed to meet first at Regina's apartment for a drink.

The Savoy located Rupert in the coffee shop.

"Sylvia! I'm so pleased you called! How are you?"

"Okay. Listen, Rupert, I'm sorry to bother you but I need help. The pace is stepping up and I think I better get myself as much protection as possible. Herb took me out for dinner the other night and mentioned that you knew some big shots in Geneva."

"I thought you were going to travel to get away from everything." Rupert was upset. "You don't know your way around Europe. If there's any chance that you're in danger, you shouldn't be there."

"Maybe, but I don't have the time to argue the point. I need information and I need protection. Herb suggested I might be able to get both at Anvers et Companie."

"Are you sure you won't go home and forget about this?"

"I'm sure."

"Okay, then that's a good idea. The guy to speak to is Paul Desrochers. I'll give him a call myself and tell him you're coming over today. He'll give you anything you need."

"Thanks, Rupert."

"Want to tell me what's going on?"

"It's too complicated for the telephone. I'll fill you in next time we see each other."

"I hope that will be soon. Any chance of talking you into a visit to London?"

Sylvia smiled into the receiver. "Maybe soon. But not today."

In a city that worshiped political power, it was not entirely surprising to find a research institute brazenly clothed in its attributes. Anvers et Companie lived in a large marble mausoleum that existed solely to show a materialist world that thinkers and scientists carried clout too.

The inside of the foyer was awe-inspiring. The hall itself went up three stories, each inch of which was decorated and embellished like an Egyptian tomb. The floor was a mosaic, made up of tiny colored stones that must have taken the better part of ten thousand slaves' lives to lay. The receptionist watched the doorways as well as a dozen tiny television screens that monitored the activity everywhere except in the washrooms. And Sylvia didn't have any real confidence in the sanctity of the toilets either.

"Sylvia West to see Mr. Desrochers." The young woman's voice was nasal. She was clearly a sophomore from one of the better American colleges, over here on an exchange program to learn European poise and a second language. "You can go up now, Mrs. West. Third floor."

Sylvia smiled and stepped over to the elevators. One of them opened as if by magic as she approached.

"Mrs. West? I'm Paul Desrochers. Rupert told me you'd

be coming around today." The speaker was a man in his forties clad in the local uniform, a navy pinstriped three-piece suit. He wasn't unattractive now, but he still bore the scars of pubescent acne.

"It's very good of you to see me." Sylvia took his outstretched hand, wincing only slightly as his fancy gold wedding band cut into her. "I won't take up much of your time."

"We're always happy to help a friend of Rupert's." He beamed at her and ushered her into an office near the bank of elevators. "Can I offer you a cup of coffee? Or tea?"

"No, thanks." Sylvia played for time until she could decide how much to tell him. "I gather you operate much as Wandling does back home?"

"Very much so. We're a research foundation that works independently of business or government. Naturally, both retain us to work on specific projects for them. Just like they do with the Wandling Institute."

"Do you do work in the States too?"

"Not usually. We're supranational in the sense of having no allegiance to a particular country or government, but we are primarily European. When we need American data, we normally work with Wandling. In a loose sense, we're often affiliated. Since you're interested, perhaps you'd like a tour of our facility?"

"Yes, I'd love that sometime. Right now, I don't want to waste your morning so maybe I'd better get down to business. I don't know what Rupert told you. . . ."

"Well"—Desrochers moved his hands deprecatingly—"he did give me a very brief summary of the problem, not that I understand it fully."

They were interrupted by a knock on the door. A middle-aged executive secretary entered holding an ashtray and a crystal water jug.

"Yes, Lorraine. What is it?"

"Will these do? The designer suggested them."

"They look fine. Thank you." He saw her out and returned to Sylvia. "Sorry. Go ahead."

Sylvia dashed over a very edited version of her story, ending with the fact that she needed information about the Geneva branch of The Foundation.

"I can certainly make inquiries for you. There's very little going on in Geneva that I can't find out about." He tried not to sound pompous. "Have you contacted the American embassy? They might know something about an American company operating here."

"They don't. I have spoken to a Peter Rosslin but all he can do at the moment is keep an eye on my safety."

"I see. Are you—" The phone buzzed. "Excuse me, Mrs. West. Yes? Oh, at least ten small round tables, plus the large one." He listened to the voice on the other end for a few seconds. "Well," he said sarcastically, "it shouldn't be too much of a strain for you to estimate attendance. And that's how many chairs."

He put down the receiver, shaking his head. "I rarely lose my temper, but when I do it's because my overpaid staff won't make the simplest decisions without me."

"Like buying new furniture?" Sylvia smiled sympathetically, thinking fondly about Bess.

He sighed eloquently. "Now, back to your problem. Where were we? Oh, yes. I was going to ask if you were sure that you were in physical danger?"

"Not positive but the evidence points to it."

"And you don't think it might be a good idea to leave the investigation to the professionals?"

Sylvia shrugged. She'd been over this ground before and anyway, it had all the earmarks of an attempt to protect her engineered by Rupert.

Desrochers tactfully dropped the subject. "I've got your room number at the hotel. I'll call you as soon as I learn anything."

"Wonderful."

"I'll show you out. In fact, maybe we should take the long way round. Give you an idea of what we look like."

He took her elbow, a gesture that normally would have been irritating but in her present state was comforting. The building was smaller than the Wandling's physical resource but more impressive in other ways. Sylvia had the impression of being at a tiny United Nations. Every conceivable race was represented, from sari-covered women with dots on their foreheads to Sheik of Araby types in flowing caftans and headdresses. The most impressive section of the institute was its computer center. According to Desrochers it was one of the most sophisticated systems anywhere and with it he could hook into any computer terminal in the western world.

Sylvia made a great show of how impressed she was, which

did nothing to harm their relations. He was justifiably proud of Anvers. Which was good. It meant that he'd knock himself out to show how capable it was of obtaining data for her.

Regina's apartment was even more depressing on a second viewing than it had been on a first. Sylvia winced slightly at the mural in the foyer and greeted the few theatergoers who had already arrived. Regina introduced her around and then took her by the hand into the tiny kitchen.

"I'm dying of thirst. What will you drink?" She turned the faucets on full blast. "It's awfully cold in here, isn't it? It's driving me mad."

Sylvia stared. It had to be at least eighty degrees in the place.

"I hate being cold, don't you?" Regina repeated.

The significance of the statement hit her. Regina of all people!

"Yes, sure," she answered weakly. "Too bad you don't have a big fireplace."

Regina handed her a slip of paper, folded twice, and motioned her to shove it into her brassiere.

Her hostess reverted to her usual form. She gulped down a glass of water and chattered gaily about some outrageous scandal she'd heard of that day. She was unnecessarily enlarging upon the more sordid details when the rest of the party arrived.

They all trotted off to a light supper, so-called because it consisted of only three courses, apparently insufficient to sustain life but adequate to carry them through to a final curtain.

Sylvia was glutted by the time they arrived at the elegant old theater. The play itself was mediocre, though its setting helped make up the deficiencies, and Sylvia was happy to slip out of the building during the intermission. She found herself near the walls of the old town and a short distance from the river. She settled herself contentedly to have a cigarette or two and only remembered the play after the intermission had been over for a while.

Regina was thankful to see her when the group filed out of the theater. "I was afraid you'd been kidnapped," she announced gaily but thinly.

Sylvia explained why she'd missed the last act.

"But it isn't safe there at night!" Regina exclaimed. The

others made light of the dangers and suggested that they all go for a walk along the river before retiring to a restaurant for another meal.

Sylvia declined their invitation, pleading fatigue, and gratefully escaped back to the hotel. She had not been entertained this time by Regina's friends. Regina was making quite a sacrifice if she had to hang around them to give herself a cover story.

The paper she'd been handed had two names on it. One was that of the investigator, the second that of a lodge. Beside the latter there was a question mark. Still, it was a lead of sorts. She hadn't been able to come up with anything better. She dialed the investigator's number.

"Hullo?" The voice answering the telephone was deep and strained. It sounded like the speaker just had a throat operation.

"Is Colin Lawrence there?"

"Who wants him?"

This was probably Lawrence himself. The name suggested an Englishman and you couldn't get more English than a cockney.

"My name is uh, let's just say that I met a friend of yours in the country and I'd like to meet you. Can you suggest a meeting place?"

"Awright. Meet me in Carouge. The Yellow Wing. Eleven tomorrow."

Sylvia started to ask for directions but he'd hung up.

She was too excited to sleep so she went downstairs to see if she could find a good map of the city and of the canton. Nothing doing, naturally; Geneva didn't believe in life after ten.

THIRTY-FOUR

Sylvia went downstairs for breakfast. She asked the waiter for directions to Carouge and was somewhat surprised at the dubious look he gave her.

"Carouge is not a place suitable for Madame."

"That's all right, I want to see it. How do I get there?"

It was a small town, almost a suburb, outside Geneva. She could take a taxi. But there was no point in taking a crowd. Uncomfortably aware that she might be carrying a shadow, she bobbed in and out of a series of boutiques looking for an opportunity to vanish unseen.

By ten-thirty she was desperate. She whirled around suddenly and hailed a cab.

"Listen, I want to go to the Yellow Wing in Carouge. But I don't want anyone to follow me. Can you get me there without a tail?"

The driver was in his forties and his eyes said he'd seen everything. He nodded in a desultory fashion as though it went without saying.

He eased the car out into traffic and suddenly took off. Sylvia clung to the seat as she watched him swing in and out of lanes, around corners and through intersections.

They went past the theater area. She recognized the old city's walls and the university. But that was the only landmark she knew. By the time they'd reached Carouge, a seedy little place filled with the first long-haired males she'd seen in Geneva, she was dizzy from the drive and totally without a sense of direction.

The taxi pulled up with a squeal in front of a dark dingy bar sporting a neon sign that no longer functioned.

"No one followed us."

Sylvia had to agree.

The bar was dank and evil-smelling, furnished with old wooden tables and plastic-covered chairs. It was humming despite the hour with overdressed men flashing diamond rings and jeweled belts on skin-tight pants and shirts. There were women inside as well, but like most animal species, here they were the dowdy sex.

No one appeared to notice her in the gloom, including the only waiter. She sat down gingerly at a filthy table.

A scratched voice behind her spoke. "I'm here, Mrs. West." She turned around quickly. "You were given my name?"

There was no response. Lawrence was evidently a man of few words who didn't choose to waste them on self-evident facts.

"I'd like to hire you to follow a man. Even if he goes out of town. Are you available right now?" Sylvia peered into the shadow of the booth that hid Lawrence. She couldn't see him unless she wanted to make a big deal out of it.

"Yuh. Who's the bloke?"

"His name is von Schagg. I don't know what name he's using here."

"Where do I find him?"

"He hangs out at the men's club up from the Grand Passage. I don't have a picture of him, but he's tall, maybe six three or four, gray-haired, forty-five or so. Very good physical condition. And probably dangerous. He came to Geneva no more than a week or ten days ago and he may be staying at the club. At any rate, I think he's a member. The doorman recognized him and he went in as though he owned the place."

"Okay. I can find him. Hundred and fifty francs plus expenses a day."

"Wow! You must be good." Sylvia was jocular but her audience lacked an appreciation of her charm.

"Yeah. I am." He stood up and the light from the weak fixture caught his face. He stood at least six six, maybe more, and weighed two-fifty dripping wet. Nonetheless, it was his face that one would remember. He'd been, from the look of him, in at least a dozen knife fights. Which explained his voice. Someone had once got his throat. She didn't like to contemplate how that someone looked now.

"You can contact me at my hotel. I'm staying at—"

"Yeah. I'll call myself George."

He left abruptly. There wasn't much keeping her there either, so she found another taxi.

She hadn't been able to locate 2034 Rue des Ormes, the address John had given to American immigration authorities as his last home in Geneva. A twenty-eight-year-old clue wasn't likely to take her very much further, but she figured that in lieu of being a talented sleuth, she ought at least to be a thorough one. The clerk at the hotel desk was intrigued by the problem. He enlisted the aid of another member of staff and the three of them spent more than an hour poring over detailed maps of Geneva and environs.

"Is Madame certain that she has the correct address?" The clerk was perturbed. It offended his Swiss sense of order and propriety that someone should have misplaced an entire street.

No, Madame was far from certain. She retired to her room.

The red light on her telephone was flashing which meant that the operator had a message for her. Mr. Jung had called and wanted to meet with her at five today.

She curled up with her newspapers, able to enjoy them now that the day promised not to be a total loss.

As she was leaving the hotel, the helpful desk clerk caught up with her. "Madame! I have solved it!" He was burbling with pride.

"You found Rue des Ormes?" Maybe she was getting too cynical. She had found it easy to reconcile herself to its non-existence.

"It has changed its name! Now it is Avenue Dufils."

"Is that so?" Sylvia spoke quietly.

"Yes, it was named after Monsieur Dufils, a very generous man who gave a large park to the city."

"Very interesting," she murmured absently.

"Madame is not happy?"

"Oh. Sorry. No, that's wonderful. Thanks again."

Madame was just bemused. She'd heard of Avenue Dufils before. It happened to be the street on which The Foundation had its Geneva office.

Jung was still in a meeting, but his secretary was expecting her. "Ah, Madame West! Monsieur Jung is very sorry that he will be late. He suggested that he could meet with you at the café you visited together."

Sylvia was on her second drink when he arrived.

"Hello, Mrs. West." He greeted her cheerfully, but as he sat down he looked around furtively.

"I appreciate your help very much," she told him. "I hope it was not too much trouble."

"No, not really. It is just that under normal circumstances, I would not give out this information. I hope that you have not mentioned this to anyone?"

"No, certainly not."

"Well, I have some bad news. I was unable to find any record of your mother-in-law in Geneva. Or in Switzerland. It is not simply that she no longer lives here; there is no record that she ever did."

"Is it possible that she just hasn't registered with you?"

"It is possible, of course. All things are possible. But it is not likely. Unless she has something to hide."

Sylvia digested this. "Could she get along without registering?"

"Oh, no. She would need papers. Everyone is registered. Sooner or later, they would require papers for some reason or other. But on occasion, the wrong name is used."

"An alias, you mean?"

"I think that is the word."

Jung was looking at her oddly.

"I can't imagine my mother-in-law using an alias," Sylvia hastened to comment. She didn't need anyone at city hall asking questions about her or her family. The embassy would love an excuse to ship her right out.

"However," Jung went on, "I have some news about Miss Wagoner."

"Oh, good. Is she still living here?"

"No, unfortunately."

Sylvia adopted a regretful expression.

"The records show that she lived and worked here, as you said. Though I do not know what she could have had to do with your mother-in-law. Miss Wagoner worked for Herman Weikert as a personal secretary during the entire time she was in Switzerland. He was the one who arranged her work permit. It is usually almost impossible to obtain."

"Then why did she get one?"

"I suppose because Mr. Weikert was a very important man. He was a judge for many years until he retired from the bench in 1959. He knows many of the politicians. In fact, he himself was a city councillor in 1960 for two years and then he retired from that too. He is now a very old man."

"He isn't dead?"

"No, I don't believe so. He was living with his daughter's family when I last heard of him. Near Geneva."

"Why would he need a personal secretary if he was retired?"

"I do not know. I heard it said that he was writing his memoirs, but I have not seen them so I suppose they were never finished. Or perhaps he did not desire to publish them after all," Jung said drily.

"Oh, why not?"

"Well, it is a long time ago now, but he was a judge in the thirties and forties." Jung stopped as though that should mean something to her.

"But Switzerland was neutral."

"We were neutral, yes. But still, we are European and we could not be untouched by the events of the time. Some of our young people did fight with one or other of the armies, and some Swiss were involved with politics even here."

"You mean, some Swiss were Nazis?"

"Not necessarily officially. But there were certainly some who were very pro-Axis. Weikert was one of them. So his memoirs would arouse a great deal of emotion, even now. Also, some of his former colleagues would not be happy to have their names mentioned just as memories are fading."

"Or dying." Sylvia recalled Madame Mathieu's words.

"Yes." Jung nodded reflectively. "Or dying."

"Do you know where he is living? Weikert?"

Jung stiffened. This was something he definitely didn't want to get into.

"I might be able to trace Miss Wagoner through him," she quickly added.

"Oh, I see." Jung paused. He shrugged. "He lived with his daughter and her family at one time. Perhaps he is still there. Their name is Kellermann."

Sylvia's heart jumped. "Kellermann. Was he a teacher, do you know?"

"I believe so. He even lived in your country at one time."

Like when The Foundation was being incorporated, for example. Sylvia tried to stay calm. "Where is their home?"

"At a lodge outside Geneva called Auberge Paradis. It's about two hours from here."

"Thank you, you've helped me a great deal. Would you like me to take anything to your mother-in-law when I go back to New York?"

"Thank you, no." Jung just wanted to see the end of her.

They separated with many good wishes on both sides. Sylvia was walking on air.

Paradis was the lodge named by Madame Mathieu's sources.

THIRTY-FIVE

Desrochers had invited her to a Saturday lunch at a trendy pub in the old town. Sylvia arrived on the dot of one and found her host already seated. The Swiss were nothing if not prompt, a quality she could have guessed at after a mere five days with John. She crossed to his table, nodding at a party of chic women she'd met with Regina. All of them, she noticed with amusement, were wearing clothes from the boutique.

"You already know people," Desrochers commented as she sat down.

"A few. Geneva is a very social place."

"It certainly is. I'm very pleased that you've had a chance to enjoy it."

Desrochers handed her a menu. "The steak-and-kidney pie is actually quite nice here." He ordered it for himself from the rosy-cheeked, plump waitress who might have just arrived from Devon.

"Make that two. And a draft for me too, please."

"Well, Sylvia, other than its social life, how do you find our town?"

"Great." She had learned to lie about it with enthusiasm. "It's particularly, uh, fascinating because of the United Nations' contingents. It's not the sort of place where you expect to see so many different types of people."

"Geneva looks like everyone should be blond, you mean?"

"Sort of."

They both laughed.

"The one thing I've really noticed," Sylvia continued, "is how many Arabs are in town. There are huge groups of them everywhere."

"That's true. More than there used to be but with the money they've got now, every country wants to be palsy with them. Israel excepted, of course."

Sylvia took a cautious sip of the beer. It wasn't half bad. Desrochers laughed at her surprise. "It comes from England," he explained. "We import a good many luxury items."

"Beer isn't a luxury at home. Sort of the poor man's drink."

"Not many poor men in here." Desrochers pointed out the interesting or influential figures having lunch around them. He appeared to know everyone. And everything about them.

"There isn't a lot of privacy in Geneva," Sylvia noted.

"Not a lot. It's too small a place. You have no idea how hard it is to maintain security at the institute."

"I guess when someone commissions a study, he wants to be the only one to see it."

"That, and the fact that a lot of companies, and governments for that matter, don't really believe their competitors use us too. In fact, it doesn't affect our neutrality but if it were known, it might affect business."

"I had no idea before I saw your place and Wandling how lucrative research could be."

He smiled. "Generally speaking, we're supported by the work we do, research, think tanks, conferences, and so on, but we get occasional help from charitable foundations and bequests. Ah, here comes the food!"

The pie was steaming hot. Too hot. Sylvia had never experienced food so hot. It suddenly occurred to her that the pies must have been heated in a microwave oven. She had been told over and over again that that was the cooking of the future but she had hoped not to live that long. She smiled wanly at Desrochers and picked at it.

"Paul! How are you?" A well-dressed man was standing at their table.

"Léon! May I introduce Madame West? Léon Karfont."

"Enchanted, madame. Paul, I have been meaning to call you but my days just disappear."

"I understand. Mine as well. We shall see each other next month, at any rate?"

"The tariff conference! Of course! I will look forward to it."

Desrochers sat down again. "Sorry for the interruption. He is a lovely man. We would be good friends except neither of us has the time to get together."

"Except on business."

"Except on business. We are managing a large conference for the E.E.C. next month and Léon is with the Department of Finance in France."

"What would he be doing here now?"

"Oh, Geneva is the hub of commerce for all of Europe. Much business is done here even if Switzerland is not itself involved. A neutral arena is always better for a negotiation."

"I see."

"But we get further and further away from the subject that concerns you most. How is your search going?"

"Better. It's definitely picking up. I was able to hire a private investigator to follow von Schagg. I mentioned him to you when I told you about The Foundation?"

"I remember."

"The detective is named Colin Lawrence. Perhaps you know him?"

"Colin Lawrence? No, I don't recall the name. I might recognize him if we met."

"He's not the kind of guy you forget." Sylvia described him.

Desrochers laughed. "No, you're quite right. I wouldn't forget him. He has been useful?"

"I haven't had my first report yet, but I have great hopes."

"I can see why. Anyway, as your other investigator, allow me to make my first report. I questioned my usual sources about The Foundation. It appears to be a legitimate charity, at least in the United States. I was told about a number of things it funds such as a nature club for young people, an old age home, that kind of thing. On the surface, it would seem to be what it claims."

"And under the surface?"

"I don't know if there is anything to find out but I'll continue to make inquiries for you. There was only one thing slightly out of the ordinary. Its conduct in Switzerland."

"What does it do here?"

"That is the crux of the matter. Nothing. It does nothing although it has the office and a few full-time employees. I'm told that it neither funds projects here nor raises money."

"Where does it get its money?"

"Private sources. Presumably in your country."

"Didn't you find it awfully secretive for a charity?"

"Yes and no. Most charities try to keep their funding sources secret from other organizations. They don't want the competition. Still, it does go about its good works very silently. Again, that's unusual but not exceptional."

"Maybe. I found out something else myself. My husband gave his last address in Geneva to American immigration when he entered the States. He gave a false address, false in the sense that he never lived there. I walked by this morning. It's been a parking lot for thirty years. And the interesting thing about it is that it is right next door to The Foundation's Geneva office."

Desrochers thought that one over. "Even so, what does that prove?"

Sylvia grimaced. "I don't know but it's an unusual fact and I'm collecting unusual facts. Like what you found out about The Foundation. No purpose in being here. No charitable purpose at any rate."

"Maybe you just hit on it. I don't know anything about American tax law. Could it be operating an office here for some tax reason?"

"You're asking me? I know less tax law than you do," Sylvia laughed. "My instincts tell me that there wouldn't be a legitimate tax reason, but don't go by me."

Desrochers looked at his watch. "Sylvia, I hate to say this but I'm due at a meeting in fifteen minutes. The real tragedy is that it's going to take me half an hour to get there."

"Oh, I'm sorry to have kept you!"

They hurried out, Sylvia insisting that she'd find her own way back to the hotel. She wanted to walk along the river for a while and she was in no rush to get anywhere.

The more she thought about what she knew, the less sense it made. Yet she had the feeling that the answer was just out of reach. Maybe she even had it right now, if only she could see it.

Rupert had left a message for her to call through international operator sixteen. He was waiting in his hotel room to speak to her.

"I wanted to hear your voice, Sylvia. How is everything?"

"Who knows? By the way, Desrochers is a doll. He's being very cooperative." Sylvia gave him a rundown on her latest discoveries. "Can you think of a legitimate reason for The Foundation to be in Geneva?"

"Not off the top. Except it is possible that Paul's information isn't complete. Maybe they do have some European project he didn't hear about."

"Surely not? He was very positive about his sources and he does know everyone."

"Okay. How about your new employee? It makes me feel

better that you've got a man mountain protecting you. How did you find him?"

Sylvia didn't want to throw Madame Mathieu's name around. "Just luck." His concern for her was flattering, but inconvenient. She invented someone at the door and got off the telephone. Wishing that there was someone at the door. At least as a student, when she'd had free Saturday nights there had been other girls in the dorm to talk to. She went jogging along the lake and recuperated by reading in bed until three.

Bess called at noon the next day. "How are things?"

"Slow. How's Maggie?"

"Better. She's getting out this week."

"Thank God."

"I have news for you."

"What? I thought I ordered you to stay out of it?"

"I thought you'd want to know about your disbarment," Bess protested with injured innocence.

"Oh, that. Okay, go ahead."

"Well, it's imminent. And your partners couldn't be more nervous about it. They hate the thought of breaking up the partnership but they're not allowed to practice with a crook, you know. They're making my life a living hell, asking after you every ten minutes."

"I'm sure you can handle them."

"And then there's the other thing."

"What other thing?"

"You don't want to know. You said I wasn't to get involved and so I suppose you don't want to know about information that might help you even if it just dropped into my lap, even if—"

"Bess," Sylvia interrupted wearily, "I give up. Tell me whatever your little heart desires."

"Okay." Bess got down to brass tacks. "Carol, that's John's former bookkeeper, has been just swell. She was only too happy to tell me about it because she's leaving the firm anyway. According to her, John fiddled his forty-two grand through the books of your favorite charity."

"The Foundation?"

"None other. The firm had a hell of a lot of their money in trust. The exact amount varies from time to time but it's reached a high of a million and a low of a couple hundred thousand."

Sylvia whistled. Hubbard Wilkinson had obviously not been the only generous donor.

"Just before John left, the firm was holding two hundred and twenty-seven thousand dollars for The Foundation. The day before he left, they took it all back. John signed a check drawn on the trust account in favor of The Foundation in the amount of two hundred and sixty-nine thousand dollars."

"Forty-two more than they were entitled to, in other words?"

"You got it. The bank had been told that a large check was coming through for The Foundation so they thought nothing of it. The check was endorsed by a stamp of the corporation, which John had access to, of course, since he kept their books and records. The police told Carol that only two hundred and twenty-seven was deposited to the corporate account. The other forty-two was taken in cash."

"That's a lot of cash."

"Yes. And the crunch is that that same afternoon, that amount was deposited to John's account. In cash."

"Stupid. He wasn't that stupid."

"Maybe he didn't care. If he wasn't sticking around?"

"Did anyone at The Foundation ever see that check?"

"Not according to what they told the cops."

"Was John's signature checked? By experts?"

"You still think he had nothing to do with all this?" Bess had pity in her voice.

"Yes, no. I don't know," Sylvia said wearily. "Thanks for the information. And now, Bess, stop investigating. I mean it! Just go back to filing your nails or whatever it is that you do these days as secretary to a nonpracticing lawyer. Just stay out of it, okay?"

"Okay, you're the boss."

"Oh yeah. Sure." Sylvia didn't feel like hanging up the phone to face her empty hotel room. "Say, Bess, do you remember that you once showed me a letter about a book called *The Conspirators Among Us?*"

"Yes, what about it?"

"Well, I bought the book."

"You what?"

"I knew I'd heard of it somewhere but I couldn't remember where. For all I know, it had been on the *Times* best-seller list."

"Don't give me nightmares."

"Anyway, whatever you've heard about it, it's worse. Filth like you wouldn't believe."

"I'd believe. That was what got me about the sneaky letter that guy Rogers wrote, sucking people in by hiding what the book was really about."

"What did you say? What was his name, the letter-writer?"

"Rogers."

"That's it! I knew something about it was bothering me. Rogers! I bet it's the same guy. What were his initials?"

"I don't remember."

"Where's the letter?"

"Upstairs in one of my purses. Do you want me to go find it and give you a call?"

"I'll wait."

"At these rates?"

"Just go on!"

Sylvia smoked frantically until Bess came back.

"He didn't give his initials. His name is Vernon. Vernon Rogers."

"Bess, you're wonderful! Really wonderful! It's starting to make sense."

She went out into the brilliant sunshine and strode exuberantly along, ignoring the other walkers until she suddenly had a strong sense of being watched. She slowed up cautiously and ambled over to a store window, dropping her purse just as she arrived at it. While she was stooped over, she took a look behind her.

A short matronly woman was engrossed in another window a few doors down. Sylvia shot up and stared unseeingly into the shop.

The woman was her mother-in-law. It didn't take a genius to figure out that it wouldn't be wise to dash right up and kiss her heartily. Sylvia found that her feet were moving her away; it required great self-control not to break into a run.

Mrs. West had been standing stiffly, self-consciously. She had wanted to be invisible quite as much as Sylvia had.

Sylvia's skin crawled but her legs kept on pumping.

They returned her to the hotel. As she entered the room, she was trying not to face the facts that were loudly demanding her attention. Mrs. West had certainly seen Sylvia. But did the woman know that Sylvia had seen her too, and avoided her?

Because if she did, Sylvia's intentions and suspicions might as well have been prominently posted in neon. And her immediate prospects were all the prospects she was likely to have.

She spent the evening in her hotel room allowing her morbid thoughts free rein. She even attempted a maudlin call to her mother just before bed. There was no answer. She debated staying up for a while to try again but as she debated, her eyes closed and settled the matter for her.

THIRTY-SIX

The water was warm, reflecting the vivid blue sky and absorbing the heat of the sun. She was swimming, accompanied by protective schools of brilliantly colored fish, streaming behind and around her. The sun was playfully darting in and out of the depths of the ocean, lighting first this patch and then that. Where it stroked the water, she could see fanciful plants on the satin floor.

The phone woke her instantly. She sat up and looked at her watch. Eight. Not a barbaric hour but hardly the ideal time to start socializing.

"Hello?"

"Just listen and do not interrupt." The voice was ragged, strained and grating. "If you want to see your children again, you will listen carefully and do just what you are told. You are to immediately stop asking questions about matters that do not concern you. You are to inform your friends in Geneva that you have tired of your ridiculous games and suspicions and are going home. You are to go home and once there, you are to collect the slanderous letters sent out to your inquisitive acquaintances."

Sylvia opened her mouth to scream something about her boys. He intuited it. "I told you not to interrupt. Listen and obey. For the sake of your children. Do not, I repeat, do not contact the police or any other authorities, including the embassy. When you have undone the damage your prying has caused, we will contact you again. Remember, any misstep, any omission, any disobedience and you will never see your children alive again."

The telephone went dead before she could say a word.

She frantically called the hotel operator and placed an urgent call to her mother.

Two cigarettes later, the line was connected.

"Mother! How are the boys? Are they with you??"

"What are you talking about, darling? I did just what you told me. What's going on?"

Sylvia forced herself to lower her voice. "Where are they?"

"Aren't they with you? I put them on the plane like you said." Mrs. Layton was bewildered. "They should have arrived last night."

"Who told you to put them on the plane?"

"You did."

"I did?"

"In your telegram. Sylvia! Stop this right now! Is this your idea of a joke?"

"No, Mother. I'm not joking." Sylvia was gripping the receiver so tightly her knuckles hurt. "What flight did you put them on?"

"Swissair 444. To Geneva. Do you mean to tell me that no one met them?"

Sylvia spoke grimly. "No, I have a feeling they were met. I'll call you back."

Her mother seldom employed the full force of her very significant personality, perferring for the most part to get her way through charm. She dropped the charm. "I want to know what is going on! And I want to know now! From your questions, it sounds like you didn't send us a telegram. But someone did. Are you trying to tell me that the children have been kidnapped?"

The word she'd been avoiding brought tears to Sylvia's eyes. "Oh, Mother, I think so."

"Because of this investigation?"

"I suppose so. I can't call the police, Mother. I've been warned not to. I wouldn't have wanted you to know but now that you do, please don't tell a soul. I'm going to have to handle this myself."

"Can you?"

Sylvia paused. "I'll have to."

It took only a few minutes to get through to London. The operator at the Savoy was very sure of her facts. "No, Mr. Thompson has definitely checked out. . . . No, he left no forwarding address."

He had obviously already gone what Herb called undercover. It was too early in New York to get hold of his secretary. Sylvia paced the room while she thought about her options.

Desrochers was in his office. "Rupert? No, I'm afraid I don't have any idea where he is. Why? Is something wrong?"

"Uh, no. I just wanted to talk to him. It is important. If you do hear from him, please ask him to call me immediately."

She booked a flight home.

Five minutes later, she canceled it.

She had thought things through and had come to the ugly conclusion that she couldn't follow her instructions. For a number of reasons, not the least of which was the fact that if she succeeded in smoothing out the ripples she'd deliberately caused, her life wouldn't be worth a plugged nickel. Moreover, the boys were probably in Geneva. She couldn't bring herself to cross the ocean without them. She was sweating. This was the biggest gamble she'd ever taken. Not that she had a choice.

She had an early lunch appointment with Peter Rosslin. It wouldn't do to act strangely; the last thing in the world that she needed at the moment was for him to become concerned enough to mix in. She dressed with shaking hands and had a double Scotch at the bar before setting out.

Rosslin was sitting at the open-air restaurant in front of the flower clock at the lake. She pasted a smile on her face, took a deep breath, and sauntered over.

"Good afternoon," he greeted her. "Well, good morning. I guess it's a bit early. I hope you don't mind having lunch now but I've got this damn meeting at one-fifteen."

"No problem. I'm not very hungry but I'll have something light." The smell of the food was making her nauseated. She ordered a small salad. And another Scotch.

"I love it here. Watching the *jet d'eau* and the flowers."

Sylvia smiled mechanically. "Yes, very nice."

"So, how's the sleuthing going? You said you'd come up with some interesting things."

"Uh, I don't know anymore. I'm not as sure as I was last week."

"About what?"

"About the political conspiracy. I may be exaggerating a few things."

"What's wrong? You sound funny."

"Funny?" She raised her eyebrows. "Now you're exaggerating. I feel fine."

"Sylvia, you said you wanted to bring me up to date. How about it?"

"I'd rather wait until I've got something more concrete, Peter. I jumped the gun a bit." She cast around for another topic. "Say, I wanted to ask you about the Arabs. I've never

seen so many in a European city." She pushed the food around
on her plate.

"Yes, there are a lot in Geneva." He eyed her dubiously.
"But, Sylvia—"

"Why are there so many?" she persisted. The other tables
in the square were very close and they were filling up. She
was panic-stricken at the thought that they might be overheard.

"Why are there . . . ? Oh, uh, I don't know." Peter tried to
think but his mind wasn't on it. "Uh, I guess because of the
UN. Well, for one thing, there are a lot of different Arab
interests and all of them are represented here. I have heard
rumors about upcoming conferences that concern them. I guess
they're here to lobby for their point of view, and if that fails,
to buy some of the people who make the decisions."

"What conferences?" Sylvia was working valiantly to keep
the conversation neutral.

"I don't know. Well, there's one coming up about tariffs
in Europe. The Arabs don't want a tariff wall against their
baby manufacturing industries so they'll probably want to have
some input. And there are others that I've just heard rumors
about."

"Oh, like the anti-terrorist one?"

"Uh, maybe."

"Look, Peter, I've got to run. I forgot I had an appointment
this afternoon." Sylvia grabbed her purse and stood up.

"But you haven't even touched your meal!" he protested.

"I'm not hungry." She downed her Scotch. "I'll be in
touch."

The woman who answered the telephone at the boutique
sounded very rushed. "No, Madame Forrester is not in."

"When do you expect her?"

"She is out of town today on a buying trip. Can I have her
call you?"

"When will she be back?"

"I will be right with you," the woman said to someone in
the store. "Tomorrow. She will be back tomorrow."

The phone rang the moment Sylvia replaced the receiver.
Lawrence had something for her but he wouldn't say anything
over the phone. They were to meet tonight at the same charming
bar.

Rupert's secretary was in his office. She didn't have a number for her boss.

Sylvia almost started to cry.

"But he usually calls me every couple of days, Mrs. West. I'll probably hear from him soon. I'll have him get in touch with you. Is there anything I can do in the meantime?"

"No, thanks." According to Herb, Rupert wouldn't be surfacing for quite a while.

Herb too had probably vanished but she had to exhaust all possibilities.

She hung up hopelessly. As she'd expected, he had checked out and the hotel had no idea where he'd gone. She lit a cigarette and stared at the wall. What was the use of having important friends if they disappeared at the drop of a hat?

She could at least use Lawrence's help. At seven, Sylvia repeated her maneuver of the earlier meeting. This time the private eye hadn't beaten her to the Yellow Wing. She sat amid the dirt, avoiding leering glances and thinking that she must find another suitable rendezvous for the future.

At the hour mark she left, trying to control her hysteria by rehearsing a few comments she'd make when Lawrence called her back.

By morning she was glued to the phone in horror. Lawrence still hadn't called. Something had gone terribly wrong.

She couldn't contact Madame Mathieu directly. For one thing, she didn't have the phone number and for another, the old woman had made it abundantly clear that Sylvia was not to reappear at her door.

Regina was in the store helping a familiar-looking woman. Sylvia greeted her and was surprised to receive only a cool response. She browsed through a rack of sale clothing but the customer with Regina showed no signs of flagging. It would look odd if Sylvia stayed much longer without trying on clothes. With a sigh, she took two outfits at random and went into the dressing room.

Regina peered around the curtain as Sylvia was pulling a too-tight jersey over her head.

"Is anyone helping you?" She still sounded formal.

"No. I wonder, do you have this in a larger size?" She'd better take her cue from Regina who was looking at the suit disapprovingly.

"I'll check if you really think this is for you."

Sylvia laughed. "Well, perhaps it's not. I could use something for fall though. Do you have anything in my size?"

Regina left to find a few selections for her to try on. Sylvia watched her retreating back quizzically. Why the cold shoulder? The proprietress returned with three dresses. Sylvia preferred pants but she could see that this was not the right moment to mention it.

Sylvia turned to her as soon as her head was clear of the neckline. "Regina, I have a prob—"

Regina interrupted her brusquely. "Yes, that's too small. I don't have it larger, so let's try this other one." She pointed emphatically to the next cubicle.

"Oh, all right. That was my favorite though."

Sylvia got out of the fitting room as quickly as possible and waited around, fingering belts and scarves until she figured she'd have to buy out the store to justify her apparent obsession.

The curtain was pulled back and the customer came out. She was wearing a ridiculous mauve chiffon evening dress that managed to wash out her coloring and emphasize her bulges at one and the same time. Sylvia's mind went back to her previous visit to the store. This was the woman in red who had been so interested in her that afternoon. No wonder Regina was acting skittish. Sylvia left the store immediately, hoping that Regina would contact her as soon as she felt safe.

It would have been a very long afternoon except for a sudden thought that cheered her immensely. Very likely the boys would have been entrusted to John's keeping which meant that their physical safety was assured. She clung desperately to the theory. Always assuming she was right that John was alive and kicking.

Regina called at six o'clock.

"I'm sorry. I couldn't get away until now. What's happened?"

"Oh, Regina, I'm sorry to trouble you. I didn't know who to contact except you. You see—"

"Wait a minute. The phone is not the best means of communication. We should meet."

"Right. Let's have a drink now."

Regina was reluctant to come around at once.

Sylvia pressed. "You remember that we were talking about getting me a date while I was in town?"

Regina caught on immediately. "Yes, you were interested in a big guy, weren't you?"

The understatement of the year. "Yes. Well, I met the guy and he was supposed to call me today. I got stood up. I guess he likes his women smaller."

"He didn't call?"

"No."

Regina had grasped the seriousness of the situation. "Oh, Jesus! I guess you were counting on his company tonight?"

"Sort of."

"Then you'll join me."

They arranged to meet at a club in the old town. It was only a short walk from the hotel.

It was dark when Sylvia set out. In a few minutes, she was in her favorite section of Geneva. The roads were narrow and cobblestoned, faced with two- and three-storied buildings of old, dark stone at least two feet thick. At night the shadows of the irregularly shaped houses protruded into the path of the visitor, sometimes taking the shape of deformed and grotesque figures that appeared to be pursuing the unwary. Few lights were on, all covered by thick, stolidly drawn curtains.

Sylvia unconsciously quickened her pace, swiveling her head at sudden movements of the shadows which were usually caused by sly cats or clouds slipping momentarily over the face of the moon. Despite the reassurances she gave herself, she broke into a half-run, swearing earnestly that next time she'd take a taxi.

Her destination hove into sight. She gasped with relief and slowed down, trying to catch her breath. Suddenly, a hand shot out from a shadow by the side of a building and grabbed her. Sylvia screamed and felt a boot in her stomach. She doubled up in pain, unable to find the strength to scream again. It wouldn't have helped. The tiny road was deserted.

She smelled alcohol and then realized she was being covered in it. Something foul-smelling was put over her head and she blacked out.

She came to, to hear the sounds of scuffle and a scream. Then everything was silent.

"Sylvia! Are you all right?"

The bag came off and she was staring at Friedman.

After a frozen moment, she threw her arms around him and started to cry. He patted her until she got herself under control.

He helped her to her feet. She shook her head a few times, trying to clear it. "I'm glad to see you. But puzzled. Where did you come from?"

"Oh, I like to turn up to save the beautiful damsel from the ugly villain."

Sylvia remembered the scream. "Was it you that yelled?"

"No." He gestured over to a dark shape on the ground. She looked at it incredulously.

"Is that a person?"

"Not unless you have no standards at all."

"Seriously, is he, is he dead?"

"Yeah. Which reminds me, we better get the hell out of here. He wasn't a nice person but I understand the Swiss police take a dim view of murder anyhow."

Sylvia went over to the body. She knelt down and felt for the pulse. "He is dead, Friedman! My God, you've killed him!" Sylvia turned the body over and saw the knife. She swallowed and then ran for the nearest wall. Friedman watched her heave for a few minutes and then quietly handed her his handkerchief.

She mopped her face and took a few deep breaths. "Thank you."

"Let's go, Sylvia."

She ignored him and returned to the body, scrambling in her pockets for a match. She lit one and looked at the face silently.

"Do you know him?" Friedman had come over to stand behind her.

"Enough information from me." Sylvia stood up. "You have some explaining to do. Like, for instance, why you're following me." She turned and walked back down the narrow road without waiting to see if he'd come after her. She wondered at her calm. Shouldn't she be more affected by a murder? Of course she was, at this point, hardly unfamiliar with sudden death, and at least this time, it was the other side's loss. She had other problems to consider. Two of them.

Friedman caught up with her on the next block. "My, how fleeting is gratitude." He saw her expression and spoke conciliatingly. "No, you're right. I didn't trust you before but I do now. I'll tell you everything but we have to go somewhere private."

"Don't kid yourself," Sylvia said coldly. "I'm grateful for your saving my life but I haven't had any straight talk from you yet, and I can't assume that your only motive was altruism. I've had one too many close calls and I'm not going anywhere private with you until I know who you are. I wouldn't trust Jesus Christ himself right now. I'll listen to you on a park bench across from the *jet d'eau* in sixty minutes. Now I've got to clean up."

They entered a small café that didn't look like it asked many questions of its clientele.

"Give me your wallet, Friedman."

He looked puzzled but handed it over. She called the sole waiter. "Do you have any champagne?"

"Yes, madame, but it is very expensive."

"Fine, a big bottle of it."

She stood up as the waiter backed away obsequiously, certain that his customers were famous, not to mention wealthy.

She drew a comb through her hair and repaired the worst of the damage she could see in her pocket mirror. "I've got an appointment now and I don't want to be followed. I'll be back with your wallet in one hour. I rather doubt that the waiter will let you leave without paying, but if somehow you're not here, I'll call the cops."

Friedman nodded glumly. She smiled fondly at him and left. He didn't show any signs of returning her affection.

Regina was still waiting.

"What kept you? I was sure you'd disappeared too!"

Sylvia was touched. Regina was really shaken up. "I had a bit of trouble on my way. A mugger."

Regina took a double Scotch in one gulp. "If that's the way you want to play it."

Sylvia let that pass. "Regina, I've got two problems." She spoke with as much control as she could muster. "My children have been kidnapped."

"Your boys?" Regina paled. "When? What happened?"

Sylvia outlined the facts. "I've been doing nothing but thinking and I keep coming to the same conclusion. I can't go home and give up whatever weapons I've got against this group! I've got to find out as much as I can so that they don't dare hurt the children. Or me. I've got to see this through."

Regina nodded. "You're right. What's the next step?"

"I think that my husband is alive and in Geneva. Which means that the kids are probably with him. Remember that someone tried to kidnap them before and at that point, he was the only conceivable person with a motive to grab them. If I'm right," she started to sweat slightly, "and I've got to be, please God, then the boys are all right. John wouldn't allow them to be hurt. The question is, can I get them back?"

"That sounds logical."

"So when Lawrence called and said he had something to

report, I was delirious with relief. We set up a meeting for last night but he didn't show. And he hasn't called back either. He wouldn't win any prizes from Emily Post but he seemed reliable. So where is he?"

"You're right about him being reliable." Regina mulled it over. "We'll try to locate him. Do you need more help right away if we can't?"

She thought of Friedman. She wanted to trust him and she'd know tonight if she should. "Uh, not right away. I'd rather find out what happened to Lawrence before I bring someone else into it. I could get blacklisted by the union if I keep on losing the help this way."

"I'll get back to you as soon as I can. Lay low for a little while, okay?"

"Under the circumstances? Come on, be reasonable."

Regina looked at her like she was a fool. "I don't know who your enemies are, but if Colin couldn't take care of himself, you're way out of your league. Anyone who could stop him is good. On your own, you don't even pose a minor challenge."

"I'm aware of that. I'll be careful, don't worry. Call me as soon as you know."

She had the distinct feeling that if her performance didn't improve, she wouldn't be getting much more help. Madame Mathieu had warned her against getting in over her head.

Friedman was still in the café. He was staring disconsolately at the clock when she walked in.

"Oh, good." She beamed. "You waited."

The bottle of champagne was empty. He hadn't left her even one glass.

She led the way to the Jardin Anglais. Friedman was still glum and they didn't talk until they got there.

"Sit down and let's have it. Now." For the benefit of curious passersby, she squeezed his hand encouragingly.

"Look, Sylvia, I know I didn't play fair with you back home but I can't tell you about it here."

"Why the hell not?"

"I'm going to give it to you straight but it's hard to talk about. It goes back a long way and it isn't a pretty story. It's going to take quite a while."

"For a start, who are you? I already know you're from

Denver." Sylvia ignored his pleas.

"Okay, if I tell you a few things, can we go somewhere private for the rest?"

"I'll see. Now, who are you?"

"I'm a cop. Like I said. In Denver. I live there, have for twenty-five years."

"Why is the Denver police department interested in John?"

"It's not."

"What?" She was getting edgy again.

He saw that and hurried on. "I'm looking for your husband for my own reasons. Personal reasons. It's not official, though I think everyone believes it is."

"Who's everyone?"

"Look, let's go to your hotel room and I'll explain everything. You can sit by the phone and call for help if I make a threatening move. I'll stay on the other side of the room. You can frisk me. Sylvia, why would I hurt you? I just saved your life, for God's sake!"

That was true. Sylvia considered it for a moment. "All right. But one move out of you that I don't like and you're going to spend the weekend and quite possibly the rest of your life as a guest of the Swiss government."

They went up without talking. Sylvia motioned him to sit on the chair by the window and she perched on the bed beside the telephone. He sat down meekly enough.

"It goes back a long way, my interest in your husband."

Sylvia leaned back against the pillows as he started to talk.

"Back many years. The story started in Europe. I have to try to make you understand how it was then. . . ."

THIRTY-SEVEN

The two young boys screeched to a halt around the corner of a tall, gray-stone apartment building. Collapsing with laughter, the bigger blond boy turned to his friend and shouted excitedly. "We got away from them again! We always do!"

The other boy was quiet. Then he spoke soberly. "Mama says that they really hurt Herschell bad when they got him, last week."

The blond boy stared at his little friend. "Why don't you fight back, Karl? There's a lot of you guys at school. If you stick together, they'll leave you alone."

Karl shrugged. "Mama says I have to stay away from them. She cries and begs me to. She says things will get better, if we just stay out of trouble."

The two fell silent for a moment, and then Karl squinted at the sky. "I'm already late for dinner. See you tomorrow, Jurgen."

They shook hands ceremoniously and walked off in separate directions.

The next morning, Jurgen waited beside the apartment building, chewing an enormous wad of gum. After a few minutes, as many youths passed him carrying their leather satchels, he became restive and bounded back into the narrow street.

He climbed the stairs of a small house and rang the bell impatiently. When no one answered, he shouted up to the second floor. "Hey, Karl! We're gonna be late, hurry up!"

An old man opened a door on the other side of the street. He watched Jurgen for a few minutes. Finally, he called out timidly, "Young man!"

Jurgen turned.

"Young man! Come here."

Jurgen crossed the street.

The old man looked around furtively. "They are gone, that family."

Jurgen looked at him dazedly. "They're gone," he repeated stupidly.

"Yes. They left in the morning. Very early, maybe two hours ago."

"Where did they go?"

"I don't know. But I don't think they'll be back soon. They had a lot of luggage in their car." He paused. "A lot of the Jews are leaving."

Jurgen walked off slowly. As usual, the boys were playing tag in the schoolyard and the shouts and laughs echoed against the moss-covered wall. On the gate a freshly painted sign was posted.

Jurgen stared at it, unable to grasp its meaning at first.

"No Jews Allowed."

It was 1938 in Berlin.

It was cold, bitterly cold. The line moved slowly, desperately, as the rifles cracked and the harsh voices screamed.

"Faster! Faster!"

The cold sank beneath the taut skins, under the emaciated frames, into the brittle bones. It gnawed at the will to live. It lingered with the hunger and dysentery. Many decided to die. They stopped dragging their almost-dead bodies forward, and a rifle cracked. They died.

The living spared no glances for the liberated corpses. They drew themselves forward, concentrating on putting one bare, bleeding foot ahead. Now the other. Now the first. One step. Another.

And with each step, some decided to die.

A skeleton in thin rags walked with his hand on the shoulder of another. The other felt him miss a step. The slower one missed another step. His companion shrugged off the hand and went on. The head sunk to the ground with its body. No one listened to the murmur.

"Go on, my son."

There were men holding the rifles. Some were old, others barely men. The war was not going well and all Germans were called into its service. Those too young or too old to be cannon fodder on the front went to other tasks. Some helped move the remnants of a people from graveyards in Poland to graveyards in Germany. A government stupefied and bloated with murder tried to hide the evidence of its swollen bloody ovens from the approaching armies.

The line crept on.

"Faster! Faster!"

A dog barked at a faltering step. There was no food for German dogs. Even the fallen bodies lacked the meat to satisfy the starving animals.

One more body fell. There were two now at the end of the line.

"Mother, just another step. Just one more."

The woman looked back with dead eyes. "No. Go on. I cannot."

"Then I'll die with you. Walk!"

Except for their words, it was impossible to say which was the older. They looked like each other, and like each of the hollow-eyed ageless phantoms.

Beside them, a rifle holder trudged on.

The son looked at him. And then stared.

"Jurgen!"

The guard looked back sullenly. "Shut up. I don't know you."

"Jurgen, don't you remember me? I'm Karl!"

"I don't know a Karl. Faster!"

The guard jammed a rifle into the ribs sticking out of the scarecrow's rags. Even the guard limped. There were no horses for the soldiers. There was no gasoline. The war was almost over for the whipped nation.

He snarled at the ghost. "I don't know you. Faster!"

"Jurgen, I'm Karl. We were best friends when we were boys together. I know you know me. I don't ask for help for myself. My mother . . . this is my mother. You remember her. She fed you after school. Every day. She fed you. Please. Let her lie as though she's dead. Don't shoot her. She can't go on. For the love of God!"

His mother fell. The guard missed a step. Another guard yelled to him. "Is that one dead?"

He was silent.

"Hey! You! Is that one dead?"

"No. I'm reloading my rifle."

The other stepped back. He fired. The frail body snapped at the waist and lay still.

The son started to run to her, but another marcher pulled him back.

"She's dead. Walk! Walk! Someone must survive. Walk!"

THIRTY-EIGHT

Friedman stopped talking. He was standing at the window, his hands against the glass as though he were a prisoner in the cattle car again.

Sylvia sat without speaking for a few minutes.

Then she took a deep breath.

"You wouldn't tell me your name, It's Karl, isn't it?"

"Yes."

"My husband was called Jurgen?"

"Yes."

She was silent again. Everything made a horrible kind of sense now. Even her children's names had been chosen from the guilt-stained past. She should never have started to dig it up. The past was a trench filled with death.

"You want to find John to kill him."

"Yes."

"Did anyone in your family survive?"

"Me."

"Only you?"

"Just me."

There was nothing to say. Condolence notes don't apply to six million dead.

"You've been following me to see if I'd lead you to John?"

"I had to assume that he might have confided in you and you might be pretending innocence. I've been with you ever since I saw you for dinner that evening, back home."

So much for that famed sixth sense fictional detectives have. "That's why you were so suspicious about the attempted kidnapping? You thought it was a way to sneak the family out to meet John?"

He shrugged. "It crossed my mind."

"You trust me now."

It was a statement, not a question. She wouldn't be alive to tell the tale if not.

"I know a fair amount now," he told her. "But you hold the

key. After the war, a lot of Germans needed to leave Germany. The War Crimes Tribunal was generally a farce but that didn't become clear for a couple of years. Meanwhile, all the Nazis wanted out. They had to have new identities, new papers. They had money. All the money they could steal from six million Jews, from millions of Poles and Russians. Their houses, land, art collections. Their bank accounts. Their gold teeth."

Sylvia winced.

"No, it's not nice. Even listening to it is painful. Living it was bad too." He spoke drily.

"I'm ready to listen to anything. If it will make you feel better."

"No, I'm sorry. I'm bitter. I know I shouldn't be harsh with you. But you lived with him for almost a decade. How could you know nothing about a man you lived with so long?"

"I don't know," she said humbly. "But there's more at stake than him. It's bigger than that."

"Yes. The group that had the money arranged to create new lives for their Nazis. They sent them to other countries, like Brazil, Argentina. Everyone knows about that. But they sent them to the United States too. They're everywhere. No country has escaped them. And it didn't end there. The groups started up again. They infiltrate the governments of all their hosts. They raise more money. They have lawyers, politicians, civil servants."

"Do you mean to tell me that they still seriously believe that they could rise again?" Sylvia was aghast. She had read about the war of course, heard about the concentration camps, about the medical experiments, about the millions gassed. But even then, it was just history. Repulsive, but history. Not something that could threaten her.

"They sure do. They're more alive than anyone knows."

"Why did John disappear?"

"Because I was after him, I think. I'd blown my cover to them a few months ago. They didn't know that I had a personal reason for wanting him. They just knew that I was a cop and that I was looking for him. I guess they thought I was acting in an official capacity. Who knows, they may even have thought I was freelancing for the Israelis. Anyway, they got nervous, and he left town."

"I still don't understand. Why would they worry about John? I mean, was he an important Nazi? Is he important to their organization now? I can't believe that. I would surely have known if he'd been heavily involved in politics over the last ten years."

"No, he wasn't a big fish. Not then and I don't think he is now either, except for being a lawyer. No, I think they were afraid that if he got caught, he'd blow the whistle on their significant members. It's like the underground during the war. Anyone who got blown knew the members of his cell and so if one person got picked up, everyone he knew had to run.

"Well, these people don't want to run. They have new lives and they don't want to endanger the work they've done. So they had to make sure he didn't fall into hostile hands. If he hadn't gone along with them, I'm sure they would have killed him."

"You're certain it wasn't John in the car crash?"

"Yes. Dead certain."

"And you think he posed a threat because he knew who the important members were?"

"Yes. He probably did their legal work or something."

"Very perceptive." Sylvia told him her end of the story, leaving out only the identity of Madame Mathieu. The old woman was entitled to peace and quiet for her last few years.

"They have the boys! Christ!" Friedman paced the room. "Wait a minute!" He turned and grabbed Sylvia's hands. "I bet they're with Jurgen. They're all right. I'd stake my, uh—"

"That's my conclusion too. I have to believe it." And she did, except in the wee hours when she thought constantly about the children and tortured doubts kept her from much-needed sleep. "That's why I've gone on with the investigation. I don't really have any other options." She shivered and picked up a sweater. "I don't doubt that John knew some of The Foundation's membership, but I think that there was more behind his disappearance. I think something big is imminent and he knew about it."

"Do you have any idea what it is?"

"Glimmerings, nothing concrete." Sylvia remembered something. "Karl, did you visit my house the day John vanished?"

"Yes, I knew that his pals were aware I was in town and that meant that your husband wasn't going to stick around long. I hoped he'd be at his office but when he wasn't, I tried his house."

"And then you called the office the next night and spoke to me?"

"I was watching from the street and when the light went on, I thought maybe he was just in hiding in New York."

It was too bad they hadn't trusted each other sooner. Both had wasted a lot of time on false trails.

"It was ironic. They got him out on the very day that I'd planned to confront him." Friedman had waited a long time. He'd taken the delay badly.

They sat quietly for a few minutes.

Friedman looked up. "I lost sight of you a few times which made me even more reluctant to trust you. Once you started for home and never arrived."

That must have been the night she'd been knocked out on the deserted road and warned to stop meddling. Friedman had chosen the worst possible night to be careless.

"Another time, I thought I had you. One of them was hanging around your house and I figured you were on your way that night. But then you drove out of there like a bat out of hell, leaving the guy behind."

"That was von Schagg's right-hand man, Leland Sterne. I was terrified!"

"I thought that he wanted to talk to you because I was in the neighborhood. I got out of the area pretty snappily myself." He had a sudden thought. "You're still holding out on me."

Sylvia was puzzled. Then she gasped. "Oh, my God! I nearly forgot a dead man! The man you killed was Di Angelo, the thug von Schagg testified for. Di Angelo obviously does, did, the dirty work." She shook her head. "He sure got out of jail fast."

"They have tentacles everywhere," Karl said sadly.

"Should we maybe consider getting help from the authorities?"

"Authorities! We'd have to have it nailed down airtight before they'd do anything. We don't even know what's going on, let alone being able to prove it."

"You're a cynical man."

"I've had a lifetime to learn all about the authorities."

She'd only had a month but she was a fast study. "Then it's up to us. The answers are out at this lodge. Rogers said he'd be in Switzerland for two weeks. I bet they're all still at Auberge Paradis."

Karl paced the room furiously, finally stopping to sink down onto the sofa. "You don't understand what these, these animals are like! We couldn't hope to succeed. It's madness, to think of going after them. Madness!" He stood up and started pacing again. "They've already had one crack at me. How many chances am I supposed to give them?"

He wasn't talking to her.

"Sylvia, I came over here for one reason. I swore on that march that I'd live. For one purpose. To kill Jurgen. He murdered my mother as surely as if he'd fired the shot himself. A woman who'd been like a mother to him. It's been the only reason to go on living. I became a cop so I could get at the kinds of files I needed to find him. I haven't stopped looking since the end of the war. I'm not going to stop now.

"But this other thing. I hadn't bargained for it. I know they're still busy with their poison but it's someone else's responsibility. I've only got one more fight in me. They killed my whole family. Surely I'm permitted to cheat them of the only remaining one of us?"

Sylvia put her hand on his arm. "I wouldn't try to force you. But I'm dead anyway unless I can find out enough to crucify them. I've gone too far now to get out and in some illogical way I don't really understand myself, I feel I've got to atone."

"As Jurgen's wife? I didn't really mean to accuse you."

"It's not that. It's more as the mother of his children."

Sylvia walked out to the balcony. The sky was filled with stars reflected in the glass top of the lake. It didn't seem possible that the same stars had watched uncritically over such butchery. It didn't seem possible that there had been such peaceful nights following upon days of slaughter.

No wonder John had been so secretive. No wonder he'd always refused to travel to Europe. No wonder he'd turned away every honor accompanied by publicity that could have come his way.

"You can't do it yourself." Karl had come out to stand beside her.

She said nothing.

"We're fools, you realize that?"

She nodded.

They stood hand in hand for a long time.

"I don't even know what his real name is. I suppose, really, it's my name too."

"No, not yours. It was Werner."

Friedman put his hands on her shoulders and turned her to face him. She looked at him quietly.

"I've wanted to kiss you since I first saw you. But I won't do it if you don't want me to."

Sylvia stroked his face. She leaned over and kissed him. They embraced on the balcony without moving for several minutes. Then she drew him inside, closed the drapes, and led him to the bed.

She was gentle as she undressed him, and then he undid her clothes. They lay side by side in the bed, touching each other and wiping their minds clear of the past and the future.

They made love over and over through the night, falling asleep only when the sun was rising over the water. Sylvia dreamed of the black forests of Germany until she woke up around noon.

She roused Karl. He'd thrown off the covers and apparently tossed and turned until the bed was completely unmade.

"You don't sleep well?"

"No. I will when this is over."

They had breakfast while they discussed the best way to get to the lodge. They agreed that they'd need a fast car, but as Karl pointed out it wouldn't be smart to leave a trail. They should cultivate anonymity.

"You're not their favorite person, Sylvia."

She felt chilled remembering the previous night. "No. Neither of us is. Do they know you're in town? Von Schagg was very interested in you."

"I don't know. I don't think so, I haven't run into any trouble."

"Remember that they've been keeping an eye on me, Karl. And so have you. They have the advantage of knowing what you look like." If it wasn't so serious, it would be funny to think of the crowd she'd been leading around.

There was a message for her at the desk. It didn't include a name. Just a telephone number from Regina. The clerk was noticeably cool when she picked it up.

"Is something wrong?" Sylvia asked.

The clerk pretended not to have heard her. If he didn't want to discuss it, she didn't see why she should push him.

Karl came down to the lobby. She told him about the clerk's new hostility.

"I wouldn't see mysterious presences in that. They often get riled when two people stay in a room registered to one."

Sylvia had forgotten that. Sure enough, the man cheered

up as she explained her oversight. It had been left to him to deal with the sticky situation and he was obviously thrilled not to have to.

It didn't seem like a good idea to call from the hotel. Sylvia went out to the street to find a pay phone.

She rejoined Karl at the magazine store in the lobby. "No one answered. I'll keep on trying but I don't think we ought to count too heavily on help from my friends."

They spent the day trying to find an apartment that would be safe for them to hide in if the trip to the lodge wasn't entirely successful. There was a dearth of housing in Geneva and the little that was available required the production of their papers. Which would negate its purpose.

"I'm losing my taste for Switzerland," Sylvia complained over their tenth cup of coffee.

"Yeah. I wouldn't have to work very hard if Denver was like this place." There appeared to be no crime in Geneva, at least not among the landlord class. Everyone they'd spoken to obstinately conformed to the strict letter of the law.

Sylvia headed to a telephone kiosk down the street, despairing of ever being able to find a safe house. This time, the number was answered. A voice she didn't know asked her to identify herself.

"I'm Sylvia. Gee, it's cold out, isn't it?"

"Yes, it is cold."

In fact, it had gotten chilly. Any moment now it was going to rain.

There was a silence. More was expected of her.

"I'd love to be sitting beside a big, roaring fire," she hazarded. That appeared to do the trick.

"All right. Who is your companion?"

They didn't miss much. "Friedman. I told our mutual friend about him." She didn't like to mention Madame Mathieu's name.

"We found Lawrence."

"What was he doing?"

"Being dead."

Sylvia said nothing. She'd suspected as much, although it wasn't cheering to be proved right.

"So be careful. We think you're close."

"I am. I need a car to go to—"

"Don't give me any details," the voice interrupted. "I can arrange a car but I don't want to know anything about it."

"Fine. I also need an apartment where we won't have to fill out a housing form. I'm pretty sure that the opposition has all kinds of contacts in the government. Can you help me with that too?"

"Not at the moment. Call back at ten-thirty. From a pay telephone, of course."

"Yes. Thank—" The line was already dead.

Sylvia told Karl about the death of the investigator.

"Tough break. Was he a nice guy?"

"I hardly knew him, but I'm sure he was anything but. If he couldn't take care of himself, I was a sitting duck." It was reassuring to have Karl with her. Though that still didn't make her an insurable item.

Sylvia looked out the hotel window at ten-twenty. It hadn't stopped pouring for four hours. A natural night for a walk. If she was being tailed, she was providing lots of hints. They should reward her for being so helpful.

The voice was waiting for her call.

"Tomorrow at ten there will be a car at the corner where you picked up the taxi."

"What taxi?"

"The one you took for a nice, long drive into the country the other day."

They seemed to know everything. It gave one confidence. If only they were coming along to the lodge.

"Right," Sylvia said, trying to sound professional.

"The keys will be under the front seat. It will be a fast car. With a big trunk. Tomorrow, after ten. And when you are ready for a place to stay, call me back."

"But we might be rather in a hurry!" Sylvia could just see herself asking to be excused from the chase while she found the right change and a phone booth.

But he'd hung up again.

Friedman wasn't exactly thrilled either. They looked at each other and shrugged. They didn't have a choice. It was evident that they couldn't find a haven on their own.

Sylvia found she couldn't sleep. Neither could Friedman.

THIRTY-NINE

Sylvia dragged a resisting Friedman into the fitting room at the department store.

"I can't go in there," he complained, trying to ignore the saleswoman's grin.

"Sure you can," Sylvia assured him. "There's a dandy exit that's hidden from the main part of the store."

"But we don't know for sure that we're being watched."

Sylvia paid no attention and strode in. He threw up his hands and followed her. She tried on a few things and sent the woman out to look for some accessories. As soon as she'd gone, Sylvia threw her blouse back on, grabbed her purse, and motioned to Karl.

The exit door was locked. Sylvia started to go back, thinking of trying another floor, when she recognized the lock. It was the same kind that had been on the back door of her dorm in college days.

She pulled a hairpin out of her purse and fiddled with it.

Karl was amused. "It's harder to pick locks than it looks."

The door opened. She smiled at his amazement. "I'd have been thrown out of school dozens of times for breaking curfew if I hadn't learned how to do that."

The car was parked at the corner. A dark blue sedan, un-impressive-looking and about as memorable as a hamburger dinner.

"Perfect." Karl was pleased. "If it has a good engine, we're in business."

It had been agreed that he would navigate and Sylvia would drive. She slid behind the wheel and, trying to look as incon-spicuous as possible, felt around under the seat for the keys. They were there. The car started and Sylvia pressed on the accelerator. They were shoved back into their seats.

"They weren't kidding when they said it was fast! It goes out of control if I breathe heavily." Sylvia concentrated on restraining it until they were out of the city. Karl had brought a map which he was studying.

"There are two roads we could take. I don't know which is the better." He opened the glove compartment on an impulse. As he'd half expected, it contained another map. "Hey, this one's marked!"

Sylvia was amused. She hadn't been allowed to tell them where she was going. They didn't want to know.

It was a two-hour drive if traffic was good. It wasn't. Sylvia muttered. Traffic was the bane of her existence. When she got home, the first thing she was going to do was move back into the city.

Suddenly Karl peered out at a sign. "Take a right, the next turnoff."

"Are we nearly there?"

"In distance, yes. But the roads aren't very good from here on."

"Figure out where we should stop the car. We can't just drive right up."

Karl looked behind him. "Well, unless the gray Volkswagen that's behind us stays on the highway, we may as well. They'll be expecting us."

The Volkswagen had been behind them for some time. Sylvia had noticed it turn onto the highway just outside the city. But there hadn't been many places where it could have passed her so she hadn't thought much about it.

As they turned, so did the little bug. They looked grimly at each other.

"Can we lose it?"

"Yes, I think so. This car could take on a Jaguar, let alone a Beetle. Unless it's souped-up too. But now that we're this close, they'll know we're coming anyway."

Suddenly the gray car pulled off the road. Sylvia slowed down to watch it in her rear-view mirror. The driver got out and leaned back into the car. She stood up with a bundle in her arms. She laid it on the hood and then proceeded to take off its diaper.

They laughed uproariously with relief. Karl wanted them to stop as soon as they passed the last small settlement before the road to the lodge.

"Let's at least get an idea of the terrain. And it wouldn't hurt to find a good hiding place for the car."

The road was now very narrow and had not been paved for a number of years. It led across a small plateau about a quarter of the way up a medium-sized mountain. They had a spectacular view all around them of mountains and foothills on which were perched barely visible private homes. The vegetation was lush, stands of evergreen alternating with fields of colorful wild flowers.

According to the road signs, a picnic area was coming up on their right. Sylvia slowed down as it came into sight. It had a parking area in clear view of the road.

"Not quite what I had in mind." Karl pointed Sylvia to a thicket of trees around the grass. She drove over, ignoring the shock of picnickers, and got out stiffly.

"Act authoritative," Karl hissed. "No one in Switzerland would dream of questioning a person of authority."

They marched across the picnic area looking as confident as they could manage. The glances changed from outraged stares to secretive curiosity.

Behind the picnic grounds was a wood. According to the map, it stood between them and the lodge, so if they could maintain a sense of direction it was a good approach to the house.

They were just setting out when Sylvia remembered the cryptic comment of the nameless voice on the telephone. Something about a big trunk. They went back to the car to check it out.

"Aha!" Sylvia pulled out a heavy vinyl bag containing several useful items. A small camera with extra film. Two pairs of gloves. A compass. And two handguns.

"My!" Karl was impressed. He took one of them and weighed it in the palm of his hand. "It's small, but it would do the job."

"They thought of everything." Sylvia had been secretly wishing that they were armed.

Karl pulled up his pant leg and drew a gun out of his boot. "I wasn't going to tell you in case it upset you." He put it back and reached for the other two.

"No you don't! At least one of them is mine." Sylvia hadn't fired a gun since she'd been at summer camp, but she felt she'd be happier with one.

"Do you know how to use one of those?"

"Well enough." That wasn't the exact truth but maybe they wouldn't have to. Karl didn't look convinced but without saying anything more, he reached for only one of the handguns.

The bag contained a final package. Karl reached in and

examined it. "They gave us housebreaking tools too. They're kind of heavy."

They agreed to leave them in the trunk. Neither knew how to use them properly anyway. And if the lodge was locked up that tight, it wasn't the ideal spot for them.

They crossed the thicket which seemed to extend for an unreasonably long distance. Suddenly, one more step would bring them into the open. They crawled on their hands and knees along the edge of the trees to survey the layout.

It was fantastic. The lodge stood about two hundred and fifty yards away. Approximately one hundred yards away was a fence, a barbed-wire affair. And just in case someone mistook that for an invitation, it was electrified. There were a number of smoking birds impaled on it.

"They can't do a lot of entertaining," Sylvia whispered. "Personally, I'd only come once." Karl didn't smile. He was white as a ghost, staring at the fence with horror on his face. "What is it, Karl?"

"Oh." He recollected where he was. "The fence. I'm sorry. They had the same kind of fence around the camps. But instead of birds dying on it, men and women did. It was one of the only ways of committing suicide."

Sylvia took a deep breath. She was beginning to understand what courage it took for Karl to come with her. He was defying a past which might easily repeat itself.

They silently continued to creep around the perimeter of the property. After a stiflingly hot half-hour of unbearable strain on their knees they saw a gate. It wasn't padlocked. But it wasn't open either, and to see that it wasn't opened frivolously, two huge uniformed guards stood by it in a belligerent pose that suggested they'd love someone to try to get in.

In case their size didn't discourage visitors, they were casually holding Israeli Uzis. Very open-minded for Nazis.

Sylvia and Karl retreated to shady cover to plan their next step. Neither came up with a suggestion and eventually they sat silently, smoking innumerable cigarettes.

"Well, one thing's for sure. We can't get in. And if we did, we wouldn't be able to get out." Karl hit the earth with his fist as he spoke. He was sure that Jurgen was inside the compound.

Sylvia had to agree. She sat up and listened. "Do you hear that?"

They crept back and saw a van coming along the dirt road

leading up to the gate. The guards appeared to expect it. It stopped only a few yards from Sylvia and Karl's vantage point. The driver got out, walked toward them, and stood still for a moment.

Sylvia's heart stopped beating.

He unzipped his pants and urinated cheerfully in the trees.

Sylvia found that she was gripping Karl's hand hard enough to permanently incapacitate it. She let go and noticed that he was holding his revolver in his other hand.

The driver walked back to the front seat of the van and pulled out a box. It must have contained lunch for the guards because they looked very happy to see it.

The three men stood at the gate, talking and starting to eat.

"Should we look inside the van?" Sylvia asked. "They're settling in for a long chat."

"Well, I think I should. You wait here."

"Hah! I'm not planning to be alone for one second until we're back in Geneva."

They inched forward. Karl pulled himself up into the back and then leaned down for Sylvia. The inside was empty except for two large sealed cartons marked with strange-looking symbols. Karl was looking at them in bewilderment.

"What are they?" Sylvia whispered.

"It looks like— No, it can't be."

"What?"

"It looks like Arabic script but what would that be doing here?"

Sylvia was about to tell him that Arabs had had fleeting roles in the mystery since the beginning when the van bounced. They stared at each other in horror. The driver must have come back. Sure enough, the engine started up and the vehicle began to move.

"Can we jump down?" Sylvia hissed.

"He'll feel it."

There was nothing they could do except hurriedly grab the doors so that the guards wouldn't notice anything amiss.

"We can only hope that it's turning around and going back to the city," Karl said in her ear.

They crossed their fingers.

There was no mistaking the sound of the gates opening. The van was taking them into the lodge.

FORTY

It seemed like an eternity before the van stopped moving. The front door slammed. They grabbed their guns and held their breath but no one disturbed them.

Very carefully, Sylvia eased herself up. They couldn't spend the rest of their lives in the van. Sooner or later, someone would want the cartons. There were no windows in the back so she very slowly turned the knob on the door. It squeaked slightly, and she stood immobile for at least twenty seconds before she dared continue. Finally the latch let go and the door swung open a crack.

There was nothing moving near the van. It was backed up to a garage. The doors were shut so no one would be able to see them get out. They grinned briefly at each other and stepped down quietly, hands in their pockets on their guns. From behind the van they could see a few small outbuildings in a semicircle around them. In the middle was a paved courtyard filled with nondescript blue vans like the one they'd arrived in. There didn't seem to be any people about and the only sounds they heard were those of birds and the leaves moving in the breeze. It made Sylvia yearn for the city.

They looked at each other. Since they couldn't see or hear anyone, they had no way of knowing which direction would be safe to take.

Or least dangerous. Every minute here was borrowed time.

Something looked familiar about their surroundings. Sylvia realized that it was just like a military compound. She expected to see soldiers coming out of the buildings in combat formation.

Just then a door opened across the yard. They froze behind the van doors. Two uniformed men came out and walked to the frame shack nearest them.

"Damn good lunch. We didn't have food like that in Rhodesia, I'll tell you." The speaker had an English accent, as did his companion.

"The grub's fine but I wouldn't mind a pint now and then.

Mighty strict, these blokes." The second man sighed. "Oh, well, the pay's good and that's a fact. We can stand a few rounds when we get home."

"It's these Muslim chaps. Can't stand liquor."

"Never knew a soldier to swear off before."

"They're good at this business though, you've got to give them that much."

"Well, they know about terrorism all right, but I can't say I've heard they're worth a farthing on the battlefield."

"Come on, we're going to be late."

They stepped on their cigarettes and disappeared into the structure. Now the courtyard started to hum. Men, all wearing the same uniform, poured out of one of the buildings and followed the first two into another. They were speaking to each other in many tongues, some of which weren't even recognizable to Sylvia. Karl pointed out the officers. A good many of them were dark-skinned.

Prudence clearly dictated a strategic withdrawal to a less popular spot. In unison, they edged toward a narrow lane between the garage and one of the small barrack-like buildings. They tried not to break into a panicky run. If they acted normally, it was possible that the soldiers would think they belonged.

It must have worked. They found themselves in a formal garden overlooked by one wing of the huge lodge itself.

"I thought I felt exposed back there!" Sylvia gasped. "We better find some cover fast or someone with a little more initiative than those apes in fancy dress will see us."

There wasn't much in sight. They were forced to dash across the garden and dive into the bushes close to the house. Sylvia was impressed with the fullness of the foliage. The gardeners were obviously excellent and ought to be rewarded.

"Unless there are dogs here, we're safe enough for the moment," Karl whispered. "Did you see all those Arabs among the mercenaries?"

Sylvia nodded. She filled him in on her previous encounters with mid-Eastern bullies.

"I can see how they would feel an empathy with Nazi aims," Karl observed drily. "And they're obviously training the troops. But what do they get out of the deal?"

"Money," Sylvia suggested.

"No, I doubt that," Karl said slowly. "They don't need money. They've got their own. Anyway, we can't do anything until dark. I'm going to get some sleep. You will too if you're smart. God knows when we'll have the chance again."

Sylvia was afraid to try for oblivion. The moment she closed her eyes, pictures of little Carl and Jay affixed themselves to the insides of her eyelids. Consciousness wasn't much better. She could bludgeon herself into believing that the children were with their father but that left her mind free to turn over a few frightening theories about this setup.

Late in the day, a man and a woman, both dressed in severely tailored suits, walked into the garden.

"Karl." Sylvia shook him gently. "That's the florist I told you about, Castle. And John's mother."

He peered out. "That's not Jurgen's mother. I knew her well and that woman doesn't look anything like her."

"People change after forty years," Sylvia reminded him.

"They don't shrink six inches. Frau Werner was tall. Not just like a little kid thinks is tall. She was at least five eight. And that woman's no more than five two."

The woman Sylvia knew as Mrs. West was certainly very small-boned, if stout. No one over three would have described her as tall. And now that she thought about it, the woman did seem more like sixty-five than seventy-five.

Sylvia looked at Karl in bewilderment. "Well, if she isn't John's mother, then who is she? And why did she come to stay with us for a couple of weeks?"

Karl didn't answer.

A group of men joined the two on the lawn.

"Karl, look at them! The guy on the left is Rogers!"

Karl looked blank.

"The insurance man who's another director of The Foundation. In his spare time he writes letters to the editor pushing a piece of filth called *The Conspirators Among Us.*" She told him about the campaign to publicize the book.

The party in the garden went inside and Karl stretched out again. It was suddenly very dark. The shadows of the trees and the house streamed across the lawns. Sylvia found herself imagining that dark figures were reaching into the bushes toward them. She shivered. They couldn't stay where they were but the thought of venturing into unknown territory wasn't appealing either.

"We better look around, Sylvia." Karl had been having similar ideas. "I wouldn't want to book into this hotel before we checked it out."

Despite her fears, she smiled. "Okay, let's go rate it for
Michelin." She poked her head out and brought it back in
abruptly. "This is not the propitious moment. It looks like the
army is going to practice its goosestep right in front of us."
She peered between two branches of the bush until she detected
a pattern. "They're putting on a show."

"Yeah, well these seats are too close."

"No, really! There's some kind of display for the folks in
the lodge."

Karl looked out as a band started to play and ranks of
soldiers strode across the lawn in time to martial music. On-
lookers at the windows clapped and cheered approvingly.

Karl was ashen.

"What is it?" Sylvia became concerned. Their chances of
getting out were slim enough without one of them falling sick.

"The music. It was popular when I was a boy."

Of course. It was the *Horst Wessel* song.

The vanguard was comprised of perfectly regimented men
in their twenties, thirties, and forties, wearing dress uniforms
of tight pants and high black leather boots, sporting swastikas
on the sleeves of their tailored jackets and on their helmets.
The formation had been led by two men flourishing a banner
of black silk on which was superimposed an enormous red
swastika. As the storm troops passed the windows of the lodge,
line after line raised stiff arms in salute.

Behind them, a younger corps dressed in lederhosen, white
blouses, and kneesocks marched proudly forward to *heil* their
leaders. They too wore the obscene emblem on their childish
breasts. Sylvia now understood the silence of the Geneva crowd
watching the parade of the nature club. These were those children.

Lastly came the mercenaries, the men they'd seen in the
courtyard, a motley crew of less than orderly pirates. They
were short and tall, blond and black-haired, European and mid-
Eastern. But they had one thing in common with the preceding
automatons.

All were heavily armed.

The company paced up and down the garden for an interminably long time, the rough boots pulling up the velvet handi-
work of the excellent gardeners, but eventually the soldiers
vanished and the music faded.

"The bastards are leaving. Now if no one asks for an encore, we can try to get out of here." Sylvia smiled at Karl and pressed his hand.

No cries for more were heard. Even Nazis got tired of *Horst Wessel*. When it seemed that everyone had returned to his or her individual hole in the woodwork, she prodded Karl.

"We'd better start. Before the dancing girls arrive."

The windows on their side of the house were mercifully closed. Most even had their drapes drawn. Sylvia stood up, creaking her muscles and bones. Karl was in worse shape, literally doubled over. Lon Chaney would have been jealous.

Sylvia was passing an open window halfway around the back of the lodge when she heard a familiar voice. "Psst!" She waved at Karl. He came back and they crouched down, trying to overhear the conversation inside. Von Schagg was talking to someone. Despite the curtains covering the opening, his voice traveled well.

"...out of the hotel. But she's still registered."

Another voice chimed in. Sylvia didn't recognize it. "I've got Jan watching it. We'll know as soon as they return."

"That will be all." Von Schagg hadn't lost his touch with curt dismissals. It was a wonder that he could keep any help at all.

"You are supposed to be so efficient," a new voice sneered. "You have one simple task and you can't even manage that! I think we may have to reconsider the American organization after all." The voice belonged to Mrs. West, or whatever her name was. She sounded like she had him by the short and curlies, and for one brief moment Sylvia felt almost sorry for poor old von Schagg.

"I thought we had made it quite clear to her," he answered defensively. "At any rate, now that we have the children, we hold all the cards."

Sylvia's heart stopped for a moment. Karl put his arm around her protectively.

"You fool!" Mrs. West was screaming. "You were to discourage her from making trouble! She's just a stupid American. She knew nothing, nothing, before she came here! Now God only knows what information she has picked up! She shouldn't have been difficult to take care of. She didn't have any definite proof that you were involved with her miserable husband. You must have made her more curious about us than she was before she met you!"

"No, really, all I did was try to distract her. It was bad luck, her seeing Di Angelo in court. It was not my fault," he protested weakly. "Anyway, we are cleaning up the loose ends now."

"And you cannot do even that efficiently! You want to take over a government and you cannot even handle a silly woman looking for her husband! You have made a mess of the entire affair!"

The dame could really dish it out. Sylvia much preferred her vantage point to Johann's. She would give a great deal to ensure that she never met Mrs. West again face to face.

The woman wasn't through with her diatribe. "Why should she be looking for Jurgen? The Americans are all soft, soft as marshmallows! The police should have discouraged her. She should have accepted the automobile accident in whatever that horrible town was called."

"Hodgins did his best. Cameron too. He tried everything but she was incredibly persistent. We did manage to keep the authorities and the newspapers out of it."

"Wonderful! They would not have been a tenth as much trouble as this bitch!" Mrs. West was getting louder.

"We are stopping her now," von Schagg protested.

"Perhaps. Di Angelo was no great loss but I do not want my forces decimated because of this Jew-lover! Do you understand me? I expect to hear tonight that this idiot woman has been disposed of for once and for all! I will leave the question of your own personal future until this is done." Her voice became ominously quiet. "I would have expected greater things from someone of your background. Your sister was able years ago to arrange two car accidents that have never been questioned. I should have imagined that Johann Wagoner would have been capable of planning one convincing crash. An old whore!" she sneered.

Karl hit his fist to the ground. "Johann Wagoner!"

"You know him?"

"In a manner of speaking. Let's just say that I had the pleasure of watching him pull wings off flies during the war."

Sylvia was putting the pieces together. It was all very cozy.

Von Schagg-Wagoner was still stammering out assurances. And trying to shift the blame. "I didn't pick the whore. Janice did."

The woman interrupted him. "And that man! He too must

be dealt with. But first, I want to question him. I must know who he is representing."

"It must be either the Americans or the Israelis," von Schagg threw in earnestly.

"I am not sure. The Americans have given little priority to tracking down war criminals since 1948. Particularly the little fish. It is more likely that he is with the Israeli pigs but my contacts do not know of him. I want to see him for a few hours."

"He may be unwilling to talk to us." Von Schagg seemed to enjoy the prospect of a reluctant Friedman.

"Yes." It cheered up the so-called Mrs. West too.

The telephone buzzed. One of them answered it but the conversation was inaudible. Suddenly the drapes were drawn back and the woman looked out. Sylvia and Karl dove against the wall beneath her, praying that she wouldn't look down.

"That was the call we were waiting for." Von Schagg joined her at the window. "The conference is going ahead as planned and our man will get the information to us as soon as it ends."

"It is to take place in Geneva?"

"Yes."

"Then he is to inform us of its progress on a daily basis. I would prefer to negotiate step by step with these Arabs. They are untrustworthy and I must be able to keep the carrot dangling."

They turned away from the window. Sylvia let out her breath.

"It is unfortunate that we need their help." Von Schagg spoke with extreme distaste.

"They have money, arms, and military skill," Mrs. West coldly rebuked him. "And they hold acceptable racial beliefs. We can dispose of them later as our Fuehrer would have handled the Japanese. It is not for you to question our alliance." She overrode his apology. "I trust that your incompetence did not extend to the files of Guardian Society?"

"No, no," von Schagg anxiously reassured her. "The documents in Jurgen's office and with the government have been destroyed. I saw to it myself. It was a great deal of trouble. It is regrettable that our important friend's name was listed as a director."

"My predecessor's miscalculation. It was not thought that he would become so successful." Von Schagg was not the only one who could shift blame. "That must be the courier at the door. Answer it."

Sylvia and Karl heard a door open and close.

"Bring them here," Mrs. West ordered. She rustled some papers and gloated. "Very good."

"It is what we hoped?" von Schagg asked eagerly.

"Yes," she answered curtly.

"Wonderful! Are there files on everyone we asked about?"

She ignored the question. "It is time to go to the meeting."

"But Jurgen isn't here yet. I thought he was to come to the last two days of our session?"

"He cannot since you are unable to guarantee our security," she snarled. "With that woman in town, he must remain in hiding. It was difficult enough to convince him to leave her. I do not want to risk an unfortunate incident."

"The, uh, argument we employed to persuade him to come here is still valid."

"I know that, you fool, but I would like him to forget that we used coercion. If threats are needed to ensure his cooperation, he will be of no further use to us."

"He'll settle in now that he's got the children."

Sylvia sank to the ground. The news that John was alive and had not wanted to leave her paled before this. The boys were alive! She had started thinking of her marriage as something that existed between a woman she no longer recognized and a man who turned out to be a stranger. But the boys were real and they were alive!

Mrs. West was still talking. "I may not be able to permit Jurgen to keep them with him. It will depend on our investigation of her family."

"I am sure she is pure-blooded," von Schagg said confidently. "I found her attractive myself and I am seldom wrong about such things."

The woman was not impressed. "You are a cretin! As was Jurgen. He should never have married her. It is more than likely that such a Jew-lover has tainted blood. Which she will have passed to her two bastards."

FORTY-ONE

They were both shaking. Sylvia took a deep breath. "Wow. We've got to get out of here and find the children."

"Do you have any ideas?"

They sat gloomily for a while without talking.

"There's no help for it, Karl. I'm coming to love this bush but we have to case the security setup. Maybe it's easier to get out than it was to get in."

"I always wanted to work with Pollyanna."

"What do you suppose is in those papers she just received?" Sylvia asked.

He shrugged.

"We ought to take a look at them," she added reluctantly.

"I know." Karl sighed. "Well, let's hope that this meeting, whatever it is, will keep everyone busy for a while."

The window had been left open. With much grunting and loss of surface skin, they pulled themselves up into the room. It was an enormous library with two walls of books and two of paintings, some of them priceless. A love of art ran through the group. The last display this lavish that Sylvia had seen had been in The Foundation's head office.

Karl walked around the room, examining its treasures.

"I wonder whose collections these came from." His mouth was twisted bitterly.

Sylvia was bent over the desk, an old beauty polished to a silken finish by years of doting attention and waxing. It was stacked high with papers.

"Karl, come over here. There isn't time to take pictures of all of this, but we can get some sample shots."

The top file contained a single xeroxed piece of paper. It outlined the structure of some organization together with the names of its department heads.

The next folder was labeled DJE. Whoever DJE was, his documentation indicated that he liked women, the younger the better. The pictures were dynamite, all the more so since his

315

biography sheet showed him to have a wife and four children.

Karl went back to the organizational chart. DJE's full name was spelled out. They continued to dig through the material and came up with more of the same sort of dossier.

Sylvia looked at him in horror. "This is blackmail material on the senior members of whatever institution the chart represents!"

Karl nodded. "It's worse than you think. Unless I'm very much mistaken, we're holding a breakdown of the security structure of the CIA!"

Her eyes widened. "Our pals could control it with this information!"

"Exactly. With access to CIA data and power, they'll be able to practically dictate the course of politics in the States. They'll have the means to affect foreign policy, not to mention national matters. Remember von Schagg saying something about asking for files? They could use dirty details from CIA files to ensure that only friendly candidates run for office—"

"Or that once elected, the officials stay friendly!" Sylvia was pacing agitatedly. "Where did they get this stuff?"

"A high-level infiltrator, I suppose. Maybe more than one. There are files on a lot of people here, not just CIA big shots. Do you know a Senator Stenning?" He held out an envelope.

She couldn't speak for a moment. "Karl! What are we going to do with all of this? If only we could take it with us."

"I think we'll have to be satisfied with taking pictures. How the hell could we hope to get out of here with a truckload of files?"

"Call a cab?" Sylvia was dead tired but she couldn't sit. "Look, I'll pick out the most important material. You start shooting."

Sylvia looked at her watch. "We've been here for almost half an hour. We better clean up in case someone comes in. I'd like to find a way out of this madhouse before the meeting comes to an end."

"I wonder what kind of meeting it is." Karl looked up to see Sylvia staring at him speculatively. "No, I didn't mean we should try to get seats. Let's just get the you-know-what out of here."

She turned out the lamp and went over to the window. She immediately jumped back. "There's a patrol out there. I vote we opt for flexibility and try another route." ·

They eased the door open. The hall was dark and apparently empty. It made sense to assume that all the guards would be outside. Why give the plebs the run of the place when as far as anyone knew uninvited guests had no way of getting in?

"Down here," Karl hissed.

They crept down the unlit stairs past barred windows on the landing. It turned out that the lodge was built on a small slope and the library was on the second floor. The front hall was daunting. It was the size of a ballroom and any interest they might have had in making a dash for it was dampened by the presence of a porter's station across from the entrance.

"Is there someone in it?" Sylvia whispered.

"I don't know but I'm not going to inquire. Since we can't see in, even if there is a porter he can't see us. So let's keep on going down. Maybe there's a door for the basement."

The stairs ended abruptly in a dingy stairwell lit by a single bulb. It led to a long hall, also dimly illuminated, that was plastered with swastikas, posters, pictures of Hitler and his cronies. It could almost have been 1939 again.

Karl's eyes were glued to the memorabilia. Suddenly Sylvia grabbed his arm. There was someone coming. They jumped into the nearest cavity they could find, a broom closet. Sylvia watched through the crack of the door as a sentry holding a rifle marched by. So much for her sensible theories about the security arrangements.

"Listen, Sylvia." Karl had his ear pressed against the back wall. "I can hear someone talking. The meeting must be next to us."

A man was ranting in a heavily accented English. Sylvia didn't recognize the voice but as she listened, she wondered how she could have believed that John was Swiss. Surely she'd seen enough war movies to know a German accent?

The speaker was highly emotional. He called upon his audience to remember and be true to the glory of the past, to continue the fight for the future, for their Fuehrer, for their race. His listeners were eating it up. They broke into wild applause and cheering almost every second sentence.

Karl's breathing was becoming labored. Sylvia could see the trickles of sweat running down his face. It was enough to hear this filth once in a lifetime. It took incredibly bad luck to have to sit through it again.

"Karl, let's go. You don't have to suffer."

He shook his head. Remembrance was not restricted to the

audience in the hall. His face grew shadowed, gaunt, as he pressed his head to the wall beside the foul-smelling mops. He was bent at the waist as though he were at prayer making supplication to a blind and deaf God. Remembering what had been too terrible to recall.

She began to understand the power of those years, the fear that anyone who wasn't a part of it had to feel, the corresponding need to be a part of it. She was invaded by the waves of energy that emanated from the orator, powerless to repel them although they aroused strong feelings of nausea in her rather than fervor.

Someone from the audience cried out. "Herr Doktor Weikert! When does it come? How long must we wait?"

Weikert. The judge, Janice's former employer.

"We will wait as long as necessary! To the disciplined, to the true Aryan son of our Fuehrer, that is not the question. Last time, it happened quickly but we were not ready. We betrayed Him. Der Fuehrer. We were not worthy. This time, we will wait until we are ready and the prize will be much greater. Not only Germany. We will have the world!"

The crowd went wild.

Weikert waited for them to quiet down. "You are the elite of America. The vanguard of the New Order in the New World. We depend on you and we call on you for even more than you have been doing. We have brought you here to let you see how close we are to success, so that you will be untiring, unceasing in your fight for our future. I now call on one of our great leaders, a son of the movement whose parents have pioneered in Australia and who has brilliantly followed in their footsteps in America, a man you know at least by reputation. Johann von Schagg!"

The audience shouted and clapped, stamping their feet until they must have bled. Sylvia had inadvertently fallen into company with the top dogs. She was beginning to feel like a bone.

"My friends, it is a great pleasure to address you today. I want to start by thanking you for the work you have all done. It is because of your faith and courage that we are as close as we are to achieving our ends in North America. And we are very close. We have many important sympathizers and even more, many who are just waiting for the proper moment to declare their agreement with us. We are tens of thousands now and we are more day by day!

"We still have a great deal to do if we are to be ready to seize the moment and take advantage of our opportunities. All over the world, like-thinking people are fighting back. The white man's day is dawning!

"Our youth and adult groups have been busy. They have recruited large numbers of discontented, disenfranchised men, men tired of the failure of the soft face of democracy which has turned out to simply mean the tyranny of the inferior breeds. Men tired of the mongrel rabble taking their jobs, their cities, their homes. These men are angry! They are ready to insist, by force if necessary, that the white working man resume his rightful place in society!

"Who are these men? They are in lowly places and in positions of influence. They are in the Senate, in the House of Representatives, in the civil service, in the courts, and in the schools. They are everywhere! We have friends everywhere! We are stronger and stronger each and every day!"

The place went berserk.

Von Schagg went on. "We must reach the American people, the real Americans. The ones who have a right to jobs, to clean cities, to a government that does not sell them out to animals. They will be with us. They are with us!

"We are ready to take the initiative, to attack! The time is almost upon us for a showing of strength, for, if necessary, a fight to the bitter end! You will soon receive your orders from your cell leaders. I know that I need not worry about you. The spirit of our Fuehrer is with you and you will not fail!

"I tell you that we now have the means to ensure that our opponents will not be able to continue their insane course of handing our countries over to degenerates and aliens! I tell you that America is ours. I tell you now that the next president will be one of us!"

At this, bedlam broke out. Sylvia had had enough. "Let's go, Karl. I need a bath."

She took his hand and led him into the hall. The only door was at the other end, past the rally. They looked at each other and wordlessly turned back to the stairs.

The door to the library was ajar.

"We closed it, didn't we?" Karl's mouth was on her ear.

Sylvia nodded. They stood outside a few minutes, listening to the house noises, hoping that if anyone was inside the room he or she would be considerate enough to announce the fact.

"I feel too conspicuous out here," Sylvia breathed finally. "I think I'd just as soon risk trying the room."

Karl handed her the camera and motioned for her to stand back. He inched his way forward, scarcely breathing. It seemed like an eternity before he reemerged, broadly grinning, to wave her in. No one was in the room. Nor were there any files. Not so much as a scrap of paper remained on the desk.

"Good job that we took the pictures," Karl commented. "But now we have to get the goddamn camera out safely."

Sylvia was at the window. "It's too dark to see anything but I don't hear anyone around."

Karl came over to peer out. They sighed in unison. It was hardly ideal but they were sadly lacking in options. Karl held Sylvia's arms as she climbed onto the windowsill and lowered herself to the ground. She bit her lip as she scraped her legs against the stone. Karl passed the camera down and then leaped out heroically. His effort was spoiled by his landing which was ungraceful and obviously accompanied by a good deal of pain.

"What have you done?" Sylvia wasn't sympathetic to injuries caused by macho heroism.

"I'm sorry. I've hurt my ankle."

"Can you walk?"

"I'll have to, won't I?" He stood up, grimacing with the effort. "Let's go."

Sylvia stood still, watching him try to maneuver his way through the bushes that were hiding them from view. He couldn't walk very well. Running would be almost out of the question.

"Shit. Well, what do we do now?"

Karl considered. "Maybe we should go back to the garages and see if we can grab a van?"

"We can try," Sylvia said unenthusiastically.

They started to make their way around the lodge.

"Karl!" She grabbed his arm. "I've just had a brilliant thought! The crowd inside sounded large, didn't it?"

He grunted.

"It would be easier and safer to mingle with them when they leave. If we go now, we'll be the only ones not staying for the cartoons. The guards at the gate are certain to be suspicious."

"There's some sense in that," Karl said thoughtfully. "They've probably laid on transport too. Unless," he added,

struck by a less pleasant notion, "unless they're staying overnight. I doubt that they've got a room for us."

"Actually, they probably do. But we don't want it." Sylvia
pointed out. "If they don't depart, then we try for a van. After
everyone's tucked in. We won't be in a worse position. Meanwhile, let's snuggle into the bushes near the front door and join
the tour if we can."

"They may have dozens of guards around the front." Karl
started to list the dangers of unknown territory.

Sylvia took a deep breath. "If I think about the risks, I'll
have a heart attack right now."

They crept around the lodge, crawling through the bushes
and shrubs until they were both badly scratched and bleeding.
The foliage ended within forty feet of the entrance. They had
a clear view of the front door and the wide stone walk leading
up to it because there was no landscaping nearby. There were
at least five other observers hanging around. In uniform.

"They're even bigger than the ones at the gate," Karl mar-
veled. "This wasn't such a hot idea. They look like they're
dying to use their new guns."

"They're not new. I'm sure they've used them a lot," Sylvia
said comfortingly.

They crouched behind their cover and estimated the chances
of joining the crowd unseen.

Time barely moved. They were increasingly uncomfortable
in their cramped positions and if something didn't happen soon,
neither would be able to stand up. Karl jabbed her. "Look! The
meeting's over! I wish I had a zoom lens so I could take
pictures of America's elite."

"There's Castle again with von Schagg. You know, he does
look a bit like Janice."

In their excitement, they didn't notice that some guards had
been talking to Mrs. West by the door. Suddenly, several
started over toward the bushes that hid them.

"Karl," Sylvia gasped, "I think our luck has just run out!"

"Run, Sylvia! Go on, start running! I can't move on this
ankle anyway. Get back to the garage and grab a van! It's your
only chance. Maybe they'll believe I was alone." He pushed
her away.

She stood still in an agony of indecision.

"Go on! We must get the camera out!"

She turned to obey him and ran right into a figure crouched

behind her. "It's too late, Karl."

The figure clapped its hand over her mouth. "Shut up! Follow me, fast!"

Sylvia clawed at Karl and dragged him along with her, ignoring his gasps of pain.

"Who are you?" The figure was robed and wearing a hood of sorts. Sylvia couldn't see his face. She was panting with the effort of keeping up and when he didn't answer, she dropped the question. It didn't seem to matter much at the moment.

They could hear shouts and gunshots behind them. The figure led them through the garden behind the lodge, carefully staying in the blackest shadows, moving in erratic lines.

"There's a car behind that building." He pointed to a shed across an open expanse of lawn.

"Very nice, but how do we get there without being shot?" Sylvia was beginning to wonder if this was a trap.

"Just run! Zigzag!" He took off first. Sylvia breathed deeply and held tightly to Karl's arm as she tried to follow their leader's example.

Karl was half running and half hopping. "I can't do it. Go on without me!" he urged.

"Drop the martyr routine," she snapped. She called to their new friend. He came back, cursing, and he and Sylvia managed to roughly drag Karl to the shelter of a few trees near the shed.

The shots were getting closer. A few of them had hit the walls of the small shack. Sylvia and Karl stared at each other in disbelief.

"Move it!" Their savior was screaming at them to keep running. They dredged up their last reserves and struggled after him, down a road hidden from the field by the shed and a few large trees. He was standing beside a long black limousine with tinted windows.

Sylvia and Karl got into the back and, following instructions, lay down on the floor. A second man got into the car. Sylvia couldn't see his face either because as he entered, he put a heavy rug over them. It was suffocatingly hot but she wasn't in the mood to complain. The driver, presumably the hooded fellow, accelerated.

Sylvia hardly dared to breathe. The car drove down the gravel road running to the gate. She and Karl held each other tightly when they felt it come to a stop.

The driver murmured to someone outside. A strange voice answered him in German. Then the voice addressed the man in the back in English. "Please go on, sir. I had no idea it was you. There is an alert because some unauthorized visitors are on the property."

The car picked up speed and continued through the gates and along the road. When she sensed that it had hit the smoothness of the paved road, Sylvia started to sit up. A foot kicked her roughly.

"This guy has no manners," she whispered to Karl.

"I don't know. I think he's a prince of a fellow."

"Please do not talk," the man in the back instructed them. "It distracts the driver."

Sylvia froze. She recognized the voice. She had heard it before from the floor of a car; this was the man who had abducted her on the lonely Long Island road in order to warn her against further interference.

She didn't have time to consider the implications of her discovery. Without notice, the car suddenly shot forward, knocking them against the back seat. They could hear the horn of another car behind them.

"Someone smarter than the guard at the gate put two and two together," Karl whispered. They clung together as tightly as the speed of the car permitted.

The driver was still accelerating. "Hold on," he shouted.

Which was fine advice for someone with something to hold on to. It didn't stop those on the floor from rolling around and being bounced off the sides of the car.

There was a loud crack. Sylvia tried to cling to the idea that it was not associated with them. If it was, it could only be either a blowout or a gunshot. Neither possibility appealed to her.

More cracks.

The chase seemed to go on forever. That ruled out a blow out.

"They're shooting at us!"

Karl was a little calmer. "They're probably more interested in the guy with us, now that they know he's a traitor."

Sylvia was unable to consider that consoling but there didn't seem to be anything else to say.

FORTY-TWO

The car made a right turn, throwing Karl on top of Sylvia and throwing the two of them against the left-hand door. It continued on at more usual speeds although it made sudden turns every few minutes. Finally it came to a stop.

Sylvia lay still, hardly daring to hope that the chase was over. But it seemed it was. The rug was lifted, and looking up, she found herself staring at Leland Sterne.

"You!" She couldn't believe her eyes.

"Allow me to help you up, Mrs. West." He leaned down and supported her with his arm.

"You two know each other?" Karl had been left to move under his own steam.

"Yes," Sylvia said thoughtfully. "This is von Schagg's assistant. Or rather, Wagoner's."

"Former assistant," Sterne corrected with a smile. "I doubt that my job will be waiting for my return."

"What are you doing? Why are you helping us?" Sylvia was recalling Madame Mathieu's caution against trusting anyone.

"I think your friend has figured it out."

"Yes, you must be with the Israelis," Karl said slowly. "But then you know I'm not."

"Sure, but I could hardly tell my employers. How would a nice neo-Nazi know that? And frankly, it was convenient that they should think that you were from Mossad. They didn't look closer to home."

"But now you've broken your cover." Sylvia was still not satisfied.

"It was only a matter of time until I'd have had to run anyway. I've come under suspicion recently. Wagoner's been having me watched for the last few weeks. I'm not sure but I think he knew that I'd gone to your house one night."

"Why did you do that?"

"To warn you. You were in great danger and I wanted you to stay out of their hands." He laughed. "You were too resourceful for me. I damn near was run over when you gunned your car and drove away!"

"So you grabbed me a few nights later and shoved me into the back seat of your car. Much like tonight."

"You wouldn't listen then either." He sighed. "You're very lucky to be alive. Beginner's luck. I've been under tight surveillance ever since, so I couldn't get to you to tell you about their plan to telegraph your mother and snatch the children."

"Where are my boys?"

"Where is Jurgen?"

Sylvia and Karl spoke in unison.

Sterne spread his hands helplessly. "I don't know. They haven't been confiding in me lately. In fact, I realized that I was in trouble when they started to hide information from me."

"You don't know what they're planning? What they think will carry them over the top?"

"No, I don't. I have figured out that it has something to do with the Arabs but that's all I know."

Karl frowned. "We noticed a lot of them at the lodge. Talk about an unholy alliance."

Sterne's face was grave. "The Arabs are providing a lot of their weaponry and they're training the shock troops. I haven't found out what they get in return. Maybe they just want to help oust a pro-Israel government."

"Maybe." Sylvia was on the verge of understanding everything but the more she tried to force it, the further it retreated. She shook her head in frustration. "Leland, who are the infiltrators in the States? The biggies?"

"I've only heard them referred to by their code names. There is someone special, someone who is crucial to their aims. I've heard them gloating over him but only Lundvar and Wagoner know his real name. And your husband," he added to Sylvia. "John knew who he was because he was mentioned on some old legal papers which had to be destroyed before you found them. I think that John probably had other dealings with this guy. John was the dry cleaner."

"The what?"

"Laundering, Sylvia," Karl explained. "Jurgen cleaned their money. Where did it go, Sterne?"

"Some of it went out openly to support various clubs and community projects. Youth groups, things like that."

"Yeah, nice clubs for nice kiddies like the nature troup in Geneva?" Sylvia asked drily.

"Something like that. Anyway, most of their money was used in secret to take over establishment institutions. John was one of the lawyers who moved those funds around."

"You mentioned a guy by the name of Lundvar," Karl interrupted. "Which one was he?"

"She. The old bitch who runs the outfit. You knew her as Mrs. West, Sylvia. Your affectionate mother-in-law. She's the real brains behind the movement but because the rank and file mightn't want to take orders from a woman, Wagoner fronts for her. He's just a slick dummy." Sterne looked at his watch. "Listen, right now we've got to arrange to get the two of you home with your camera."

They stared warily at him.

"I watched you while you were in the library. There's a one-way mirror from the next room."

They still said nothing.

"Look, you were lucky it was me. We've got to get that film back to the States fast. A leak can always be traced by the information that's passed and this one might be urgent. I can't do it myself because your people get irritated when they find out we've been operating on their territory. It's quite understandable, of course, but it's damned inconvenient. They would be happy to get the dope but then they'd have to make some reprisal against Israel. A delay in an arms shipment, a cut in aid. It isn't healthy here for either of you anyway. I can get you on a plane tonight. And my people will clean up this end of things."

"No." Karl spoke flatly.

Sterne looked at him compassionately. "I know about your family and I'm sorry for you. But Werner isn't exactly an Eichmann. This information is a hell of a lot more important than he is. Surely you see that?"

Karl wasn't even listening.

"Okay." Sterne didn't want to argue. "At least Sylvia can go home now? You want her out of danger, don't you?"

Sylvia wouldn't let Karl speak. "I'm staying with Karl. And I wouldn't go back without Carl and Jay anyway."

"We'll get your children out. Leave it to the professionals, Sylvia. The kids will be home by the end of the week."

She ignored him. "I can make sure that the camera gets to the right people. I have a contact who will do the job."

Sterne wasn't convinced.

"It's that or nothing," she continued firmly.

He nodded resignedly. "If you insist. Mike will take you to a safe place that your friends arranged."

"Where can we reach you if we need to?"

"You can't. I'm off this particular job as of this moment. Now that I'm blown, I'll probably be going home. Or else I might be assigned to straight security duty in Geneva. There's some big event coming up and they're using all available bodies."

He stepped out of the car. "Sylvia, your kids are with your husband somewhere in Geneva. Find them and get out of Europe. Don't delay a moment longer than necessary."

He turned and walked away toward a field that didn't appear to lead anywhere. They watched briefly.

"Okay, Mike. Let's go," Karl ordered.

The car continued down the road they'd stopped on. It was actually more of a path than a real road and the ride was memorable primarily because of the huge potholes that the car fell into every few yards.

"That's it." Mike pointed across a field. In the light of early dawn, they could just make out a farmhouse a few hundred feet off. He waited for them to get out.

Sylvia emerged into a still-misty cool morning and breathed the country air deeply. She forgot for the moment that every bone in her body was bruised, if not broken, from the activities of the last twenty-four hours and luxuriated in being alive, surrounded by the fragrant smell of long grasses and the sounds of innocent birds and crickets. "Oh, Karl, we're going to like it here."

She started across the field and noticed that she was alone. Karl's ankle had suffered badly from the trip and he was forced to cling to the side of the car just to stay upright.

Sylvia came back to lend a hand but he really needed to be carried. Mike got out grudgingly and took hold of Karl's other arm. Together, they got him to the building.

A tiny, plump woman came out to greet them. "Ah, I was not certain that you were coming. We were told that you would probably fly home today."

"Well, it's a long story. We're staying all right. My friend has hurt his ankle. Can we get him inside?"

They deposited him on a big bed plumped high with down-filled pillows and comforters in a cheerful room just off the kitchen. Sylvia set to work to remove his shoe.

"Ah no! You are tired too. Come with me and then I will

take care of your friend." The woman shooed Sylvia away from Karl and led her to a room on the second floor of the farmhouse. It was much like Karl's bedroom, although done in yellow rather than blue.

The bed looked inviting. Sylvia couldn't recall ever having been so exhausted. She began to undress.

Dave! She'd been so tired that she nearly forgot. She couldn't afford to waste time. It would take him long enough to get here.

She stumbled into the living room. Mike had vanished and in his place was a pleasant-looking man who introduced himself as Armand, their male host.

"I must use the telephone. I have to call the United States. I can pay for it but it's urgent."

"No, it is not permitted."

Sylvia thought she couldn't have heard right.

"No," he repeated. "It is unsafe. You will tell me who you want to call and what to say. I will see that it is done."

She was almost comatose. In her present state, she wouldn't trust her own evaluation of a man in a long black cape with horns on his head. What did she know about these people? Who could she trust?

Armand noticed her hesitation. "Is it cold in here?" he asked.

Sylvia's befuddled mind refused to remember where she'd heard that before.

"It is very cold, is it not? It would be nice to be up in the hills with a lovely view and a fire?" He stared at her meaningfully.

She got it. She paused for only another second. They had to trust Madame Mathieu's crowd because they had no alternative.

She gave him Dave's number and the message.

"Go back to bed. All will be well," Armand assured her. "Go to sleep."

Sylvia returned to her room, although not without misgivings. Nonetheless, as soon as her head touched the pillow she was asleep.

She woke up ten hours later with a feeling that she'd worked out the puzzle while she'd slept.

She had. It all came flooding back to her. She sat up and went over it again with a heavy heart. It all fit. She had to be right.

She put on her clothes and went down to Karl's bedroom.

"Wake up, Karl. I've got the answer."

"What? Huh?" He looked her up and down. "Nothing's worth being woken up for."

"You're wrong. I've figured everything out. Are you awake?"

"I am now." He took her hand. "You don't look very pleased."

"I'm not." She sat down beside him. "The key to the whole thing was John after all. He was the link between all the elements. I don't know if he was a dyed-in-the-wool Nazi but they certainly used him to their best advantage. The Foundation kept all their dirty money in his trust account. Both the dough that came from sources they wanted to keep secret and the money they wanted to spend without broadcasting the fact. And who was his other big client?" She took a deep breath. "The Wandling Institute. He didn't even have to deal with a bank to transfer funds from The Foundation to Wandling. He just had to make a few bookkeeping entries.

"All along, I trusted Rupert. He knew every single thing I was doing. No wonder I was blocked at every step of the way. I acted like a stupid teen-aged girl, believing that he was interested in my charms. I was played for a fool. And I suited the part." She twisted her mouth wryly. "That note in The Foundation's file? The one that suggested John had had an appointment with von Schagg-Wagoner the morning he disappeared? It showed another initial: R. For Rupert. John was to see both of them. That's why the diary vanished. Janice did the dirty work but Rupert was the mastermind behind it."

"It's logical," Karl mused. "Wandling is so prestigious that no one would think of questioning anyone concerned with it."

"That's right. And Wandling's people get sent to every branch of government. Lorne Reyes just went to the White House, for Christ's sake! Wandling carries a lot of clout because it's supposed to be neutral politically. I've seen the way important men ask Rupert's opinion all the time. The place is wealthy, influential, powerful in all kinds of ways."

"My, my, my." Karl was impressed. "What a mind."

"There's more."

"More?"

"The bad news." Sylvia walked over to the door and shut it. "Karl, we've had a sense all along that something really major was in the works. And Sterne said it had to do with the

Arabs. What are the Arabs concerned with right now?" She answered her own question. "The anti-terrorist conference. They'd give a great deal to know what security measures are presently in effect. And they'd probably give a lot more to find out what conclusions and agreements are reached at the conference.

"I'll take any bet you want to lay that Rupert is a delegate to it. His institute has just completed a major study of the problem and he's over here working on some very hush-hush matter. If I'm right, he'll turn all the data over to those animals and they'll use it to buy help from the terrorists, their new allies."

Karl was pale. "The Nazis will be able to demand their own price for the information."

"Absolutely. They'll be rich beyond imagining. And we've only had one major terrorist attack in the States. It wouldn't surprise me if all of a sudden there were a lot more. Enough to discredit a government that was oddly paralyzed and couldn't respond effectively. Enough to justify a national state of emergency under martial law. Not to mention that if it was the United States that leaked the conference results to the terrorists, no other country in the world would continue to trust it."

"We have to stop it from taking place!" Karl was pacing around the bed. "Who can we trust? The embassy, maybe?"

Sylvia smiled sarcastically. "I don't think that would be a very good idea. We can't trust anyone, Karl. They've infiltrated too many areas. We'd be taking a terrible risk that we would hit on another of their creatures."

"That may be, but we don't even know where or when it's going to occur. Mrs. West or whatever said something about a conference in Geneva but that covers a lot of territory."

"Not really. Not if you know where to look."

FORTY-THREE

Dave was on his way. Armand had hinted that he'd been less than pleased at not having heard from her before but he'd agreed to fly over. It would take a couple of days to set up a meeting.

It was a long hot two days. They should have passed pleasantly enough. Sophie, the woman of the house, fed them extravagantly and entertained them with scandalous tales about the local dignitaries' doings and undoings, but both Sylvia and Karl were regrettably poor guests. They were impatient to get back to the job at hand and Karl was additionally irritable about his ankle. Sophie assured them that nothing was broken but it was horribly swollen. She treated it with poultices of herbs that looked like superstitious old wives' remedies and smelled worse. Nonetheless, by Sunday morning, it was starting to resemble a human ankle again.

Sophie came into Sylvia's bedroom after breakfast. "You are leaving at two o'clock."

"Dave isn't coming here?"

"Oh no! That would not be safe. You will be taken to meet with your friend and then," her kindly face fell, "you will go to another place."

The hours dragged but eventually a battered Volvo arrived. Sylvia hugged their little hostess, trying to hide her all too obvious pleasure at getting on with things.

The driver was new to them but he shared Mike's taciturnity. They were allowed, this time, to sit on the cramped rear seat for the three-hour drive through the mountains. Sylvia was finding that it was indeed possible to tire of the magnificent Swiss scenery when they pulled off the road and parked outside a sleazy shack sporting a torn German sign.

"Where are we?" she asked Karl.

"A restaurant of sorts."

She was glad she'd had a big lunch. "Uh, Karl, let me go in alone. I'll call you when I'm sure Dave's with us."

331

She went inside without waiting for the response. It was just as well that Karl didn't witness Dave's greeting. He dashed over and hugged her tightly.

"I was so worried about you! Why didn't you call? Are you all right?"

When he'd calmed down, they sat at one of the rickety tables in the bare room. They were alone; in fact there was no indication that anyone else had been in the place for months.

"Did you find John?"

"Not yet but that's not the main point." She described the organization she'd unearthed. "They're making a play for power in the States and there are a lot of important people involved. The leaks in our government make the proverbial dike seem waterproof."

Dave whistled. "Can you prove it?"

"The film can. They've got enough to blackmail every congressman on the Hill. Sort of makes you lose your faith in our elected officials."

"Yeah, but they're the only game in town."

"Not if this crew has its way. And they've got the money to buy anyone in their path who won't be blackmailed. You can find out more about them from Janice. A little chat with her would not be out of place."

"Who?"

"Janice Wagoner, John's secretary. It turns out that von Schagg is her brother. He changed his name, probably because of some of his hobbies during the war. Janice had a great deal to do with the Naylor and Gibson car accidents. According to my sources, a woman came into the newsroom looking for Naylor just before his death and five will get you ten that it was our girl. Maggie Brewster can give you the name of the reporter who talked to her. I don't know if he can make a positive identification that would stand up in court, but the threat alone might be enough to scare her into talking about her cronies."

"Is this really the noted defense counsel speaking?" Dave was amused.

She sniffed. "Or if that fails, see if any of the Times Square hookers can put the finger on her. Has Sweetie shown up yet?"

"Well, actually, she has." Dave looked down at the table. Sylvia's face was not pretty. "What happened?"

"She was dragged out of the East River about a week ago.

The coroner said she was dead when she went in. Strangled. We've got no leads."

"Is she buried yet?"

"No, the medical examiner's office hasn't released the body. You know how slow they are."

"I'll cover the funeral costs. Get her a nice one." Street hookers usually went into paupers' graves. Pimps' goodwill didn't extend past the last trick. "I got her into this, me and my big mouth."

"It's hardly your fault that she was a witness to the come-on to Cass."

"No, but it was my stupidity and vanity that caused the fact to be bruited about."

"So see Janice and the hookers." Dave was making notes. "Aren't you coming home with me?"

"Karl and I haven't finished the job."

"Who's Karl?"

"Oh, I have a partner. I meant to tell you but we got caught up in the details. His name is Karl Friedman. He's a cop from Denver who's been following this crew for personal reasons. He's a survivor from the camps himself."

"Poor bastard." Dave spoke compassionately, obviously picturing a wizened old man.

"He's outside now." She called for Karl. "By the way, Dave, if anything can be printed, I promised Maggie that it would be her story."

"Okay."

Karl had entered. The two men sized each other up and immediately bristled like a couple of jealous tomcats.

"Karl Friedman, Dave Masowski. Now, Dave," she added quickly, "here's the camera and the film. Be careful. We don't want any more deaths."

"Speaking of deaths, Mrs. Wilkinson was found murdered the day you left New York. I sure hope you didn't know anything about it before you went?"

"Of course not! How terrible! Do you know who did it?"

"Yeah, Di Angelo. Our prison system is really swell. He had to do a whole couple of weeks before they let him out on parole. After all, we want to give everyone a second chance. He had hardly any record to speak of unless you want to speak of six and a half pages worth." Dave was bitter. "The stupid son of a bitch left his prints. It's only a matter of time before we get him and then he's going inside for good."

Sylvia and Karl exchanged a glance. She spoke hastily to change the topic. "Yes. Well, when you go home, you better talk to Cameron and good ole Sheriff Hodgins in Vesper City. They're involved up to their fat red necks."

Dave's face froze. Crooked cops were his personal vendetta. "I'll be going back tonight, Sylvia. Listen, I think you ought to come back with me. There's no point in hanging around Europe any longer and it sure isn't safe."

"I can't."

Dave interrupted her. "I know he's your husband, but do you really want to find him now that you know all this?" He gestured toward his notes.

"It's not John. Dave, they've got my children."

"What?" He was on his feet and shouting.

"It's a long story but that's the gist of it. I can't go home without the boys and to find them, I've got to find John."

"Christ almighty! No, you've got to stay, I see that." He paced the small room, raising clouds of dust from the untended floor. "You can't do it alone, Sylvia! It's too dangerous. Maybe I can help. I met a Swiss cop at a convention once and I hear he's fairly senior now."

"We've got it under control," Karl drawled. "But thanks for the suggestion."

Dave continued as though no one had spoken. "I'll stay with you. We'll get them back, don't worry."

"We don't need your help."

Sylvia leapt in to prevent bloodshed. "Thanks, Dave, but Karl and I made a deal. I help him find, uh, an old friend he's searching for and he'll help me get my kids back. I'll be fine, I promise you. And it's crucial that you take the film safely home. More crucial than my safety and even than the boys'."

"It's too dangerous for you to be running around Europe," Dave argued stubbornly. "You should be calling in the cops. Karl, you don't want anything to happen to Sylvia, do you?"

"It won't. I'll see to that."

They were talking as though she was as fragile as fine crystal. Sylvia repressed her irritation. "Look, Dave, I'm going to be all right. We can't call the nearest police station because half of them sympathize with these half-wits. And you've got a job to do back home."

Dave wavered. But Karl couldn't leave well enough alone.

"She's staying with me, buddy, and you're taking the film back to the good old U.S. of A." He stood up and limped to the door. "I'll wait for you in the car, Sylvia."

Dave turned to her. "Are you staying with him?"

"It's not that simple. I explained why I've got to see this through."

He looked at her steadily. "Okay, if that's the way you want it." He nodded curtly and walked out. Sylvia heard a car start up and leave. For a moment, she was flooded with guilt at not having explained things better. She forced herself to stand up and get moving. She had no time to think about anything except the immediate future.

Their driver was leaning against a wall of the building, smoking a pipe.

"Have your friends arranged for another place for us to stay?"

He took the pipe out of his mouth and considered his answer. "I'm taking you to see someone else first." He wouldn't say anything more.

They stopped at a small stone inn on the outskirts of Geneva. The driver turned around and looked over their heads. "She's going in alone."

Karl looked dubious.

"It'll be all right," Sylvia assured him.

"I'm coming in after you if you don't return in fifteen minutes."

She was directed to a cozy smoking-room overlooking the formal gardens of the hotel which were small but spectacular. She stood at the window, enjoying the riot of color, until the door opened behind her.

"Regina!" Sylvia rushed over to embrace her. "I'm so glad to see you again!"

"Me too." Regina stepped back smilingly. "You've done very well. You're quite the heroine hereabouts."

"Thanks, but I'm not finished. I'll get out of your hair as soon as possible but I need help from you once more."

"You'll need it twice more. And we will be pleased to give it. Madame is very happy with you. She asked me to tell you that she has changed her mind about Americans. They are tougher than she thought. And less innocent."

Sylvia smiled bleakly. "She was right about the innocence but it doesn't take much to lose it."

"Truth is always better than fantasy."

"Not always. I think I was happier in dreamland but nobody asked me my druthers."

The woman let that pass. "We have an apartment for you in Geneva. Will you need it for more than two nights?"

"No."

"And for the second thing. You won't find it easy to get out of the country. The exits are being watched. We have papers for you and your children. And for Friedman too, of course. When you are ready, go to Alitalia's counter at the airport and talk to either a blond woman or a blond man. One of them will always be there. They'll get you out. It may be indirect, but it will be safe."

"I don't know how to thank you. And Madame."

"You already have." Regina smiled. "Do you have a name you'd fancy for the papers?"

"Layton." Sylvia answered without hesitation.

Regina caught on fast. "Your maiden name. It's a nice name."

They beamed at each other.

"One last request, Regina. I need an address in Geneva." Sylvia outlined what she wanted.

"No problem. It will be delivered with your false documents. We won't meet again this trip, but if you ever come back, be sure to come let me dress you."

"You know I will."

They held each other tightly for a moment, and then Regina swept out in her usual extravagant fashion.

They were taken to a large apartment block in an old suburb of Geneva. The apartment itself might have been anywhere in the world. Even age had not bestowed personality upon it, merely a colorless layer of dust. The furniture in their unit was heavy and ugly. It looked uncomfortable and it was.

No one appeared to have lived in it for some time. The register had it owned by a Miss Larousse who, it seemed, had quite understandably looked around her one morning and given up, leaving with only the clothes on her back.

The only sign of recent human visitation was the fully stocked refrigerator. Sylvia and Karl were ravenous and they set right to work preparing dinner.

Karl pushed the last dish away with a satisfied sigh. He smiled across the table. "That mattress looked soft. Want to check it out?"

"It's not healthy to sleep on a soft bed," Sylvia agreed. "Let's investigate the situation."

They entered the bedroom hand in hand. The bed was a double, quite solid enough for their purpose. Karl was eager to make this a memorable night for Sylvia.

He succeeded.

Afterwards, he lay back and stroked her arm while staring at the ceiling.

"What are you thinking about, Karl?"

"Jurgen."

She was silent for a moment. "Well, we're nearly at the end of the road."

He sat up suddenly. "Did you hear something at the door?"

They peered out of the bedroom. Two envelopes lay on the floor, pushed under the front door.

"That will be our new passports." Sylvia picked up hers and carried it with her to the bathroom. She closed the door, turned on the water and opened the envelope. Inside the passport was a piece of paper. She memorized the address and flushed it down the toilet.

Karl was standing in the kitchen preparing a pot of tea. "Want some?"

"Sure."

"Sylvia . . ."

"Yes?"

"Are you sorry about what happened this afternoon in the restaurant? I mean, sending your cop home?"

"My other cop, you mean," Sylvia teased.

"Well, one of your other cops!"

She put her arms around him. "No, I'm not sorry. Not after this last hour, anyway."

Karl ran his fingers through her hair. "You're so beautiful. Sylvia, I—"

"Don't say anything, Karl. Not until everything's over."

He smiled tenderly at her and carried the teapot into the bedroom. She stood still for a moment, watching him with a sad expression on her face.

She wasn't sorry, but there was every chance that he would be.

FORTY-FOUR

Friedman kept watch out the back window of the taxi in case their trail had, unaccountably, been picked up again. "Since Sterne mentioned something about heavy security duty this week, I understand why you think the conference is on the cards. But what makes you think you know where it's going to be held?"

"I overheard this conversation about ashtrays and round tables. It's a long shot, I admit, but my instincts haven't let me down yet."

There were police cars blocking the street. Sylvia nudged him triumphantly. "What did I tell you?"

"Maybe there's been an accident."

Sylvia pulled out the requisite number of francs as Karl stepped onto the road and studied the barricades. "I think that this is not the time to play by the book. Look like you're my secretary."

He strode off toward the obstruction. Sylvia rehearsed a few pithy comments but hurried along at his heels pretending to take notes in her daily diary.

Karl was talking over his shoulder, dictating. ". . . the Commissioner that the use of the plainclothes men is less effective when female officers are not interspersed among the crowd. The weapons that are deployed in Geneva are . . ."

He nodded curtly at the uniformed men at the corners of the blockade, allowing his coat to fall open so that his service revolver was clearly visible. Sylvia caught her breath as he marched on, noticing that one of the officers was looking after him with a frown. She darted after Karl and almost made it through.

"*Un moment, madame.*" The keen-eyed guard stepped in front of her and ordered another officer to chase after Karl.

They started to argue with the policeman. Karl wove a complicated story about being with the CIA security forces, threatening the officer with demotion if not outright dismissal.

His explanations were having no effect. Sylvia was desperately casting around for an alternative plan of action when she heard a familiar voice.

"Sterne!" She yelled and waved her arms. "Sterne, come over here!"

"Hi, what's up?"

Sylvia outlined their predicament. "Please believe me. I've got to get in there. It's too long a story now but it's vital! Really vital!"

Sterne raised his eyebrows and unexpectedly grinned. "Who am I to argue with the lady who single-handedly takes on the devil?" He turned to the obstructive officer and showed his credentials. "These two are with me. I'll take responsibility for them."

The second man shrugged. He didn't care as long as his ass wasn't on the line.

"Sterne! Get over here!" A brawny man wearing a baggy suit and an air of authority was looking severely at their savior.

"Shit, I've got to go. That's my boss. Uh, I'll meet you at the front steps as soon as possible and you can tell me what you're planning to do." He was gone before Sylvia could begin to point out that her information was the most important issue of the day.

"Sylvia, it's crazy out here. Let's go over to the building."

Karl wasn't exaggerating. It was clear that all the scurrying security men had been warned to expect an immediate entry into the civilian world if anything whatsoever went wrong.

Black limousines at least twenty feet long were pulling up at the stairs in front of Anvers et Companie. As soon as one would screech to a halt, four doors would burst open and six to ten dark-suited men holding guns would leap out and look aggressively around. Eventually, they would nod to each other, and one would open yet another door out of which would step a man in a dark three-piece suit holding a briefcase that was chained to his wrist.

The bodyguards would escort him up the stairs to the front door of the building at which time several other guards, these in brown uniforms so liberally displayed around the area, would take over.

It looked a lot like a wedding, the one set of donors dubiously giving the bride away to another set of strangers.

The stairs themselves were littered with security police dressed in civilian clothing, looking exactly like security police. Half of them carried miniature walkie-talkies into which they hissed and whispered. Everyone in the area carried either a briefcase or a weapon and they all were men. She had to be the only woman for blocks around.

Karl assessed the situation. "It looks to me like most of the participants sent in their own security forces to stand guard over the place. Those other guys over there," he pointed to a trio by the fountain, "are French. Not Swiss French, Paris French. And there are Britishers and our folks. And Israelis, of course. They all may look dumb, but it's well organized." He moved his arm toward the myriad goons at the front door. "Take a quick peek at the roof."

Sylvia tilted her head up and saw the sharpshooters outlined against the bright sky. She swiveled around. "They're on all the buildings on the street."

"I'm going to find Sterne. We need his help."

"Okay, I'll be here, waiting for Herb."

"Look haughty. Otherwise, some smartass will try to throw you out."

She watched a very distinguished black man with silver hair step out of one of the cars. His guards were the biggest around; six-six was the runt of the litter. It was enough to make a girl wistful.

"Sylvia! What are you doing here?"

She was riveted to the spot.

Rupert was standing on the next step, beaming down. He put an arm around her, apparently oblivious to her instinctive flinch.

"What a surprise! What a nice surprise!"

She smiled, summoning the iron control that had so often hid her shock in court when a witness had come out with entirely unexpected evidence. Or when her own client had.

"What are you doing here?"

It wouldn't do to be too frank. "I, uh, I thought I'd come to see Paul Desrochers." Hopefully he wouldn't stop to wonder how she'd slipped past the barricades. "I can see it isn't a good time. What with all this." She swung her arm as though she had no idea what was going on.

"What did you want to see him about?"

"Nothing important. Just a few questions. Well, I can see that you're busy too, Rupert. I won't keep you." She tried to move away.

"No, don't go. I don't know how to get in touch with you."

His arm was still firmly around her shoulders. "Let's go somewhere a little quieter. I want to talk to you." He started to move her up the stairs.

"No!" She recollected herself and lowered her voice. "I'll meet you later, if you like. I have an appointment now." She smiled unconvincingly.

He relaxed his arm briefly. It was enough. She slid away and hurried off, pretending not to hear his calls. She dashed around the corner of the building, trying to find a spot where she could watch for Herb but avoid being corralled by Rupert again.

Unfortunately, the building was a perfect rectangle entirely lacking in nooks and crannies, and the so-called landscaping comprised only dwarf trees and legions of overflowing flowerpots that wouldn't have provided cover for a leprechaun.

Her only hope was to keep moving. There were a lot of people milling about although few of them were dressed in yellow. And a surprising number of them, considering that almost all were police, were less than six feet in height. She tried to stay with the thickest concentration of tall men, but since the crowd ebbed and flowed like a particularly erratic tide, she had quite a time of it. Cars continually drew up and discharged scads of men but Herb was not among their number. And where the hell was Friedman?

From time to time she caught sight of Rupert, standing at various points at the top of the stairs, craning his neck for a glimpse into the mob. She found herself staring at the ground as though she was an extremely modest ostrich. If she couldn't see him, he couldn't see her.

"Oh!" She let her breath out with a loud rush. "Herb! Thank God! I've been waiting for you for ages. Thank God you're here!"

"What is it? What's the matter, Sylvia? Why are you here?" He handed a few files over to an assistant and moved with her out of earshot. "Are you all right?"

"Yes. I am, now that you're here."

He was very concerned at her emotional state. He patted her awkwardly until she seemed calmer and then repeated his questions.

"I'm here because this conference must be stopped, Herb!" She saw Rupert again, this time only a few feet away but mercifully staring in another direction. She grabbed Herb's arm and pulled him away. "There's a traitor in our delegation.

Rupert's going to pass the conference results to the Arabs. He mustn't be allowed to see any of the privileged material! You have to stop the proceedings."

"Rupert? A traitor? What are you talking about?"

"John's disappearance wasn't what it seemed. He was involved with a neo-Nazi organization and Rupert's part of it. They're buying help from the Arabs and they're paying with the stuff that's coming out of these meetings."

Herb was white-faced and incredulous. "Wait a minute! I'm not sure I understand you. Are you trying to tell me—"

She saw Rupert again. "Herb, can we go inside? I'm afraid of him. He's looking for me."

"Who?"

"Rupert. He knows I know about it."

Herb looked up and saw his friend talking seriously to a few very powerful-looking security men. They were nodding and looking down the stairs. "Come on," he said without hesitation. "There's a side entrance. We'll sneak in there."

They crept around the perimeter of the edifice, trying to attract as little attention as possible from anyone. The guard at the side door insisted on seeing several kinds of identification before he'd allow them through.

"Don't let anyone else in this way. If they make a fuss, call Mr. Desrochers," Herb instructed the man as Sylvia slipped in thankfully. "And on no account admit that you let us through. Come on, Sylvia, we'll find someplace to talk. If you're right, we've got to get outselves a game plan."

They tried a few doors on the first corridor. All were locked.

Herb turned a corner and stepped back immediately, right onto Sylvia's foot. "Shh!" His finger was on his mouth. "Those men with Rupert? They're in the halls!"

He grabbed her hand and they ran down to the basement. A small office, clearly used only by stenographers and other lowly forms of life, was open. They slipped inside and locked the door behind them.

"There are closed circuit cameras all over this building," Sylvia whispered before he turned on the lights.

Herb found the camera, draped his suit jacket over it, and flipped the light switch. "Okay. Now. What's this all about?"

"Oh." Sylvia's legs gave out. She collapsed onto a desk chair and lit a cigarette with a shaking hand. "I found one suspicious client in John's files. A charity called The Foundation. It's a front for a neo-Nazi group that, unbelievably, is very active in the States. And Rupert's one of them! With Wandling under his control, he's able to infiltrate every level of government. You know the clout Wandling carries!"

Herb nodded slowly. "Yes, but I can't believe that Rupert . . . Why I've known him for years."

"I trusted him too," Sylvia said bitterly. "I shot my mouth off and was responsible for at least two deaths. He knew everything I was doing."

Herb took her hand. "There's no point in castigating yourself. I think, actually, that you were very close-mouthed. Even if you're right about, well, about Rupert, you have nothing to blame yourself for."

"I was close-mouthed with you. That's because I didn't trust you at first. I had Rupert's help so I didn't need to decide about you and you seemed very interested in John's disappearance. But I told Rupert everything."

"I was very interested in the mystery. I, well, it sounds like hindsight but I've had the feeling for some time that all was not right with John. I was very upset when he disappeared because I promoted him and I knew he did work for Wandling. If there was something fishy about him, I shouldn't have allowed him to get so close to national secrets."

"That's why you asked me about his refusal to join the Presidential Commission?"

"That was one of the things I found disturbing, yes. And then of course, a great many things about the disappearance itself. I—" He stopped.

"What were you about to say?"

He spoke in a troubled voice. "I just remembered that Rupert introduced me to John." They were silent for a moment. "Where is John now? And why did he run away?"

"He was forced to leave New York because he knew too much about The Foundation. With this conference coming up and with what he knew about Rupert, he was potentially dangerous to them. It was complicated by the fact that someone was after John. It's a long story, but—"

"Hold it. Let's stick to essentials for the moment. Are you sure of your facts?"

"Yes." She looked him squarely in the eye. "I wouldn't make allegations like this unless I was very sure."

"Okay. That's good enough for me. We've got to protect ourselves in the conference. News that we have a potential spy in the American delegation could do untold harm to our international credibility. We're not the favorite participant by a long shot. We've got to stop him from finding out other countries' secrets and passing them along. But we've got to do it without letting on publicly. Who else knows about Rupert?"

"Just Friedman."

"Who?"

"That's part of the long story. A guy I've been working with, to put it briefly. But he wouldn't spread it around."

"Where is he?"

"On the grounds, somewhere."

"Okay. I'll get word to him to meet you here. I've got to get cracking. The participants are supposed to pick up a file of material and most of it is top secret. We don't want Rupert anywhere near it. Sylvia, stay in here and keep the door locked. I'll knock three times when I come back. Don't let anyone else in. Okay?"

"What are you going to do?"

"I'm going to go out and talk a few security men into detaining Rupert. We don't have time to phone for instructions."

"You can't go out there alone! It's dangerous."

"They may not know we're together. Anyway, what choice do we have? The security men won't act on your say-so." He smiled reassuringly and slipped out.

She lit another cigarette, checked that the door was locked, and started to pace. If Herb couldn't convince the security men to hold Rupert, he would be able to get word to his cronies and God only knew what would happen to her children in retaliation. She realized that she was sweating.

"Oh, my!" She'd forgotten to tell Herb about Sterne! The Israelis might already know about the leak. She had to find Herb. She didn't like the idea of venturing out of her warm cocoon but he mightn't return for a while. She stubbed out her cigarette and took a deep breath.

The corridor was empty. She made sure that the door was unlocked so that she could escape back in if necessary and, taking off her shoes, crept out. There were noises coming from inside some of the basement rooms, typewriters probably connected to translation services, but she met no one wandering the halls.

A door just beside the stairs on the first floor was slightly ajar. A familiar-looking profile was visible. She stopped. If

Lorne Reyes, one of Rupert's boys, was here, the American delegation was riddled with spies. Reyes was speaking to someone. She moved away from the door so that he wouldn't see her if he turned, and leaned casually against the wall.

"She's in the building? Wonderful. Now we'll be able to get rid of her before she does any more harm. It's time to take care of her for once and for all." Reyes chuckled unpleasantly. "She's got it all figured out, has she? Well, she's logical if nothing else. Personally, I prefer my dames well-fleshed and slightly retarded."

His companion laughed in agreement.

"We've got to get Friedman alive. Mrs. Lundvar wants to talk to him. Do the guards know to be careful?"

A grunt.

"All figured out?" Reyes was enormously amused about something. "And the plant is Rupert? Are you sure she said 'plant'? Maybe what she really said was 'patsy.'"

"No. She's got him pegged as the mastermind. Is Paul on his way? I want to clear it up as soon as possible."

Sylvia had to hold on to the wall to keep from collapsing.

Reyes' companion was Dutton. Herb Dutton to whom she'd just handed her girlish confidences.

She started to back away, keeping a careful eye on the door.

"Oh!" She had bumped into Desrochers.

Paul Desrochers. Whom Reyes had just called in.

"Sorry, Paul. See you." She continued to move away, a great deal more briskly.

He reached out and caught her arm. "Where are you going, Sylvia?"

"Just on my way to meet Herb," she lied with as much eye contact as she could manage.

"I'm right here."

She spun around to find Herb and Lorne on her heels.

They backed her into the room in which they had just had their tête-à-tête.

"If you're thinking of screaming, don't," Herb warned. "I'll be forced to hurt you and besides, this room is soundproofed. Every room in the place is. Anvers gives value for its money. Paul," he ordered without taking his eyes off her, "go make the necessary arrangements."

Sylvia didn't like the sound of that.

"And Lorne, you'd better tell my party that I'm delayed with emergency government business. I'll be there as soon as possible."

The two men hastened out.

Sylvia couldn't think of anything to do except try to brazen it out. "Herb, what's going on?"

He raised his eyebrows. "Don't go playing the innocent, Sylvia. You know, I'm actually sorry. You were far too nosy for your own good despite your many warnings, but I quite liked you. Until you took to hanging around with that Jew."

"It was you all along! Not Rupert!" She took a deep breath and lit a cigarette, acting as cool as she knew how. "You played him for a fool because he was decent enough to trust you. You ran Wandling through him. Placed people with him, like that creature, Reyes. People who eventually went to important jobs where they could be useful to you and your slimy friends."

"Now, now. No name-calling." He smiled coldly. "If we were able to control Wandling, it was because Thompson was soft. Soft and stupid like most Americans. He didn't deserve to be in charge. We made sure that the right sort of people worked there and that Wandling stayed influential. Left to Thompson, it would have decayed to the point where it ceased to matter. We made sure that important contracts came its way, that the institute had money and influence. I hate to shock you, but the strong deserve their power. The meek will never inherit the earth. Nor," he snarled, "should they."

"You have to cheat and lie to get anywhere. Americans don't want your kind. Nazis have gone out of style, Dutton."

"We'll take our chances." He was supremely uninterested in her opinion. "Even your husband was one of us."

"And it was you who arranged for Rupert to use John. It wasn't Rupert who discovered him."

"True. I created John. I made him important enough to handle Wandling's business. I even offered him a major appointment that he was instructed to refuse. I'm good at my job, I admit it. Are there any more questions?"

Naylor, Gibson, Cass, Sweetie, Ingrid, Laura Wilkinson, and Colin Lawrence added up to one conclusion. These guys were real killers. The fact that he'd been frank and honest with her was not an encouraging sign.

She gasped. Without warning, he'd slapped the cigarette out of her hand. "Where is your sheeny boyfriend?"

Her eyes didn't flicker. "Go to hell."

He hit her again, this time across her face.

"I don't know where he is. There's no use in hurting me, he's got all the information too. Enough to hang you, Dutton. You're finished. No matter what happens to me."

"He's here and my men will be bringing him in any moment."

Her heart missed a beat. Then she laughed. "Sure. Why ask me where he is? I don't believe you. Go ahead and do whatever you want to me. It won't save your yellow skin."

"We're not going to do anything to you." He didn't take the trouble to make it sound convincing.

Sylvia desperately wanted another cigarette but she was afraid to move. And she'd be damned to hell if she showed him that he got to her.

"Ah, Paul. Good." He turned to her. "Well, we're going to say good-bye now, Sylvia. It's been very interesting doing business with you."

A brawny man in a brown security guard's uniform grabbed her arms and pushed her against a long, pale wood desk. Desrochers was holding a bundle of thick cord. Very slowly he unraveled a few knots in it and proceeded to tie her legs together. He apparently enjoyed the exercise; his hands stayed longer than was necessary on her bottom. He then moved up to constrain her arms. The expression on her face must have put him off because it wasn't until he was entirely finished that he rubbed his hands over her breasts.

She jackknifed at the waist, kicking him sharply on his shins.

"Ouch! You bitch!" He started to hit her and then leered. "Never mind, honey, you'll pay for that later." His hand shot up her leg.

Herb was looking at his watch. "Okay, boys. Fun is fun but I have a meeting to attend. Let's complete this, shall we? What you do later is up to you." He might not have been in the room during the boyish hijinks.

Desrochers sobered up immediately. "Of course, Mr. Dutton." He reached behind him and came up with a hypodermic.

He moved toward her waving it about. "Sleeptime, honey."

Sylvia screamed and threw herself to the floor. Without the use of hands or legs, she had little balance. She concentrated on rolling this way and that and, when approached, on kicking out violently, using what momentum she could summon from bending at the waist and snapping back.

Desrochers attempted to grab her legs. "Get the cunt's head!" he screamed to the guard, watching vacantly from the door.

Sylvia continued to struggle desperately but the two of them outweighed, outnumbered, and outmaneuvered her. The guard smashed her across the face and then sat down heavily on her stomach.

She gasped and used every ounce of her remaining strength to try to heave the man off. He did move, only to settle further up on her chest and make it almost impossible to breathe.

Desrochers was showing her the hypodermic and all his teeth. "I'm going to enjoy this." He leaned down, muttering obscenely about what she had to look forward to when and if she woke up.

Sylvia spat, hitting him squarely on the nose.

He pulled his arm back to wallop her just as all hell broke loose. The door crashed open and suddenly the room was crammed with hurtling bodies, shouts, and gunshots.

The guard had taken to his feet, pulling on the gun at his waist. He wasn't fast enough. He uttered a short cry, somewhere between a curse and a gurgle, and slid to the floor beside Sylvia. She immediately rolled under the desk, peering out and trying to make sense of the noise and confusion. From her vantage point, she could see only shoes, black polished ones and brown scuffed boots, moving to the time of the pistol fire.

There was another abrupt terminated cry and a body she'd never seen before dropped on top of the guard, blocking her view entirely. After a frozen moment, she started to inch her way painfully toward the open door, oblivious to the kicking and pounding her maltreated body took as it crawled through the tumult. It seemed to take forever; shouts and explosions surrounded her on all sides. She screamed. A bleeding man collapsed in front of her, his glazed eyes only inches away. Her heart started beating again as she realized that his stare wasn't for her. He was looking at Cerberus. She dragged herself forward again, ignoring the red drops that had fallen onto her hands.

She was almost at the door when she was stopped.

"Sylvia! Thank God!" Karl was bending over her. "Thank God! Thank God!"

"Untie her, Karl," Rupert suggested kindly. He was standing behind Karl.

"Where did you come from? What's happening?" She didn't comprehend the events of the last five minutes. "Rupert! Are you all right?"

"The more relevant question is, how are you?" He smiled at her affectionately.

"Fine. I'm fine. I guess." She stood up with the help of Karl's strong arm and rubbed her wrists to start the circulation going again. "How did you know where I was?"

"We didn't or we'd have been here sooner. We've been searching the building. When your friends grabbed me," Rupert gestured toward Karl and Sterne who had joined their little party at the doorway, "I was already confused about your running away from me. It didn't take long to figure out that you thought I was part of the conspiracy, a piece of deduction that Karl confirmed. I had the advantage of knowing that I wasn't. But if someone highly placed was a fifth column, there was only one other possibility."

Sylvia looked sheepish. "I feel very ashamed for doubting you. It was just that I told you everything as it happened. And you showed such an interest in Karl. The same reasoning that convicted you applied to Dutton but I didn't twig to the fact that he could have, er..."

"Manipulated me? Why should you? I didn't catch on either. And there I was, trying to protect you by getting his help and spilling the beans to your worst enemy." He flushed. "Anyway, once it was clear that you'd disappeared, I convinced these two to look for you first and sort it out later."

"It's a good thing you did. There mightn't have been a later," Sylvia observed thankfully. "At least not for me."

A short stocky man in a business suit that didn't seem to go with the very large gun in his hand came over and spoke to Sterne in a low voice.

"Right. Thanks. Rupert," he broke in, "Dutton's bought it and Reyes is hurt bad."

Rupert brightened. "We might be able to get out of this."

Sylvia looked questioningly at Karl.

"If we can cover up the fact that members of our delegation were connected to the Nazis, the good old U.S.A. won't look so bad. In fact, we'll be heroes for saving the security of the conference," he explained. "Sylvia, can I talk to you for a second?"

They moved out of earshot.

"I know where Jurgen must be."

"Do you?"

"He's at that woman's! Mrs. West, uh, Lundvar."

"Could be."

"Sure he is. It's the only place that makes sense. All I need now is her address!" Karl was rigid with excitement. "I'm going to take a couple of guys and go over to The Foundation's office to get it. It might be better if you waited for me here."

"I'll buy that," she agreed. "I've had enough shootouts to last me for a while. Come back for me."

"You still want to see him?"

"John? Not particularly. I want my children."

He leaned over and kissed her. "I just about died myself when I thought you were hurt. When this is over, we're going to take a vacation, just the two of us."

She smiled wistfully. "That would be nice."

He stroked her face. "I was very upset when I wasn't sure that I'd see you again. There was something I wanted to say."

"You don't have to say it now, Karl."

"Yes, I do." He smiled at her. "I love you."

She watched him leave. She was still wearing the wistful expression.

FORTY-FIVE

Sylvia waited until there was a lull in the hubbub around Rupert. "I've got a loose end to tie up," she told him. "Do you mind if I take off?"

"We have a lot of questions for you."

"They'll wait until we get home, won't they?"

"I suppose so. Do you need any help with your loose end?"

"No. It's something I have to do myself." She headed for the door.

The street was still cordoned off. She hailed a taxi a few blocks away and gave the driver the address Regina had found for her.

It was another beautiful summer's day. The city was moving slowly in the heat. Young women in bright sundresses ambled lazily along the streets of the Budé with their baby carriages and toddlers. Traffic was crawling.

It seemed that only Sylvia was in a hurry. By the time the cab drew up outside the apartment block, she was sitting on the edge of her seat.

A woman was going in with two bags of groceries and a rambunctious boy. She was trying to open the glass doors, control the child, and not break her eggs. Something was about to give.

"Here, let me help you." Sylvia took the key from her and turned it in the lock. "C'mere, honey." She grabbed the boy firmly and marched him through.

"Oh, thanks." The woman was obviously an American UN bride. The place was full of them. "Could you do the next two doors too?"

"Sure."

"My husband wonders why I'm tired when he gets home. He says he works! And he's got a desk, a chair, and a devoted secretary." The young woman was whiny. Sylvia didn't blame her.

"Here's your elevator." She shoved the child in after his

351

mother. "Can you handle it from here?"

"Sure. He says he's tired when his day is finished. Finished! Mine..." The doors closed on her complaint.

Sylvia took the next elevator up.

She walked down the hideously carpeted hall and stood in front of a door. It was a minute or two before she raised her hand and knocked.

Silence.

She knocked again, this time more firmly.

"Allo?" The voice came through the door but she recognized it. She had a lump in her throat.

"Qui est là?"

"It's me."

A pause.

"Sylvia!" The door opened and they were staring sadly at each other.

"I didn't want to go, Sylvia, believe me."

"I believe you, John."

"They made me leave. They didn't give me a choice."

"I know. Someone was after you and they were afraid that you'd spill the beans about Dutton. They couldn't risk that, not with the anti-terrorist conference coming up."

"My God! You really do know everything!" He couldn't meet her eyes.

Sylvia walked inside the room and shut the door behind her. She scarcely noticed her surroundings. John was not quite as she'd remembered him. He was still tall and handsome, but he seemed thinner and somehow less significant a presence.

"I had an appointment that Monday morning to see von Schagg and Vernon Rogers. When I got to the elevators, I found them waiting for me. I had to go then and there. They threatened me."

"They weren't kidding. They're killers, your pals. They left bodies strewn around New York."

"They're not my pals. I didn't want to have anything to do with them after I came to the States. Especially after I met you. I wanted to forget the past and start over but they wouldn't let me."

"I know. Janice was always there and then there was the visit from your phony mother to make you toe the line."

"I tried refusing all along the way. I wanted to be independent as far back as law school but they insisted that I accept their generosity." His voice broke. "Generosity! I've been trapped by their generosity for thirty years."

"You should have come to me and told me about it, John. Was I really such an ogre that you couldn't confide in me?"

"I couldn't bear to show you how stupid I'd been. You always looked up to me. You leaned on me even if you didn't like to admit it."

Sylvia stared at him wonderingly. He'd participated in a totally different marriage than she remembered. "I'm strong, John. I always have been. That was one of the main troubles between us."

"Whatever." He slid over the subject. "I had hoped you'd never need to know about all of it. Even this past year, when this, uh, this Israeli agent was following me and they told me to be ready to leave on a moment's notice, I kept on saying I wouldn't go." He expelled his breath. "But I knew I'd have to. They threatened me. And you and the children. I was afraid of them for all of us."

"Where are my children? I'm taking them home with me. For good."

He gestured helplessly. "The boys are here. Of course you can take them. They want to go home, all they've done is ask for you. You won't believe me but it wasn't my idea to bring them to Switzerland. Mrs. Lundvar wanted to convince you to stop interfering. I told her I didn't want to take the children away from their home. I only wish I could go back with the three of you." He averted his eyes. "I suppose there would be no point in that anyway." He turned and looked questioningly at her.

"Not much, John. I've had a lot of time to think about things."

"What went wrong, Sylvia?"

She threw out her hands. "What didn't go wrong? You hid yourself from me. When I tried to describe you to the police, I realized that you were just a shadow. I couldn't live with a shadow so I kept all my emotions for my work. Everything natural about me irritated you and I wasn't able ever to live up to your expectations. And I guess I didn't try very hard."

"It was my fault. I know that."

She shrugged awkwardly. "I don't think fault is the right word for what we did to each other."

"Well, it doesn't matter now. I can't go home, they've seen to that. They forged my name to a check so it looked like I'd embezzled money. No one would believe that I didn't, and even if I explained it I'd never be able to practice law again."

"Why did you send for the money? If you hadn't written that bank draft, you'd be in a much better position."

"I did it to prove to you that I wasn't worth searching for. They warned me that you were making trouble. I was a poor husband to you, but at least remember that at the end I tried to protect you."

"What will happen to you now?"

"They'll send me somewhere else with another new identity—oh!"

"No, it's all right. I know about that too. You're Jurgen Werner and I guess I'm Mrs. Werner. I know all about your past."

He froze.

Sylvia watched him for a long moment.

"I've got only one more thing to say to you. You don't have much time. The man who's been after you this past year is on his way to the apartment now."

"The Israeli?"

"No. He isn't an Israeli. Your friends overreacted. His name is Karl Friedman."

"Karl Friedman." John repeated the name stupidly.

"Your childhood friend. He's coming here for personal reasons. The irony of all this is that Mrs. Lundvar would have been perfectly safe if she'd left you in New York. But you'd be dead. He's coming here to kill you because he blames you for his mother's death. He's spent the last thirty years looking for you."

"I didn't do anything! Let me tell you about it! There wasn't anything I could do."

"I know the story." Sylvia was drained of emotion. "You were part of the whole thing. You were actually part of the whole thing. I couldn't accept that if I lived to a hundred. It makes me sick just thinking about it. You were to blame, you and your kind, for allowing such obscenities."

She turned away, Karl's last words echoing in her ears. She closed her eyes and blotted them out. "But I can't say for sure that what happened with Karl's mother was a capital crime. I can understand Karl. I can sympathize with him. But I couldn't stand by and let you be killed for it. Give me my children and start running."

She was much too numb to do more than react mechanically to the boys' hysterical greeting. She knelt down and held them, remembering two other little boys in another time and place.

When they had stopped crying and clinging to her, she took each by a hand and walked out of the apartment without another word.

They got into a taxi.

"Where to?"

She wanted to give the address of the safe house. If only she could see Karl one more time. Maybe she could explain it to him. Maybe he would still love her.

She felt her eyes well up. There was nothing she could say. Karl would never forgive her and she could never be sorry.

"To the airport. We're going home, kids."

FORTY-SIX

Bess met them at Kennedy Airport. After a fond reunion, she broke the news that Sylvia was to proceed straight on to Washington for what the bureaucrats called a debriefing. The boys were far too insecure to be left at home so the four of them caught the next flight out.

Sylvia was too exhausted to fall asleep. Besides, although she tried valiantly, Bess couldn't hide her eagerness for the details. Sylvia filled her in, being especially cool and collected when she mentioned Friedman.

Bess wasn't fooled for a second but she was tactful enough to change the subject. "There's been action here too! It's been very exciting although Dave isn't exactly forthcoming. I, uh, gather he wasn't thrilled about the way things went in Switzerland. Anyway, loads of people have been picked up. Janice and Cameron and that cop in Vesper City."

"Hodgins," Sylvia put in absently.

"Right, him. But the most important thing is that it turns out that Cameron's the one who framed you."

"You mean the Bailey allegation?"

"Yup. The Baileys have been promised immunity and they're going to testify for the D.A. at Cameron's trial!"

Sylvia took a deep breath. It was a treat to think that Benjamin and Mansfield were off her back. "Did we get an apology?"

"From the Bar Assocation? You have to be kidding. They still think it was tacky of you to have been framed. All Benjamin said when he called was that the Association has decided not to pursue the investigation! Do you believe it?"

Typical. Sylvia shrugged and stubbed out her cigarette as the No Smoking signs came on.

"Sylvia," Bess added, with a hand on her friend's arm, "I won't labor the point but thanks. What you did, well, it was very important to me."

They smiled at each other as the plane touched down.

Sylvia went right to the telephones and called the number Bess had been given. She was told that she'd be met at the hotel.

Washington was hot, so hot that except for the lower-level civil servants and everyone's secretaries, the town was deserted. The humidity felt like a hundred percent and even the ubiquitously whining air conditioners couldn't keep the inside air dry.

Two tall clean-cut and square-jawed men in their mid-twenties were in the hotel lobby when the taxi drew up. Both Sylvia and Bess picked them out instantly. It wasn't hard; they were caricatures of G-men, faces as open and unlined as a newborn babe's. And as expressive.

"Mrs. West, will you come with us, please?" The blonder of the two flashed a polite, toothy smile.

It was impossible to mistrust such outstanding examples of Midwestern America. It was also impossible to like them. She nodded, kissed the boys, and wearily trotted off, still wearing the bedraggled suit that she'd been in for what seemed like a lifetime. She had hoped to wash her hair and herself but as it turned out, it would have been pointless. The moment she got into the nondescript Chevy, it became all too evident that these fellows were not senior enough to rate air conditioning.

The drive would have been pure torture if Sylvia hadn't been too numb and too tired to care. She sat in the back, hardly noticing the lack of inside door handles, staring out at the steaming city and trying not to think.

"We're here, ma'am."

Sylvia looked up. The sandy-haired escort was holding her door open. "Oh, thank you." She got out stiffly, wondering if her rapidly aging body would ever recuperate from the ardors of the past month.

They led her into a boxy office building, a stone and tile edifice without a name in front or a directory in the lobby. The elevators worked only with a key. Both men reached into their breast pockets, competing slightly for speed. Blondie won. Inside, Blondie allowed his clone to mutter the magic code into the telephone that started the machine.

At the end of a long bland hall they came to a long bland boardroom. As soon as Blondie opened the door, a rush of icy air hit her. She gulped it gratefully as four men she'd never seen looked her over. Fortunately, Rupert chose that moment to walk in, forestalling her now-chronic mistrust of strangers.

"Hi, Sylvia. You look beat."

She smiled weakly and allowed herself to be introduced around, not that she caught or remembered any of the names. All four men were wearing the same navy suit, and as if some music inaudible to her was playing for them, all removed their jackets and rolled up their sleeves on the same beat. One was sporting an obviously expensive made-to-measure shirt. She pegged him as the sophisticate from the White House; the others were probably CIA and FBI. Certainly they were face-less and as memorable as enriched white bread.

The so-called debriefing consisted of telling and retelling her story for five and a half hours. When the same man asked the same question for the fifth time, Sylvia put her head in her hands.

"Maybe we should adjourn until tomorrow," Rupert suggested with an anxious look at her. "Mrs. West hasn't had much sleep lately and she's been through a lot."

Sylvia would have thought that that was the understatement of the century but her four inquisitors didn't look convinced.

"Just a few more minutes, Mrs. West," the third from the left muttered unconvincingly. He repeated his question.

She sighed and answered it. Again.

Eventually, the men looked at each other and nodded. It seemed she had been fully debriefed. Sylvia hid a smile. It sounded like a slightly more exciting activity than had actually occurred.

"Okay, now it's my turn. I've got a few questions before we leave," she said firmly.

They raised their eyebrows in unison.

"Where did the CIA leak come from?"

"I'm sorry, Mrs. West," the White House dandy said. "We are not cleared to give you that information."

"For Christ's sake! If it hadn't been for me, the leak would be a flood! At least tell me if I'm right in assuming that once he got to the White House, Lorne Reyes had access to the information?"

No one nodded, let alone said anything. But a few eyes flickered.

She pressed on. "Have the files been recovered from Switzerland?"

Silence.

She looked at Rupert and repeated the question.

He flushed and decided to ignore the outraged glances of

his confreres. "Yes," he said defiantly. "We were able to get them. Actually, the raid wasn't made by our boys."

"Sterne's crew?"

"Uh huh."

The outrage had changed to stunned horror. At least one of the Torquemadas appeared to be seriously considering whether or not to charge Rupert with a heinous breach of government regulations.

Rupert sailed blithely on. "We notified all the potential victims and we'll keep in touch with them. There wouldn't be any point in attempting to blackmail any of them now."

Sylvia frowned. "I don't understand. I assume you've cleaned up The Foundation so how could there be any future blackmail?"

"Well, we've certainly made a number of arrests here in the States," he said vaguely.

"But not in Europe? What about von Schagg and Lundvar?" Sylvia's voice was loud. To hell with refinement.

This time Rupert joined in the looks going around the table. "Well, Sylvia," he observed, leaning forward confidentially, "you have to be realistic. We can't get them without extraditing them, and it would be disastrous internationally to publicize this unfortunate mess."

"No one would trust a country that could be so easily in-filtrated, you mean?" Sylvia asked bluntly.

Winces were unanimous.

"In a manner of speaking." One of the four spoke up, im-plying that it was boorish to speak in that manner. "After all, we have been able to handle all American nationals. The only one not yet arrested is Reyes."

"And he's very ill," another interjected. "Very ill. I would be surprised if he recovers."

All of the men were staring at various parts of the wall. It didn't look good for old Lorne.

"But the organization will still be able to function!" Sylvia protested.

"Not here."

And that was that. She was unable to get any more details out of even Rupert. Eventually she threw up her hands and stood. "If you're through with me, gentlemen, I think I'd like to get some sleep."

Rupert saw her down to the car. The Bobbsey twins had been kicked out of the boardroom before a single important word had been uttered. They were now standing at attention beside the Chevy.

"Just one more thing, Sylvia," Rupert murmured. "You won't see a great deal in the papers about this."

"Somehow I suspected as much."

"In fact, there hasn't been a single story."

"How did you handle Maggie Brewster?"

"Her editor did it for us." Rupert opened the car door. "Sylvia, I'm sorry about everything. John and this last month. You know."

"Yes. Thanks."

"I would like to see you again. Uh, you know where I am. Anytime."

The pain came flooding back. "I don't think so, Rupert."

He looked down at his hands. "Well. If you change your mind."

"Good-bye, Rupert."

New York's weather wasn't much of an improvement on Washington's. The ride out to Long Island left all of them cranky and damp. Bess had come too, insisting that Sylvia wasn't going to take care of the boys alone for at least another couple of days.

Which was just as well. Sylvia's mind was playing tricks on her. Every time she thought she was listening to something that Bess or one of the kids said, she would realize with a start that she'd been daydreaming about Karl.

Bess froze at the front door. "Sylvia, why isn't the house locked up?"

"It should be." Sylvia pushed ahead, motioning for Bess to wait outside with the children. She cautiously walked into the living room and stopped dead.

In the background, Bess was ushering the kids upstairs. A part of Sylvia's mind was thankful for the tact. The rest was totally absorbed in watching Karl.

Neither said anything for a long time.

Finally Sylvia spoke. "I never thought I'd see you again."

"I just found myself here."

Sylvia was afraid to speak.

"I'm still not sure why I'm here," he went on. "I'm filled with a dozen conflicting emotions. At first, I wanted to hurt you. And then I didn't want to think about you at all. My whole life, every minute existed just to find Jurgen. I couldn't believe that you knew that and still did it."

He stopped talking to get control of himself. Sylvia watched silently.

"I never thought about afterwards. I suppose I knew that there wasn't anything else inside me and when he was dead, I would be too. Or might as well be." He turned away. "And then I met you and there was something else in my life, something for after. A future. But it was for after."

Sylvia walked over to him and made him look at her. "There still can be a future. Please, Karl, think about the future. Let the past go. Let the ghosts sleep."

He didn't answer for a long time.

"I look at you and I see him. I don't know if I'm alive enough to have a future."

"You can try."

"I can try."